Also by Deborah Swift

The Silk Code

The Shadow Network

DEBORAH SWIFT

ONE PLACE. MANY STORIES

HQ
An imprint of HarperCollins*Publishers* Ltd
1 London Bridge Street
London SE1 9GF

www.harpercollins.co.uk

HarperCollins*Publishers*
Macken House, 39/40 Mayor Street Upper,
Dublin 1 D01 C9W8

This paperback edition 2024

2

First published in Great Britain by
HQ, an imprint of HarperCollins*Publishers* Ltd 2024

Copyright © Deborah Swift 2024

Deborah Swift asserts the moral right to be
identified as the author of this work.
A catalogue record for this book is
available from the British Library.

ISBN: 9780008586898

For Jean
fellow traveller to unpathed waters
and undreamed shores

'With the help of a clever persistent propaganda,
even heaven can be represented to the people as hell,
and the most wretched life as paradise.'

Mein Kampf, Adolf Hitler

Chapter 1

Lilli tucked her scarf into her coat and braced herself against the chill of the November day. The examinations would start next week, so as she hurried down the steps from the main building of the university, she was still repeating the lines of Shakespeare under her breath.

> *For I have sworn thee fair, and thought thee bright,*
> *Who art as black as hell, as dark as night.*

The lines of the sonnet rang bitter-sweet after the cringing humiliation of losing her boyfriend Bren. Brendan Murphy – five years older, with rangy good looks and the easy confidence of a postgraduate student. He was an Irish student in Berlin, there to top up his German language skills, and they'd bonded over Goethe and Hermann Hesse.

Until Hilde, that was.

Even now, months later, as Lilli lugged her bag of books across the rain-wet compound, she was watching out for Bren and cursing Hilde Bollmann. Hilde, who'd swooped in with her blonde ponytail and flawless skin, and almost spirited Bren away from right under Lilli's nose. But now Hilde had gone too, moved out of Germany, vanished like so many other students who were worried about the strange way Germany was going. But Bren had never rekindled his romance with Lilli, and it still hurt like toothache.

Lilli sighed, and hurried on, but seeing a crowd ahead, slowed to a crawling pace. Crowds were never good these days. Her path was blocked. She hesitated, fear uncoiling in her gut. The Brownshirts were always hanging around on the university steps and she'd learnt to side-step to avoid them. The warning came to her as a stench that seemed to swamp the street – harsh at the back of her throat like burning oil. Lilli had a quirk in her perception, something they called synaesthesia, and always felt atmosphere in colour and smell, just like she heard music in colour and shape.

Bracing herself, she strode forward. Today there were more of them, gathering like flies.

Best ignore them.

Further down the street, the Brownshirts were massing in smaller knots, staring at the girls who walked past. She wove swiftly between two parked cars to avoid them. The atmosphere was febrile, belligerent. She heard a tall, gangly boy make a ribald joke as she passed on the pavement. All girls suffered the butt of their attention. Ahead of her, two other young women were pushed into the road with shoves and shouts.

Lilli tightened her grip on her bag of books and walked on, her head up, but stony-faced, as if they didn't exist.

'I'd have that one,' said the shortest youth in the group when she hurried by, head down, huddled into herself for protection.

One of the other lads laughed loudly, but then stifled it. He was about seventeen years old, she guessed, a lot younger than she was, but taller, with the swagger that comes from being in a gang. Lilli felt her shoulders tense, but lowered her eyes like the girl ahead of her. It wasn't worth courting trouble. The low winter sun sliced between the buildings, dazzling her, and she hurried on with a hand shielding her face.

A boy with darting eyes and thick fleshy lips stuck out a foot, aiming to trip Mindel, the girl who was walking in front of her – a slim, dark-haired girl of about fourteen, whom Lilli knew from choir practice. Like her, Mindel wasn't a member of the Bund, the League of German Girls. Mindel tried to dodge the boys' attention, but another long-limbed boy stretched his foot out further so she stumbled and fell headlong, both arms out in front. The boy booted her in the ribs.

Lilli cringed at the thud as his boot connected, but instinctively stopped to help as the youths sniggered and jostled. One of them kicked again at Mindel, grabbed her notebook and taunted her, holding it high above his head, shouting, 'Jump for it!'

'Louts! Give it back!' Lilli shouted.

Mindel snapped to her feet in an instant, scraping up her books. She kept her eyes to the ground and didn't even try to get her notebook back, just dodged onwards, leaving it in her tormentor's hands.

'Ignorant swine,' Lilli muttered under her breath.

'Get her!' a boy called.

Lilli shot sideways and ran, feeling someone grab her cardigan, but she kept running and it ripped from their hands. 'Juden', came the yell. Jews.

'Are you all right?' She caught up with Mindel around the corner. 'Let me see your hands. Your knee's bleeding.'

'I know. Leave me alone. I just want to get home.'

'Where do you live?' Lilli asked, catching her by the arm.

'Rosenstrasse. But I won't go back there yet. They wait for me and throw stones. I'll go to the bakery. Frau Brockdorf's kind and will let me wait there, though her shop has hardly anything left in it now.'

3

'Do you want a handkerchief for that graze?'

A shake of the head. 'They always do it. They know my father's house, and it's too near the Nazi Party's new Assembly Rooms. But there's something different about them today. They're bolder. They've never done that before, kicked me in plain sight.'

'You're sure you'll be okay?'

'Just a bruise.' A nod and a wave before she shot away down the side street, but Lilli had felt her fear, like a shiver of blue-grey.

Lilli continued towards home, checking over her shoulder that none of the boys had followed her. As she arrived warily at her front door, she noticed several more of the Brownshirts loitering at the end of the street. They were holding sticks in their hands, a fact that made her insides turn liquid. They were facing away from her, thank goodness, as she silently prised open the gate at the front of the house and took out her key.

Her breath grew faster and shallower because she was aware they could turn to see her any moment. The back of her neck bristled as she unlocked the door. Once inside, she turned the key in the lock, wiped the sweat from her hands onto her skirt, and bounded breathlessly up the apartment steps to the first floor.

It was time to leave, like Hilde. She must tell Papa.

The door to their apartment was open as usual, and Papa was at his desk amid the metallic smell of solder, with the innards of a radio in front of him. An untidy pile of papers was stacked at his elbow.

He looked up distractedly. 'That time already?' He rubbed a hand through his hair, and then pinched the bridge of his nose where his glasses sat. 'I haven't been to the shops. I got involved.'

It was nothing new; he often forgot things. She peered over his shoulder at the calculations, pages of figures scrawled and crossed out; dozens of equations, like a language only he could understand, along with discarded diagrams of circuitry. To see him sitting at home like this made her sad.

'Hello, Papa.' She patted him on the shoulder. 'There are

4

Brownshirts outside,' she said. 'They look like trouble. Papa, we need to talk about leaving.'

'Give me a minute while I finish this,' he said.

She sighed, frustrated. She sensed change coming like an approaching wave, a roiling cloud like ink in water, yet Papa turned his back on it hoping it would go away. But the truth that stares you in the face has its own timing, and sometimes, it won't wait to be heard.

'Papa?'

'In a minute.'

Still Papa refused to think it had come to this. She sat down next to him and peered at the wiring in the device he was working with. It was a Bakelite body with a single round speaker in the front. On the sideboard they had the official Nazi Volksempfänger radio, much lauded by Goebbels, and produced by a rival company. Her father was always wanting to improve on the design. The set in front of her, with its trailing wires, employed three vacuum tubes, which should make it fairly powerful.

'Is it longwave?' she asked him, used to these conversations about the insides of machines. She helped him in the long winter evenings, fascinated by the concept of invisible radio waves.

'Mmhm. About 150 to 350 kilohertz.'

'And what about the aerial?'

'Three jacks, for antennae of different lengths, so we can optimise reception on the different frequency bands.'

'There are Brownshirts loitering outside, Papa,' she said again. 'They tried to beat up Mindel. For nothing.'

'Is the front door locked?'

She nodded and watched him take a small sharp-nosed pair of pliers to the wiring inside the radio. He just didn't get it. She tapped a foot, frustrated that he didn't pay more attention to the world outside. Most of his colleagues had gone, yet they were still here. A law in 1933 had made it illegal for any non-Aryan, specifically Jews, to be a professor or teacher in Germany and so

5

fearing they would target him because he was married to a Jew, Papa had given up the university and gone to work at Blaupunkt, developing new radio receivers and headphones. But now, even Blaupunkt had, in their words, 'let him go'.

'We have to let you go,' they'd said sadly, their faces not sad at all. They closed their doors to him despite his skill. So many scholars, and most of his colleagues with Jewish connections, had fled Germany.

Every day her instinct told her it was time to leave, but Papa was always too distracted, preferring to brush things under the carpet. Mama would have chivvied him. But Mama was gone, dead of cancer five years ago, and now they were alone in this sinking boat. Lilli knew the Nazis had started targeting what they called 'Mischlinge', those of mixed Jewish and Aryan heritage, for deportation, but Papa was sceptical.

'I'm a good German citizen', was Papa's mantra. 'German through and through, and you're an exceptional student, the cream of your class.' He thought now Mama was dead that the Jewish part of the family could be swept away, or ignored. Though he hadn't joined the Party, and it terrified Lilli that he hadn't.

She drew her chair nearer so she could hold the soldering iron. Maybe it would speed him up if she helped.

'It's all right,' he said. 'I can manage. Go get yourself some bread and cheese.' Outside, shouting and the noise of a car horn. 'Ignore it,' he said. 'Nothing to do with us.'

She picked up a plate, and went to the larder but the bread bin was empty.

'Is there no bread?' Papa called. He'd heard the clank of the bread bin lid. 'Would you go across to Frau Kirchner, borrow a slice?'

'I think we should lock the apartment door, Papa. Will you give me the key?'

'In a minute. Just bob over to Frau Kirchner, would you?'

'Haven't you eaten, Papa?' He would have forgotten again. Since her mother had died, food was always a little unpredictable; it was never the first thing on her father's mind.

'I don't like to ask Frau Kirchner again,' Papa continued, waving ink-stained hands, 'but tell her I'll return it when I get to the bank, all right?'

Lilli stepped out across the landing to knock on Frau Kirchner's door.

As she passed across the landing, she saw from the window that a bigger crowd of Brownshirts had gathered at the end of the street. They were milling around, obviously waiting for something. A car was overturned there, its windows smashed.

She knocked insistently on Frau Kirchner's door until she opened up. Frau Kirchner was a solid-looking woman of about forty years, dressed in a brown knitted twin-set and pleated skirt. The piano stood open near the door, for Frau Kirchner was a piano teacher and often she and Lilli would play and sing together. Papa was keen on her music; he said music was the sound of mathematics, but Lilli found it too stimulating, all the notes jangling in colours and shapes. She preferred to sing, where she could control it all.

Lilli asked Frau Kirchner politely for a bit of bread.

'I can let you have the end of a loaf,' Frau Kirchner said. 'I baked yesterday with that sawdust they call flour. Wait, while I go and get it.'

A sudden bellow, shouts and thuds, crashing glass. Both of them looked to each other and rushed to the window. A gang of Brownshirts were breaking the windows opposite with their sticks. One aimed a kick at the remaining teeth of glass until it fell in.

'Whose house is that?' Lilli whispered, horrified.

'The Kalinskys. She's Polish. She used to have the milliner's on the corner, before they …'

Frau Kirchner didn't continue. There was no need. Lilli knew what she was going to say. *Before they trashed it.* The *Juden* sign was still scrawled over the door in yellow paint.

Neither of them could look away. A crowd of men were trying to shove past one another in their eagerness to force entry into the house. One of them, a fair-haired, skinny youth, was climbing over the windowsill, tearing a net curtain out of the way.

'What are they trying to do?' Lilli asked.

Frau Kirchner shook her head dumbly. The house opposite seethed with pushing men, until finally the Kalinskys were dragged out of the door. Herr Kalinsky gripped a suitcase to his chest. He'd been battered around the face, and blood dripped into one half-closed eye. The Brownshirts kept on hitting him, like a mule they were whipping into motion.

An excited red-faced youth dragged Frau Kalinsky out by the hair.

'Leave us al—!' she cried. But her words were quashed as four of the men threw her on the ground and raising their arms, beat her down until she curled into a ball.

'What shall we do?' Lilli whispered.

Frau Kirchner shook her head but didn't move, her eyes fixed on Frau Kalinsky. 'Nothing. We can't get help. They're like beasts, not men. Come away. It's none of our business.'

None of our business.

It was never their business, but Lilli was mesmerised. In a few short moments, the rabble divided into two groups, one still intent on beating blood from the Kalinskys, the other striding across the street towards their house. Both mobs were the same buzzing, dark haze she'd seen earlier, like a swarm of stinking locusts. In seconds, about fifteen youths had gathered on the pavement below.

As if entering a battle zone the men lurched as one towards the door.

'They're coming!' Lilli whispered, tugging at Frau Kirchner's arm. Then turning to the door, 'Papa!'

Frau Kirchner leapt to shut the door and lock it.

Lilli tried to grab the key, but too late. Thuds and shouts. More

8

breaking glass. She turned to Frau Kirchner in fury, but screams from the elderly Frau Hartzug in the downstairs apartment made her freeze where she was.

'No! Get out of here!' Frau Hartzug's voice.

It was the space of a heartbeat before they heard men on the stairs outside. 'This way. There are more Jews on the first floor. Apartment four. That's what the Irishman said.'

Irländer. *Irishman?* There was only one Irishman she knew. Her ex-boyfriend. *They couldn't mean Bren, could they?* A vision flashed in her head, of Bren's expression as he swept past her, arm in arm with Hilde, deliberately ignoring her presence, as if she were an insect.

How many Irishmen were there in Berlin? her thoughts shrieked.

An assertive voice. 'Herr Bergen. Jewish sympathiser, the Irishman said. Married a Jew and refuses to join the Party. This way.'

Had Bren told them about her father? He wouldn't do that to them, would he?

Lilli lunged towards the door, but Frau Kirchner held her back, put a hand over her mouth.

'Quiet,' she hissed in her ear, as Lilli struggled. 'Do you want to end up like Frau Kalinsky?'

'Papa's in there,' she cried, frantic.

Already the Brownshirts were outside in the hallway, she could tell by the thuds, scuffles, and scrapes. Sounds that rose and fell like jagged mountain peaks. She heard them baying, banging, and kicking to be let in to her apartment.

'What is it?' Papa's voice behind their door. 'What d'you want?'

'Open up, or we'll break it down.'

No answer. Lilli had her fist stuffed in her mouth. A bang as she heard the door give way and slam back against the wall.

The rough voice of a young man. 'Herr Bergen? Get your coat. Come with us. Quickly.'

She heard her father's reply. 'This is an outrage. I've done nothing wrong.'

'You're a Jew-loving bastard. You married a Jew. Where's your daughter?'

Lilli gasped, but Frau Kirchner had her gripped tight.

Papa's voice. 'She's not here. Not home yet from the university.'

A lie. Papa never lied.

At the same time there were cries of 'Look at this!' 'I'm having that clock.' 'I'll take that gold watch!' 'Give me that, I saw it first'. Above it all, the sound of her father's confusion, his protests. 'I'm a friend of Otto Griessing, you can't do this. I work for Blaupunkt.'

He didn't work for anyone. The fact he kept lying bit a hole in her heart.

Don't lie, Papa.

'You can take one suitcase.'

'I'm not leaving.'

Then the noise of crockery smashing. Lilli lunged towards the door, but Frau Kirchner had hold of her by the hair, one hand over her mouth.

'Don't touch that radio!' Her father's frantic shout from across the hall.

'Let go!' Lilli wrestled free. But immediately Frau Kirchner's hand slapped hard over her mouth. A sudden smell of marzipan, burnt almonds.

'Shut up!' Frau Kirchner hissed in her ear.

'Out!' came the order from outside amongst all the noise. 'We've got to do the whole row.'

'Any more in this building?'

'No. The rest are paid-up Party members.'

'My papers!' Papa's panic-stricken voice. 'What about my work?'

'Downstairs, now!'

Lilli squirmed and wrestled to go to the door, but Frau Kirchner had an iron grip, Lilli's mouth was covered by her hand, until the commotion and thumps on the stairs fell to quiet. Then she let her go.

Lilli fought to get past her to the window, but Frau Kirchner pulled the curtains tight shut and stood before them blocking her way.

'What will they do to him?' Lilli asked.

'God knows. The world's gone mad. Take him to a camp, I expect.'

'I'm going with him, let me look!'

'No. Don't be a little fool. Count your luck! They're like savages. Stay here quiet a while. You heard your father; he said you were out for good reason. He'd want you to stay safe.'

Lilli held her breath, straining to hear. There were still men next door. She imagined them prowling in her apartment. She heard them moving, like wolves in the forest, smelled smoke, heard the banging of the wardrobe door, the scrape of drawers.

Finally the thud of boots going downstairs and an eerie silence.

Frau Kirchner peered out through the curtains, her face white and drawn. 'They've moved off. There's about a hundred of them out there now.'

'Can you see Papa?' Tears leaked from her eyes.

A shake of the head. 'They're taking people away. Half the street. Even the Kalinskys.'

'I should go with him,' Lilli said again.

'You were lucky.'

'No,' Lilli said. 'You'd no right to stop me.'

Frau Kirchner's mouth tightened into a hard line. 'Go on then. Go after them. I won't stop you if you want to break your father's heart.'

Irländer. She thought of Bren Murphy. 'Papa, what have I done?' Lilli put her face in her hands and began to sob.

*

Late that night, still shocked to the core, Lilli looked out into the street at the glint of broken glass and the dark stain on the

11

Kalinskys' doorstep. She shouldn't have confided in Bren Murphy; should never have told him about her Jewish heritage, about how Papa was redundant and eking out his time at home. Now Papa was paying the price for her indiscretion. She cursed Bren Murphy, but most of all she cursed herself, her fingers tightening into claws around the bedsheets. She should have trusted her gut instinct, made Papa find them somewhere to go before it was too late.

Sleep in Frau Kirchner's stiff spare bed was impossible; interrupted by the noise of fire sirens and shouting from other streets, sounds that had shapes like torn paper. Lilli spent most of the night bolt-upright in bed, terrified the rabble of Brownshirts would come back.

The next morning she had just managed to doze off when the crackle of the radio woke her; the low voices, and then Hitler's more strident one spouting propaganda. As soon as Lilli appeared, Frau Kirchner switched it off. Her face seemed older, more wrinkled than Lilli remembered. 'So much anger in the world. What are we doing? What are we teaching our young people?' Frau Kirchner demanded.

Lilli squeezed her hand to comfort her, suddenly the one in control. 'I need to go and look.'

'No. Stay here.'

But Lilli insisted on going back to her apartment.

In the hallway, one of her father's papers floated abandoned on the top stair. The lock to the door was missing, torn from its housing, leaving splinters of wood on the doorframe. By habit, she reached to touch her mother's precious mezuzah by the door, but it had been ripped away and the prayer scroll lay in torn fragments on the floor.

Lilli stepped over it, disgusted to find cigarette butts had been ground into their best carpet. She paused in the middle of the room, her eyes wide. Every drawer was open, anything valuable had gone, even the brass menorah candlestick. She closed her eyes, as if that might make it all disappear. But no, her mother's family pictures had been ripped from the wall and stamped on, so the cracked glass had cut through the canvas.

She covered her nose. The place stank, and the shape of it was like a creeping worm. Someone had defaecated in the corner and her bedroom reeked of piss. She bent over to pick up the radio her father had been working on, but of course the delicate vacuum tubes were smashed, the wires ripped out, and someone had made a bonfire of the papers from the desk.

'Put that down and get your clothes and your coat. You can't stay here.' Frau Kirchner appeared at her shoulder, her voice loud in the silence.

Lilli was too dazed to disagree. It wasn't the state of the apartment that had pole-axed her, but its emptiness. The newspaper was still on the floor, the crossword puzzle almost completed in her father's neat hand.

The beige cardboard suitcase that used to be her mother's was in her wardrobe. What should she take with her? Lilli couldn't think, it was as if her thoughts were stuck in cotton wool. She threw some clothes into the case: a random jersey, a handful of underwear, stockings, a pair of flat shoes and her nightdress from under the pillow.

She couldn't bear to look at anything else. She just wanted to get out of there, out of the stink of them, the men that had done this. She heaved the case towards the door.

'Come on now,' Frau Kirchner said, wresting it from her hands. 'I'll make us some hot coffee. I might even have some milk. Then we'll decide what to do.'

'Do?' Lilli was blank, too shocked to comprehend.

'Yes. We'll have to get you out. I didn't understand before. Thought it was just rumour. But now I see what we're dealing with. And you heard them, they'll be back, if we don't get you away.'

'I can't. There's nowhere to go.'

'Coffee first, then we'll think.'

Hands wrapped around the coffee cup to stop them from

13

shaking, Lilli said, 'You shouldn't have stopped me. I need to find my father.'

'No. What will you do? Go after him? They'll beat you, like they did the Kalinskys.'

Lilli stood up. 'But he's on his own, and he's ...' She wanted to say, 'not good at looking after himself,' but it sounded disrespectful so she bit back the words.

'If you stay here, they'll come back. And then send you somewhere else; somewhere with the rest of the women, somewhere he can't find you.' She grabbed Lilli by the shoulders. 'They separate the men and the women. Do you understand?'

She tried to turn her face away from Frau Kirchner's insistent gaze. She hadn't wanted to understand. Not really.

'Now, have you any relatives outside Germany?' Frau Kirchner asked.

'None.'

'Nobody at all outside Germany? A friend? Anyone?'

'Only Maddie. My English penfriend. I stayed with her once for a month, when I was about fifteen. To improve my English. And two years ago, she tried to get us to go over there, but Papa refused. He didn't want to move from Berlin. He said we'd be badly treated in England because the English don't like the Germans since the Great War.'

'You have her address?'

'It's in there.' She indicated her apartment. 'In the family address book – in the drawer under the recipe books.'

'Best fetch it then, if it's still there.'

Lilli steeled herself to go back. She only prayed Papa hadn't taken it, or worse, the Brownshirts. Papa had never once opened that drawer, but Lilli used to open it to look at her mother's pencilled lists of ingredients, and to remember her baking. The idea of sugar and flour were mixed with those of her mother, like memories from another world. Now she walked gingerly over crunching glass, to find the drawer leering open but the address book, *praise be*, still hidden under the books on bread-making and preserves. Nazi men were not interested in cooking.

She pressed her lips together to prevent her emotion overwhelming her, and took it back to Frau Kirchner. On the way back she looked out of the window where a gentle rain was falling. A man carrying a briefcase strolled past, under an umbrella. It was impossible to believe that people were still going about their business as if nothing had happened.

She placed the address book on the table and opened it at the correct page.

'Madeleine Kettering, Butcher Mews, London N1.' Frau Kirchner read aloud. 'If we can get you to Paris, then you can go by boat to London.'

'I don't want to go to London.'

'It's not safe for you here. On the radio this morning they're claiming there were riots, and protests about the assassination of some embassy official in Paris, a German – Vom Rath – and that's what the beatings are about.'

'You know it's a lie,' Lilli said. 'That's just the excuse they're giving, heaven help us.'

'It's convenient for them.' Frau Kirchner curled a lip in disgust. 'They're blaming the violence on this Jew, saying he started it. So it tells me this – Hitler's condoning it. Because of that, I can't have you stay here either.'

'What about my classes? It's translation today with Herr Groening.' Unthinkable that she would not be going back to university. Even to English lessons. She'd wanted to study telecommunications engineering at the Technische Hochschule, and her father had encouraged it, but the Party had decided women could only study what they called 'soft' subjects, so she was studying English.

If it hadn't been for English, she would never have met Bren, and then she would never have told him— *No. Don't think of him.*

Frau Kirchner sighed. 'Listen,' she said gently, as if speaking to

15

someone deaf. 'I have a friend with a car. We'll get you to France. From there, you must make your own way.' She closed the address book, took hold of Lilli's hand, and placed it firmly on top of it.

'This book, I'll burn it. These people could be in danger because of their connection to your mother. Memorise the addresses you need. You can do that, can't you, Lilli?'

Lilli nodded, too awestruck to speak. Her visual memory was something Papa had always been proud of. Her ability to remember circuitry and recall without effort the facts and figures from a page, even the page numbers they were on. Now though, she knew the problem would not be remembering, but learning how to forget. It struck her all at once. Before there were two of them against the world. Now there was just her, and she was alone.

She flicked through the pages, suddenly mourning the loss of these people – names she hadn't even realised were gone until now. Frau Kirchner put the address book into the stove, pushing it into the flames with a poker until the book flared before collapsing to ash. Lilli pressed her hand to her mouth. Her mother's handwriting, her father's friends and colleagues, everyone they knew, they all dissipated into the smoke as if they had never existed.

Chapter 2

England, 1940

Maddie was a student nurse on shifts and lived in a two-room apartment on the ground floor of a crumbling Victorian terrace. On their nights off, Lilli and Maddie sat together in the evenings, before the popping coal fire, ears glued to the wireless, avid for news about Germany and the progress of the war, but it was frustrating that nothing seemed to be happening, and everywhere people were calling it the 'phoney war'. Although England and Germany had been at war since September, London had been quiet, and for the last six months the ache in Lilli's chest for her previous way of life in Berlin had never eased.

Lilli thought of her father every day, wondered where he was and if he thought of her. She realised she had retained only an idealised image of him; that she hadn't taken enough notice of the particulars of his face. She fought to cling to the memories – how he used to nick himself shaving in the morning, of the frayed edges of his cuffs, of how he'd pace in front of the window when a problem foxed him, the propelling pencil stuck behind his ear.

As soon as it was confirmed on the radio that Germany had

invaded Belgium and the Netherlands, Lilli turned to Maddie. 'That's it. I'm going to join up as a volunteer warden,' Lilli said.

'Don't be daft,' Maddie said. 'They won't have you. Not being German and brought up in Germany.'

'Why not? I'm a refugee. They know that. They gave me papers so I could work as a domestic, didn't they?'

'But that's all you're allowed to do. Nothing that would be a risk to security.'

'How would rescuing people from German bombs be a risk? It's worth a try. I have to do something.'

Though Maddie tried to dissuade her, Lilli was adamant. Being in domestic service was all very well, but it didn't ease her heart, didn't stop the anger eating away at her. She missed her father's riddles, his games of chess, his quick intellect, even his vacant faraway smile. And she was angry that her future had been whipped away. She should have been studying something by now, not clearing out old ladies' dirty sinks and wiping down kitchen shelves.

She went to the library to ask the librarian where the nearest recruiting office was. It would have to be the Women's Royal Voluntary Service, the only unit women were allowed to join.

'There's a recruitment office in Selfridges department store,' the librarian said. 'Looked strange in amongst the furniture displays. Not thinking of joining up, are you? You're our best customer.'

*

Two bored-looking women in heavy face powder and khaki uniform stared out from behind their desks.

'You will need to fill in birth, nationality, age, current address, and place of work, and details about your health and physical fitness,' the blonde one said. 'Have you a pen?'

Lilli took one from her handbag and within a few moments had filled it out. Under 'current occupation' she had written 'domestic' but didn't write down German, instead she wrote down Welsh. She hoped that might explain her accent, though she'd never been to Wales in her life.

She gave Maddie's address, and filled in her name as Lily Berg, naming her mother as the only parent, with 'deceased'.

The other, dark-haired woman barely glanced over it before rubber-stamping it. 'A letter will come within a few weeks inviting you for interview, to assess your suitability, after which you will have to report for training,' she said. 'Your train fare will be paid. Make sure to attend because you are now officially under WRVS orders.'

She handed Lilli a rubber-stamped copy of the agreement.

Lilli pocketed it and walked out with a spring in her step. At last, she'd be doing something useful.

*

The letter of acceptance took ages to arrive, and Lilli leapt on the post every day. Finally, the brown envelope with WRVS written on it and an official postmark dropped onto the mat. She was to report to No. 4 School of Recruit Training in Wilmslow, Cheshire.

'It's come,' she said to Maddie, jumping up and down and hugging her. 'I'm going to be a warden! Training starts next week.'

'I'll miss you when you go,' Maddie said. 'It'll be quiet without you bossing me about and telling me what to do.'

'I don't boss you.' Lilli was hurt.

'Aw, Lilli, it was a joke. It's what we English do – joke about everything. It's how we deal with the hard stuff in our lives. Will you tell them at the Tip Top Club?'

The Tip Top Club was where Lilli had a part-time evening gig as a singer. Reg, the pianist, was Maddie's uncle and they'd gone along one night to hear him play. Lilli had joined in, sung a few numbers, and that was that.

'I'll let Reg know tonight,' Lilli said. 'And I'll tell Mrs Grainger I won't be cleaning for her again.'

'She won't be best pleased, the old bat. Domestics are hard to get now, and she treats you abominably.'

'She's all right. I give as good as I get. And she's lonely, that's all. I might even miss her.'

Maddie laughed. 'You won't miss cleaning her outdoor privy though!'

Lilli couldn't wait to do the training. Living with her father had taught her if she wanted to do something, it would be up to her. No one would do it for her. The thought of her father was enough to galvanise her. She always felt like she was betraying him if she got too comfortable.

The clock in the hall struck half-past eight.

'I'll go up now,' she said to Maddie. She'd need to change, and put on some make-up before going to the club. She opened the wardrobe to choose between her only two dresses, one home-made, one second-hand.

The noise of shattering glass made Lilli startle and turn rigid, and barbed shapes shot up in her mind's eye. Loud noises always had the power to transport her back to Frau Kirchner's parlour, before the war. 'The Night of Broken Glass', they were calling it now, according to the English papers. As if glass was the only thing that had been broken.

Lilli hooked up the blackout blind with a finger. Rain had made the pavements slick and shiny. A curse and a loud miaow. Just a neighbour, tripping over the cat and knocking over the milk bottles on the doorstep. She watched the cat shoot off into the darkness, yellow eyes gleaming, and the man fetch a dustpan and begin sweeping.

She dropped the blind back, remembering. Even now she'd heard nothing more from her father. Letters from the years before the war had been returned unopened, and now no letters could escape the censor and there was only dark silence from home.

A glance at the clock. That time already! She'd have to hurry or she'd be late. She wriggled into the slippery green dress – one she'd sewn from an old quilt cut into pieces – and did up the side buttons. She admired her reflection. It would do. She'd re-stitched the satin fabric on the bias so the patchwork shimmered in different lights.

Quickly she slicked some cochineal mixed with Vaseline over her lips, and threw on her coat. It was threadbare and ruined the effect, but it was the only one she had.

She'd have to run, carrying her platform shoes, to be in time for her spot in the limelight. Not that it paid very much, but once the lilt of the piano started, she could lose herself in another world, a world with no broken glass, no sirens, and no bombs.

On the way out she dragged the curtains over the blackout blind, and called out as she ran downstairs, 'I'm going, Mads, don't wait up!'

Maddie's voice came from behind her door. 'Don't forget your key.'

She hadn't put on the lights, so she felt in her pocket to check, hooking the straps of her shoes over one arm. She stooped to pick up an umbrella and was just about to leave when a staccato rap on the door made her yelp and step back.

The small panes at the top of the door were blacked out, but something about the hardness of the knock made her wary. A sharp, black flash that sounded like a Gestapo knock, even though she was in England. She hesitated.

'Will you answer it?' she called to Maddie.

No answer.

'Mads?'

Maddie came out of her room with the newspaper under her arm, slopping to the door in her slippers. 'You could see who it is,' she grumbled. 'Probably someone collecting for the Sally Army.'

Lilli let the square, no-nonsense figure of Maddie push past her to unlock the chain and the Yale lock, just as the insistent knock came again.

'All right, all right, I'm coming.' Maddie yanked the door open and three men forced their way into the hall. One in a wet trilby hat followed by two policemen.

'Lilliana Bergen?' asked the man in the trilby.

'No, I'm Madeleine Kettering,' Maddie said. 'That's Lilli. What do you want?'

The three men surrounded Lilli before she even had time to blink.

'What is it? What have I done?' She tried to back away, a chill rippling down her spine. This was how they came for people, back in Germany.

'I'm sorry, miss,' the man in the trilby said, 'but all enemy aliens have to come with us. Orders of the government.'

Enemy aliens? No, it must be a mistake. 'You've got the wrong person. I'm a refugee. I came here to escape the Nazis. I've been in London more than two years.'

'We have our orders,' one of the policemen said. 'You can take a suitcase with you though, one suitcase.'

The words hit her like a fist. *One suitcase.* That was what they said to Papa. And she'd no word of him since.

But this was England, not Germany. 'It's a mistake, I tell you. I have all the correct paperwork. Ask anyone. I've a job here, friends here. I'm about to go to work. You can't possibly believe I—'

'We'll give you five minutes to pack,' the second, burlier policeman said.

'Let me speak to someone,' Maddie said. 'She's done nothing. She's about to train as a warden with the WRVS. The letter came today. Wait there, I'll get it.'

'No!' Lilli tried to protest but Maddie had gone to get the letter from the mantelpiece. The men looked a little more uncertain.

'Here!' Maddie said, thrusting it into their hands.

One of the men looked at the envelope. 'Lily Berg? According to our records, you're Lilliana Bergen. Who is this Lily Berg? And it says you're Welsh.' He turned to Maddie. 'She's not Welsh, is she?'

'They got it wrong. It must be a mistake …' Lilli tailed off. She was caught, and couldn't answer.

'I can vouch for her good character,' Maddie said, 'and so can her employer, Reg Benson; she works as a singer and as a domestic for Mrs—'

'It doesn't matter,' said the man in the trilby. 'All that will be looked into later.'

'It's an offence for a refugee to use a false name,' the big policeman said. 'She's to come with us. Fetch your things, miss, or we'll take you without them.'

Lilli looked at Maddie desperately, unable to believe what she was hearing.

'Five minutes.' The trilby man tapped his watch in a manner designed to intimidate.

She ran up the stairs again, her heart thudding. What to pack? Practical clothes. She was still wearing the silk dress, so she grabbed a cardigan and knitted jersey, plus a blouse and a skirt from the rail in the wardrobe, and another pair of flat shoes, the ones she used as a cleaner.

She was stopped in her tracks by the photo of her father, staring out at her from its silver frame.

Oh, Papa, she thought. *Where will they take me?*

She swept it up and pressed it to her heart, then thrust it into the inside pocket of her suitcase. From the dressing table she retrieved the gold Star of David on a chain that her mother had given her as a child. She never wore it, as it drew too much attention, but she couldn't leave it behind.

'Ready?' A man's voice from downstairs.

She grabbed her sheet music from the bedside table and at the last minute remembered her nightdress and squashed it in on top.

When she came down Maddie was complaining about how it was ridiculous, and she'd lose money from not having Lilli's wages coming in.

'Then get another lodger,' the man in the trilby said. 'One that isn't a German.'

'She's a refugee,' Maddie protested. 'She came to get away from Hitler.'

'Same difference.' The burly policeman shrugged.

A police van idled at the kerb in a wreath of exhaust smoke. The officers yanked open the back doors and pushed Lilli to get in. Inside shivered another woman, an older lady, whose white face and carpet bag stuffed to overflowing, told Lilli she'd been caught equally unprepared.

'Where are they taking us?' Lilli asked.

The woman shook her head violently, her mouth sealed shut.

Lilli turned to see Maddie yelling, 'I'll report you! It's disgusting! You can't do this!' and thumping on the side of the van. A noise that felt like small explosions. Then Maddie's desperate voice; 'Lilli! Write, hear me? You'd better write!'

'No talking.' The heavy-set policeman clambered in to act as a guard. His face was set in an expression of hostility.

The other woman just stared with frightened eyes as Maddie kept on banging. The metal doors slammed, and was locked from the outside.

Papa? Lilli sent up a silent prayer. She'd heard nothing from home, even though she'd sent countless messages back to Frau Kirchner in Germany, sheets covered in her blue-black writing. Dozens sent via the neutral Post Box 106 in Lisbon.

She'd written every week, until Frau Kirchner wrote back to tell her gently that nobody had ever returned and it was best to just get on with her life.

You are lucky to be out. Go and live life to the full, Frau Kirchner wrote, *because you never know what's around the corner.*

Now those words seemed to be almost prophetic.

*

After Lilli spent a night shivering in an ice-cold police cell, the door opened and a policeman thrust her suitcase inside. When

Lilli undid the catches, everything had been jumbled together. She felt in the pocket for Papa's picture, but couldn't find the heavy weight of it. The silver frame had gone, the picture jumbled loose amongst her underwear. No sign either of the gold Star of David.

Incensed, she banged on the door. 'You thieves! Give me back my things!'

Nobody answered. Lilli dressed as quickly as she could, fearing someone would come while she was undressed, her arms and legs full of gooseflesh in the chill damp. Skirt, jersey, coat. She put everything back in her case in a semblance of order. Only just in time – with a clank and grating noise the door of the cell opened.

'Ready? The coach will take you to Liverpool.' The burly one again.

Liverpool? All she knew about Liverpool was that it was a port. Her stomach dropped. Not back to Germany, surely? Not back to where she'd be in the hands of the Nazis! How would her father find her then?

She planted her feet. 'I'm not going. I'm a refugee. There's been a mistake.'

'The only mistake is that someone let you Krauts into England in the first place. Now move.' He grabbed her arm, and the thinner policeman hoisted her case roughly onto his shoulder.

They bullied her outside to where a coach was idling, and threw her case into the under-coach stowage.

'Get on,' the policeman said.

The coach was already full of women, staring out with blank faces. None of them smiled as she clambered aboard. The engine revved, and the coach lurched into reverse. Lilli grabbed onto the seats as she staggered down the aisle, with that queasy feeling of being rootless again, of belonging nowhere.

Chapter 3

Lilli found a seat on her own, but further down the quay the coach stopped again and even more women got on. She was joined in the double seat by another older, pinched-faced woman in a worn-out coat and hat.

'Good morning,' Lilli said. Then tried again in German, 'Guten Morgen.'

The woman ignored her and stared fixedly ahead as the bus stuttered off in a grinding of gears. What would they be thinking at the Tip Top Club when she hadn't arrived? They'd be thinking she was unreliable. Singing slots were hard to get, and plenty of other women were after the work and the extra cash. And what about Mrs Grainger? She'd wonder why Lilli didn't come to do the cleaning.

They'd only gone a few more miles and down a long, slow hill when the front of the coach began to belch smoke. The driver pulled over and the young round-faced policeman at the front of the bus got out. Lilli peered out of the window. A metallic creak as the driver raised the hood, and immediately smoke poured out in a black cloud, accompanied by the throat-catching smell of burnt petrol.

'Why've we stopped?' someone called.

Lilli stood up to crane her neck. 'Engine trouble, looks like,' she said.

The woman next to her ignored her.

'Excuse me,' Lilli said, pushing past her. She made her way to the front of the bus and clambered down.

'Hey!' The driver who was now bending over the engine stood up. 'Get back on the bus.'

'I know a bit about engines. Can I have a look?'

Rain had just started pelting down from a grey sky.

'Get back on the bus, you heard him,' the policeman said, trying to take hold of her arm. Rain was bouncing off his helmet. 'We can't have you all wandering about.'

'But the smoke means its overheating somewhere,' she said, resisting and holding her ground, despite the stinging rain. 'I expect the hill overheated it.' She pointed to the brake drums that were burning off brake fluid. 'Look at the steam!' She scoured her memory for the right English terminology. 'Good thing the drums didn't expand past the brake shoes, or your brakes would fail.'

'You're talking rubbish,' the young man said, hunching against the wet. But he stood aside all the same as Lilli rolled up her sleeves. Rain sizzled and evaporated on the engine.

'Have you got a rag?' she asked the driver. 'It will be hot.'

'I'm not letting you mess with my engine! Could be sabotage for all I know.'

She narrowed her eyes, and enunciated in her best English, 'My father was a professor of engineering. Do you want to stand out here in the rain all morning or do you want to get this coach back on the road?'

The driver scowled, but hurried around to the front of the cab, calling, 'Bleeding nuisance. Can't trust these old Crossleys. They're always breaking down. We have to make the 10.15 ferry, or Lord knows what I can do with this lot.'

Lilli stiffened. *Ferry*. 'Where are we going?' she called to the policeman.

He ignored her question as the rain dripped off his helmet.

Perhaps she shouldn't help. But if she didn't, they'd just send another coach and they'd all be cold and hungry. Better to find out sooner than later. The driver returned and reluctantly handed her the rag.

It took twenty minutes for the engine to cool. Lilli found the blockages in the brake vents which were preventing cooling, and unplugged them.

'There,' she said. 'It should be fine now.' Her hair was dripping, and all three of them were soaked. She wiped her wet and oily hands on the rag and passed it back to the driver, before climbing back aboard.

None of them thanked her.

When she walked back to her seat the women all stared at her with glowering faces, as if by helping the driver and policeman she'd stepped over some unspoken line. The woman next to her stared at her oily hands until the coach finally arrived at a town, and they passed through an army checkpoint.

Slowly they trundled down a pot-holed road filled with army vehicles and motor lorries. She guessed they were nearing the port.

'Everybody off!' shouted the policeman.

The coach was only one of many lined up in the dock car park in the stink of fish and engine oil. Lilli clasped her small suitcase to her chest as the luggage was thrown out into the wind and rain, surprised to see how many other buses were disgorging their passengers.

A line of blue-uniformed policemen herded the bleary-eyed women from the other buses towards the boat waiting at the quay. They must have all been woken early, just as she was and chivvied through the cold dawn onto these freezing buses. Some had small shivering children with them, their faces peaky and scared.

Lilli dragged her attention back to the queue. By now there were dock workers and office workers surrounding the cordon behind the police, an unruly crowd of men and women spitting and yelling abuse through the bluster.

'Good riddance!'

A young mother ducked her head as someone threw a stone, and another with her toddler hitched onto her hip hurried past as a man ran alongside shouting, 'Filthy Nazis!'

Lilli kept with the main throng who huddled together as some sort of protection. They were all women, she realised, all carrying just one case. Not a single man amongst them.

Where were they going? The whisper ran through all the women, who were looking for clues on the ship, but it had no destination marked on it. The vision of the men in brown shirts beating her neighbour was seared into Lilli's memory.

They were hounded aboard onto a cramped vessel far too small for the number of women, and to make it worse, the rain and wind increased as the boat got under way. Out of the window the sea rose and fell, choppy and grey-brown as stone. The lashing rain and lurching deck soon drew all the women below. There Lilli shivered, sitting on the floor, unable to find a seat.

A woman who was on the wooden bench opposite, her legs clamped neatly together, said in German, 'I'll be glad when we're home in Germany again.' *Heimat*, she called it, 'homeland'.

Lilli swallowed, feeling nauseous. Germany could never again be her homeland, not since she had witnessed what had happened to Papa and the Kalinskys.

The woman, her fine blonde hair scraped back in a bun, examined Lilli's dark hair and stocking-less legs with disdain and tried to move away, but there was no room to go anywhere; they were crammed in, like herrings in a barrel.

Beside her, one of the little boys wet his pants, and the smell, a shape like a mushroom cloud, seemed to add to Lilli's already queasy stomach. Before long she had to wobble to her feet and stagger, clutching her mouth, to the conveniences at the back of the boat. There, many more women were being sick, even though none of them had had anything to eat.

Still, rather here, than with the woman who thought of

Germany as her homeland. She scrubbed at her oily hands and cupped them to drink some water.

The mothers, their faces strained, tried their best to occupy the children and pretend that they knew where they were going. 'A lovely holiday,' one woman said brightly, though her eyes were as troubled as Lilli's.

After a few hours the engine slowed, the sea swell grew less and the women all crowded to the windows to see what was happening.

Land heaved into view.

Already? This was a shock. Were they to disembark here?

'Gather your belongings and make your way immediately to the deck,' came a voice over a tannoy. Then the message was repeated in German. The shock of the German language galvanised Lilli into movement.

She pushed with the rest towards the stairs and up into the squally light.

The first thing that met her eyes was another line of English policemen, waiting on the quay.

'Where are we?' Lilli asked her neighbour, the woman with the toddler.

'No idea. Ireland, maybe?' The word Ireland reminded her of Bren Murphy, the man who'd betrayed her.

But then the word began to spread through the women. 'Isle of Man.'

She'd heard of it, of course. As a holiday destination. The only trouble was, from the faces on the quay and the way half the beach was cut off by barbed wire, she suspected this was going to be no holiday.

*

A row of desks was ahead of them, under children's drawings of Union Jacks and hand-drawn posters saying, 'Careless Talk Costs Lives.' Behind each desk sat a man waiting to check their papers and belongings. The queue was long, and many of the children were crying or wailing with hunger. Next to her, a hefty woman in spectacles said to another that the police had come for her husband with no notice, and he'd been handcuffed then sent somewhere else to a different camp.

The mood of outrage and resentment made them all restless. England was supposed to be a safe haven. They'd lied to them. Now Lilli was beginning to see that in England she was still considered the enemy, even though she had more reason than any English person here to hate the Nazis.

'Name?'

It was her turn. 'Lilliana Bergen,' she said.

'Single or married?'

'Single.'

'Reason for being in England?'

'Refugee. I'm half-Jewish. It wasn't safe for me to stay in Germany,' she said simply.

The man didn't react. But after all, he must have heard the same thing over and over. 'Put your case on the table.'

She did as he asked and he opened it up and rifled through it. She'd no idea what he was looking for. He picked up the picture of her father, smiling out at him from ten years ago, but he just shoved it back in the side pocket as if it was of no value. She wanted to shout, 'Careful with that!'

He slammed the case shut. 'Handbag?'

She passed it over and he went through it. She was astonished to see him take out her gold-plated powder compact and set it to one side. It wasn't worth much, it had been her mother's, but she was fond of it. He checked her passport and the letter that gave her refugee status, and then took out her purse. This he kept to one side too. He handed the bag back without her compact or change-purse.

'My purse?' she said.

'You won't need money,' he said. 'You'll be given a guinea a week's allowance.'

There was eleven pounds in her purse, all her savings from her singing job. 'But the purse was a gift, from my mother.'

A heavy sigh. He emptied the leather purse into a sweet-shop jar by his chair, shaking out the pound notes and sending the coins clinking to the bottom. It was half full already, and she wondered where it would all go. He thrust the purse back at her. 'Any jewellery?'

'No,' she said, angry. 'The Nazis made us give it all up. Then the police stole my necklace. Now you've stolen my money and my compact. Have you no shame? It's nothing but profiteering.'

Another woman behind her in the queue, shouted, 'Daylight robbery, pure and simple. I've lived in England fifteen years. When I worked as a nurse you were happy enough to take my money in taxes all this time. We don't deserve this.'

The man glanced down at his paperwork, but his mouth tightened into a tense line. 'It's government orders. Nothing to do with me.' He thrust the handbag across the table towards Lilli as if shoving her away.

Government orders? To steal a woman's trinkets? Lilli felt like saying, *then refuse to do it, you toad*, but she knew better than to get a name for herself. 'Keep your head down', had been Maddie's advice since the war started. 'You have to remember, all Germans are the enemy to English people.'

'You're billeted at Bella Vista just off Bay View Road,' the official said. 'You'll be sharing Room 6 with two other women. Mrs Blattner and Miss Grohl. Up Bridson Street, turn left, keep walking until you're nearly at the Prom. It's on your right. The landlady is Mrs O'Brady. Next.'

She was free to go. Angry and disorientated, she headed out into the fresh, briny air. It was still raining, but there was no sign of any soldiers, no one to stop her out on the street. She should be in London, going to work, scrubbing Mrs Grainger's kitchen floor then going home to do the crossword with Maddie by her warm coal fire. It was strange to be let free so suddenly and she felt at a loss. Should she follow orders and go to the billet they talked of, or should she try to run somewhere else? But the Isle of Man was cut off from England. Where could she go to?

If she could, she'd join the army to stop the rise of the Nazis. If she could do anything to get revenge on them, she'd do it. But now they were telling her *she* was the enemy.

*

Bella Vista was a tall Victorian villa painted in white stucco. Five steps up to a front door surrounded by a fake Gothic arch to match the fake arches on the windows. It looked well-to-do, not run-down as she expected. She rang the doorbell and waited until a woman came.

'Oh yes, come along in,' Mrs O'Brady said, in a broad Irish brogue. 'I've been expecting you. Tea's laid out in the breakfast room. Give me your case and I'll take it up.'

'No.' Lilli clutched the suitcase to her side. She wasn't prepared to let it out of her sight ever again. It was all she possessed. And the Irish voice reminded her powerfully of Brendan Murphy.

'All right, dearie, calm down. You go through and have tea. I expect you're hungry. Two slices of bread and jam each, that's what you're allowed. But as much tea as you can drink. Plenty of time for everything else later. Get yourself a nice hot cuppa first. There's a few more in there already.'

And indeed she could hear the tinkle of teaspoons on china. A homely sound, the shape of bells. When she pushed open the door, two other faces looked up at her with interest. Neither were women she recognised, but both smiled as she went to one of the tables. The tables were laid out with bread and margarine, jam in a pot, milk, and a big teapot under a cosy.

The sight of it made her swallow back tears. She was so glad to see something sane after these two days of madness.

She took off her coat and poured herself tea, and ate two

pieces of bread and jam, trying not to wolf them down. She was ravenous. Only then did she look up to see that there was a big bay window to the front of the house, where the road fronted a low wall, over which was an expanse of green grass. Below that the most impossibly beautiful cove. Through the drizzle she could make out golden sand, and the sea lapping gently into a natural bay enclosed by high cliffs. The sun was breaking through now, and just visible to the right, on the clifftop was a white pencil of a lighthouse, unlit of course, and a few white cottages.

'What a view,' one of the other women said.

'I can't believe I'm here,' Lilli said. 'One minute I'm in a prison cell, and the next, I'm in paradise.'

'Same,' the woman said. 'I'm Dorte, Dorrie now I'm here, and this is my sister Frieda. We spell it without the "i" now she's in England.'

'Or was,' said the other woman, shorter and plumper than her sister. 'Was in England. Now we're here, wherever that is. And we don't know when we'll be allowed back home. Bethnal Green. We worked at the tailor's on Chance Street. Till a few weeks ago, anyway. Then they put us in Holloway prison, with the fascists and the murderers.'

Lilli exhaled with relief. So they were refugees like her. 'Lilli Bergen. I worked as a cleaner. I used to be a student. English. But I never finished my course.'

'Like my husband. He taught economics in the university. But he's in a camp somewhere here too now. Can't see him of course. There's barbed wire right across the island. One side to the other. A bloody great fence. Kurt's on the other side of that wire, and there's thousands of men like him on the other half of the island.'

'And the locals hate us,' Freda said. 'They call us "effing Jerries" and say they should send us back where we came from, and I yell back, and say, "Where? Bethnal bloody Green?"'

'Sorry about your husband,' Lilli said. 'What do you think they'll do with us?'

'Nothing, I hope,' Dorrie said. 'Let us sit tight until the war's over. Unless the English decide to bomb us all, or the Nazis invade.'

'You ready now?' Mrs O'Brady stuck her head around the door. 'I'll take you up, show you the bathrooms and what's what.'

They trooped upstairs following the large behind of Mrs O'Brady, who was giving instructions as she went.

'There's rations for everyone but you'll cook on a rota. Lunch will be what you can make – sandwiches or leftovers. Soup some days.' She stopped to point out the WC and the bathroom. 'No more than three inches in the bath. And it'll have to be cold because the electric water heater's broken and we've no men to fix it. Rota will be on the wall. Once a fortnight. Blackout blinds to be down after dark and lights out at 9.30. Otherwise you're free to come and go as you please.'

She stopped to send the sisters into a small room at the back of the house with two single beds. 'There's a sink in every room, but laundry's only to be done on Mondays. Lines out the back for drying. Soap's rationed, you'll get an ounce each when the commissioner comes round.'

Mrs O'Brady left the two sisters deciding who was to have which bed and pushed open a door into a bigger room at the front. Three beds. Two were already occupied by two women in dark coats and hats. They were talking, their backs to the door.

'Ah, Mrs Blattner and Miss Grohl. Here's your other sharer, Miss Bergen.'

The women turned.

Oh no. One of them was the woman who wanted to go 'home' to Germany. Lilli didn't want to share a room with her, but it looked like there was no option. The third bed, the one squashed behind the door, was obviously to be hers, as the other two were sitting on the ones near the window. She reminded herself to be grateful. After all it was a bed, and Mrs O'Brady seemed kind enough.

Lilli smiled at the other two women who were staring blankly at her without expression. 'Very pleased to meet you,' she said.

'I'll leave you to get acquainted,' Mrs O'Brady said, shutting the door as she went.

'What did you say your name was?' The blonde woman's question was not one of someone wishing to make friends.

'Lilliana. Lilliana Bergen.'

'From?' she pressed.

'From London.'

'No, no. Your German address.' She raised her eyes heavenwards as if Lilli was stupid.

'Berlin. I left when things got too difficult to stay.'

'Thought so,' the other woman said. She was a hard-faced brunette in a stiff felt hat. She whispered to the blonde behind her hand. 'She's one of them. I can always tell.'

'Yes, I'm a Jew. So what?' Lilli stuck out her chin. 'We're all equal here in England. Nobody tries to beat us up, or burn down our houses here.'

She turned her back on them, threw her suitcase onto the bed, and started to unpack it.

Behind her she heard heels clack across the floor and the door opened, slamming into her shoulder. 'Mrs O'Brady?'

'What is it?' An annoyed voice called from below.

'We can't have this woman in here with us,' the blonde woman complained. 'She's just insulted us.'

Lilli whipped around. 'That's a lie!'

Mrs O'Brady, tea towel over her arm, looked harassed. 'Now Mrs Blattner, what's all the fuss about?'

'This woman swore at me and accused us of burning down her house.' Mrs Blattner's English was impeccable.

Mrs O'Brady frowned. 'Beggars can't be choosers. All Germans are to go where they're sent. I can do nothing about the room allocations. They're set out by central committee.'

'They don't like me because I'm Jewish,' Lilli said. 'I was perfectly happy to put up with wherever I was sent, but no, they want to create trouble.'

Miss Grohl huffed. 'If you believe that, Mrs O'Brady, you're a fool. It's always the Jews who make trouble,' she said, pursing her lips. 'Ask anyone. It was the same in Germany. You'll soon learn.'

Mrs O'Brady put her hands on her hips. 'Oh is that so? As far as I'm concerned you're all trouble. You're all enemies of England, so you are, that's why you've been locked up, and if you don't stop with this nonsense I'm sure they'll find a better camp for you to go to. One in Australia.' With that she puffed away and her tread echoed down the stairs.

Lilli's stomach was clenched tight as she unpacked her night-dress and put her indoor shoes under the bed. She was about to prop up Papa's photograph on the small bedside cabinet, which was jammed behind the door, but hid it under her pillow instead. She didn't want these Nazi women looking at him.

Desperate to escape their disdainful presence, she ran down-stairs, and out of the front door.

The island was a prison, that much was clear, and worse, she was supposed to live with women who she suspected wanted the whole Jewish race wiped from the earth. No one had told her how long she'd have to stay here, and with no end in sight, how would she stand it?

She strode down onto the hard-packed sand, and spotted a dark swimming cap bobbing in the sea, and arms scything through the water. A swimmer? In this rain? It was coming on summer now after all, so maybe it wasn't too cold.

There was a sign which said, 'No Swimming', but she ignored it. The other woman was swimming, wasn't she?

Within a few moments Lilli had stripped down to her under-wear and folded her clothes into a neat pile on the edge of the sand.

A few seconds later she sprinted into the waves, gasping as the water hit her stomach, but then she plunged in. The saltwater was a shock that made her bob up for air, and she had to keep swimming to keep warm. But nobody stopped her or paid her any attention. She swam out for about fifty yards until she was surrounded by the green-grey sea. Farther out was a wire mesh cordon to stop boats landing, but she didn't swim out that far.

Instead she closed her eyes to feel the slap of the waves. They were unaffected by the war. They rose and fell just the same. It was just her and the sea, the tide lifting and sinking under her. She lay out on her back, not caring that her hair would be ruined, and gazed up into the rain a long time. Was it raining where Papa was? After a while she realised it was not salt water on her face, but tears.

The clang of a church bell, a sudden bloom of blue, reminded her it was getting late. Crying would do no good. When she got indoors she went into the bathroom for a look at the electric boiler. She needed hot water. She lifted the front panel away and squinted inside.

Mrs O'Brady was right; it was an antiquated thing, not like the ones in Germany. But maybe she'd be able to do something. In a drawer under the sink she found various odds and ends, including a blunt pair of scissors and a screwdriver. The plug looked ancient. 'Bakelite', it said on it. She unscrewed it.

It was a simple fuse; that was all. It made her laugh that they'd all had cold water for weeks because of a simple fuse. A pack of spares in the drawer soon fixed it. She turned on the water and the element heated straight away. Hot water gushed out.

Grinning, she imagined her father saying, *Good job, Lilli.*

If only it were so simple to fix the world.

Chapter 4

England, 1941

Neil Callaghan watched the countryside zip past the windows as the train sped south. It was his first time on a journey like this since he'd narrowly escaped death in a London bomb blast. He kept a tight grip on his walking stick, nervous about travelling because his legs were still weak, and the right one was apt to give way.

Once he got out of Scotland everyone seemed to be in a hurry, the stations were full of troops, and when he changed from the East Coast Main Line at Potton, he was jostled at every turn.

'Sorry, sorry,' he kept repeating. His slow crawl, leaning on his stick for support, caused a log jam amongst the crowds on the busy platform.

When he had to change trains, a porter helped him up into the train in a condescending manner and he was dismayed to find it was packed with soldiers, all able-bodied and going somewhere.

'Invalided out?' asked one young man, a cigarette dangling from his lip.

Neil nodded. It was too hard to explain; simpler to match the assumptions.

'Aww, tough luck, mate.'

He bore it – the banter and the smoke – until finally the servicemen got out at Bedford in a noisy kerfuffle of kitbags and swearing, and Neil breathed out at the sudden space in the carriage. The train from then on was slow, and apart from a few women shoppers, empty. He counted out the twelve stations on his timetable, then, juggling his stick and his briefcase under one arm, hobbled down the corridor of the train, grasping the leather straps with his other hand as he went.

From the window he saw the platform sign for Old Bletchley, but it had been painted over. He stared at the blanked-out sign as the train chugged in. He'd heard of Bletchley though, from his boss Beauclerk, in his previous work in the Special Operations Executive. Very hush hush, few even knew the coding centre existed.

At last a grinding of brakes, a lurch, a hiss of steam, and the train clanked to a stop. Neil clung to the door and lowered himself awkwardly down the stairs. A glance up and down the platform. Deserted, except for a few scurrying passengers and the guard, who waved the train on down the Varsity Line.

Sod it. Someone was supposed to meet him off the train and take him to meet a man called Sefton Delmer. He wondered what it was all about. He hoped to hell and high water it was nothing to do with that dreadful business last year. Ugh. Best not think about that.

At a loss, he made his way towards the booking office, trying not to put weight onto his right leg, which was the one that gave him the most pain. No one waiting. From there he went out through the arches onto the cobbled forecourt, but there was no sign of a car. Had he got the date right? He leant up against a wall and propping up his stick, delved in his briefcase for the letter.

It was while he was doing this that a car hooted its horn and

Neil started, knocking over his stick. A young woman in a grey-blue WAAF uniform jumped out.

'Let me!' she said, bending to retrieve his stick for him. 'I take it you're Mr Callaghan?'

'Yes,' he said, attempting a smile.

'Good-O. I'm company assistant Harrison. Lovely day, isn't it?' She leapt to open the back door of the car, a dusty and battered grey Vauxhall, and helped him ease himself in. Her vivacity made him feel ancient. 'It's only about four miles,' she said. 'We'll be there in a jiffy.'

He sat back and watched the landscape roll by; white clouds breaking up to patches of blue, and the red campions swaying in the hedges amidst clouds of may blossom. He hadn't been able to find out anything about Sefton Delmer, except that Delmer was once a journalist for the *Daily Express*, and he vaguely remembered his name in conjunction with some reporting of the Spanish Civil War. Was it him who'd written about the Nazi invasion of Poland, right at the start of the war? Or was that someone else? He couldn't remember.

It was all very mysterious, being summoned like this by letter. After all, he was no use to anyone, hobbling about with two smashed legs. These days it took him fifteen minutes to struggle up a flight of stairs. He hoped whatever it was would have something to do with coding, because that was what he did before – well, before that awful year when his life had gone off the rails. He shuddered. Just the thought of it had the power to make him sweat. If they were going to drag all that up again, he'd be in serious trouble.

He concentrated on the view through the dusty window. The car turned left between two sentries, and down a short drive to a country house with a church tower at the front.

'Wavendon Tower,' Harrison said, as the wheels crunched to a halt on the gravel. 'Isn't it spectacular? I'll take you in to meet Mr Delmer.'

Neil eased himself out onto a gravelled drive. So not Bletchley and coding after all. The plot thickened.

He was led through a gloomy corridor and into a library where a coal fire gave out sooty smoke in the corner.

Delmer, bear-like and bespectacled, stood up with his hand out and a big smile. Neil leant his stick against a chair and grasped hold. Delmer's handshake was firm and warm. He had that air of easy confidence born of getting what he wanted.

'Do sit,' he said. 'Harrison will bring us some tea.'

Neil was glad to get off his feet and into one of the leather armchairs.

'I expect you're wondering what this is all about,' Mr Delmer said, wedging himself into a too-small armchair. 'Have you heard of the Political Warfare Executive?'

'I've heard of it, yes, but I'm not really sure what they do.'

'Ah. Exactly the position I was in a few weeks ago.' Delmer laughed. He had a broad open face and eyes that were very alive. He was a little overweight, which was unusual in these times, and balding already, though he was only, Neil guessed, in his late thirties. 'Basically,' Delmer went on, 'it's psychological warfare we'll be involved in. You know I was a journalist?'

The 'we' bothered him, as if his job was a foregone conclusion, but Neil nodded.

'Well, now I'm going into broadcasting. Radio. We're going to make a radio station that will spout our propaganda. With me so far?' He didn't wait for Neil's answer. 'The idea is to undermine Hitler – pretend to be his fanatical supporters, grow a base of his listeners, and then, once we've reeled them in, do everything we possibly can to damage German morale.'

'If you're looking at me to do this,' Neil said, 'I don't think my spoken German's good enough. Not for radio broadcasting.'

'No, Mr Callaghan. We're going to use captured prisoners of war, people who've fled Germany and have a grudge. They'll all be native speakers. The thing is, we need someone listening in;

someone who can make sure these people are following the script. A chap who can alert us if they say or do anything out of order. A minder, if you like. And of course I can't be everywhere, so I need some German-speaking helpers. People who pick things up quickly. Are you willing to have a go? It's a desk job. Beauclerk thought it might suit, since you're … less mobile these days.'

Just at that moment, Harrison brought in a tray of tea. She gave him a wink before passing him the plate of biscuits.

Neil wondered if Beauclerk had told Delmer about his less-than-salubrious past. It seemed not, and he certainly wasn't going to enlighten him. After last year, he wasn't sure he could cope with any more Germans, even the thought was terrifying.

'I'm not sure I'm really ready for it,' he said, searching for an excuse. 'The bomb really knocked my confidence. I have bad days, you know, when I can't—'

'I don't think I'm being clear. We need you, Mr Callaghan. And MI5 said you would be glad to help, particularly as you made a few … how shall we say? A few faux pas in your last post.'

So Delmer did know. And now he was piling on the pressure. Guilt kicked in, as Delmer must have known it would. And shame. Neil straightened his tie and tried to think positively. Maybe this time it wouldn't all go belly-up and he'd be able to do something positive for his country. Reparation for his wrongs, if you like.

He had no choice. And somehow that was a relief. That he didn't have to choose a side.

'I'm in,' he said. He grabbed a Marie biscuit from the plate and took a bite.

'Oh, good chap.'

It felt like both a jail sentence and a celebration. Neil passed Delmer the plate of biscuits, and Delmer picked one up in his ham-fist and crammed it in his mouth, showering crumbs on his trousers.

'Huntley and Palmers. Where do they get them?' Delmer said through his munching. 'Can't get biscuits for love nor money

43

where I live. Once we've had our tea, I'll take you on a tour of the place.'

Neil took a gulp of his drink. It couldn't be too difficult, could it, supervising people talking on the radio? He wondered who the technicians would be, that he'd be working with. Whoever they were, he'd have to make damn sure nothing of his previous disastrous SOE career ever came out.

*

On the tour, Delmer stopped by a rattling printing press, manned by two women in oily overalls. The drum of the machine was spewing out fake German ration cards. On the table in front of it was a pile of bright yellow booklets which, when translated from the German, read, 'Sickness Saves'. There were great stacks of these under the table too. Neil was beginning to grasp it, that this was some sort of disinformation game.

'Fake ration books,' Delmer said, picking out a sheet from the tray. 'To sow confusion.'

Neil picked up one of the yellow handbooks and glanced through it to find the words in German: 'Better to be ill and live, than be brave and die'. He closed it. 'Do they actually read these?'

'*The Malingerer's Handbook*? God yes. They work only too well,' Delmer said. 'They were supposed to keep German men out of the army. Less of them, more of us, see? Trouble is, this false illness malarkey soon spread, and the Germans translated our pamphlet, the cheeky bastards, and sent an identical one in English back to our troops. So those are being discontinued. The paper will be pulped and re-used. We have a unit that makes our paper look like German paper.'

Sefton Delmer took him out of the building and into another shed-like place with a full newspaper-sized printing press racketing away, and a group of young men poring over German newspapers. Two older balding men in shirtsleeves were at desks, each plugged into radio headsets. They were scribbling down words as if their lives depended on it.

'Gathering material,' Delmer said. 'Anything German we can subvert or make useful.' He waved to get one of the men's attention. 'Oy, Max, come and meet Mr Callaghan – Neil.'

Max, a rangy man with very dark hair that almost brushed his collar, unplugged his headphones and hung them around his neck. He looked Neil over with interest. 'Nice to meet you.' His voice had a faint German accent. Neil was uncomfortably reminded of Otto Hefner, the friend turned enemy who'd blackmailed him when he was at Baker Street.

'Found any dirt this morning?' Delmer asked Max.

'A few leads. We're working on a thing about Kommandant Stift, the man who was too much of a coward to lead his men to the front. We've dug up a bit more gossip about his past, through one of his teachers. The teacher was prepared to talk so long as he could stay anonymous. Seems Stift was a bully as well as a coward. We've got a few juicy stories to keep the station going over the first few weeks.'

Delmer turned back to Neil. 'Yes, I forgot to say, we're broadcasting to the German troops as Gustav Siegfried Eins – GS1 for short. We hope eventually that the troops might pick up that those initials could also stand for Geheimsender 1: Secret Transmitter 1, or for Generalstab 1: General Staff 1. We want them to think it's secret, or that they're listening in on their superiors. Nothing like making them think they've picked up illicit broadcasts from their own side.'

Clever. Neil brightened. This was just the sort of intellectual game that appealed to him.

'Word of mouth is the best publicity. We want to create a bit of a buzz,' Max said.

'By the way, you'll be billeted nearby at Simpson Village,' Delmer added.

'Not here?'

'Don't worry, Harrison has instructions to drive you there and back for the first week or so while you get acquainted with everything. Then once we're fully staffed, there'll be a bus to take workers over. Or bikes.'

Bikes? With my legs? You're joking.

But it all seemed pretty well organised, and it appealed to the strategist in him, this business of controlling the media. Whoever would have guessed it, that this stuff was going on in these sleepy wee Bedfordshire villages, what with Bletchley and Wavendon Tower and now this Simpson Village. 'How much do the Nazis know about all this?' he asked.

'Oh, they know about it, all right,' Max replied. 'They sent a spy to try and find out what we were doing once, but he was caught at Bletchley station when he tried to buy beer in the railway bar at two in the afternoon. The bartender got suspicious, gave him a beer, but then sneaked off to telephone the police and have him picked up. Dummkopf obviously didn't know the English licensing hours.'

Neil laughed. 'At least he gave him time for his beer before they took him in.'

'I understand you'll have to get organised at home,' Delmer said, breaking the jokey atmosphere. 'It's a fair way from Scotland, but we'll expect you down here again by the start of next week. I'll send your travel permits on, and the address of your billet.'

'If there's any chance of a place with no stairs I'd be grateful.'

Sefton Delmer looked taken aback but recovered himself quickly. 'I'll see what we can do.'

'Since Major Hanley moved out there's a ground floor room with us at Mrs Littlefair's,' Max said.

'Then tell her to reserve it.' Delmer rubbed his hands together. 'Fortunately the recording studio's on the ground floor. We'll get you set up at a listening station and then you'll meet Harry Robin, he's our technical whizz.'

'And I'll see you there too,' Max said. 'I like to listen to my wild inventions on air.' He gave Neil a wicked grin, and Neil couldn't help but smile back.

On the way out, Delmer said, 'Know enough for now?' He paused for Neil to catch up.

'I think so. But I suppose I've only one question, which is, does all this really work? Do the Nazis swallow these lies?'

'Sometimes yes, sometimes no. But we aim to change the mainstream German narrative; that whole idea that Germany is invincible and the Führer has public interest at heart. That story drives all compliance – but we want to show the exact opposite – the corruption within the SS. Show them Hitler doesn't care a toss about the average German, only himself. Divide from within, that's our plan – the right kind of poison news can be just as deadly as bombs and bullets.'

Chapter 5

Brandenburg, Germany, 1941

Bren Murphy was one of seven men in the hut making explosive devices using sugar, potash, and flour stuffed into a pipe.

He poured the mix of powder down the funnel, enjoying the sound like sand running into an hourglass. His hands were already reaching for another pipe. Always restless, he relished this training with the Brandenburg commandos, a stiff regime designed to equip them for undercover missions in enemy territory.

Bren glanced at his fellow commandos, all hard at work for the National Socialist Party. He wished the doubters could see them in training – many Germans looked down on the Brandenburg units with derision because they were mostly ex-pats brought back from Europe. He of course was not an expat, not even German, but an Irishman with a PhD in German. Most Wehrmacht men were too soft – they wouldn't last five minutes on the tough assault courses the commandos had to tackle.

Bren flexed his muscles, still stiff from night-time runs through the forest with a forty-pound pack, and continued with his task. He leant into the table, mixing the ingredients with his red

India-rubber gloves and using the funnel to get the stuff inside another tube. He tried not to breathe in the dry gunpowder dust that hung in the air. He stood back, ripped off his gloves, and admired his handiwork. A five pounder – it would knock the smile off someone's face, and half the neighbourhood too.

Practical tasks had always suited him, and anything with an edge of danger. But now, after three weeks in the camp, he wanted action. He couldn't wait to get posted.

'You done already?' His friend Alix Hoffnung asked in perfectly accented English. Alix was another English speaker, who'd been educated in Oxford.

'Yup. Done it before. I've shoved in a little extra. Guess it'll blow a few people out of their boots.'

'God in heaven! Don't let the Kommandant catch you. Don't suppose we'll be allowed to try it out on the testing range,' Alix said. 'There won't be time.'

'Yeah, the training's gone quick.'

'D'you use bombs in Ireland?'

Bren nodded. 'Same sort of thing. Mostly nitro though if we could get it.' He'd been part of the IRA as long as he could remember, from being a nipper. Brought up on it, like everyone else in his street. The Nazis wanted to crush the Brits, just like the IRA. Difference was, the Germans were better organised and better equipped for it too.

'What did you target?' Alix asked.

'Same as the S-plan here. Anything to cause disruption to the English. Electricity sub-stations, trains, government buildings. But one of them went wrong and I had to get out smartish. After that, they upped the surveillance.' He paused, remembering. 'Bicycle bomb. Last August, in Coventry – killed five civilians – one hell of a mess. Supposed to make them take us seriously.'

'And did it?'

'I'll say. Worked too well. Papers had a feeding frenzy and turned everyone against the IRA. Of course it was all backed by the Abwehr, so that's how the Gestapo got wind of me. Von Hippel tracked me down in Dublin and asked if I wanted to serve with him.'

Alix stoppered his metal pipe with the bunch of rag provided, and stripped off his gloves. 'We should be out of here in a few days,' he said. 'Wish I knew where I'd be going.'

'I don't care,' Bren said, 'so long as it's not Ireland. Or the Eastern Front. Hoping for England; get even with the bastards.'

'I'll miss all this.'

'What? Five o'clock wake-up calls and sawing through underwater bridges in minus two?'

'God yes. That was awful.' Alix paused. 'No. I mean having company; like-minded comrades. Out there, we'll be on our own.'

'Just the way I like it,' Bren said.

'What, no women?'

'Only if there are no ties.' His mind went back to Lilli, to her face when she bumped into him with Hilde when he was supposed to be at football practice. That look of shock and incomprehension. But he couldn't hang out with her any more, not once he knew her mother was Jewish. It would have tainted him with the Party for good.

No, she was a pariah. In the end he'd told his PhD supervisor the Bergens were Jewish sympathisers, and it had earned him a bunch of Brownie points with the Gestapo, and consolidated their special interest in him as a trusted member of the IRA.

'First thing I'll do if I ever get to England,' Alix said, a dreamy expression on his face. 'Find a screw.'

'Make sure it's a clean one then. I've heard dodgy whores are the Brits' secret weapon.'

Alix grinned and stuffed more explosive into the pipe.

Chapter 6

Wavendon Tower, Bedfordshire, 1942

When the evening broadcast was over, Neil escorted the German prisoners of war to the coach to take them back to the camp. The fact he had a limp and used a walking stick seemed to disarm them. So far, to his relief, they had all followed the prescribed script exactly.

'I just wonder how my wife's doing,' one of them said, 'now there's nobody to bring in the coal from the store. I think about her lugging the coal bucket up our cellar steps, and I just want to go back and help her.'

Neil murmured a few platitudes, before he watched the man go, perturbed. It was hard when the business of war clashed with the business of being kind.

As he walked back to the studio, in the encroaching dusk, the bats flitting by overhead, he realised that this was the best job he'd ever had, this work with Sefton Delmer. That he actually liked listening to people. He liked the challenge of sifting through the broadcasts and helping Max tailor the best material, and he got on well with his secretary, a middle-aged Austrian lady called Miss Blum, who was tasked with typing all the German up into a script.

He was about to go and see her to check if the transcript was ready for archiving when Delmer stopped him in the corridor.

'This new station. Soldatensender Calais,' Delmer said. 'We're going to need a woman.'

Neil blinked. He'd no idea what Delmer was talking about. Delmer often forgot to fill him in on his thoughts, as if Neil could somehow just divine them from the ether.

'Soldatensender Calais. I see.' Though he didn't.

'To get the ordinary soldier to listen, we need a woman,' Delmer said. 'I discussed it with my wife. She listened in, and she says it all sounds too dry. Not enough music, no female voices. Our programme needs something to attract – no, seduce – the listener. I've got one of my men scouting around the enemy alien camps looking for someone suitable.' Delmer didn't seem to need a reply, so Neil just nodded along as he continued in his expansive arm-waving manner. 'Get Max to look out for some things from Germany that might be of women's interest.'

'What like? Anything specific?'

'Oh, I don't know. Knitting, flower arranging, stuff like that.'

Neil suppressed a smile. He immediately thought of his sister Nancy, who was surviving on her wits in enemy-occupied Holland. She was a match for any man, and she'd slap him if he said anything like that.

'What about articles about the women doing men's jobs now they're away fighting?' Neil said. 'Not only would that be more interesting to the men, but we could also massage it a bit – make it serve our purpose of making the German troops restless, thinking they will all be replaced by an army of women when they get home.'

'Brilliant. That's just the ticket! And we could have them worried about the prostitutes in France, and what the men are up to. As much smut as we can get.'

Smut. The vicar's son in him protested, but he gritted his teeth. 'Right. Yes, I'll get onto it. I'll give it to Max, it might actually put a smile on his face for once.'

Later he asked Max, 'What's this Soldatensender thing?'

'Oh, that. Delmer's new baby. For German troops in France. To get right under the skin of the occupation, and give them as much false information as we can.'

'Ah. More work, then.'

Max looked up at him. 'I love it. The more rubbish they believe, the more I love it.'

*

Lilli dunked a carrot in cold water and began scraping it, her hands so blue you could see the bones. Summer was turning to autumn and there was an unwelcome chill in the air, but they all had to pitch in with these tasks on a rota. The days at the camp on the Isle of Man chafed, but had become routine. In the end, her room-mates, the two Nazi women Mrs Blattner and Miss Grohl, complained so much that they were visited by one of the army captains who told them in no uncertain terms that unless they accepted where they were, they'd be sent to Holloway prison. That shut them up, though they blamed Lilli for it and made her life hell with as many petty complaints about her as they could invent.

Lilli finished the carrots and left them soaking in the big pot on the stove.

An electric heater had gone wrong and they'd asked her to fix it. The lack of men meant she was much in demand for small repairs, but she didn't mind because it kept her busy and stopped her thinking.

Still, she wasn't sure what to do – it being a 'convector' and not just radiant, so she hurried down to the public library.

There she hunkered down to the bottom shelf, dragging out a weighty volume of the *Encyclopaedia Britannica*.

'C' for convector. Ah. Here was something. She soon had the answer and she spent the day happily tinkering with a screwdriver and pliers until the heater was working again.

When it was finished she got on her coat and beret, for it was Thursday and the evening for 'ballroom dancing'. A kind of social club had been set up in the Rushden Scout Hut, and tonight she was meeting Freda and Dorrie to play cards, socialise, and dance. The room was already busy with women leading each other round the floor, chatting in small groups, or playing beetle and rummy at the folding tables.

'Hey, Lilli, wanna dance?' Freda asked.

'Sure.' There was a gramophone that they took turns to mind, and in the corner an old upright piano, a little out of tune. The records in their brown cardboard sleeves were mostly old classical music, but there were one or two of what the English called 'music hall' songs. To Lilli, these songs had the colour and shape of old Bratwurst, but she kept that to herself. Of course it was odd that there were no men to dance with, and they had to partner each other, but at least it was practice.

A waltz was playing so they guided each other round the floor, taking turns to lead.

'D'you know what today is?' Freda asked, as she steered Lilli round the corner.

'No. Your birthday?'

Freda laughed. 'My birthday's in August, don't you remember? No, it's the third of September.'

'So?'

'The anniversary of the start of the war with England, silly. The third of September 1939.'

Lilli stopped dancing, let go of Freda's waist. 'Three years ago? It seems like only yesterday.'

'But in another way, like aeons,' Freda said. 'Do you think we'll ever go home?'

Lilli shrugged. 'I don't want to think about it. I don't even know where "home" is any more.'

Freda shook her by the shoulders. 'Home is where we're safe. Where we can go where we like and do what we like, and always come home to family.'

She looked like she was about to cry. Lilli thought of Papa and reached out to squeeze her in a tight hug.

After that, by tacit agreement they gave up dancing and walked over to the piano.

Freda said, 'Go on, Dorrie, play something for us. I'm sick of these same old records over and over.'

'It'll be too sad. It'll remind me of home,' she said, 'and we're not allowed German stuff.'

'Maybe an old tune would be good today. Three years. Maybe we can hope the war will be over soon and the politicians will see sense.'

'Not unless someone shoots Hitler,' Dorrie said glumly. But she took a deep breath and sat down at the piano to play. The piano reminded Lilli of home too – so far, she hadn't even dared to touch the keys. Dorrie began a Beethoven accompaniment, one for the song 'To Hope' that had been banned by the English as 'too German' to be played.

There was a small gasp as she began, and the whisper 'Beethoven' ran round the room.

Gradually the women gathered to listen, standing in silence by the piano. Lilli knew the German words, but didn't open her mouth to sing. The sound of the piano was so poignant, the music like swirling clouds, or the murmuration of birds.

As the last note died away, they cheered and whooped.

'Play us another,' Lilli said. 'But something less sad.'

'Yes, something we can jitterbug to,' Freda said. 'I want to let off steam. I'm tired of the same miserable records.'

Dorrie crashed her hands down in the opening chords of 'Chinese Moon'.

Lilli jolted to attention. The music was like a slice of sunshine. She used to sing this as a standard at the Tip Top Club. From being a toddler, she'd always loved to sing, to be in control of the notes as they formed shapes and colours.

Her feet began to tap, her body to sway. After the introduction, unthinkingly she launched into the vocals. Her rich contralto voice echoed in the draughty hall.

'Go, Lilli!' The women took partners to dance, and at the end, yelled, 'Bravo! More!'

Dorrie started another popular number, and Lilli opened her heart to sing. After that it all became a blur.

Excitedly she asked Dorrie, 'Do you know, "In the Mood"?'

Dorrie answered with the opening chords, and everyone tooted the horn part. Delighted, Lilli kept on singing, number after number, all the songs she knew from the Tip Top Club. When eventually she stopped, it was to see that word had spread that there was a party going on and the hall was full. In the crowd she spotted the sour faces of Miss Grohl and Mrs Blattner. The next time she looked, they had gone, but more jiving women seemed to have materialised in their places.

She finished the song and embarrassed, gave a small curtsey to a spontaneous, raucous round of applause. Dorrie started 'Lili Marleen' and Lilli began.

The door flew open and Mrs Atkinson from the island committee burst in, closely followed by Miss Grohl and Mrs Blattner. 'Stop that noise!'

Dorrie stopped mid-bar. The hush was electric. Lilli glared at the two women at Mrs Atkinson's shoulder. Obviously Miss Grohl or Mrs Blattner must have reported them.

Mrs Atkinson grew purple in the face. 'The community centre is closed. Closed, d'you hear?'

'Everyone out!' shouted her second-in-command, Mrs Barber. 'Rations will be cut if we have any more nonsense.'

A chorus of 'Aw! Shame!' Another reminder, as if they needed one, that they weren't free, even to do something as innocent as sing a few songs.

Mrs Blattner looked to Miss Grohl with a smile of satisfaction.

The next evening when they went back to the hall to have a few games of beetle and housey-housey, the piano had gone. The gramophone was still there, though, with its dusty pile of music hall 78s. Unfortunately, no one felt like dancing.

*

A few weeks later Lilli was doing the laundry in what Mrs O'Brady called the scullery at the back of the house. It was a windy October day, and she hoped to get her bedsheets out onto the line to dry. She stared through the mist into the back alley with the dustbins and the line hung with other people's vests and slips, and sighed. Life was passing her by. Twenty-three years old, and still the war dragged on; a cold winter of short rations and misery that seemed never-ending. Lilli was longing to do something, anything, to end it. She looked back into the suds and rubbed harder.

'Lilliana Bergen?'

Startled, Lilli turned through the steam from the washing tub.

'You were the one singing when that other girl was playing the piano. Mrs Grohl told us.' It was Mrs Atkinson, the one who always wore a faint sneer of disapproval under her jammed-down felt hat.

'That's right,' Lilli said, still clinging onto the laundry tongs. 'It was just a bit of fun.'

Mrs Atkinson frowned. No doubt she thought her impertinent. 'There's someone from London coming to meet you tomorrow.'

'Why?' She dropped the tongs into the water. 'Have I done something wrong?'

'He wants someone who can speak German and sing. You seem to fit the bill. Now don't ask me what it's about, because I don't know. And I've been asked to keep the whole thing quiet, so before you ask, there's nothing else to know, except you've to come down to the office tomorrow. He's coming by boat. Two-thirty sharp.'

'By boat? To see me?'

A sigh of frustration. 'That's what I said. But remember what I told you. You've to keep quiet about it, all right? Not a word to anyone.'

When she'd gone. Lilli pondered on it. Were they going to complain that she'd been singing German songs? The old panic set in. Would they lock her up somewhere worse?

She didn't sleep much, worried she'd be carted off again to jail. But the next day she dressed in her tidiest skirt and least-darned jersey and brushed her hair till it shone. She'd try to make a good impression, whoever the man was. Maybe it would go better for her that way.

It was a cold, windy day, so after her ration lunch of thin soup and a margarine sandwich, she hurried over to Mrs Atkinson's 'office' which was really the front bedroom of another Victorian boarding house. It had been hastily furnished with two filing cabinets, a big desk, and an assortment of mismatched chairs. A clock hung on the wall; Mrs Atkinson ran everything strictly by the clock.

Lilli glanced up at it. Two-thirty. Bang on time.

A man was already hunched there, perched on one of the chairs, with his head in his hands.

He stood up as she entered. Youngish, with a fashionable broad tie that seemed to have got wet somehow. His face was grey. 'Mr Clarke,' he said, introducing himself. 'I'm sorry, I had a bad crossing. You'll just have to pardon me while I get some air.' And he rushed off down the stairs. They heard him throwing up into the gutter.

'Poor man,' said Mrs Atkinson. 'Looks like he's a bad sailor.' She went to fill a glass of tap water. 'Fancy, and all this way just to see someone like you.' She made it sound like the seasickness was all Lilli's fault.

It didn't bode well. The whole thing seemed to be off to a bad start.

They waited until they heard his footsteps returning.

'Sorry about that,' he said, pushing his handkerchief back into his pocket. His eyes were red and watery.

Mrs Atkinson handed him the glass and he sipped warily. 'You say there's a piano here,' he managed.

'There was,' Lilli said, still wondering what it was about. 'But they took it away.'

Mrs Atkinson sniffed. 'It's been put back,' she said. 'Since Mr Clarke asked for it.' Her tone was one that said, *And it was a lot of bother.*

Mr Clarke ignored Mrs Atkinson. 'Then let's go there, Miss Bergen. I could do with the air.'

Was he a pianist? He looked like an office clerk. Would he ask her to sing? She led the way along the front, and indeed the sea did look rough; heaving grey breakers smashed against the beach. Mr Clarke kept his gaze on the pavement as he followed her in silence, occasionally stopping to press his handkerchief to his mouth again. 'You go in,' he said. 'I'll just be a moment.'

She left the mysterious Mr Clarke hanging over the railings still looking green.

The hall was empty, as it often was in the daytime with the women doing their chores. It smelled of dust and the old velvet curtains on the stage. The piano looked lonely with no crowd around it. She sat down and ran her hands over the keys. Glory be! It had been tuned! She didn't want to play because her playing was rudimentary and made such jagged images. She'd always preferred to sing.

She gave herself a note or two to find the key, smiling as the notes rang out in pure lemon and gold, then launched into 'Blue Moon', a slow unaccompanied rendition, and she let the notes linger.

She was halfway through when she sensed someone behind her. She paused mid-note.

'Don't stop, Miss Bergen.'

She continued to the end, her voice haunting in the echoing hall.

'Can you sing German jazz? Something raunchy that would appeal to a Nazi soldier?'

She frowned. Was it a trick question? 'I'd rather not.'

He sat down at the piano stool, and crashed his hands down into a ragtime bluesy stomp, complete with rapid trills and syncopations.

She was baffled. It was a tune she'd never heard before.

'Don't know it?' His thin face had gained some colour and he made a snorting laugh. 'Never mind, Miss Bergen,' he said, turning from the keyboard. 'You've got the job. You've a belting voice. Time to talk about what to sing later.'

'Sorry, but I don't understand.'

'We need you, Miss Bergen. There's a job waiting with our special English radio station for a woman who can sing in German. A professional. Someone who will volunteer to help the English war effort.'

'By singing in German?'

'Yes. We will provide you with accommodation and a small allowance. You'll be based in the English countryside.'

This was unexpected. She backed away, wary. 'Is it another camp?'

'No. You will be a free woman while working for us. Well, with only a few restrictions.'

'And if I say no?'

'Well, you'll just stay here. But it will go on your record as being, how shall we say, unhelpful.'

'You mean I don't have a choice.'

'Miss Bergen, your records show that you are Jewish. I take it you want to do everything you can to stop the Nazi persecution of Jewish people wherever they live. So, it is a choice. Sit here and do nothing, or come and help us.'

He turned back to the piano and began to crash away, murdering another tune. She winced as the notes made staccato peaks. His cufflinks flashed as his hands pounded the keys. Should she go? She'd got used to it here, and the world out there, the world at war, was frightening. At the same time, the thought of joining the war effort, or reaching people by radio seemed too good an offer to miss. Even the word 'radio' reminded her of her father, and wherever he was now, he'd have a radio with him and be tuning into whatever he could get.

She watched Mr Clarke hammer the keys. Yet she still wouldn't be free. She would still be under the thumb of the English. Was this better than being under the thumb of her own countrymen?

He finished with a crescendo of chords. 'Well, Miss Bergen?'

'This radio station you're talking about, why would they want me to sing in German?'

'I can't tell you. Not until you sign something. But I can tell you there'll be other Germans there, and other Jews, and state-of-the-art equipment, and all the latest in radio technology. Tempted yet?' He gave another thump on the piano.

That clinched it. She let the chord die away. 'Thank you, Mr Clarke. When do I start?'

Chapter 7

England, 1942

Two army officers escorted Lilli and Mr Clarke on the *Maid Marion*, the specially requisitioned fishing boat to Heysham. It stank of engine oil and fish, and in the distance she could hear the firing of guns and the occasional flash of fire. Winter at sea: rough, dark, turbulent, and frankly, terrifying. No wonder Mr Clarke had been seasick. He spent most of the trip in the toilet cabin below, and then after they'd staggered off, and got the train, he was still green until they had to say their hurried farewells at Preston.

'Goodbye, Miss Bergen. And best of luck,' he said. He stuck out a hand and they shook like old friends. It was the first time in a long while she'd been treated like an equal, and she found it oddly moving.

This feeling was short-lived when she was told to get in the car driven by a tight-lipped woman in FANY uniform, who slammed the door after her and was obviously in a bad temper. Lilli bore with it, as the woman, Second Lieutenant Webster, stalled at junctions and swore while grinding through the gears.

'Leave the clutch down a little longer,' Lilli said, 'then it won't stall.'

'Who's driving?' Webster spat back. 'Me or you?'

The long journey through many *road closed* signs, diversions, and fallen trees and branches didn't add to her mood.

'How much further?' Lilli asked.

Even this attempt at conversation stalled, when Webster said, 'Just get some sleep, won't you? I need to concentrate.'

The journey seemed interminable; the view from the window obscured by mist and grey drizzle, the country roads all looking the same with the signposts blanked out, and the only comfort break was a stop in a lay-by with cows peering over the gate. The woman driving her wouldn't tell her anything about where they were going. 'It's classified', was all Webster would say, and exhausted by the journey and lack of answers, Lilli fell asleep in the back of the car.

'Oy! Nearly there.' A sudden voice above the squeak of the wiper.

Lilli struggled to come to, peering out of the window in the low evening light. 'Simpson Village,' Webster said with satisfaction. 'Godforsaken bloody place.'

Lilli's first impression was one of intense disappointment. Simpson wasn't even a village, just a few brick cottages strung along a lane of bare trees. Not a shop, a post office, or a pub in sight. Even the Isle of Man had been better than this. The place looked like a real dead end.

'This is you,' Webster said, pulling over to drop her off on the curve of the road. 'Number three.'

Lilli dragged her single suitcase out of the boot – it was her mother's, the same one she'd had ever since she left Germany.

'You'll need this,' Webster said, thrusting a buff-coloured booklet into her hand. 'And you'd better behave yourself if you don't want to be shipped straight back to the Isle of Man.'

Two blasts of the horn and the car backfired and kangaroo-jumped away.

She opened the booklet. Some sort of pass with a photo copied from her old ID. Suitcase in hand, and feeling somewhat abandoned, Lilli walked up the pot-holed road looking for number three, and was glad to see it was one of the bigger semi-detached houses, with a front garden neatly trimmed, and clean windows.

She banged on the front door, and a bony arm reached out to drag it open. A tall, dark man filled the doorway and looked her up and down. 'I'm Max,' he said. 'You're Lilliana, right?'

'Lilli,' she said.

'Mrs Littlefair's out. It's her WI night. She said you were coming, and to show you up to your room.'

A German accent, not an English one. He was thin, with a sharply angled face and fine black hair that fell in his eyes. 'Yours is at the back I'm afraid.' He beckoned her in and up a flight of narrow stairs. 'Two of us Aspi folk are sharing the front. Me and Ron Bottomley. And another's on the ground floor. Neil Callaghan. He got hurt in a bomb blast and can't do stairs.'

Max pushed open the door and she was glad to see it was a single bedroom. Privacy at last. How she'd longed for it. 'Thank you,' she said. 'What's Aspi?'

'The Aspidistra transmitter that we use at the radio station. We call it Aspi for short.'

She didn't get why the English could call it such a long name and then have to call it something else 'for short'.

'They want me to sing,' Lilli said.

He nodded. 'We need a few more female voices, or it would look odd, and not like a real radio set-up. Most of the POWs are men. They'll be excited to see you.'

'You're a POW?' Had he been in the Wehrmacht? She felt her smile die on her face. She'd been prepared to like him.

'Good grief, no. Refugee. You?'

'Same.' The relief made her smile. 'I was in a camp on the Isle of Man. Thought I'd never get out.'

'Jewish?'

'Does it matter?'

'Not here, no,' he replied. 'There's quite a few Jewish refugees like me at the station. And Catholics. In fact, anyone the Führer took a dislike to, which I have to say seems to mean just about anyone interesting.'

She let herself relax. He was not a Nazi.

'There's a corned beef sandwich under the fly cover in the larder. Mrs Littlefair said to tell you. Help yourself to Camp coffee from the bottle. But it's disgusting stuff, so you'll probably try it only once. And it'll have to be black, we've no milk.'

He turned to go into the room opposite.

'Max?' she called after him. The relief made her almost euphoric. 'Thank you.'

He raised a hand in farewell and disappeared into his room, before sticking his head out again almost immediately.

'I nearly forgot. We have bicycles to get us to the RU at Simpson's. We leave at eight o'clock sharp, or Mr Delmer gets in a funk.'

'What's RU?'

'Research unit. That's what they call the studio so the locals don't know exactly what we do. They don't like the idea of the enemy in their midst.'

Aspi. RU. It was all baffling. She hoped she'd be able to keep up.

*

Lilli had slept like a baby, and only woke to the banging of feet on the stairs. There was time only to grab a piece of Mrs Littlefair's charred black toast and margarine, and a mackintosh, before following the others to the bicycles propped up in the rain by the garden shed. Max was with his room-mate Ron, a thick-set English chap with a face full of freckles.

'Do you want to bike with us, or wait for the coach?' Max asked Lilli.

'Is it far?'

'Not really. But Callaghan and some of the others from the other villages prefer the coach. I like to keep fit, because I'm at a desk most of the day.'

'I'm game to cycle,' Lilli said. She'd put on her only pair of slacks, just in case.

Ron exchanged a conspiratorial grin with Max.

They wheeled out their bikes, leaving her struggling in the downpour with the most antiquated-looking bicycle that had probably once belonged to a delivery boy.

She pushed off and pedalled like fury, cursing the bike which weighed a ton and had no discernible brakes, along with a tendency for the chain to stick. Immediately she named the blasted thing Goebbels, the man her father despised with a vengeance. Once off the road, she found the track to the radio station was through a dense forest, which at least gave a little cover from the pelting rain, though it was steeply uphill, and she thought her lungs might burst. Ahead of her, the men's legs pumped easily up the incline as they stood on the pedals. She gritted her teeth as she saw Max look back, and she put her head down to pedal harder.

Later, as she sped downhill, she realised they'd gone in a circuit, that they were almost back where they started, on the flat. By the time she arrived, their bicycles were propped up against a tall wire fence and they were barely out of breath.

'You beasts!' she said, as she slid off the saddle, panting. 'You never said it was all uphill.'

'It's not,' Ron said. 'We took you the long way round. We have to avoid the village because villagers don't want Germans like Max hanging about.'

'Anyway, it's an initiation test,' said Max. 'You are now officially a Radio Rat.'

'And what exactly is that?' she asked, indignant that they'd played a trick on her, and fearing it might be an insult. She knew her hair was dripping and that her face must be hot and red.

'A sort of club,' Ron said. 'Of the people who work here and take no nonsense from their bosses.'

'Huh. How old are you all? Seven? You'll be telling me next you have a …' *What was the word?* 'A hideout,' she finished triumphantly.

'Could be,' Ron said cheerfully. 'But we make do with The Plough. We have to be careful though, because we're not supposed to drink in local pubs. They're scared of us getting drunk and letting out all their secrets. Get your pass ready, we'll need them.'

The cycling up the hill meant she had to open her raincoat and fan her neck before she could push the bike any farther. She hadn't banked on arriving this dishevelled to meet her new boss, Mr Delmer.

But Lilli hadn't time to worry; Ron and Max were heading towards two stone gateposts and a wall with a barbed-wire fence. There was a sign warning people to *Keep Out* and a Ministry of Defence badge. The grounds had the air of a country house, with a manicured lawn, formal primula beds and ornamental trees, though the whole area was surrounded by barbed wire and armed soldiers stood at the guardhouse. They passed through a new metal gate, where there was a sentry box to keep the soldiers out of the rain. An Alsatian dog barked and strained at his leash. It was the opposite of a welcome.

'Oh look out, here comes the coach and Delmer's car,' Max said. 'Best get inside. Callaghan's a stickler; he won't take any fooling around. Takes it deadly seriously.'

They showed their passes, parked the bikes in the rack, and nipped along the path towards the house, as the coach pulled up behind them. Now they were past the fence, the house looked impressive, like something from an old Victorian melodrama. Virginia creeper grew up its walls and it had a tower like a church on one side. 'Welcome to Wavendon Tower,' Ron said.

It was a far cry from the Isle of Man, at least, thought Lilli.

Inside the door they led her down a long corridor.

Max shouted out the names of the rooms as they passed; 'Switchboard, Laundry, House-staff Dining Room. Boss's Office, Library, Newsroom, Recording Room 1, that's the small one, and here we are.'

He pushed the door open. *Recording Room 2*, said the plaque on the door. It was nothing like she could ever have imagined. This had obviously been a drawing room, judging by the elaborate plaster ceiling rose, only now there was brown cardboard pinned to the walls, and the furniture was strictly utilitarian: metal-and-canvas chairs, and a work surface made up of four tables with metal legs shunted together.

'Watch where you put your feet,' Ron warned her. The floor was covered in snaking wires, all taped down to the floor, and big sharply angled floodlights were pointing in from the corners. It looked exciting, like a film set.

Above the fireplace, now boarded up, hung two clocks, one labelled *London*, the other *Berlin*. It brought her up short.

Berlin. Where Frau Kirchner lived in her tiny apartment on Ludwig-Koch Platz.

The sorry state of Germany was suddenly present in the room with her. To make it worse, the only familiar item in the room was a piano, a German Blüthner, exactly like the one Frau Kirchner used to have. Lilli walked over to look at it, instantly transported back to the day her father was taken.

'Lilliana?'

Max was calling her over and pointing at the coat stand. Lilli swallowed hard and went back to hang up her wet coat and beret. She scraped the hair back from her face, wiping it with a sleeve.

'You okay?' Max asked.

'Fine,' she said, though her heart was beating double time. A few moments later she heard uneven footsteps and tapping in the corridor.

'Ah, that'll be Mr Callaghan,' Max said, glancing at the clock. 'Always on time.'

He was a tall fair man with one crooked leg and a distinct limp. He was leaning on a stick, and his brow seemed already furrowed by worry. He spotted her straight away and introduced himself as the unit manager in charge of personnel. 'Mr Delmer'll be along in a minute,' he said. 'He's gone to talk to the canteen staff.'

'And get himself a butty, no doubt.' Ron nudged Max.

'Or two, knowing him.' Callaghan smiled. 'I'll need to do some recording tests.' He was brisk and business-like, and it seemed he wanted to get to work right away.

He got set up in an efficient manner, plugging in the microphones at one end of the table before concentrating on the switches and dials on the bank of gun-metal grey consoles that ran down the side of the room. How Papa would have been fascinated by all this! Lilli longed to go over for a closer look, but it would have looked presumptuous on her first day.

'First, a voice test,' Mr Callaghan said, putting on headphones. 'Max, can you give Miss Bergen some material to read?'

Max passed over a German newspaper. Lilli glanced at the date. It was only two days old. She was incredulous. How had they got this? It was the newspaper *Der Führer*. That horrible Nazi rag. Just to see the printed emblem of the eagle and swastika, the heavy black type, gave her a chilling sense of dislocation.

She remembered the overcoated men huddled around the newsstands, the underlying fear and tension as they scanned this paper for the latest directives from above, the lists of who would be fired, and who would be 'transferred', never to return.

'Second article on page three, try that,' Neil Callaghan said.

She couldn't focus, she wanted to read the whole paper cover to cover, to see what was going on in Germany, and yet the thought of reading the Führer's version of the news revolted her.

Her hesitation made Mr Callaghan turn. 'You can do it,' he said, more gently. 'Don't be shy. We know it's a fearful load of tosh. Just start. It gets easier after that, I promise.'

She began to read, the German words flowing easily from her

tongue. 'Schnellbootangriff auf Deutsches Geleit Abgeschlagen.' A report from war correspondent Gustav Herrmann about a naval attack on a German convoy. According to this, the attack had been victoriously repelled.

A hand-scribbled note was stuck to the paper with Scotch tape. 'Lies. Sunk. No survivors. See over.'

Briefly, she wondered how this Gustav Hermann could live with himself, writing this propaganda for that despicable man Hitler. She carried on reading.

'Sounding good. A little louder please,' Neil said. 'And brighter. Try to make it sound like excellent news. And read the extra script taped to it overleaf too, please.'

The extra sheet said, in German, '*Our men who died in the explosions have been buried at sea. Unfortunately due to a govern-ment shortage of body bags, they were buried overboard in batches, without …*' She read it out with a growing unease. Could this be true? She felt sorry for the relatives of these men who had such an undignified end, but she kept on reading into the mic until Callaghan told her to stop.

'First rate,' Mr Callaghan said, taking off his headphones. 'Your voice is very easy on the ear. We'll have to give you a name. You can choose something. Make it sound seductive, something that conjures up the spirit of Old Germany. Something that would please a Nazi soldier.' He smiled at her, and his smile was surpris-ingly boyish. She'd thought him older because of his limp. 'We want to get as many impressionable Wehrmacht soldiers believing in our broadcasts as possible,' he went on. 'You'll broadcast every evening for the music session, and be on call to read bits of news, like the item you just read. Delmer wants information, music, information. Like a sandwich. And only half the news will be true, the rest fake – doctored to our needs.'

'Will I get the material in advance?' she asked. 'I don't want to be stumbling over the words.'

'As far as humanly possible, yes, but it has to have the feeling of being live broadcasts, see? So sometimes we won't be able to, because the news is so fresh. Just do your best and I'm sure it will be fine.'

The door swung open in a hiss of air. 'Ah, here's Mr Delmer. Just in time to hear you sing. Can you sing jazz?'

'Love it. But it's a long time since I sang any.' It was banned. Anything from Berlin's 'hot clubs' was, because of it having African roots, and because the best horn players and saxophonists were Jews.

'Sing us something in German. The jazzier the better,' Mr Delmer called. He'd taken off his heavy overcoat and was sitting on the other side of the table.

'It's not jazz, but how about "Lili Marleen"?' Lilli asked. 'We had a recording of that in the Isle of Man. I've no music for it though.'

'Doesn't matter,' called Mr Delmer. 'Do it without for now, straight into the mic. We'll get you some music and musicians to play for you, before we broadcast anything.'

'Actually, I know it,' Mr Callaghan confessed. 'And I can play basic chords, if you don't mind it being a bit rusty.'

From the reaction of everyone else, it seemed that this was a surprise. Mr Callaghan took off his headphones and limped over to the piano. Standing, leaning against it to stay upright, he ran his fingers along in a trill, and then played the first few chords. Lilli saw it as a ripple of green, like hay in summer. Thank God, nothing like Mr Clarke's bashing at the keyboard.

Mr Callaghan turned and made a nod to Lilli to begin. After humming to try to find the right key, she closed her eyes and began, holding the mic stand in one hand and the mic as if it were a delicate egg. The piano music seemed to open something in her heart and she crooned quietly, as if to herself, imagining the lantern and the lamplight and saying farewell to someone she loved.

Vor der Kaserne
Vor dem großen Tor
Stand eine Laterne
Und steht sie noch davor,

So woll'n wir uns da wieder seh'n,
Bei der Laterne wollen wir steh'n
Wie einst Lili Marleen. Wie einst Lili Marleen.

As the verses went on, she found herself thinking of home, of the university, of her friends, and wondering if she'd ever see them again. Bitterly, she wondered what had happened to Bren Murphy. And Helmut, the friend who used to accompany her on the piano accordion at the 52 Club in Berlin, who used to try to sell her copies of the *Die Rote Fahne,* full of fanatical communist ideas and zeal. Like all communist sympathisers he was rounded up and arrested. So many friends gone.

Her eyes prickled and the room became blurred. By the time the last verse came, she could no longer sing without sobbing and came to a stop. The piano music ceased instantaneously, and the bunker was filled with an intense silence.

The few seconds stretched like a solid wall.

Finally, a handclap. 'That was marvellous.' Mr Delmer stood and walked towards her, offering her a handkerchief. 'Well done.'

More spontaneous applause. 'God, she's good,' she heard Ron say behind her. 'What a voice.'

Everyone came up then to congratulate her, and Lilli tried her best to accept the compliments gracefully. But at the same time, that hunted feeling deep inside, the feeling of having lost something precious and not knowing where to look for it, made all her smiles and thanks feel false.

She turned to thank Mr Callaghan for his playing. He was staring at her, his body very stiff and upright, his eyes glassy. She saw him swallow and then turn to pick up his stick. She had an instinct he was in pain, just as she was, and she wanted to say something to him. She set off towards him, but he limped away to his desk as if deliberately avoiding her. She stopped mid-track. She wasn't sure what to say, and now the elusive moment for thanks had fled.

'Who would've thought it?' Max said to Ron in a low voice. 'I never knew old Callaghan could play like that.'

Delmer came over to talk to her about the sort of material he wanted her to sing. 'Nice voice, but far too polite.' She opened her mouth to protest, but he was continuing. 'We want bawdy stuff – stuff that will hook the lowest kind of common soldier. The rougher the appeal, the better.' Delmer tapped a fleshy finger on the table. 'No one can stop gossip. If I was to invent some sort of bogus military doctor who said Hitler had the pox, it would soon get around – spread like wildfire. We want to give credibility to that creeping kind of rumour.'

Lilli frowned, unconvinced. Did they really want her to be singing the worst kind of dross?

'Come and sit,' Delmer said, reading her expression. 'Forget decency. We want modern stuff the Nazis forbid. The soldiers will spread the word and make the Germans see that their leaders are self-serving and corrupt – break the link between the men and their overlords. Cover, cover, dirt, cover, dirt, that's the way we want to go. Are you game?'

'If it works, yes. I'll happily sing every swear word in the bloody dictionary if it brings the Nazis down.'

Mr Delmer leant back and roared with laughter. 'Great news.'

She glanced over to where Callaghan was sitting, still in his raincoat with the damp shoulders. Again, he was watching her reaction. She flushed at her language and looked at her knees.

'Tomorrow night we'll begin rehearsals, so we at least get the first few right. After that we'll be on the hoof, so to speak. We've got a whole German band lined up for you, prisoners of war.'

'Try not to spit in their coffee, Ron,' Max said.

'No need,' Ron said, turning away from the console. 'They won't be getting any.'

Prisoners of war. Lilli tensed. She hadn't considered she would need to talk to actual Wehrmacht soldiers.

Chapter 8

Lilli paused on her bicycle to watch the German POWs arriving the next day on the old military coach. They were a sorry-looking bunch, wearing too-thin clothing, their hands blue with cold from labouring work on the nearby chicken farm. Young men whose swagger had all gone, replaced with a humbleness that stuck in Lilli's throat. She couldn't forgive them though. Who knew what atrocities these men had perpetrated in the name of the Third Reich?

She'd been given sheet music and the bawdy words to a song that made her wince, though she'd rehearsed hard to learn it enough to perform. She tried not to look at the musicians, all POWs, as she belted out these vulgar songs in rehearsal, still in her coat, for there was no coal and the room was so cold she could see her breath. One of those German prisoners could have been responsible for dragging women and children from their homes and bludgeoning them. Her anger made her voice guttural and sharp, her consonants bitter and staccato.

Once she'd finished, she slunk to the side of the room feeling drained.

'Excellent,' Delmer said. 'Just what we wanted.'

She tried to feel pleased, but the sight of the POWs congratulating themselves left a bad taste in her mouth.

Also on air was an actor called Len Hubbard, a man with a burgundy silk cravat knotted at his neck and an impeccable suit. Lilli asked Ron about him and discovered he was a German expat actor living in England, formerly known as Len Sieg, who'd been recruited to do the continuity between items.

'Get me a cup of tea, would you, darling?' he asked Lilli, after she'd rehearsed her second song, clearly expecting her to jump to it.

'Lilliana is on air tonight at the same time as you,' Mr Callaghan said frostily, 'with our opening number. So best get it yourself.'

She tried to shoot Mr Callaghan a grateful look, but he had his headphones on again and was engrossed in the script for the evening show.

At last, six o'clock came. In three hours it would all be over.

She took off her coat and leant towards the microphone ready to sing. Behind her the band were tuning up. Her first number was to be the milder 'Schön ist die Nacht', 'Beautiful Night'. A very popular tango tune among the youth in Germany, but very unpopular with the Nazi Party, who thought tango not wholesome enough for mass consumption.

'Stand by,' Callaghan called as the studio light turned red.

The room fell to silence.

'Three, two, one … and we're live.'

Len Hubbard's voice intoned in German, 'Here is the Soldatensender Calais broadcasting on wavelengths of 360, 410, and 492 metres, linked with the German shortwave bands of 30.7 and 48.3 metres. We bring music and news for our comrades in the Command Areas West, and Norway.'

The band struck up the introduction, and soon, Lilli was transported again deep into the song. Because of her synaesthesia, singing was a sensory, whole-body experience for her. At school she hadn't understood that not everyone saw or felt music the way she did, not until Papa had brought home a study paper from the university, and she'd read it with dumbfounded understanding.

Here in the studio, it seemed odd to be singing in an ordinary jersey and slacks, and her feet in her galoshes, instead of in her glamorous evening wear. But she soon forgot her appearance in the vision of the night she was conjuring. At the end of it she turned to nod terse thanks to the band; they nodded and smiled, no doubt delighted to be here, rather than in the rough huts of the POW camp.

Afterwards she sat at the back of the studio to hear the broadcast of the news. Gleaned from German papers, and read aloud in her native tongue, it sounded exactly like a radio station from Germany.

The broadcast transported her from this dingy country house to her warm kitchen at home, the radio blaring as she chopped onions and lit the gas on the old enamel stove, while her father marked papers. She shivered and folded her arms over her chest. She had to remind herself that everything had changed. She could never go back to Berlin.

The news, recited in Hubbard's strident tones, was:

'*Further to allegations that our brave troops are freezing to death on the Eastern Front from lack of kit – here's some good news! Our trusty housewives of the Frauenschaft have rallied to the call and are knitting up a storm, making scarves and mittens and socks. If only German High Command would expedite permission for the items to be sent immediately, instead of having the parcels stuck in the depot, tied up with legal red tape.*'

When the item finished, and Lilli had to rub her chilly hands and stand up to sing again, she was still wondering whether this was actually true. She couldn't help but feel for those poor men, sitting in a Siberian winter, hoping fruitlessly for knitting from home.

Several more items followed, and Lilli sang twice more, introduced by Hubbard as Lilliana Linde. She was determined to keep her first name and her mother's maiden name as a clue to her father as to where she might be, though she knew this carried some risk, should the Germans ever succeed in invading England. Papa would have a radio, wherever he was, of that she was certain, and her hope was if he ever heard her voice coming from a radio, he would pick up on the name and recognise her and know she was safe.

Finally, the broadcast ended. '*This is Soldatensender Calais along with Atlantiksender, wishing you all a very good night.*'

The band played a jaunty tune, until the green light snapped on again.

'Off air,' announced Callaghan.

Everyone whooped with the euphoria of it being over.

Lilli sat down, deflated. Until that moment, she hadn't registered the tension in the room.

'What a performance,' Callaghan said to her. 'You'll have them begging for more.'

'Thank you. What's Atlantiksender?'

'Our sister station – broadcasts to U-boat crews.'

'But not all of Germany?'

Mr Callaghan laughed. 'Give us time. The number of listeners will grow, I'm sure.'

'Was it true, that part about the soldiers freezing to death?'

'No,' Max said. 'Not the way we made it sound. Conditions are harsh, but we pushed that narrative, so families think the troops are not being looked after by High Command, and that the Nazi government is preventing their troops from getting what they need.'

'It works. I was feeling sorry for the soldiers myself, and I hate the bastards.'

Mr Callaghan smiled at her choice use of words. 'They're men who've been caught by Nazi propaganda and ideology. Like a religious cult. We want to smash that up.'

'By more lies and propaganda,' she said.

He winced. 'True. But name another weapon that can do so much damage and yet seem so benign.'

'I don't think the soldiers have been brainwashed,' she flashed. 'You excuse them too easily. The ones I saw in Germany were perfectly aware of how cruelly they were behaving. Beatings for fun, destruction just to bully people. It was ugly.'

'The POWs here have all been vetted,' Max said. 'They've either renounced Nazism, or were against it from the beginning.'

'Well, they would say that,' she snapped back, 'if it meant saving their skins, and getting a comfortable little job like this. Better than shovelling chicken shit, or hammering in fence posts, isn't it?'

Callaghan butted in. 'It's all right, Lilli. It's not exactly comfortable for any of us. We have to weigh up the risks, yes. But we've got a job to do, and it's part of a whole strategy – a shadow network undermining the real German network. And if we're using POWs, we have to keep a certain neutrality here, see that everyone's human, the Geneva Convention and so on,' Callaghan said. 'Or the thing'd break apart. That, or we'd all go mad.'

'Madness, is it now?' said Ron, overhearing. 'So what's new?'

Lilli was more taken with Callaghan's soft expression than his words. She saw he was struggling to hold everyone together and decided reluctantly to give him the benefit of the doubt.

'You joining us at The Plough?' Max asked.

'Is it far?' She was wary of another punishing cycle ride.

'It's all flat, or downhill,' Ron said.

'Then yes, but you'll have to wait for me. I don't know where I'm going.'

'Enjoy,' said Callaghan, turning back to his desk and beginning to shuffle his papers.

'Aren't you going to join us, Mr Callaghan?' Lilli asked him. 'It sounds like a celebration.'

'Call me Neil. The rest do.' Though actually, she'd noticed they didn't.

She kept her gaze on his face, still expecting an answer.

'I'd rather have a quiet night in,' he said.

'Our first broadcast from Soldatensender Calais and you want to duck out of the party?'

He swivelled to face her. 'If you must know, the coach won't go out of the way – government orders. And I can't cycle. Legs just aren't up to it. Probably a good thing that one of us is sober for tomorrow's session anyway.'

'Ron says it's downhill,' she insisted. 'You won't need to pedal. Just sit on top and enjoy the ride. Hey, Max,' she waved an arm, 'can you find another bike for Mr Callaghan?'

'Neil,' he said. 'But I don't need—'

'Oh yes you do,' she said. 'Max, find another bike for Neil will you.'

In the space of a few minutes while he locked up the building, she'd arranged for a bicycle to be brought over from the transmitting hall in the next building. It was a better model than hers, with a light on the front, which hers didn't have. Once they got through the security checks, she tied his stick to the cross bar with his own tie and parcel string that Ron had produced from his pocket.

'Oh. I take it you can ride a bike?' she asked.

'You bet. Or at least I could before …'

'Get on then.'

'All right, miss bossy britches.' But he was grinning.

Was she bossy? Maddie had called her bossy too. She supposed so, in comparison with these English people who never said what they thought. She pushed off after the other two, wobbling as she tried to go slow enough to escort Mr Callaghan. *Neil*, she reminded herself.

She needn't have worried. Once Neil was in motion, he soon zipped away down the hill like he was born to it, his red wartime lamp throwing a column of brightness against the stony path, his breath pumping out white clouds, legs stuck out sideways like a kid on a paper round.

She daren't go half as fast, scared she'd skid and go over the handlebars. When they got to the bottom of the hill the road levelled, and it was still a few hundred yards into the village and the pub. Oh no. She hadn't thought of that. To her frustration, Max and Ron had pedalled on but Neil was forced to stop.

She drew up alongside him.

'Gosh, that was fantastic,' he said. 'I used to ski, and it's the same sort of feeling.'

His cheeks were pink and he suddenly looked five years younger. 'But I can't pedal, so it looks like I'm stuck. I'll have to leave the bike and walk. You'd better go on ahead, it could take me ages.'

'It can't be that far,' she said. 'Tell you what, I'll leave mine in that hedge, and I'll stand in front of you and pedal yours.'

'I should have thought it through. And even if I get there, how will I get home?'

'Something will happen,' Lilli said breezily. 'We can't leave you there all night. Get on.'

Awkwardly she hitched one leg over the cross bar and stood down with all her weight. The bike inched its way, wobbling down the road. Twice it fell sideways and Neil had to put out a stiff leg to save it. But finally they made it to the pub, and into the lounge bar, which was the only place that would serve 'ladies'. Max and Ron must have gone into the snug.

Neil got the drinks. 'Only fair,' he said, 'as you did the driving. What'll you have?'

'Just a beer.' He looked taken aback. She'd forgotten women didn't drink beer in England.

As he brought them back she noticed one leg was completely rigid and the other slightly bent inwards. He walked slowly so as not to slop the beer. She blushed at the idea she'd almost rail-roaded this man, now her boss, into such an undignified activity.

'Cheers!' he said.

They clinked glasses.

'Have you worked up there long?' she asked him.

He turned to check the barman was in the other bar and out of earshot. 'I worked for Delmer before, on his earlier radio station, Gustav Siegfried Eins. Similar outfit to this, another shadow network of propaganda and dodgy news. It seemed to work, so they're doing it again. This one's more sophisticated though.'

'Really? Sophisticated? What about that story they're planning tomorrow about the state of the Wehrmacht latrines?'

He laughed. 'Delmer likes that toilet humour; it appeals to the troops, who repeat all the worst parts amongst themselves.' He took a sip of beer. 'I mean, the transmitter's better, in other words the signal can go further. The big nobs saw Delmer's idea was working and stumped up for a decent transmitter, a more versatile one. Six hundred kilowatts with a longer range. It can get right under the skin of the German output.'

'Wait, wait. Six hundred kilowatts? *Six hundred?*'

He paused. 'Yep. Our other transmitters are no more than a hundred and fifty. Technical jargon, sorry. Ron's domain.'

'No, I get it.'

'Your English is very good. They tell me you've been in England a while.'

'I meant I understand about the power of the transmitter. I used to mend radios. I know a bit about them.'

'Really? Where did you learn to do that?'

'My father. He was a radio designer. An expert. Till they sacked him. Didn't like the fact he'd married my mother. She was Jewish, you see.'

'So what does he do for work now?'

She stared. 'Work?' A hollow laugh. 'No, they took him away. I don't know where he is now.'

She saw his face fall.

'And your mother?'

'Long gone. Cancer, about ten years ago.'

'God, I'm sorry. What an idiot. I didn't realise.'

She took a sip of her drink. 'My father's a very clever man.

81

He'll be making a radio somehow wherever he is.' Her voice was brittle to disguise her pain. 'And I want my songs to reach him if I can. I like technical things. I wanted to be an engineer, but the war …'

A silence as he toyed with his glass. 'How long have you been in England?'

'Five years. Three in London, two in the Isle of Man as an internee. I had to mend a lot of things there because everything was run by women. It feels strange now, that the radio station seems to be entirely male, even though there's a war on.'

'We're part of the Political Warfare Executive – a reserved occupation. We're all pretty harmless. And there's the secretaries, and women on the switchboards and in the canteen. Miss Blum who types the scripts is an absolute whizz.'

'But none in the studio.' She paused, looking at him with raised eyebrows as he took this in. A sigh. 'It just takes some getting used to. Being here, I mean. And also just the fact that it's someone else's idea of what I should do.'

'What would you really like to be doing, if there was no war?'

She gave a rueful huff. 'A bit like asking what you'd do with three wishes. Learn about engines. Learn what makes things work. Given half a chance I'd like to be operating one of those consoles in the studio.'

'Really? But what about your singing?'

'I love it. It's how I show people how I feel. But I'd rather perform to an audience that has paid to hear me sing, not one where my voice is thrust down their unwilling throats.'

'I'd pay to hear you. You have a tremendous voice.'

'At first when I came to England I didn't think I'd be able to sing again. It was like my voice had been locked up in Germany.' She blushed and then looked up at him. 'It was good to have you accompany me when I tried out. I was so nervous. I thought they might send me back to the Isle of Man if they didn't like it. And it would have been hard with no accompaniment. My own piano

82

playing is basic at best. I used to have a friend who'd accompany me on the accordion, and I miss our sessions. Do you play much?'

· 'Not now, no. I learnt the piano as a child. My parents insisted.'

'Like mine. My father used to say, "Music is maths made audible." But I was a stubborn child, I never practised enough. I have this thing where I see notes as shapes or colours, and it can interfere with what I'm playing.'

'Really? Like how?'

'Hard to explain. But some sounds are shapes to me, like globes or cones. And some are colours. Like my senses have got all mixed up. They call it Synästhesie … synaesthesia?'

'I've heard of it, but never met anyone with it before. It sounds rather exciting.'

'I'm used to it. But too many sounds and it can get over-whelming. Like I can't listen to brass bands – it's like being hit on the skull with a baseball bat.'

'I've always played the piano. My sister Nancy learnt too, but she soon gave it up. I kept on with it until I got more interested in the cello, and now that's my main instrument.'

'The cello? Ooh, I love the sound of the cello. It's like smooth creamy coffee.'

'What about the prisoner's band? What shape are they?' He was listening intently, head cocked to one side. She was suddenly very aware of how he was looking at her, as if nothing else but their conversation mattered.

She felt her cheeks grow hot. 'The band's all right, but the colour's like mud.'

He laughed. 'Don't let them hear that!'

'Oh, it seems so long since I heard a proper orchestra. I'd like to hear you play.'

'I don't play much now.' He looked away. 'Not since my accident. I got caught in a bomb blast.'

'Is it painful to play?'

'No. Not physically,' he said. 'But the music … Well, before

83

I worked for Delmer I had a rough sort of a year, and it just hurts too much.'

She was silent at this admission. She knew exactly what he meant. Music was unbearable for her sometimes too. They stared at each other a moment longer, unable to look away.

The snug door flew open. 'There you are!' Max cried. 'We thought you'd got lost. Whose round is it?'

'Yours,' Ron said, appearing at his shoulder.

*

They settled into a routine then at the station, cycling to Wavendon Tower in the frosty winter mornings, trying not to skid on the way home. She grew to appreciate how hard Max and Ron worked to find material for them to broadcast, and that Neil bent over backwards to find suitable people to appear on the programmes, so that it didn't get too stale. Some of these were German prisoners but Neil was always polite, even to men who'd been captured as Nazis, and were wearing the red alert patch on their uniforms. At Christmas he even arranged for the POWs to have drinks – separately of course, it wouldn't be right to fraternise with them without some sort of boundary.

Lilli had gleaned over the last few weeks that Max was a Jew who used to be a professor of History at the University of Munich, and that Ron, his complete opposite in appearance – short, square, and sandy – was a Northerner and a radio expert who used to run a regional newspaper. Ron's schoolboy German gave her much cause for amusement. But Neil was a mystery.

He wouldn't talk about his past at all, nor about his family, except to say he had a sister who was working as a FANY. Even at their digs, Neil was aloof, in his downstairs lodgings, whereas the rest of them bantered away in German. Neil was a man who gave little away, unlike Max, morose but sharp as a blade, and the cheerful Ron from whom she'd got a life story almost immediately.

But she hadn't forgotten that moment in The Plough with Neil, the moment when their eyes locked and time seemed to have stopped.

After a few months of broadcasts, during which they tried to spread as much dirt as they could about high-up Nazi officials, Neil came in from his side office, where there was a desk and telephone, and said, 'Gather round, everyone, there's news from the Executive.'

They did as he asked, intrigued by his serious expression.

'The War Office are impressed,' he said. 'So impressed that they've been building a new facility for us, a proper broadcasting studio just down the road at Milton Bryan.'

A flutter of interest and a few gasps of surprise.

'We'll have state-of-the-art equipment, a proper green room for artists and broadcasters, and a staffed canteen. Two locked rooms too for our POWs. Even better – our output will increase from just a few hours to almost twenty-four-hour coverage.'

'Will you need more technicians?' Lilli asked. 'Because I—'

'Will that mean we have to move?' Max asked, interrupting her.

'No, it's not far. We can keep our billets. Mrs Littlefair's jam is still on the menu! But as a team we'll be organised differently. You three will be going down to Milton Bryan, Max to be on hand with breaking news, as fresh as you can get it, Ron to assist in the technical aspects of the recording equipment, and Lilli to read news items and sing.'

'Will they need more technicians?' Lilli tried again. 'Because I'd be keen to apply.'

She saw Ron give an amused look to Max, but Neil answered her straight; 'I don't know, best ask Delmer. I won't have as much to do with it, I'll be staying on here, as my role is mostly organisational.'

'If it's not you, then who'll be overseeing the operation at the new place?' Lilli asked.

'One of Delmer's assistants – Karl Robson, or if he's away, Ron I presume.'

'Why don't they ever tell us anything?' Ron said, outraged. 'I've only just got to know this system and they expect me to run something new? What sort of tech set-up have they got there?'

'Don't know exactly. Just that they've already installed all the wiring and—'

'Without even consulting us?' Ron threw up his hands at Max, who rolled his eyes. 'Robson's away this month, at another research unit, so it'll be muggins here again sorting it all out, I suppose.'

Neil sighed. 'All I know is, the GPO have installed the switchboard and private wires to link us up with the Aspi transmitter, as well as our other broadcasting sites at Potsgrove and Gawcott. And Max, get this – they've set up direct lines to the agency at Reuters, and the Press Association. Even better, they're connected to the POW interrogation centre at Wilton Park. It'll save loads of time on travel, and bring us bang up to date with German news.'

'Will you be able to find out about individual Germans?' Lilli asked. 'My father got rounded up and …' She paused. The choke in her throat made it impossible to continue.

'No,' Neil said softly. 'As I told Max, who's in a similar situation, I'm afraid we can't look for individuals. Much as we'd like to.' His eyes were sad. 'There are just too many missing, and the Germans are keeping those records close to their chests. We just have to hope the war will end soon.'

'I see.' Lilli tried not to show how much that hurt.

'But I'll still be in touch with you all by telephone, and monitor every broadcast,' Neil said. 'I'll pop down occasionally to the studios too, just to keep in touch. But I'll be the link between the output at Milton Bryan and the transmitter.'

Lilli was disappointed. She was only just getting to know the elusive Neil Callaghan. Somehow she felt safe with him. He wasn't brash or trying to throw his weight around, even though he was her superior. She liked his soft Scottish voice, the way he treated everyone with courtesy, and the fact he was moved by music the way she was. She'd miss him, even though she hardly knew him.

*

Lilli stopped her cycle outside the new studio with its brick-built Art Deco frontage.

'Blimey,' Ron said, puffing up behind her. 'It looks like a cinema!'

Max skidded to a halt. 'Let's hope it's not all for show,' he said.

Inside, it was thrilling to inhale the odour of new gloss paint and the wood smell of the new parquet flooring. 'Gosh, I feel like a film star,' Lilli said. 'Look at those lights!'

Max craned his neck up the stairs, which boasted impressive electric chandeliers.

They clattered up the steps and into the studio with its sound-proofing tiles, and a purpose-built inner sanctum with glass walls more than one-inch thick.

When he saw the new shiny studios, Ron turned to Max, fell towards him, and said, 'Hold me up. I might faint.' Then he shot off like an eager dog on a walk. He was in his absolute element leaning over the consoles, touching the shiny metal with reverent hands.

Harold Robin, the technical expert, arrived to give them a guided tour, and explained to Ron what he called 'the gubbins' or inner workings of the site. Lilli was close on his heels, drinking in his every word.

'Is it true it's six hundred kilowatts?' Lilli asked.

'In terms of power,' Mr Robin said, ignoring her but addressing Ron, 'the Aspidistra transmitter is the dreadnought of the ether. But here,' he patted a console, 'this is where the brain power will be.'

Ron was pink with the idea of being the great god Harold Robin's second-in-command and being given carte blanche to troubleshoot if things went wrong.

The communications room next door was a sea of switchboards and wires, with two other young women at the controls, Maureen and Heather. Maureen was a plump but glamorous brunette, and Heather a more down-to-earth type with her hair fastened back with kirby grips.

Lilli was momentarily envious; she would have loved to have a go on the switchboard, but then realised she was lucky to be there at all, she could still have been behind the wire on the Isle of Man.

'What a place!' Max said. 'Though I'm afraid of messing up,' he confessed to Lilli over coffee in the newly built brick annexe that served as a canteen. 'In one way it's great I'll be able to call up the officers directly and demand the most promising men from the camps, the ones who were journalists or broadcasters. But some of them are wily bastards.'

'No surprise there, then,' she said.

'One of them last week had even re-written his script parroting a load of Nazi propaganda, arrogantly thinking no one would check. Needless to say, Neil had him shipped straight back to camp and onto hard labour.'

'Yes, but in Berlin you can't escape it, the adulation of Hitler and the scapegoating of anyone who disagrees. Hitler's glory, Hitler's world plan, Hitler's new order. There's no room for any other view. If you object, they scream traitor at you.'

'People do have a choice though,' Max said. 'I used to despair at the stupidity of the average German, because if they really cared they could just tune in to somewhere else.'

'Not any more, they can't,' Lilli said. 'When we you last in Berlin?'

'Before the war, got out in 1937 when I saw which way it was going.'

'Then you're way behind. There's only one radio station in Germany now. The Gestapo came to confiscate our old radios, and guess what? They generously replaced them – with the Führer's "free gift" to the people. The German official Bakelite wireless with only one station – his. You can't refuse or you get arrested for "un-German activities".'

'So how do people get any other news?'

'Illegally. Human nature, isn't it? Tell us to do something and we immediately want to do the opposite. Hidden radios are everywhere, but people daren't admit it. My father made dozens.'

'Radio is a route to the inside of people's heads. Sometimes I think Delmer's a madman. Other times I think he's a genius. It seems like we're not doing much, but it's the solid weight of opinion we're trying to shift. But it's slow – like the drip-drip effect of water wearing away a rock.'

'I wish we could make it go quicker.' She stirred a spoon around to dissolve the dried milk in the sludge of coffee. 'Are your family still over there?'

He held up a hand. 'Please. Best not to talk of it.'

She reached out a hand to him. 'I know. They took my father.'

'No, you don't know.' His mouth twitched. 'They executed mine.'

She started and looked up at him, but he'd turned away.

The pause went on a long time.

She weighed the implications, with visceral fear for her own father's fate. 'Do you think the war will end soon?' It was the question she desperately wanted an answer to.

Max turned back with glassy eyes and gave a gentle shake of the head. 'It's too far spread now. It's like trying to put a genie back in a bottle, the Nazis have arms everywhere.'

'Except here,' she said.

'Except here,' he agreed.

*

Neil was alone in the studio, sifting through the day's plans for the broadcast. It was bitter even indoors, with ice frosting ferns on the inside of the windows, so he blew on his hands before turning the pages. He was looking for the parts where Lilli would sing, and noting what songs Delmer had chosen.

What a load of trash. He'd feel embarrassed giving her these. Crude songs full of barely disguised innuendo. He searched through the scores looking for something he thought would suit her voice. Something with more class.

'Is Ron not here?' Lilli's voice from behind startled him.

'No. Meeting with Harold Robin at Wavendon. Delmer's busy so Webster drove me down to bring you your music. She's gone to the canteen until I'm ready to go back.'

Lilli came and sat down opposite him. Her face was chalky, her eyes unreadable. 'Max just told me about his father.'

He winced, feeling unaccountably that it was somehow his fault. At the same time he was aware his face was going red. 'Awful. I asked Delmer whether there was any way we can broadcast that sort of news, that innocent people are being executed for nothing at all.'

'It wouldn't work,' she said. Her voice was matter of fact. 'The Party would invent some wrongdoing that gives them an excuse.'

Neil nodded. 'That's what Delmer said. The trouble is, when France and Belgium fell, Hitler's supporters felt good to be on the winning side. Who can blame them?'

'Can't you get Delmer to step it up? It seems so slow.'

'I thought exactly the same. But he says that we have to go "softly softly". If the Germans get wind we're not a proper radio station it would ruin all our work just when we've built up trust. He says the Nazi regime took years to build, and so it will take years to undo.'

'My father might not have years.'

It was a statement without emotion, and somehow that made it even more chilling. There was an awkward silence, and one in which Neil was far too conscious of Lilli's white hands on the table, and the fact they were alone together.

He rifled through the musical scores and cleared his throat. 'I thought this one for tonight.'

He pushed it over. It was 'Du bist die Einzige für Mich', 'You're the Only One for Me'. As soon as she'd pulled it towards her, he realised it was sending a message, and cringed with embarrassment. What a fool.

But she looked up at him, her eyes full of light. 'Oh lovely! One of my favourites!'

He let out his breath and couldn't help smiling.

'I know it well, so it won't take much rehearsal. Can we go over it now?'

'Now?'

'You'll play for me, won't you?'

Elated, he sat on the piano stool and put the music on the stand, lifted his hands in a flourish, and played the first few chords. Surprisingly, they sounded good.

As her voice rose above the notes, he was filled with an unasked-for happiness. This was what life was for! There was no artifice in this, just her voice and his notes and the freezing chill of the room.

'Du bist die einzige für mich,' Lilli sang. And with one hand on the top of the piano, she caught his eye.

For a moment she was singing it just for him. A sweet pain in his heart. He increased the tempo and his hands seemed to fly over the notes.

After the last crescendo they both burst into laughter.

'Gosh, that was marvellous,' he said.

'Because I like it. It's what I might choose – a bit less … how can I put it … crude than the ones Delmer wants.'

'And I bet it'll be more of a hit with the listeners,' he said. 'Everyone needs a bit of joy in their lives.'

The words hung in the air between them like jewels.

*

The next day Neil was at Wavendon going through news items and thinking of Lilli and how it had felt when they'd played together. He was smitten with her, and it was no earthly use, because she was way out of his league. The more he liked her, the more tongue-tied he got. Not only was she lively and outspoken, even querying the great Delmer on what he was up to, but she didn't seem to understand quite what a stupendous voice she had. And of course every other man in the place would think exactly the same, he thought glumly.

He pushed his fair hair away from his face and tried to concentrate, while at the same time wondering what Lilli was doing. He hobbled over to the canteen, careful on the slippery path, hoping to see her, but there was no sign of her. It was a relief actually, because what on earth could he say to her? She was such a big presence. Everyone turned to stare when she entered the room, and he just couldn't do chat-up lines, not without feeling like a fake.

Someone had left the local daily paper on the table in front of him. Apparently twenty-two German divisions in Stalingrad had been encircled by the Red Army, which was good news, but didn't help anyone over here in Europe. He flicked through to the end to read the personal pages; columns of obituaries and missing people.

Awful, the displacement war brought.

He glanced at the things for sale – a bigger-than-ever list, some of it just scrap. Suddenly something caught his eye. There were dozens of motorbikes for sale. Folk couldn't get petrol. It was as if a light went on.

If he could ride a push-bike, he could ride a motorbike! Maybe that would make Lilli take notice. And working for the PWE, he could get petrol.

With a grin, he took his pen out of his pocket and drew a big circle around the advert for a BSA 500cc in Brunswick Green. He tore off the advert and put it in his pocket, and without finishing his coffee, scooted back to his office to make the call.

Chapter 9

Brendan Murphy was on a cold, draughty train to Birmingham. Travelling was always risky; there was no way to get off if the police caught up with you. Impatient, he fiddled with his watch as the countryside rolled by, drearily grey, outside his carriage window. By now Bren had been in England two years and was completely familiar with the German military intelligence and espionage service, which supported the IRA. He'd been back twice via plane to Berlin, to their cramped headquarters known for its stink as the Fox's Lair.

He watched for the ticket inspector because he had no ticket. Now even though he was used to adopting the persona of a rather pushy sales rep, he still had to stay on his toes. Invisibility was hard for him. Trouble was, he was not bad-looking. People tended to remember him, and it was a problem.

Via Harper and Green, he took orders from Pfalzgraf, the code name of Hauptmann Marwede, head of the section dealing with political subversion in the West. He'd met him once on the third floor of the Fox's Lair in a room with *II N/W* painted enigmatically on the door.

'Never use the same name twice,' Pfalzgraf had told him.

So Bren had a series of false names – common Irish names

like Flannery, O'Malley, or Duffy. Today he was Duffy, a rep of Robinson and Co, the Bristol paper manufacturer. Not that he ever went anywhere near Bristol. His job was to use the real Robinson manuals and samples he'd been supplied by the Abwehr, and take orders for paper, as an excuse to get into the factories and photograph them, or disable key targets through sabotage.

He'd smile and act charming to the factory boss, and take orders that would never be delivered. Outraged complainants would be directed to the telephone number of Harper and Green, his Nazi contacts, who told the victim of the fraud that the paper was on its way but held up by a shortage of pulp and wartime difficulties.

But now, Harper and Green wanted to see him, and as he was still alive, it must be a new assignment. His pulse quickened at the thought of it.

Voices further down the train – the ticket inspector was coming. Bren grabbed his case and nipped to the WC compartment and shut the door. The floor swayed and the undercarriage squealed as the train slowed.

After ten minutes or so, he poked a head out to see the inspector moving away down the corridor. Bren exhaled, but allowed himself a smile. Nothing he liked better than getting away with it.

The train slowed as they got towards the city, creaking and puffing past the soot-blackened marshalling yards and munition dumps.

Bren stretched, picked up his briefcase, and buttoned up his overcoat, then leant out of the window to reach the handle of the door.

Birmingham was full of bustle and troops. Full of that hated English accent.

Bren's IRA contact in Birmingham was Fergus O'Donnell, another Irishman who ran a betting shop. Checking no one was following him, Bren got on the 53 bus, hopping off in a grimy bomb-blasted suburb, where he hurried to a run-down betting shop on a corner.

He eyed it up from the outside. Two brick-built terraces knocked into a shop – one of the illegal neighbourhood book-makers that relied on gambling on the Irish horse races, because those were still broadcast on the radio during the war. Some dog tracks were open too, as the government had brought back grey-hound racing – a so-called outlet for men labouring in munitions factories and heavy industry.

Bren pushed his way to the makeshift writing shelf through a sea of oily boiler suits and flat caps, and scribbled the bet down; the code – *Green Goddess 5.30 Kilbeggan*

The betting shop stank of stale smoke, and the noise from the blaring radio made Bren taut with irritation. He queued for his turn, then slid the docket across to the ginger-haired man behind the counter.

As soon as he saw it, O'Donnell squinted up at him through eyes bloodshot with smoke. 'Round the back,' he croaked. 'Second door on the left.'

Bren set off carrying his kit bag, as O'Donnell grabbed his gangly son, who was chalking up the bets, and told him to take over.

Bren pushed open the door straight into O'Donnell's parlour. O'Donnell appeared from the connecting door to the shop and shook his hand. 'Brendan, is it?'

Grand to hear that Irish accent. 'Aye.'

'Take a seat. I'll get on the blower, tell 'em you're here.'

Bren eased himself into the grubby moquette armchair before the tiled fireplace. In the hallway he heard O'Donnell say, 'Your man's here … yes … yes … sit tight? All right.'

O'Donnell came back pushing his shirt sleeves further up his tattooed arms. 'They're coming. You just have to wait. They won't knock. There's a dram of knock-off whisky in that cabinet, if you fancy a drop. I have to get back. My lad's a bloody eejit with the money. Only fit for writing odds.'

'Thanks.'

'Make yourself at home then.' A moment later and he was gone. Bren heard the muffled excited commentary from the radio next door as he pulled open the cabinet.

'And it's Gulliver's Boy, at four to one, Gulliver's Boy, from Saucy Lass ...'

The shelves were empty except for a few old ashtrays, some china dray-horses, and a bottle of Bushmills with only a finger-width left at the bottom. No glass.

It was clear no woman lived here, Bren thought, looking around the room. None of the knick-knacks he'd associate with a woman. Just a few copies of *Racing Times* and the *Birmingham Post* lying on the table, stained with rings from coffee cups and ashy dust from an overfull ashtray.

Bren took a swig from the whisky bottle and let out a sigh of satisfaction. He was still on edge. Being always on the run, always a false persona, meant his wits were stretched, but now he was here, he could ease off a bit. He was clearly in the right place. He'd dodged turnstiles to get to Birmingham, but he was pretty sure no one had followed him.

It took his contacts an hour to get there, by which time, despite his better instincts, Bren had finished the whisky. Strangely, it was the first time he'd actually set eyes on his contacts in person. Two men, both city types. They gave him their names, Harper and Green, names that were undoubtedly false. In their city suits, all sharp creases and silky ties, they looked odd, perched on the old sofa in this mess of a parlour.

'We've got a job for you,' Harper said.

His English was impeccable, upper class. He could have come from Eton. It didn't endear him to Bren.

Harper put a briefcase on his knee and opened it. 'We want you to find this man, and eliminate him.' He clicked open his briefcase and drew out a black-and-white photograph attached to a typed sheet. 'Neil Callaghan.' He passed it over.

The photograph was a poor copy but looked like one from a

passport or official document. The man in the photo, fair-haired, unsmiling, stared out at Bren with that curious, expressionless face that was no use at all in finding anyone.

Green, a suave-looking fella with gold cufflinks, added, 'We think he's at his home, Stranraven in Scotland, so that's your first port of call.'

'Is he dangerous?'

Harper gave a dry laugh. 'He murdered one of our men, Otto Hefner, a high-up member of the Party, friend of Canaris of the Gestapo.'

His respect for the man in the photo increased. 'Why?'

'Shot in the street in cold blood. Callaghan was working for us, but turned chicken. Then he disappeared from his lodgings and there's been no trace of him since at any London address.'

'We'd given up on tracking him down, but now we think we've found him,' Green said.

'Rumour has it, he was in some sort of accident, because by chance, when looking for someone else, we found his name in the Marylebone Hospital records, and they told us he was discharged home to Scotland. He got messed up badly, so walks with a stick, but he's still a threat to us. He's got intelligence on our men in the British Union of Fascists,' Harper said, 'and on the way our network functions. He's a security risk and traitor to the Party.'

'So, a trip to Scotland. Sounds straightforward enough. What then?'

'We'll contact you again with more instructions once that's done.'

'No more factories then?'

'Not for now, no,' Harper said.

'If it's a home visit I'll need a gun with a silencer.'

'Funny you should say that.' Green opened up a bag and drew out a case. It contained an English pistol, a Welrod, with an integrated suppressor. He placed it on the table along with a box of ammunition.

Bren picked it up and passed it hand to hand, took off the safety catch, smiled and pointed it at Harper. Harper did not flinch, but his lips tightened.

Bren's spirits immediately lifted. This was what he loved, the power to make people freeze.

*

Two days later Bren was on another train, this time carrying an overnight bag and briefcase. Green had given him a cover story that he was a health inspector, looking at health and safety in emergency accommodation, because of the large number of bombed-out residents. He had new papers, manuals on safety, and a raft of paperwork and a clipboard supposedly showing previous inspections, all collected in a new briefcase they had supplied. He was now Flannery, and he enjoyed acting the part, peering myopically through thick-lensed glasses that made everything genuinely blurred.

At Stirling he got off the train, and went into the library to ask about premises that had been bombed. To his frustration it seemed Stranraven was a godforsaken little village with no bomb damage anywhere near it, and not a suburb of Stirling as he'd imagined. It seemed to be mostly farming and country pursuits like fishing. He'd stand out there, like an eejit, dressed in his suit and tie.

Trust Green and Harper to give him a useless cover story. He doubted they'd ever been out of the city in their lives. Fortunately, like everywhere else these days, Stirling indoor market had a second-hand clothes stall and he soon furnished himself with a pair of old trousers, a cord waistcoat and an ancient tweed jacket.

Another stall supplied him with galoshes, which looked new, but which he could muddy up without any trouble. He went into a pub for a lunchtime drink and changed there, nipping out before anyone could notice the switch. The clothes fitted passably, though the jacket was baggy over the shoulders, and smelled of old horse. Carefully, he loaded the gun and transferred it to the pocket of the jacket before leaving his bags in the left luggage at the bus station.

After he waited more than an hour at the bus depot, an old clapped-out bus took him to Stranraven. Out here there was no chance anyone could have followed him. He was out of spy territory, a lone agent, just the way he liked it.

'I'm looking for an old friend,' he said to the bus conductress, in what he hoped was a passable Scots brogue. 'Neil Callaghan. Thought I'd call in and see him.'

'Ah yes, you'll be wanting the rectory. Right by the kirk, you can't miss it. We don't see as much of him these days, not since the accident.'

'Aye, must be terrible,' Bren said.

'Keeps himself busy though, I'll say that for him. Parish council, refugees, collecting for charity. Spitfire appeal and all.'

Bren nodded and let her ramble on until the next stop where someone else got on.

The rectory. He'd no idea Callaghan was anything to do with the church. Protestant, no doubt. One of the bastard Unionists who'd taken away a chunk of their Ireland.

Even as Bren got off the bus, he could see the church. An austere stone building with arched windows set with plain glass. He remembered his childhood Mass on Sundays, with the incense swinging and the kaleidoscope of coloured reflections from the windows gilding the congregation with light. His father doing up his top shirt button and chiding him to sit still.

No, don't think of it.

He walked towards the church, curious to look inside. He saw the rectory adjoining, and that there were lights on inside on this gloomy day. He hesitated. Protestant churches were an abomination. Still, he would go and look, see what kind of a God this Neil Callaghan worshipped.

The door was open, and he stepped in, galoshes squeaking on the stone flags. The door swung back and latched itself closed behind him. He shivered, felt in his pocket for the gun. The church was cold and damp, with plain whitewashed walls and an altar with no adornment. It looked bleak, and he couldn't imagine it filled with people.

'Hullo?' a Scottish voice said. A man emerged from a side door, an older man, stout, in an old jumper and tweed cap.

'Just taking a look,' Bren said.

'Aye, she's a fine old church. Been here since 1824.' His manner was pompous, self-satisfied. 'You should come on Sunday. She's better in action. Congregation's got bigger since the war; we're the nearest church for miles.'

Bren nodded. 'I was told the Callaghans live here; in the rectory.'

'That's me, Reverend Callaghan. How can I help you?'

A frown. He wasn't wearing the dog collar. 'Then I'm looking for your boy, Neil. He's an old friend from London.'

'Neil?' Callaghan's face fell. 'Ach, you should have let us know. He's not here. He's gone back to London.'

Bren was taken aback, but soon regained his equilibrium. 'Oh, shame. I'd hoped to catch up with him. Where's he living now? Maybe I can look him up.'

The vicar was silent, his mouth working; he'd caught something in Bren's manner. He took a step away. 'I don't know exactly. War work, something hush hush, you know how it is.' He raised his arms in a shrug. 'I don't have an address, though of course he said he'd write.'

Bren felt something snap inside him. He drew out the gun and clicked off the catch.

Callaghan stared at it, eyes wide.

'You'll tell me where your son is,' Bren said. 'I want to know exactly where and what he's doing.'

'Come on, son, no need to point that at me. I'm harmless.' He gave a nervous laugh. 'What is all this?'

'Your son's got some questions to answer. About the death of one of my friends.'

'Who? Neil? Impossible. He'd never hurt a fly.' The vicar was blustering now. 'He was working for the civil service. Got hit by a bomb—'

'I know all that. Where is he now?'

'I told you, I don't know. He left by train yesterday, to …' he hesitated, 'to Aberdeen.'

'You said London before.' Bren stepped nearer. 'Which is it? London, or Aberdeen?'

Callaghan's eyes searched left and right, looking for some kind of escape. 'Aberdeen.'

He was bluffing. Stupid sod.

Callaghan stood up taller. 'Now then, let's not do anything hasty. Just put that gun down and I'll say no more about it. In case you hadn't noticed, you're in a house of God.'

His patronising schoolmaster manner flipped something in Bren's chest. The scene became hard-edged, and a tight feeling constricted Bren's breath. He could barely get the words out. 'House of God? The false English God that calls on you to kill little children in his name?'

As if in slow motion, Bren registered Callaghan putting up his hands but the man was too late. The bullet had already left the gun with a mere *phut*. The slight thud as it hit Callaghan in his chest seemed too small a noise for what had just occurred.

'What in God's name …?'

Bren watched as Callaghan sank to his knees, but Bren was fixed in place, his legs unable to move. The gun was warm and heavy in his hand. A glare of sunlight sliced in, as Reverend Callaghan clutched at his chest as if to keep his heart inside.

Bren saw none of it. He was the five-year-old he used to be, wincing at the sound of gunfire in the street, the rat-a-tat of the English machine guns as they corralled everyone into North King Street, Da grabbing him roughly by the shoulder and thrusting his

101

face to the dusty plaster wall. At first Bren thought it was because he'd pinched a Woodbine from his Da's pocket and he was going to be leathered again with Da's belt. As Da slammed him into the wall the smoke stung his eyes, the cigarette burnt his lip then crumbled from his mouth. He could still taste the plaster dust.

The juddering noise of the machine gun was too loud for him to make any sense of it. Da jerked against his back and then, Da falling onto him, his fingers scraping the wall as if clinging onto it. Then silence, and crawling out from under that blood and that weight.

Da's back was ripped and sodden, but he, five-year-old Brendan Murphy, was alive. Only there was no one left in 19 North King Street who would care.

He tried to get Da up, to move him. But he was too massive to move, like a fallen boulder.

Bren had wandered bewildered up the road, the day the English came. Every house had lost someone. He saw hysterical Mrs Flannery come home from the shop and drag out his best friend, six-year-old Barney. He was limp, his head a mass of blood. She'd had to drag him by the ankles from where he'd been shoved under a heap of rubble in the yard, like he didn't matter.

Bren blinked the images away. The gun was still heavy in his hand. He watched Callaghan stop his thrashing, until he was still as his da had been that day in 1916, big Joseph Murphy – Da who would never again slap a Woodbine from his mouth, never again take off his belt to leather him.

Bren swallowed and kicked at the body on the church floor to check it was dead. 'English bastard,' he said.

He slid the gun back in his pocket. He knew by instinct he shouldn't have done what he just did, but his mind was already making excuses.

The same excuses he'd used all through his life. *He had it coming.* Bren walked away with a slight tremble in the pit of his stomach and stood to wait at the bus stop.

The silencer was a good one. Nobody had come. And now, he could hear nothing but the crows cawing in the trees. But he'd have to try to track Neil Callaghan down, and what should have been a simple job had just got a lot more complicated. He shouldn't have done it, but when the rage came on him, he couldn't help himself. There'd be a hue and cry, but by then he'd be gone. And people would only remember a mysterious stranger, dressed in an old stinking jacket covered in horse hair.

Chapter 10

Milton Bryan, Bedfordshire

Lilli wrapped her checked coat tighter over her chest before breezing down the corridor and out into the air. After the fug of being inside for the broadcast with the heat of all the electrical equipment and lights, it was a shock to be out in the cold again. She shivered as she hurried towards the gate and the rack where she'd left her bicycle. She showed her pass, and was nodded through by the guard with his flashlight, and was just taking hold of her handlebars when there was a grinding roar, and a motorcycle drew up.

The noise died, a shape like barbed wire, but it was a moment before she realised the man with the scarf wrapped around his nose and the goggles over his eyes was Neil Callaghan. He was dressed in a calf-length leather coat that had obviously seen some wear, and creaked as he struggled to kick down the stand. Eventually he managed it, and pulled down his scarf.

'What d'you think?' He waved his arm at the motorcycle.

'Impressive!' she said.

'It's all your fault,' he said, grinning. 'You know, that time after our first broadcast, the time I rode down on the push-bike.'

'Me? Don't blame me if you kill yourself on that thing!'

'It's brilliant. Always crawling along on a stick is no fun. When I was a kid, I used to go at thirty miles an hour on skis. The chap selling it gave me the coat and goggles too. Now I can zip about wherever I want.'

She went to examine the motorbike. 'A BSA. Neat. Can you get petrol?'

'If it's for the war effort, yes. But there's a bit of leeway if I squeeze it, because I'm registered as disabled and in a reserved occupation. I thought you might like a ride down to Simpson Village.'

'But what about Goebbels?'

He squinted at her, confused.

'My old bike. I call him Goebbels because he's determined to make my life hell.'

He laughed. 'Good to see you can still laugh at them.'

'It's either laugh or cry.'

'You'll give it a go, then?'

'You bet.' Lilli climbed on as he shunted forward so she could ride pillion. She'd never been on a motorbike, and she thanked God for her slacks, which were the latest thing for all the women at the base, and far more practical in winter for riding a bicycle.

With an ear-splitting roar, Neil opened the throttle and they were away. She clung on tight, fingers digging into the leather, for after just a few breathtaking seconds she understood that Neil Callaghan on a motorbike was quite a different animal from Neil Callaghan in the office. They tore down the road, with him leaning into the bends until she longed to cry out to him to slow down. His headlight was just a thin sliver so it was like going through a dark tunnel. Grit blew in her eyes, which were watering so much that she could see nothing but a blur of trees whooshing past. Shocked, she gripped tight to his leather coat, praying for it to stop. Near the bottom of the hill, he applied the brakes in a screech of rubber and a military lorry rumbled past missing her ear by a whisker.

He turned to look over his shoulder. 'You all right?' he asked.

She nodded dumbly, wondering if she could get off here. But too late, the engine was already grinding back to life and the machine shot forward, leaving her clinging on again, helpless to do anything except close her eyes and clench her teeth.

From her limited view she saw parked cars flash past, pedestrians turn to stare, before they shot between a bus and a farm gate with barely room to breathe.

At their lodging house she got off, legs shaking, to rub a hand over her wild hair and blow her nose.

'I told you she's a belter!' Neil said, eyes shining.

Flipping lethal, you mean. She rubbed the grit from her eyes.

'Let me help,' she said, seeing him struggle to drag the bike to the garage. She yanked open the doors as he awkwardly hauled the motorcycle inside.

The tin-roofed garage at Mrs Littlefair's was obviously hardly used, but contained a few boxes of aluminium cans, saved for the Spitfire appeal, a stack of old rubber tyres, and a heap of rusty garden tools. Neil's stick was propped up next to them, and now she took it up ready to pass it over to him.

As he wiped down the bike's bodywork with a cloth, she asked a few questions about the engine, and he turned surprised.

'How do you know all this?'

'My father. He let me tinker with his car. Before the Nazis told him he wasn't allowed to drive. And I was the mechanic everyone turned to in the women's camp.'

'Really? I'm going to strip it down this weekend. Get a look inside. Would you like …' He bit off the words, then he said, 'We could go out one night, if you fancied it.' He didn't turn to look at her. 'To see a film. There's a picture palace in Newport Pagnell.'

She hesitated. She didn't want to get on that motorbike ever again. But she was curious about Neil. About his love of music, about what had happened to him. She felt they had

106

some sort of connection she couldn't explain. And to tell the truth, she wouldn't mind a look at the engine, as long as it was switched off.

Now he did turn, the rag in his hand, waiting for an answer.

'I'd love to,' Lilli said. 'Let me know when, and what's on. And I'll help you strip down the engine if you need another pair of hands.'

'Oh gosh, that's splendid, I mean, thanks.' He stood a moment just looking at her, twisting the rag back and forth. 'And I'll check the local paper, see what's on at the Elektra.'

*

Neil walked around the rest of the evening in a kind of euphoria unwilling to go to bed. He was still counting his luck that Lilli had agreed to go out with him, when Mrs Littlefair came to fetch him to the phone. Neil was startled. Nobody phoned him here. Especially not at eleven o'clock at night.

'It's Tom,' came the gruff voice on the other end.

'Tom! Great to hear from you.' Tom Lockwood was Neil's old friend from the Special Operations Executive in Baker Street, and the only one who kept in touch with him from the time he'd rather forget.

'Look, Neil, there's been some sort of accident.' Tom sounded shaken. 'You mother just rang me; they didn't know how to get in touch with you, and I had to call on a few favours to even prise a number for you out of Delmer.'

Neil twisted the receiver cord around his finger. 'What is it? What accident?'

'Your father. I'm afraid he's dead. They took him to hospital in Stirling, but he was dead on arrival.'

He couldn't take it in. Tom's voice sounded far away. Neil blinked. 'Right. What did you say?'

'I'm sorry. It's awful news.'

The fact of it hit him like a smack to the face. 'Oh God. I'll have to go home. My mother … What was it, a heart attack? I told him he shouldn't get so stressed—'

'Not a heart attack. He was shot.'

Neil almost laughed. Shot? Ridiculous. Who would shoot his father? He was a vicar, a pillar of the community.

'Neil?' Tom's worried voice.

'Yes, yes. I'm here. Was it an accident? Is Mother all right?'

'She's pretty traumatised. They think it might be someone trying to steal from the church. That's where they found him, you see.'

'Why? It doesn't make any sense. What have they stolen? There's nothing to steal there, it's a poor rural kirk.'

'Neil, I can come and get you, drive you up. I know the trains are hard for you.'

'No, no. I've got a motorbike. I can—'

'Talk sense. You're not going all the way to Scotland on a motorbike. It would take days.'

'I just need to get my head around it. I'll need to talk to Delmer—'

'Delmer knows. I had to tell him so he'd give me the number to call you. He was bloody awkward, security and all that. I'm coming to get you, okay? Just stay there and I'll drive down – be with you as soon as I can tomorrow. They'll let me have petrol, compassionate leave.'

'If you're sure—'

'Just you get some sleep, and I'll see you first thing tomorrow.' The line went dead.

Neil stood for a moment, unable to make it real. His father couldn't be dead. He was too big a person to be dead. And shot? That didn't make sense either.

He was standing there when Lilli came past on her way to the kitchen. She paused on the way back, with a cup and saucer in her hand. 'Neil? Are you all right? You were just staring into space.'

'I just heard, my father's died.' The words didn't seem true. They seemed like lies.

'Oh no. Oh I'm so sorry. Look, take this. It's tea. Hot tea. You go and sit down, and I'll bring you some sugar.'

Dazed, he took hold of the saucer and carried the tea back to his room. What would happen to the broadcast? He was supposed to be briefing three more POWs tomorrow. His schedule was full. And he was going to take Lilli out. The cup was shaking. He put it down on the bedside table, sat in the only chair, and put his head in his hands.

A few minutes later, a gentle knock and Lilli appeared with a sugar basin. 'Gosh, what an awful shock. I've pinched some sugar from Mrs Littlefair's secret hoard.' She put a generous spoonful in the tea and stirred, then perched on the edge of the bed.

I should have tidied the room, he thought.

'Had he been ill, your father?'

'No. It was sudden … unexpected.'

She nodded.

He couldn't bear to say the word 'shot'. It brought back his own terrible memories. He took a gulp of tea that scalded his tongue. 'A friend's coming to drive me back home to Scotland. He'll have to set off awfully early.'

'That's good.'

'Lilli, I'm sorry but, I'll be away and we can't—'

'Never mind all that, we can do it when you get back. I'll still be here.'

Why would anyone shoot his father? He only half-heard her reply because a thought had just punched him in the guts.

Otto Hefner. Dread made his spine tingle. He'd thought he'd got away with killing him, but no. Neil's thoughts chased frantically in circles. The British Union of Fascists must have put two and two together and realised he was responsible for Otto's death. His stomach sank as the idea took him in its icy noose.

It was clear. This shooting of his father was no random

accident, or robbery. It was some kind of retribution for the death of Otto Hefner, and his father had paid the price.

Immediately Neil shut off the light and went to the window to lift the blackout blind. The road outside was pitch black. He scanned the road for any movement, but nothing.

'What is it?' Lilli asked.

'Nothing. Just checking the road.'

She frowned, and said, 'I'll leave you to drink your tea. I'm really sorry about your father.' She put a hand on his arm. 'I hope you have a good journey tomorrow.'

He barely took in her words. He was uneasy. If they could find his father, they could find him.

*

Lilli left Neil in his room. His father must have meant a lot to him. He'd been shocked but then he'd suddenly got jittery and looked out of the window as if something might be out there. Grief did odd things to you. It was a thing that couldn't be shared, no matter how much you tried. She'd been grieving her own father all these years, even though she'd had no word of his fate. She couldn't assume he was dead, but nor could she assume he was alive, and, if she thought too much about Papa, the tension made her want to scream or tear something.

That night she couldn't sleep, worrying about Papa. So the next morning she was groggy as she went out to collect her bicycle from the back of the house. She was just untying it from the drainpipe when a disturbance in the privet hedge made her start.

There was a boy's face staring at her through the branches. A pale boy with brown hair and a grubby white shirt.

'Hello,' she said.

'Hello.' He kept on staring. She guessed he was nine or ten years old.

'Do you live next door?'

'Yep. Worse luck.' He was still peering through the hedge. 'Will that man be coming out soon? The man with the stick?'

'Not today.'

'What happened to him? Has he been a soldier or what?'

'It was an accident. A bomb.'

'That's why they sent me here. Because of the bombs. Will he be coming out soon? He said I could have a go on his motorbike.'

'No. Someone's coming to collect him in a car. He's got to go home.'

'Wish I could go home,' he said glumly.

'Where's home?'

He kicked at the privet. 'Forty-six Lancelot Road, Wembley,' he recited. 'But they sent me here and now I have to stay with the Baileys.' He made a face. 'They're teachers and they don't like me to make any noise.' The word 'teachers' was spoken with venom.

Her heart went out to him. She knew what it was like to be displaced. 'Are there many of you from Wembley?'

'Nah. None of my friends got sent here. They all went to—'

'Raymond?' A piercing female voice shouting from next door. The boy rolled his eyes. 'Better go.'

'Raymond! Get inside this minute! What're you doing out there? You should be getting ready for school!'

'Coming, Miss Bailey.' A sigh, and he lifted his hand and his face disappeared from the hedge.

She felt sorry for him. She'd spoken to the Bailey sisters, Madge and Enid, on a couple of occasions – polite conversations as they were coming in and out of their house. She'd been on the receiving end of their air of general disapproval, and she remembered thinking they were like two old women who'd been brought up in the Victorian era, all fussy lace collars and long tweed skirts. Their house was screened by net curtains and the high privet that ran right around the house.

When she'd been in London she'd seen mothers packing off their children to the country, but had never imagined them coming to the outer reaches of suburbia like this. Poor Raymond, she didn't suppose the Bailey sisters would be much fun.

She heard a car draw up as she was wheeling out her bike, and Neil, pale and serious-looking in a suit and black tie, hurried out of the house to meet his friend. Neil threw his overnight bag onto the back seat, then got into the car, looking all around as if expecting to see someone there. He seemed agitated when he saw her in the drive. She lifted her hand to wave as Neil's friend, a tall man in glasses, accelerated the car away.

She went to fetch Goebbels. Poor Neil. What a thing to go home to.

And she'd really been looking forward to getting to know him better. Her thoughts were interrupted as Ron and Max whizzed by, shouting, 'Come on, slowcoach!'

Chapter 11

At Milton Bryan, when Neil was away, things got slack. It was as if he embodied the seriousness of the war, and for the week he was gone people forgot why they were there. When you'd seen what was at stake the way Lilli had, it was disturbing. The broadcasts went out just the same, though there were errors and blips in the transmission. She hoped Delmer hadn't noticed and that wherever he was in Scotland, Neil had not tuned in.

'I've to go to Aspidistra at the weekend,' Ron said over breakfast the next day. 'There's some sort of trouble with the frequencies. That's why we got all those outages.' He sounded like this was the best news he'd ever heard. 'They're giving me petrol for the car, yippee! And as Neil's away, it could be a jaunt. I wondered if you fancied a run over there.'

'You bet,' Max said, smearing his toast with dripping. 'So long as I don't have to fiddle with wiring or understand what the heck you're talking about. Is it far?'

'About a hundred miles.'

Max nearly choked on his toast. 'You're kidding me. We can't really go there and back in a day, not with all the diversions.'

'I know. That's why I need company. Someone to read the map.'

'Where will we sleep?' Max asked.

'I thought we'd get rooms near the Aspidistra base. There are two boarding houses, I've used them both before, they're nothing fancy, but clean enough. It will make it more relaxed if we stay over. Lilli, do you want to come?'

Lilli was dubious. 'I'd love a chance to see the transmitter. But only if there's another woman; someone to share with.'

'How about asking Maureen from the switchboard?' Ron said.

'Ah, so that's what all this is about,' said Max, giving Lilli a nudge. 'Ron wants an excuse to bring Maureen.'

'I do not!' But his red face told another story.

Lilli liked Maureen, who always chatted cheerfully to her when she arrived at work, and she'd noticed Ron stopping off to chat with her every day on his way into the studio. 'Okay, I'll ask her if she'll share. But won't we need some sort of clearance to go on the site?'

'Yep, you'll need a high-security pass. We all will, but I told you, you're a Radio Rat now.' He leant in to whisper, 'Why d'you think I'm pally with the forgery department.'

'You old cheat!' Max said.

Ron protested, 'They all do it. Slip 'em a ten bob note and there's no questions asked. So long as it's me and not some Jerry that's asking. There's no harm done, it just makes life easier.' He grinned. 'And more fun.'

'Only you could think it fun to break into an underground bunker full of radio consoles and radio geeks. Can't you get us passes for the Ritz or something more exciting?'

'You wait, you'll be impressed, promise.'

Lilli was gratified to think she and Max were not considered 'Jerries', and she was also curious to see the transmitter she'd heard so much about. She imagined it to be a bit like the Eiffel Tower, tall and impressive, like radio masts from the USA. The ones she'd seen in Papa's magazines. She wished Neil could come too, but even if he wasn't away, she realised it was probably completely against any regulations.

So on Saturday Ron went to pick up his car from its rented garage and when he got back to the house at Simpson Village, Max and Lilli were waiting on the doorstep, shivering in the February chill. Maureen was already ensconced in the front seat, so Max and Lilli piled in the back as if Ron were the chauffeur. After only a few miles, Lilli sat back and relaxed. The car was an Austin, and Ron was a sedate, careful driver, slowing before every junction, and waving his arm out of the window to make his hand signals. Nothing like the way Neil tore up the road on his motorbike.

'Give her some throttle,' Max said, bouncing on the back seat. 'We won't get there until tomorrow at this rate.'

'Can't risk pranging her,' Ron said, steering round a bend in his leather driving gloves. 'I barely got any miles out of her before petrol rationing. And she's a beauty. Listen to that engine. Purrs like a cat.'

They passed through Luton and then skirted around London on the bypass. Max had the map on his knee and was shouting out instructions every time they got to a junction. The lack of signposts made it hard to navigate. Never mind confusing the enemy, it confused the locals just as much. They didn't stop except to get petrol with their ministry coupons and for Max to have a quick smoke in a lay-by.

Maureen was chatting away with Ron, but kept turning round to ask them their opinion. They passed many convoys of armoured trucks and at one point they were flagged down by a policeman. Ron politely showed his pass, and the others held theirs up to the windows.

The policeman signalled them to drive on, and Lilli let out a sigh of relief.

'Good job they didn't look too closely,' Ron said. 'Mind you, the police wouldn't know an MOD pass from their elbow.'

'Ooh Ron, they could have put us in the cells.' Maureen didn't sound as though the prospect bothered her. To her, the cells and being arrested were a joke, but the idea of it frightened Lilli and reminded her of when they arrested her and sent her to the Isle of Man. She still remembered that cold bare cell and the feeling of helplessness. She glanced at Max, whose mouth was also set in a straight line.

It was after lunch when they arrived at the market town of Crowborough.

'Let's stop for coffee,' Maureen said.

'Nah, we can get a coffee in the canteen onsite,' Ron said, 'and you can do that while I look into the problem.'

'I'd like to come with you,' Lilli said. 'I know a bit about radios.'

Ron turned and glanced at her before turning back. 'Sorry, but I don't want any distractions.' His tone was mild, but she felt the rebuff and it hurt.

A few miles outside the town, the car began to climb, and they were on a tarmac road leading up through densely packed pines, and drizzling rain. An army checkpoint on the road stopped them, but the guard on duty seemed to know Ron.

'Not seen you for a while,' the man said. 'Mr Robin expecting you today, Ron?'

'No, Saturday's his day off. He sent me to troubleshoot.'

'Right you are, I'll put up the barrier.'

And that was it; they were through.

Ron parked in a dirt lay-by next to other mud-spattered cars. He jumped out and held the door for Maureen, who looked pleased and rather hot under her fur collar as she thanked him. 'Gosh, it looks like a prison camp,' she said. 'Do they need all that barbed wire?'

'I'll say so. The transmitter alone cost more than a hundred thousand pounds.'

'Sheesh. Where is it? I thought you said it was big?' Maureen peered through the fences.

'It is. They had to dig a fifty-foot hole.'

'My God, must have taken some digging,' Max said.

'Canadian army did it.' Ron made them sound like royalty. 'They had six industrial bulldozers and it took them six weeks.'

Obviously Lilli's idea that the mast would be sticking up like a monument was wrong. There was not much to see but trees. By following Ron's lead, they held up their passes and went through the first gate in the barbed wire outer compound and after about a hundred yards, past a circular brick building. But to Lilli, the barbed wire reminded her of the Isle of Man. She tried to squash her unease that their fake passes might be discovered, and as a German, it would be hard to prove she wasn't a spy.

'That's the aerial allocator,' Ron said. 'It feeds the stuff from the various transmitters to all those aerials you can see.'

Lilli squinted through the drizzle at the various pylons. 'It looks like it needs a lot of maintenance.'

'Ron's preserve, he's a real radio freak,' Max said.

'Come on, let's get out of the wet.' Ron had grabbed Maureen's arm and was striding ahead.

Lilli hurried uphill, following Ron further up a track. This place was certainly in the middle of nowhere. More wire, and another guardhouse. She caught sight of some wooden huts and what looked like a brick water tower as well as two ominous brick-built gun emplacements.

At last they were striding towards a big metal door that seemed to be set in the side of the hill. 'There she is,' Ron said, pointing to the bunker. 'The biggest Aspidistra in the world.' He pulled off his trilby hat to look up through the rain at the top of a metal construction of steel and wire.

'What's an Aspidistra?' Lilli asked, confused.

'It's a sort of house plant that the English are obsessed with,' Max said. 'Don't ask me why. But there's an awful song by some music hall star called "The Biggest Aspidistra in the World", so that's why they've called the mast Aspidistra. Because it's so huge. Don't forget it's mostly buried underground.'

'It's not an awful song,' Ron said. 'Gracie Fields is a legend. She's from Rochdale, near where I come from.'

'It's a horrible song,' Max said, goading him.

Ron made a face. 'Ignore him, we all do.' He grinned. 'Look. Those other three big masts, the ones with the metal guy-tethers, they're the antennae.'

Lilli had guessed as much, but just nodded.

At the door was another checkpoint.

'Good grief. It's like Fort Knox,' Max said, nervously.

'Has to be,' Ron said. 'Security and all that.'

The fact Ron was well-known and introduced them all as his companions from the Political Warfare Executive, smoothed their way, and after showing their credentials, they pushed their way in past the concrete pillars, exactly as if they were going inside the hill.

Lilli turned to Max and smiled at him in relief.

Down gloomy pea-green and cream corridors, all curved Art Deco lines and electric light, towards a collection of grey metal doors. Lilli glanced at the labels on the doors, *Engine Room, Ventilation Plant, Engineers Only.*

They were in an underground bunker, surrounded by grey metal consoles, filing cabinets, and a big industrial-looking table, spread with several large maps of what looked like the coast of Ireland and the Irish Sea. Flag markers of different colours bristled from the surface.

Lilli tried to quash the feeling that she shouldn't really be here.

Facing one wall, two women were typing away on clattering typewriters. 'They're typing up information from London,' Ron said. 'There are telephone lines from this centre direct to all the networks; the BBC, the PWE, and the Air Ministry, and to us of course at Milton Bryan.'

A man who obviously recognised Ron came over and sat down with him at the table, as Ron dumped his large tool bag, got out his briefcase, and began pulling out newspapers and notes.

Ron was immediately engaged in a conversation about frequencies which Lilli tried her best to follow by looking over his shoulder. Apparently the transmitter had the amazing ability to change frequencies within an instant.

Maureen grabbed her arm. 'Let's go and find the canteen,' she whispered.

Max tapped Ron on the back to get his attention. He'd obviously forgotten they were there. 'We'll see you later.'

Ron nodded distractedly and went back to the charts of wiring he was examining. Lilli wished she could stay and try to make sense of it, but Maureen was pulling at her sleeve.

By the time they got out, the rain had started; a squally freezing shower. They ducked their heads and ran towards the brick-built hut and burst through the door showering raindrops from their shoulders. Rain peppered down on the corrugated iron roof, the sound and shape like a million ball-bearings.

As it wasn't lunch time, the woman behind the counter was glad to have their custom. They crowded in, hoping to find something edible, and they were in luck. Meat and potato pies were just out of the oven and Lilli was so hungry, she devoured the hot pastry in a few bites, even though it was mostly carrot and potato with a lot of pepper and only a whiff of meat. They ordered three steaming coffees and sat warming their hands and drying off.

The canteen was empty now, and the woman at the till had gone back into the kitchen. Outside, the rain still pelted down.

Lilli had just picked up her coffee cup when Ron threw open the door, his coat held over his head. 'Quick. Leave your drinks. Mr Robin's here. You shouldn't be in here. You'll have to leave. If he sees you, we'll all be in deep trouble.'

Max shot to his feet. 'He'd know me for certain.' His face had paled to grey.

'You have to go now!' Ron shouted, flapping his arms at them. 'While he's still inside.'

'Now?' Maureen glanced at the window, running with rain.

'He's doing a spot inspection, since we had those outages. But he said he'd come to the canteen for lunch. You can't wait in here, and you can't go back in, in case he sees you. Come on, move! We'll all lose our jobs if he finds out we've falsified our passes.'

Or worse, Lilli thought.

They stood up in a clatter of chairs. 'Shall we wait in the car?' Maureen asked.

'No!' Ron's voice was a squeak. 'Not the car! There's nowhere to hide there. Mr Robin's parked his car too close to mine.' It was the first time Lilli'd ever seen panic on Ron's face. 'Wait just beyond the car park in the trees. Stay out of sight, and I'll come and get you when he's gone. Whatever you do, don't come back in, and stay out of sight.'

'But we'll get soaked,' Max protested.

'Just go! When you get to the gate, walk like it's normal,' Ron hissed.

Maureen looped her arm in Lilli's and they headed for the gate with Max loping behind.

'Mr Bottomley will be along soon,' Max said to the guards at the gate, as they went out. 'We'll wait in the car.'

They were nodded through and they hastened through the driving rain towards the car park. Sure enough, Mr Robin's black car was close to Ron's Austin. Lilli glanced back. Rain stung her eyes, but she was glad of it, for it meant the men at the gate paid them little attention, but headed back into their dry sentry boxes. Maureen pulled on Lilli's arm, and they hurried up the slope, on a small slippery track through the trees. Once out of sight they could look down on the complex.

'Now we look even more suspicious,' Max said, 'lurking out here when we said we'd get in the car. Ron and his flaming stupid ideas.'

'Don't blame Ron,' Maureen said. 'He wasn't to know Mr Robin would turn up.'

'Ssh!' Lilli said. 'There are people coming out.'

It was Mr Robin and Ron, seemingly chatting amiably as they walked towards the canteen. Ron glanced up once towards the trees, but then followed Mr Robin.

'Damn, they could be ages,' Max said.

Maureen huddled miserably against the trunk of a tree, trying to keep out of the rain. 'Is there nowhere else we can wait?' she asked. Her carefully rolled hair was flat and dripping.

Nobody answered.

In the silence they heard footsteps approaching from further up the track.

Max waved at everyone to get down. They hid as best they could, squatting behind the trees.

Thank God the rain was bouncing down and the soldier who was patrolling the perimeter fence barely looked right or left. He was hunched as he walked to keep his face out of the rain. Lilli held her breath as his boots crunched by less than twenty yards from where she was hiding.

The machine gun over his shoulder made her legs tremble.

When he'd gone past, she saw the others' faces were like ghosts too.

Another agonising wait of about twenty miserable minutes, before in the distance they saw the familiar figures of Harold Robin and Ron strolling from the canteen towards the cars. To Lilli's horror, Ron then climbed in his car. Mr Robin got into his, and signalled Ron to back out first.

They watched as Ron drove away down the drive, followed by Mr Robin.

'Shit. Now what?' Max said.

'He'll come back for us,' Maureen said, but her voice held a note of uncertainty.

In fact it was a good half an hour before Ron returned by which time they were all soaked and shivering, despite the tree cover from the pines, and terrified another patrol guard would come past and see them huddled there in the woods.

'You flaming idiot! That's the last time I go anywhere with you,' Max said, when they were finally all in the car. 'What if someone saw us?'

'Not my fault,' Ron said. 'What else could I do? I gave him the impression I was there alone, so I could hardly pile you all into the Austin, could I? I had to wait until I could pretend to get petrol, and then turn off.'

'What the heck was Mr Robin doing there?'

'Some bod from MI6 had the bright idea of turning Aspidistra into a jamming transmitter against German bombers, and it fouled up the output. He was trying to reconfigure the frequency.'

'Oh, is that all?' Max said, rolling his eyes. 'Now it's all perfectly clear.'

They all laughed.

'Come on,' Max said, 'my trousers are stuck to my legs, we've been here so long.'

Lilli had never been so relieved to drive away. She vowed she'd never go near that transmitter again.

*

The hotel they were staying at was a bed and breakfast obviously more used to travelling salesmen than tourists, but the rooms were clean and tidy. They all signed the book.

Lilli was sharing a twin room with Maureen, and Max and Ron were in together.

'Gosh, even my underwear is wet,' Lilli said, flapping her skirt to dry it.

'I'm glad we came,' Maureen said. 'He's nice, isn't he, Ron?' She lounged back on one of the twin beds and kicked off her wet shoes. 'What d'you think of Max?'

'Not my type.'

'Why not? He's handsome, isn't he? And you must have a lot in common.'

'I just get the feeling he's not interested, that's all. He's a good friend, but there's no spark.'

'Have you ever been in love?' Maureen asked.

'Once, yes. In Germany.'

'With a Nazi?'

'No, don't be silly,' she flashed. 'With just an ordinary boy. I was young, it was at university. He was kind of wild and I found it attractive, the fact he'd been expelled from his school, but still got enough qualifications to study. He was from Ireland, and it gave him a kind of mystique. He talked about the roughness of the Irish streets, the fights, what he called the craic, and he gathered a group of male admirers straight away. But now I look back; he was always kind of angry with the world. At the time though, I could only see his popularity. He flattered me; he was charming and very attentive. I was young and he made me feel special.'

'How did you get together?'

'At a party. He was on the doorstep smoking a cigarette and I tried to push past him. He stopped me, called me beautiful, and wouldn't let me pass until I'd kissed him.'

'Ugh. A mouth full of smoke.'

'I know. It sounds horrible, but it was sexy. He blew the smoke out real slow, and he had this twinkle in his eye, and of course he was known as the big guy in our gang. It was power, I suppose. I could sense his power and I wanted a part of it.'

'What happened?' Maureen had sat up now, leaning forward to hear more.

Lilli sighed. 'We courted a while, but then he went off with someone else. He was someone who liked to be where the action was happening, and now that was in the Nazi Party. He dropped me for someone who looked more like the Nazi ideal. Blonde, blue-eyed.' The words brought out the sting all over again. 'He was always surrounded by admirers, and he never told me anything; just dropped me. They'd brought in this new rule you see, that even Mischlings were not to be tolerated.'

'Mischlings? What are they?'

'People of mixed blood. I'm half-Jewish.'

'The toad,' Maureen said. 'He'd drop you for that?'

'I don't think Ron would ever be so unkind,' Lilli said, trying to change the subject. 'He's not one to let a girl down. And he seems stuck on you.'

'You think so?' Maureen's eyes sparkled. 'How can you tell?'

'Just the way he looks at you, that's all. He was really keen for you to come with us.'

Maureen tossed her head, and a slight smile played on her lips. 'What was your chap's name? Your Lothario?'

'Brendan.' Saying the name again brought a rush of hot embarrassment and hatred. She'd hated being dumped, it had been so humiliating. 'But I'll never see him again, thank God. He'll be cheating on someone else by now.' She didn't say that he'd betrayed her, though the thought of it burnt like acid.

But she couldn't get rid of the memories; that feeling of excitement mixed with the sense of terror. She remembered a date with Bren like it was seared into her brain. Hitler had just come to power and it was a Germany full of hope and expectancy for the future. She'd chosen a blue-flowered spring dress and platform shoes, and they were watching the girls parade, the Jungmädelbund. Bren glanced down at her as if weighing her up, and she realised with searing clarity that the future was only for blond-haired Aryans and not for dark-haired girls like her.

And even after Hilde, she still thought she meant something; still trusted him, right up until the moment she'd heard those Brownshirts, and their talk about the Irländer who had sent them to raid her house.

Chapter 12

Bren strode out of the Bedford public toilets dressed in a Nazi-supplied General Post Office uniform, with a bag of mail slung over his shoulder. Somehow, Harper had tracked his target, Neil Callaghan, to Bedford. The post office rig-up was courtesy of his new contact Estofal, whom Harper had set up by telephone, and who'd left the brown-paper parcel at the GPO for him to collect. That fact made Bren smile. Local postman – the perfect excuse for pedalling anywhere he liked. He'd got a forged medical certificate stating he had angina and heart problems, so that would be his sob story as to why he wasn't fighting.

By that evening, he was on a bar stool in the Red Lion, ready to get on Callaghan's trail. He ordered a Guinness, which came lukewarm, but he stayed propping up the bar, hoping to pump the barman for local knowledge.

The barman was bored and friendly. 'Ain't seen you in here before,' he said.

'No. New round. Used to be in Lyme Regis, but got transferred.'

'It's a nice little spot, busy for a local place now, what with the war.'

'So what goes on round here?' Bren asked, cradling his pint. 'Anything interesting?'

'There's Woburn Abbey. All sorts of things go on there.' The barman leant in past the pumps. 'You'll be making a lot of deliveries there, 'cos there's about five hundred women billeted there. WRNS mostly, they go in and out in special buses. Why, I've no idea. We're miles from the sea.'

'How peculiar.'

'It's a rum do. All behind closed doors – some special intelligence thing, I gather. Though of course we're not supposed to talk about it.'

Woburn Abbey. Bren made a mental note. 'Sounds interesting. Do they drink in here then?'

'No.' He laughed and shook his head. 'Too posh. But we get 'em occasionally from Wavendon Tower – there's another outfit going on there too. Don't know much about it, but I suppose it's something else for the war effort. There's armed guards on the gate.'

'Really? Who owns it?'

A shrug. 'No idea. Taken over by the War Office.'

*

The next day, wearing his GPO uniform, Bren marched into the Bedford Sorting Office, said he was new and asked for the mail for Wavendon Tower and Woburn Abbey.

A helpful postwoman showed him the two pigeonholes. He shoved the mail into his bag, hoping there'd be something addressed to Callaghan. The sorting office was busy, and the other women who were doing the sorting barely glanced at him. The uniform seemed to be all they needed to see.

Fifteen minutes later, he was back on his bike with two genuine mail sacks slung over his back. He grinned. The real postman would be mighty confused when the mail was gone. War was great for spies; confusion everywhere. Something missing? Blame the war. Accidental death? Blame the war.

In his dingy hotel in Bedford, all old cabbage smell and musty curtains, Bren sorted the mail. Strangely, all the mail for Woburn or Wavendon came with London postmarks. Definitely something off there; it was being censored, monitored, and then forwarded, he guessed. No mail for Callaghan, but for Wavendon, many items for a Mr T. Sefton Delmer.

He didn't open the mail because he wanted to deliver it as an excuse to survey the sites.

He contacted Estofal via his insurance agency telephone though he knew it was risky. Once wouldn't matter as it was the first call from this public call box. 'Get Harper and Green to find me everything they can on T. Sefton Delmer,' he said. 'Arrange for them to meet me in the Black Bull in Bedford Friday night. I should have news for them by then.'

After that he went back to his hotel and begged an ironing board and iron from reception. If there was one thing he could not bear, it was crumpled shirts. Attention to detail; that was what mattered.

*

During the next week, Bren kept the two sites under surveillance, cycling back and forth with their mail, eking out the batch of letters. At one point, he spotted another postboy, who looked about seventeen years old, cycling towards him in his uniform. After a moment's panic, Bren just waved nonchalantly as if going in the other direction.

'Oy you!' shouted the soldier at the gate to Woburn, raising a gun in warning. 'No deliveries! All mail to be left at the gate.'

Bren let out an expletive under his breath. He could see the building through the trees, but he had to hand all the mail to the sentry at the gate. These bloody great country houses, a sign of all that was wrong with the English and their inherited wealth. He frowned as yet another posh car rolled by, with a man in the back seat driven by an elderly chauffeur.

He cycled the few more miles to the other site, Wavendon Tower.

Bren hovered around the gate, pretending to sort the mail. A few private cars swished by, driven by WAAF officers. None of the occupants looked like Callaghan.

A louder engine noise made him pull his cycle onto the verge as a coach lumbered up. A group of young men and women, university types, got off at the gate, chatting and joking as they got out their passes. While the coach was still disgorging its passengers, a motorcycle roared through the gates in a sputter of grit and dust. It didn't even stop at the gate, the sentries just waved it by. A tall fair man pushed up his goggles, unwound his scarf, and struggled to put down the stand. He gave the bike an admiring look before he limped to pick up a stick waiting by the door.

'Bingo,' whispered Bren. Odds on that's Callaghan, he thought, summoning the photograph to mind. Too many coincidences otherwise.

He watched Callaghan go inside before cycling away.

*

On Friday night Bren was watching the doors at the bar of the Black Bull when Harper and his sidekick Green arrived. He'd avoided the lower-class Red Lion, where his alter-ego the postman drank. After getting in the beer, and putting themselves in a back corner out of earshot, Harper brought out a photo cut from a newspaper. He tapped the picture.

'Sefton Delmer, ex-journo, used to be with the *Daily Express*,' Harper said.

'So why's he based at Wavendon Tower?' Bren asked.

'An informant slipped us a note to tell us they're employing German POWs so we guess they're doing something that needs native speakers of German – exactly what, we don't know.'

'Callaghan's in with them too. I saw a man meeting his description going in there – to Wavendon Tower.'

'That fits,' Green said. 'He's got good German-speaking skills. They're saying it's local radio, but our informant disagrees, because nothing German's come on the airwaves. Also the bus driver told Estofal he picks up from another site too, the old MOD base at Milton Bryan. We want to know what's going on. We suspect some sort of black broadcasting, but we can't be certain until we get a man in there.'

'We want you to infiltrate it somehow,' Green said. 'Get to know someone who works there.'

'What about Callaghan?'

Harper gave him a cold stare. 'That's something we need to talk about. Let's go outside, we'll take a walk in the park, okay?'

They drained their glasses and headed out. They walked without speaking, each step making Bren more uneasy.

They strolled through the entrance to the park, now bereft of its wrought-iron gates, until they were on a side path with no one else in view.

Harper stopped as if to survey the lawns. 'Our main priority now is to find out what Delmer's up to, but it seems to me someone here's a bit too loose with the trigger.' He turned and looked directly at Bren. 'Pfalzgraf is most displeased. We're spending precious resources working to close down a murder inquiry where a Scottish vicar died in very mysterious circumstances. I'd like to remind you that we can be equally trigger happy if an agent becomes more of a liability than an asset.'

Bren was indignant. 'Fella caught me by surprise. He'd seen too much of me; the sort of questions I was asking about his son. He was a risk.'

'Not enough of a risk to be dead. He was a bloody vicar! The cops are crawling all over it.'

'I told you. I couldn't leave him to blab – he was suspicious of me.'

'You got an anger problem? No more assassinations, hear me? Especially if it will blow your cover.'

'So I'm not to hit on Callaghan?' Bren was disappointed. 'But you said—'

Green interrupted. 'You're to hang fire until we know exactly what's going on there. For now we're more concerned with the bigger story – finding out about the network – what operations are going on behind that barbed wire. And we don't want you to blow our cover.'

'Cover? What cover?'

'We want you inside Wavendon Tower with this Sefton Delmer. You're to keep your post office persona, but now you're Johnny Murphy, an Irish ex-actor, working for the GPO,' Harper said. 'You were in cabaret in Germany, but came back to England in 1938 at the first sign of hostilities and got a job with the post office in London. You'll be glad to know you've still got angina, but you've been transferred to Bedford.' Green patted the dossier under his arm. 'It's all in here.'

'Johnny Murphy? I've a cousin called Johnny.'

'That's him.'

Bren snorted. 'You've obviously never met him. He's a cretin. So how will I get inside?'

Harper looked his uniform up and down. 'Deliver the mail? Use your damn initiative. They must need a clerk or office boy.' Harper gave a dry bark of a laugh, as if he knew this was the sort of job Bren would hate. 'Seriously? You need to find out where Delmer goes when he's off duty, act like you're the ideal employee. Estofal might be able to help.'

Green passed the file over. 'Destroy the dossier as soon as you can,' he said. 'But keep the documentation. There's cash there too. No gambling though. Not with our cash anyway.'

'How will I get intelligence to you?'

'Not to us,' Green said. 'Our man Estofal will be your contact.

But now we're on the job, you'll use a drop box to contact him, okay? You'll never see us again. We don't exist, right?'

'Got it. But there was mention of a fee—'

Harper's voice held a warning. 'Don't push us. You've cocked up once. Our advice is to lay low a couple of days. Learn your stuff. Solidify your story. Get yourself in to Wavendon or this new outfit at Milton Bryan. Estofal will help you integrate into the area; he's been watching the activity in and around Bedford for a while. He's got a few teams running. Okay?'

Bren nodded because it was what they expected, but inside he seethed.

'Good luck,' Harper said and held out a hand.

Bren shook it. It was cold and dry.

Green watched a dog run past, and its owner in pursuit. As if talking to himself, he said, 'Accidents happen to careless men. And bear in mind, if you get caught in these studios, spying in wartime is a hanging offence in England. And I repeat – that vicar who was shot – Pfalzgraf was less than pleased. It drew attention where it wasn't needed. It would be a shame if it were to get out, who'd done the deed, wouldn't it?'

A moment where Green turned and raised an eyebrow at him, before he walked away, with Harper falling into his stride.

That was a threat, no doubt of it. Bren clenched his hand around the file and watched them walk away, two city gents in hats and polished leather shoes. Still, he had the measure of them. Both pen-pushers; useless in a fight. When he'd been in the IRA he'd got used to it, the taste for a rumble – the excitement, the adrenalin. The feeling of being one step ahead.

He found a park bench, sat down, opened the folder and began to read. Ugh. A typed booking confirmation for another week's accommodation in the same seedy lodging house close to the Swan Hotel.

*

In his hotel room Bren found a letter waiting for him addressed to Johnny Murphy. He slit it open to find a message from Estofal.

Bedford Public Library
From Track to Highway by Gibbard Jackson.

He guessed that must be the drop box.

Bren sat on the bed and thumbed open the dossier in the file – fake Irish passport, moniker Johnny Murphy, actor. That made him smile, cousin Johnny couldn't act to save his life. Ration card, new GPO identity card. A wallet with notes. He speed-read the information on the typed sheet.

The cover story was thin, and lacking much detail. He'd have to flesh it out in his mind, before attempting to contact Delmer. Detail, detail. Delmer was a journalist after all, with a nose for a story.

*

The next morning Bren was at the library as soon as it opened, looking for *From Track to Highway*. It was so obscure that it was lodged under 'miscellaneous interest' and the label inside showed it had never been taken out. He flipped the book open looking for his message. Under the section on 'Turnpike Trusts' he found a scribbled note on a thin lined piece of paper. It simply said, *4111013*.

Got it. He took the paper and crumpled it in his pocket, then scribbled a note that said *OK* and left it between the pages.

When Estofal returned he'd see it and know to turn up. The code was simple. Four was the month, April, eleven the date, as the first had already gone, and the rest the time, and as instructed, Estofal used an odd time for the minutes, not thirty or fifteen.

That would be Thursday, at 10.13. A few days then to try to make contact with Delmer. If his instinct was right, he'd probably drink with the snobs in The Swan. One of his buddies there might know where to find him.

Chapter 13

Lilli was glad to see that the lights in Neil's room were on, a thin sliver around the edge of the blackout blind. So he must be back from Scotland.

The next morning at breakfast Max had a paper in front of him. 'Look, folks, I found this yesterday.' He pointed to the headline on the second page. 'Vicar murdered in callous robbery.'

They crowded round to look. 'Stranraven. Where Neil comes from. And he told me his father was vicar of the local church.'

'No.' They were incredulous.

'I saw Neil after he'd got the news,' Lilli said. 'He never said anything about him being murdered.'

The door at the front of the house creaked and then they heard it shut. Max hastily folded the paper and shoved it under his seat.

'Morning,' Neil said as he took his place at the breakfast table. Everyone looked at each other, not knowing what to say.

'How's your mother?' Lilli asked eventually.

'Bearing up,' Neil said. 'It was a shock. And I'll have to go back up for the funeral. But there'll be a postmortem, so it could be a few weeks. The war's made everything more difficult.'

The table fell to silence. Lilli watched Neil eat a small piece of toast and drink a half cup of tea before he left the table. She

133

jumped up and hurried after him. 'The little boy next door,' she said. 'Raymond. He's been waiting for you every day. You said he could have a go on your motorbike.'

'So I did. Said he could sit on it and I'd take him just up the road and back.'

'I let him have a go on my push-bike yesterday. Had to hold him up, but he must be so bored with nobody to play with.'

'Just wait while I get my coat on.'

He disappeared into his room and emerged wearing his leather coat.

'He'll be waiting round the side.' Sure enough when they appeared, the boy was already there. This time in his grey knitted pullover and school uniform shorts.

'Here you go,' Neil said.

Raymond squirmed through the fence, face aglow, and Neil lifted him onto the saddle of his BSA.

'This is wizard!' Raymond mimed driving and they watched him play, while keeping a sharp eye on him.

'We saw an article in the paper about your father,' Lilli said. 'It said he was murdered, shot by an unknown assailant. That's terrible. Why didn't you tell us?'

'So everyone's gossiping about me, are they?'

'No. We're just concerned. It's a horrible thing to happen.'

'It can't be changed now. Nothing will bring him back.'

'But they'll catch the man who did it, won't they?' Lilli said.

'The police are asking all sorts of questions. Actually, I find it intrusive, all their poking around. My mother's at her wit's end. Witnesses say they saw a stranger get off the bus, before it all happened. A tall man in a tweed jacket and flat cap. But that's all we know.'

'No sign of a motive?'

Neil turned away. 'No.' He'd closed off the conversation, and that hurt. But for it to be murder, what an awful thing to have to deal with.

A ring of a bicycle bell alerted Lilli to the others who were ready to leave.

'Hey, Raymond!' Neil said. 'I'll drive you just up the road and back. Then you're to go inside to the Misses Bailey, all right?'

Lilli got on her bike and was about to push off when she saw Neil hitch Raymond onto the pillion. 'Hold tight,' Neil said.

She watched a moment, relieved to see Neil go at a sedate pace to the end of the road before turning back and helping the scrawny Raymond dismount. Neil would be a good father, she thought and it set off something inside her; her own sorrow for Papa. She was about to cycle after the others when she glimpsed the uniformed postman watching Neil's motorbike too, from the post box. He was straddling his bicycle, his face shadowed by a cap.

She pushed off and was going to wave to him, but too late, the postman had turned and cycled away.

*

Lilli was in the corridor outside Delmer's office at Wavendon Tower, thinking about the Aspidistra transmitter. It was good to have seen it, even if the tour had been nerve-wracking. The transmitter was the only way she knew to get a message to her father. But she knew it wouldn't be allowed. Every broadcast was checked and double-checked by Neil or by Delmer. If she was to broadcast a personal message to Papa it would undermine everything they were trying to do here to make the Germans believe they were a genuine radio station.

Yet not to try to reach him when the airwaves were open to her would be unthinkable. She refused to accept that she would never see Papa again. If only she could get access to the equipment, she might stand a chance. She'd written to Delmer to ask if she could have an appointment to see him, and now, after a nail-biting wait of three weeks, he'd finally agreed to see her.

Lilli knocked at Mr Delmer's door and when he called, 'Come

135

in,' she mentally crossed her fingers and entered. The office was cramped, with a solid leather-topped desk on which sat a dozen telephones, a dictaphone, and a reel-to-reel tape-recorder. She picked her way past too many chairs, and piles of discarded newspapers in heaps on the floor. What a fire risk, she thought.

Delmer welcomed her with cheerful good humour. 'Do sit down, Miss Linde.'

She braced her shoulders. *Here goes.* 'I was wondering if there were any vacancies on the technical team for a broadcast engineer,' she said.

'I think Ron's got everyone we need. Is it for someone you know?'

'Actually, it's for me. I was wondering if I could transfer.'

Delmer's brow furrowed in puzzlement. 'Is there a problem? Has someone upset you?'

'No, not at all. It's just that I'm interested in technical things. My father was an engineer and I've been watching Ron, how he logs the readings from the transmitters.' Even as she spoke, Papa's face loomed in her mind. Desperately she continued, 'I know a bit about circuitry, and I'm good with diagrams. And practical work – soldering and wiring, all those skills. With my experience, I could be an asset.'

Delmer's face was blank. It was as if she hadn't spoken at all. 'But you're our singer. We need you on air.'

'I could do both,' she insisted. 'I was going to study engineering at university, but then the war came and … well, I ended up here. I'd just like to be a bit more involved with the electronics side of broadcasting.'

Delmer tapped a finger on the desk, still frowning. 'It might upset the men if a woman were to be brought in. Everyone's happy as they are.'

She waited, her hands clamped together, hoping if she just sat tight, he'd relent.

His face suddenly brightened.

Was he going to say yes? She leant towards him.

'But you see it's quite impossible.' He looked at her almost with relief. 'We could never have a German person anywhere near the equipment. Danger of sabotage, don't you see?'

Inside she crumbled. Had he plucked this out of the air as a solution to not upsetting the men? She made one last try to persuade him. 'But I'm already working here, with access to it all anyway, and so are many other German prisoners of war.'

'I know you are. I meant no offence. Of course I know you're not a risk, but it would look that way to the Political Warfare Executive. They wouldn't want me to take any chances.' He raised his arms in a shrug as if the decision were completely out of his hands.

He must have seen her disappointment, for as she stood, anxious to get away from this humiliating experience, he stood up to usher her to the door, and talking hurriedly all the time. 'But you're a fantastic singer. The fact we can't allow it doesn't mean we're not grateful for the role you have as Lilliana Linde. The German soldiers love our station, sweetheart.' He smiled encouragingly and patted her on the shoulder. 'Everyone agrees you're marvellous in that role.'

She hurried out, and heard the door click behind her. For a moment she stood in the corridor and then pummelled her fists on the wall, rage overtaking her. They didn't trust her. After everything she'd done, Delmer still saw her as an outsider.

Papa, she thought. *I tried.*

Still shaking, she got on her bicycle and worked off her frustration pedalling like fury to the studio at Milton Bryan.

*

Neil had returned from Scotland. He'd had to go home for the coroner's report on his father's death, and the funeral, but now that he was back, he was gaunt-faced, as if all the life had been

137

drained from him. Apparently the verdict had been 'murder, by a person or persons, identity unknown'.

He'd knocked shyly on Lilli's door as soon as he got back and they set a date for their delayed cinema visit. Saturday. It filled her with both a thrilling sense of excitement and toe-curling nerves, and almost made up for her disastrous interview with Delmer.

Lilli couldn't help but watch Neil when he came up to the studio at Milton Bryan that evening. She shot him a sympathetic smile and was pleased to see him brighten.

'I've got a new announcer,' Max said, as they ate dinner. 'An actor. Used to be in cabaret in Germany. I think he'll be great. His German's impeccable because he lived there, but also studied the language. He'll be broadcasting tomorrow.'

'What about?' Neil asked. 'Can you get it to me for checking, later?'

'We've got this neat piece about Sweden being full of fleeing Germans – it seems communication with the Abwehr in Sweden is all over the place.'

'What's the story?' Lilli asked.

Max swallowed a mouthful of corned beef hash. 'We're putting out the rumour that for every German soldier killed in action, at least five more have deserted. It's aimed to crush German morale in the occupied territories.'

'I can't believe the Nazis would be so inefficient. They thrive on lists. If you're on one of their lists, it means you'll soon disappear,' Lilli said.

'Is there any evidence that the Jerries are running away?' asked Ron.

'Minimal. But it'll put the wind up the German women at home. They'll be demanding to know the fate of their sons, and when the Gestapo can't tell them, it will cause unrest.'

'Ach. Why is it always the women that are put through that sort of pain?' Lilli asked.

The men looked at her blankly.

'Why target the women? What's the point of that when what we're really fighting is not the women, but the Wehrmacht, Hitler, all his Gestapo.'

Max slapped down his napkin. 'Ha! The idea that all the women are innocent victims of this war is a total lie. My family were rounded up because of a word from our neighbour – a woman. That kind soul who went to church every week and was a pillar of our society? She betrayed my father without even a backward glance.' He was getting heated now, could barely get the words out. 'D'you know she actually rang the Kommandant personally and told him where my parents were hiding? So don't you dare feel sorry for the women!'

Neil put out a restraining hand. 'Max, let's—'

But Max couldn't stop. 'D'you know what they did? My father's dead with a bullet in the back of his head and the rest of my family – well, no one knows where they've been taken.'

Mrs Littlefair put her head round the door. 'Is everything all right? I heard shouting.'

Silence in the room.

'We're fine,' Lilli said. 'Lovely bread today.'

Mrs Littlefair went out, but she shook her head in a worried way.

'Look, everyone,' Ron said quietly, 'terror does odd things. Women who support the Nazi regime need to know not all their men want to do this. That some run away. That's the whole point. Think of it as un-brainwashing.'

'But I don't want to end up like them,' Lilli said, 'manipulating and pushing lies.'

Neil looked directly at Lilli. 'You won't. You haven't got it in you. It's only for work, not life. And don't think of it as lies,' he said. 'We're telling a bigger truth. That the Nazis really don't care for the people they rule over.'

'Oh get off your high horse, Neil. War's bloody and we all know it,' Max said. 'There are no good guys and bad guys, just men wanting to save their own skins.'

Chapter 14

The rehearsal that afternoon was tense, because Delmer was in to watch and they all felt his scrutiny, Lilli especially. But today she was loving the swing of the rhythm. After the morning's row with Max, she'd swallowed back her questions, because they were always the same ones. Was fighting lies with lies really the answer? Just be grateful, she thought. So what if you can't be an engineer? We're all away from barbed wire, in a place where only the music matters. She buried her opinions and worries under the blare of jazz trumpets and the incessant gutsy beat of the snare drum.

Lilli was halfway through a syncopated 'Endless Night' when a gaggle of men came in through the door. She saw Max take one of the men, a tall, well-built individual, to introduce him to Sefton Delmer, and from the corner of her eye, she saw them shake hands. She continued singing into the microphone until the man turned to look at her.

A ripple of shock made the note waver.

Bren Murphy. No mistaking him. She'd never thought to see anyone she knew from Germany ever again. Their eyes met. The shock made a column of blinding light shoot upwards in her mind's eye.

Bren froze, as if he wanted to simply disappear.

She continued to sing, her mind racing. Bren had been the boyfriend she'd told Maureen about. The man who she was ninety-nine per cent sure had betrayed her and her father. In an instant, the emotion came back, a hot mix of shame that he'd dumped her, and dumb anger that he'd betrayed her. Yet she still remembered the taste of that first smoky kiss, how she'd felt the pull of his casual confidence. She could never forget him. Nor would she ever forgive him for what he did.

The music was drawing to its final note. She held it a moment longer than usual. She'd show the bastard how good she was.

The men clapped, a small show of applause.

'Lilli, come and meet Johnny,' Max said, pulling Bren forward.

Johnny? He was Brendan. What was going on?

'Johnny Murphy, meet Lilliana Linde,' Max said, 'our singer.'

She opened her mouth to say, 'We know each other' but Bren's eyes bored into hers, clearly trying to tell her something. 'Very pleased to meet you, Lilliana,' he said quickly. 'That was a fine rendition.' His accent, the way he said 'foin' instead of 'fine', set off a flush of old emotion.

She made a small nod, but she knew her face was stuck in the blankness of shock. So he wasn't going to acknowledge their past. He was treating her like a stranger.

'Johnny's got the news section directly after you, so we thought we'd just do a test run,' Max said, not noticing her confusion. He took off his glasses to clean them.

She tried to catch Bren's eye again, but he wouldn't play. The band meanwhile were putting away their instruments in their cases and heading for the canteen. Lilli would usually have joined them, but today she couldn't tear her eyes away from Bren Murphy. Was Johnny just the name he'd chosen for himself to broadcast?

'Bren?' The word came out as a whisper.

He shook his head emphatically at her, then turned away, cutting her dead.

She slipped on a coat, for in the evening it was chilly, and thrust her hands deep into her pockets. Five years ago she'd resigned herself to the pain of losing him, the first cut amongst so many losses. The fact he was actually here in England made her head reel. How the hell had he got here?

Max came over to usher Bren away, and got him set up at the table with a mic. A script was placed in front of him, then Ron told him to go ahead.

Bren began. 'This is Konrad Benz, broadcasting for Kurtzwellensender Atlantik …'

Lilli listened with fascination to the introduction, unable to keep her eyes from Bren's face. He had always been good at voices; he used to impersonate all the masters who'd been at his school, and in their little gang had been adept at the voices of all the well-known German radio personalities. His face was older now; harder, more chiselled, but he would still have the presence to make girls stare. His pale brown hair was short, bristling at the back of his neck.

The radio mic crackled and gave off a muffled thud. Bren tapped a finger onto it.

'Go ahead,' said Ron, who was at the control desk. 'Should be right, now.'

'Abend, meinen herren,' Bren began in a low growl. He sounded exactly like a battle-hardened U-boat sailor, stuck under cold water with a Kommandant who had no idea what his orders were. The diatribe was shot through with swear words that made her wince, but there was no doubt he was convincing. It was like eavesdropping into the belly of a U-boat. When he finally turned the page and there was no more, he asked, 'Will that do?'

He was met by a barrage of praise. 'God, you had me fooled,' Delmer said. 'That's just the right tone. I can't wait to hear what the reaction is from Germany.'

Bren was studiously avoiding Lilli's gaze.

'Where's he living?' Lilli whispered to Max, taking him aside. She needed to know if he was in the same village.

'Murphy? He's got lodgings in Aspley Guise about five miles away. A few others that are helping us are there too. No room in Simpson Village with Mrs Littlefair.'

She was relieved. Her heart was all a-jangle.

Some discussion ensued about putting in extra sound effects from the BBC archive to give veracity to the sound, and of adding more reverb. Finally, Delmer, much taken with 'Johnny', said, 'I'll drive you over to your lodgings now. The two others in your billet are having a tour of the printworks. The stuff they'll make will support your broadcasts – we're working right now on Druckerberger an Die Front, deserters at the front. It's a campaign to hammer home the notion that Wehrmacht officers are tired of the war – make Germans think they're deserting in droves.'

Bren nodded and followed him out, without even a backward glance at Lilli.

Lilli swallowed, bereft again. It was strange being in England, and seeing his face. It brought back her whole youth in Germany. Made her nostalgic for the place it had once been, the once-safe country they'd shared. The country of bierfests and secret walks in the forest, of stolen kisses under the stars. Before that terrible summer when Bren changed, and the street was full of broken glass.

Was he a Nazi sympathiser? Or had she been mistaken, and it wasn't him who told the Brownshirts where they lived? Too many questions. Her head reeled with them. Why was he here? Bren had always said he hated the English, so what was he doing working for them? Had he been in the German army? A prisoner of war?

'What's the name of that new chap, again?' she asked Ron.

'Johnny Murphy,' Ron said. 'He's going to be good.'

She started again at the name. 'Max said he was in cabaret. So not a prisoner of war?'

'No. Irish. They're neutral. But Delmer's persuaded him to come on board. And you saw him on the mic – seems to be just the ticket.'

But there was something odd about it, or why change his name? Should she tell someone he wasn't Johnny Murphy, but Brendan Murphy?

The thought filled her with discomfort. No. She should talk to him; hear his side of it first, even though it was impossible to ignore how he'd dropped her overnight, and then in only a few weeks, betrayed her father to the Nazis. She'd try to catch him alone, find out what he was doing here.

Chapter 15

Damn, damn, damn. Bren sat back in Delmer's car, avoiding conversation. The two other men didn't notice and were talking for him over the noise of the engine. He needed to think. When he saw Lilli Bergen's face in that studio he hadn't been able to believe it. The same soaring voice, the same intense brown eyes and nervous energy. But now what was he to do? She'd rumbled him straight away, and though he just about held it together, her presence in the radio outfit made him sweat.

He wiped his damp palms on his thighs. How the hell was he to know she'd turn up like this?

The car veered left, causing him to fall sideways into the man beside him, a young German in a threadbare suit, wet on the shoulders from the rain.

'Sorry,' Bren said in German.

The young man, introduced as Hermann, continued to talk in German to Delmer about the sort of heavy typeface the Führer was fond of on his propaganda.

Bren tried to relax and let the talk wash over him. He'd done his job, and managed to get on the broadcast. But it was only a matter of time before Lilli would blab, and then what would he do? He was suddenly aware that he was in an enemy country, and if they found out his agenda, it would be the end – a short rope and a long drop.

He'd have to get to her. He knew she was Jewish, had always known it. But it had become a problem to getting on once the Führer started his persecutions. He'd nothing against the Jews personally, though he knew they were a good excuse for the reign of terror and control that Hitler was unleashing over Europe. Lilli had been fun. Not his first sexual conquest, but he'd enjoyed her innocence and her outspokenness.

He'd ruined it of course. Young men are always driven by a desire for conquest, whether in the matter of women or of war. Hilde hadn't been worth it, just a quick fling, but afterwards he couldn't bring himself to repair it with Lilli; it would have meant admitting he was wrong. And besides, the world was full of beautiful young women. Hopefully less stupid and more beautiful than Hilde.

The car rolled on through the dark. In the side window he saw a reflection of his own mask-like face.

He had felt a twinge of guilt about Lilli, but not enough to bother him until now. He'd let it slip her mother was Jewish to his gang of Brownshirt friends when they asked why he'd given her up for Hilde.

It was boasting. Hilde, virginal, beautiful Hilde, was one of the most sought-after girls in the Frauenschaft, whereas Lilli – she would never advance his career.

The Party officials had seized on the information about the Bergens like terriers with a bone, and the next day reported with glee that Lilli's father had been arrested and was being sent to a ghetto with the rest of the Jews. They'd soon catch up with the girl, too, they said. One more for the camps. They'd been talking as if this was a hunt, and they'd been tallying their quarry.

It had shaken him, but he soon pushed it aside. There were more fish in the sea. For the last few years he assumed Lilli was in a camp too, or dead. So he'd used that as an excuse not to think of it.

Yet here she was, in England, staring him in the face, working for the bastard English. Though she'd never know, would she, that he'd told the Brownshirts where to find them?

The car engine slowed, and Bren came up from his thoughts like a drowning man. The car slid to a stop, and the three men got out. Waiting for them on the doorstep in the rain was a tall upright man in his fifties, Brigadier Harris, an elderly gent with a moustache and a no-nonsense manner. It was clear he was to be their minder, along with his over-lipsticked wife.

Bren stepped into the narrow hall after the others, inhaling the sour smell of boiling rhubarb.

Already he felt hemmed in. He'd have to find himself lodgings of his own. Couldn't have the brigadier breathing down his neck all the time. Still, it'd do for a few nights while he got his bearings, and got pally with Delmer.

Once in his room, he slapped his suitcase down onto the bed, closed the blackout curtains, and pulled the cord to switch on the light. Not bad. A front bedroom with a window overlooking a quiet road, its gas streetlamp unlit.

The bed was firm, but the springs creaked under the crocheted blanket as he sat down, pressing his hands to his forehead to help him think. He dug to the bottom of his suitcase to get out his leather writing case. Furnished innocuously with Basildon Bond writing paper, envelopes, stamps, and a handy cardboard date calculator, the writing case had a secret compartment behind the writing pad to stow coded memos from his contacts. He took out Estofal's number. He'd risked calling him once, but couldn't do it too often; Harper's instructions.

He paced, weighing it up. He'd call him. He couldn't wait for the rendezvous next Thursday, he'd have to see him as soon as possible, tell him about this clandestine radio operation.

An odd name, Estofal. What nationality was he? He couldn't tell by his voice on the phone, even though it had a slight accent. Spanish? Portuguese?

Now he memorised the number and set light to it, using the handily provided glass ash tray on the chest of drawers next to the bed. Then he walked out down the lane in search of a telephone box, and by the cross-roads he found one and called him.

'Who is this?' Estofal was wary.

'Murphy. I need life insurance. Some things have come to light you need to know. Can we meet?'

'Yes, I'll send you a quotation as soon as I can,' Estofal said. That presumably meant he agreed to sort out a meeting and leave the date and time in the agreed drop box.

'Leave it until after the weekend,' Bren said. 'Monday, maybe. I'm busy until then.'

'Okay. Will sort out a time.' A click and the whirr of the dialling tone came back.

Bren walked back to his lodgings, footsteps loud on the tarmac road. Before any meeting he'd have to solve the 'Lilli' problem – not to mention finding out what Neil Callaghan had to do with any of this.

He weighed up whether Lilli could meet with some sort of accident. But he heeded Harper and Green's warnings – if a young woman went missing it would cause a hell of a fuss, and he didn't see how it could be done quietly. And truth be told, seeing Lilli again had made him nostalgic. He hadn't had a woman in his bed for months, and the thought of it was tempting. Better to make up a tale of undying love and get her on his side if possible.

*

The next morning as Bren scraped margarine over his toast, he made a quick assessment of his supposed colleagues, Hermann and Hans from the printing and propaganda department. Hermann was in Luftwaffe uniform, but Hans was now dressed as a civilian. Young, naïve, and not the vaguest idea about politics or war. They shared a room and had become friends, which suited Bren fine. He didn't want to have to be a pal to them.

Silently, Bren watched Hermann decapitate his egg. By listening, he gleaned that Hermann had been a student of English and journalism in Frankfurt before being put in a Messerschmitt, but was shot down over Kent, where he'd had to bail out. There was a moment when he almost regretted they couldn't be friends.

Bren ignored the English *Standard* newspaper on the table, as did Hans, who was a bad-tempered Austrian with a grudge against Hitler because he'd been conscripted against his will. He'd surrendered in France at the first sign of trouble. Both Hermann and Hans were ready to throw off any principles they'd ever had, to grovel to their English masters in this new radio enterprise.

Bren watched Hermann pick up the paper, and plough his way through its propaganda.

Why was everybody so ready to treat the English as master? Was it the accent? That peculiar high and mighty way with the vowel? The hee-hawing? It was baffling. The Irish at home had the same problem, treating the English like gods. To see these two Germans kowtowing to the brigadier and his wife as they brought the toast made him sick. He regarded them both over the paper with silent loathing.

At eight-thirty a coach came to pick the three of them up and deposit them at the radio station gates where they had to go through a series of checkpoints again to get back inside the compound.

Come on, come on, we haven't got all day. Bren was tense, shifting from foot to foot, ready with a barrel-load of excuses in case Lilli had said anything to anyone else about who he was. As soon as he was in the studio building, he was on the lookout for Lilli, determined to stall her.

'Guten Morgen, *Johnny.*' Lilli emphasised the name.

Her arrival behind him took him by surprise. He swivelled, to find her right in front of him. Her penetrating eyes held a challenge.

'Top of the morning to you too, Miss Linde.' He'd try his Irish charm. 'Looking forward to today's rehearsal. Do you read the features as well as sing?' he said, aware that the rest of the men in the studio could hear their conversation.

She smiled but her eyes were ice-cold. 'Sometimes. If they need a woman, yes. For things like cookery, how a German woman can make do and mend. Advice columns,' she said, fixing him with a glare. 'Like what to do if your boyfriend leaves you for another woman.'

He tried not to react. 'Sounds exactly like my sort of thing.' He grinned and winked.

'You'll fit right in then.' She brushed past him to go to pick up the day's script, which was on the table.

Oh no you don't. 'Hey, wait a minute. I've a feature I'd like to run past you.'

'Oh?' She turned and her gaze locked on his.

'Is there somewhere we can …?'

'The canteen should be open,' she said. 'And I could do with a cup of coffee. A strong one.'

She set off, with him following her like a dog at heel. He admired her long legs and shapely bottom in those newfangled high-waist slacks women seemed to wear now. He'd spent the night thinking up his approach. Would his ruse work? Lilli was a bright spark; she'd be hard to fool.

The canteen was in an annexe and furnished with cheap deal tables and army issue chairs. People were busily finishing their coffee and heading out of the door as Bren and Lilli went in. 'Sorry, love, breakfast's over,' said the harassed-looking woman behind the counter.

'It's all right. Just tea, thanks,' Lilli said.

So not coffee after all, but the terrible English tea habit. Bren longed for the German coffee from his university days, strong and black. 'Make that two,' he said, aiming to re-establish a bond.

She led him to a table well away from anyone else.

Here it comes, Bren thought, bracing himself. *Keep your wits about you.*

*

Lilli placed the tea tray firmly on the table, and sat down, angry thoughts rampaging around her head.

Bren slid into the seat opposite.

'Well? What's with the false name, Bren?' She spoke to him in English.

'I wanted a new start. I didn't want to be the loser I used to be.'

'Crap. You were never a loser.'

'The Nazis thought I was. That's why I left Germany and went to Ireland. But it won't be forever and one day I'll go back to Berlin. I had dreams of running my own language school over there.'

'So? What's that got to do with anything?'

'I need the false name. It's my war identity. Imagine what'll happen when I go back to Berlin after all this is over, and they find out what I've done? That I've deliberately deceived them all, betrayed them with lies and untruths? Better to pretend I stayed in Ireland.'

'Why would you ever want to go back to Berlin? It's not the same country any more. That country has gone. Germany's a country led by a madman, and he's determined to erase anyone who doesn't share his warped ideas. He'd rather every city was in ruins, than to talk sense.'

'The war won't last forever,' Bren said. 'We're still young, with all our lives ahead of us. It's not our war, it's a war of old men like Hitler and Churchill.'

'Not our war? When armed men force us from our houses? When they arrest my father for nothing at all?'

She knew she had raised her voice and people were staring. She reined it in.

His face was bland, concerned. 'I didn't know that.'

Yes you did, you traitor. She lowered her voice again to a whisper. 'Why did you have to change your name? What's wrong with Brendan?'

'I met Delmer by chance in the Swan Hotel.' He glanced behind before answering. 'When I said I'd been in Germany, Delmer suggested I audition. I didn't know then what they'd ask me to do, so I played safe. It's only like an actor having a stage name.'

'But why do you want to do it at all?'

'I thought it would be fun.' He threw up his arms and smiled. 'I've always liked acting. And Delmer's very persuasive. Sounded like a good way of getting back at Hitler.'

She frowned. 'I haven't forgotten Berlin. I thought you were falling for it. National Socialism. You hung out with those Brownshirts – Willi Wendt and Gustav Brauninger.'

'I knew them a bit. And it was easier to pretend to get along with them, you know how it was.'

'What about the bosses here – Delmer and Callaghan? Do they know your real name? Surely they must have checked you out? Didn't you have to sign the English Official Secrets Act?'

'I signed. They think I'm Johnny Murphy, and they checked him out. So it would look mighty strange to go back on it all now.'

'What d'you mean, checked him out? Who is he?'

'My second cousin. There's a lot of Murphys in Ireland. Too many Johnny Murphys to check, and my cousin's the same age as me. Look, I get it; I was stupid. But now I'm stuck with it. You'll keep my secret, won't you?' He reached out his hand to take hers.

His touch sent a shot of unbidden desire through her. It shocked her, the fact of it, and that she wanted to believe him. She fought it off, appalled that a handsome face could hold so much sway.

'God, it's good to see you, Lilli,' he said. 'I never stopped thinking about you, you know.'

She snatched back her hand as her face grew hot. 'Someone might see.' *I'll never forgive you, you bastard.*

152

'I thought of you so often.'

'It's been a long time, Bren,' she said. 'You could have kept in touch.' She couldn't keep the barb from her voice.

'When the war came, it upended everything,' he said. 'I knew if I didn't want to join the Wehrmacht I would have to get out of Germany so I went to Ireland. And I wasn't sure then if …'

She was sure he was going to say, *if they'd deported you*. But then she knew he couldn't say that; it would sound too callous. She watched him squirm, caught up in his own lies.

Lilli looked into his face, the features still striking, but grown harder and more defined. When his gaze finally connected with hers she saw the familiar desire rise up in his eyes, the swamping look that meant he was going to want to kiss her. But she quashed her response with icy precision. 'Do you still see Hilde?' That question, why had she blurted that out? The question that really meant, *Why did you leave me for her? What was so special about her?*

'She got married and had two kids. No idea what she's doing now.' He paused. 'And anyway, she didn't mean anything. Not like us.'

She recognised the flattery. He obviously thought that was what she wanted to hear.

'Are you seeing anyone, right now?' he asked.

'You must be joking. I've spent the last few years on the Isle of Man in a women's camp for what the English call "enemy aliens". There wasn't a man in sight.' The thought of Neil Callaghan stuck in her thoughts, the light in his tawny eyes.

She picked up her tea and glanced towards the door as two more people came in.

'This tea's terrible,' he said.

'At least it's tea, and not dandelion.'

'How can you tell? It's so weak it could be anything.'

'So, I've to pretend we've only just met?' she asked him.

'It could be good. Remember when we first started going out? Wouldn't be a bad thing to do that again, would it now?' He raised his eyebrows and smiled. Suddenly he was the old Bren and she was back five years ago, looking forward to a night out dancing at the jazz club. 'I've never forgotten you, Lilli.'

You forgot me enough to send the Brownshirts to take me to a camp.

She'd play along though, find out what it was all about. She pinned on what she hoped was a wistful expression. 'They were special times.' She paused. 'We'd better go back,' she said. 'We don't want to set tongues wagging.'

Bren obviously took this as a good sign. He led the way to the door and held it open with a flourish. 'I couldn't believe it when I saw you here,' he said. 'What a bonus! Can I take you out somewhere, for dinner or something?'

She stopped. She didn't want to spend more time with Bren than necessary, but she'd need to play the part, if she was to find out the truth. 'Who will I be dining with? Bren or Johnny?'

'Johnny,' he said firmly. 'Bren was a fool, and didn't know a good thing when it was right in front of his nose.'

*

Lilli watched Bren for the rest of the day whenever she thought he wasn't looking. He was both the same, and not the same. His long wrists, strong and brown, ending in hands that always looked like they itched to do something. The way his hair curled around the neatness of his ear. She'd never get used to calling him Johnny. All that guff about wanting to leave the 'war version' of himself behind. He obviously thought she was stupid.

But Bren was here for a reason, and instinct told her that the reason was all about what served Bren, and nothing to do with saving England from the Nazis.

She thrust the thoughts away and busied herself with rehearsing for the evening's broadcast, trying as hard as she could not to look Bren's way, though her gaze seemed to be pulled back to him as though magnetised, searching for the boy she remembered; his restless figure that now looked fidgety, the same nonchalant good looks a bit too studied. Just the sight of him – how he moved with purpose to every stride, that undercurrent of unpredictability – would have been enough to set her heart on fire all over again, were it not for the fact she suspected he'd put her and Papa in danger without even a second thought.

I don't know what you're up to, she thought, *but I intend to find out.*

She picked up the sheet for the evening broadcast from the music stand to read it through, but her mind was still on Bren. He came and went with various pieces of typed propaganda, and each time the door opened her heart lurched.

Just before the broadcast, Neil and Max came in, scripts in hand.

'How's my songbird?' Neil asked. 'Ready for tonight?'

'Ready as I'll ever be,' she said, glad to see his shy smile.

'I heard Murphy, the new fellow, through headphones over at Simpson's,' Neil said. 'Ron cued me to let me listen in. Delmer's very keen on him. He sounds the business.'

'He's very good.' She couldn't meet Neil's eyes. She found herself staring at the floor.

Bren was watching them, so Max called Bren over to do the introductions. 'Neil Callaghan, this is Johnny Murphy. He'll do some of the announcements alongside Len, but also be on Atlantiksender, our sister programme, as our submariner.'

'I heard you last night,' Neil said. 'You're just what we need.'

Bren smiled widely and held out a hand, which Neil took and shook.

After introductions were made, they all settled to their positions for the evening broadcast. Lilli watched Bren size up the other men, like he always did, and then relax, as if they were no threat. All except for Neil; he kept staring at Neil when he thought no one saw him. It bothered her, that he was watching him like that.

Neil came over to speak to her again. 'I checked out the programme at the Electra in Newport Pagnell,' he said, 'and it's *Sahara* – an American thing with Humphrey Bogart as a tank commander in Libya. All male cast, I'm afraid. Will you mind?'

'No, not as long as it's good.'

'Starts Wednesday. The evening show's at seven. You've got a night off; I checked. Shall we go?'

'Wednesday? Lovely. Yes please.' Bren raised his eyes from the script and was looking over to where they were talking.

Lilli ignored him, and continued to make arrangements for Neil to pick her up. She was operating on some sort of automatic. The fact Bren had reappeared in her life had thrown everything to sixes and sevens.

'I only came over to hear you sing,' Neil said, 'but now I've something else to look forward to.'

'Rubbish. You only came to give that infernal machine a run out from Wavendon.'

He laughed. 'I'm thinking of getting a bigger bike now. Something with more oomph.'

'God help us. Do you want to kill yourself? You've already smashed yourself up once.'

'Not me. The Luftwaffe and their bombs.'

'Well, try not to finish the job yourself.'

'Ha, ha.' He grinned at her.

That night, Lilli was first on air, with her rendition of 'The Last Time I Saw Paris' sung huskily in German. Bren was at the table in the studio, preparing his script, his eyes fixed on her as she sang. It made her shiver, but also because she could see Neil, his headphones on, watching her intently too, from the console. Bren was watching Neil with that weird unnatural attention. The tension between the two men was almost visible. She saw it as a long purple line, taut as a wire.

Suddenly she couldn't breathe, she thought she might be having some sort of attack. She finished the song quickly and headed for the ladies' room.

She splashed her face with cold water and took a few deep breaths. She wished she wasn't here, she wished she was somewhere else where there was less pressure. She felt alone, like a child lost in a forest.

She'd hoped that her voice might reach her father, that someone might know how to find him. It will take time, she reassured herself. Don't lose faith.

Had Bren betrayed her? She couldn't accuse him, for she had no proof. Only a single word from a dark stairwell on a noisy night in Berlin. *The Irishman.* But that word wouldn't leave her – what had happened to her father was because of it. She would find out all she could, and then, when the time was right and she had proof, she'd make sure the Irishman got what he deserved.

Chapter 16

On Wednesday, Lilli struggled off Neil's motorbike pillion, her legs still wobbly from the thirteen-mile screech to the market town of Newport Pagnell. At one point they'd followed an ancient bus and her nostrils were still full of exhaust fumes. She helped Neil park the blasted bike at the back of the Electra cinema and took off her headscarf.

Once inside the tiled foyer they had to wait as there was a long queue, and by the time they got to the booth, only one ticket was left.

'You take it,' Neil said. 'I'd hate you to be disappointed. I can wait for you outside.'

'No, don't be silly, you take it,' she said. 'I'm not so bothered. To be honest, I wasn't that keen on the sound of it. I know nothing about the tank war in Libya.' Her mind was still half on Bren, and what he might be doing. She pushed him from her mind.

'Well, if you're not bothered, I'll have it.' A man in a raincoat pushed past them to the booth and handed over his money.

Lilli and Neil exchanged glances and laughed.

'That's that then,' Neil said. 'You should have said! I didn't like the sound of it much either – too gung-ho for me really.' He paused, gave a shy shrug. 'But I wanted an excuse to take you out.'

She smiled up at him. 'Then that's both of us. What shall we do? I'm not ready to go home yet.'

'There's a coffee bar not too far down the road. We could at least have a coffee before we go back.'

'All right,' she said. 'Will we walk?' She was already dreading having to get back on the motorbike.

'Yes, it's only a step, and I'll be able to manage.'

She let him lead the way, though it was slow. Neil was a good-looking man, she thought. Long straight nose, a bit of a Greek profile, though his face seemed shadowed by pain. He swung himself along on his stick at speed, wincing every time his right leg hit the ground.

The coffee bar, Marco's Italian Ices, near the paper shop on the high street, sold sarsaparilla and ice cream and coffee, and had long mirrors all the way down one side to make it look bigger. Lilli shuffled her way into the bench seat and took Neil's stick, smoothing down her hair while he ordered. There was loud Italian music, some sort of opera, playing on a gramophone behind the counter, so Neil had to shout to the middle-aged Italian woman who took his order.

A younger waitress in a tight skirt brought the coffee over and gave them the paper tab, but Neil paid her no attention. Bren would have stared, she realised.

'Really sorry about the film,' Neil said again. 'Next time, I'll book.'

'You weren't to know it would be so busy.'

He smiled back at her. Nice eyes, she thought.

'How's it going with the broadcasting?' he asked. 'You still sound sensational. I listen in every day. Did you used to sing professionally?'

'In London, yes, a few years ago.' She leant in to whisper, 'Before the British decided I was a threat to National Security. I sang in a night club. It was a hobby really, just a couple of hours a week. Two forty-five-minute sets.'

'I bet it was popular.'

'Not particularly. It was a quiet place, full of regulars who mostly came for Reg, the pianist, but I enjoyed it. Reg was an old timer, and used to improvising. Same tunes, but never the same arrangement twice. No music, just his ear to guide me. Nearly killed me at first, I was never sure what I was going to get.'

'Sounds horrible.'

'No, not at all. Reg was a master. It kept it lively, meant I had to interpret things differently each time. What about you, what did you do before this? Before the war?'

His face closed off a moment. He frowned. 'I used to be a lawyer. But I'd only just qualified when the war started, and it sent everything belly-up.'

'So how do you get from being a lawyer to being in broadcasting?'

Again that slight hesitation. He leant in closer to talk over the music. 'I was in a sort of desk job before, but Delmer heard I could speak German, and that was it.'

'Yes. You speak it well. Only a slight accent. Where did you learn?'

He looked at her sharply, and sat back. 'It's not that good. All I have to do for Delmer is check no one's going off script.'

She immediately thought of Bren. He'd not be easy to order about. He hated authority. 'Have you ever had anyone do that? Ever had anyone broadcast for you who turned out to be ...' She mouthed the words, *A Nazi?*

He looked down at his coffee and stirred it with methodical turns of the spoon. Then he looked up. 'No.' His face was closed off.

There was an awkward silence. As if she'd made a gaffe.

She apologised. 'Of course not; I didn't mean to imply—'

He cut off her apology. 'I thought you might like to come with me to this.' He fished in his pocket, uncrumpled a piece of paper, and laid it out on the table. 'I remembered what you said about wanting to hear an orchestra.'

Grand Concert Friday May 15th
Woburn Village Institute
featuring the Aerospace Orchestra
Extracts from:
Vaughan Williams Pastoral Symphony
Vivaldi Four Seasons
in aid of the Red Cross
Refreshments by the WRVS Tickets 1/6d

'I've always liked Vivaldi,' she said. But already she was worrying about Bren and what he might think. *Don't think of him.* The fact that Bren was in England set her on edge.

Neil was still talking. 'This time I'll get the tickets in advance. Unless you want another night in here,' he joked.

'I wouldn't mind. It's kind of cosy. Though I'm not sure I could stand another night of Italian opera.'

'True, that singer sounds like she's in pain.'

'She probably is!' Lilli said. 'Italian opera's like that. But the Aerospace Orchestra sounds like it might be jolly.'

'Don't get your hopes up, they'll probably be dreadful amateurs.'

'Did you leave your cello in Scotland?'

'Yes. I hardly ever play now; the war's sort of taken over.' His face fell. 'Do you ever feel that? That it's taken over everything and left you a different person than you were before?' His eyes held hers.

'Yes,' she said softly. 'And I don't know who I am anymore. People keep labelling me with different things – Jew, refugee, enemy alien. But I'm not any of those things. It feels like I'm waiting to find out what my real label is.'

He took her hand. 'You don't need any label. You're just Lilli. Beautiful Lilli.'

Her eyes filled with tears, but she blinked them back, and kept on staring at the table.

Eventually, he let go of her hand and passed her a napkin so she could blow her nose. 'Sorry,' she said.

'Don't be silly. You should be proud of yourself. Come on, let's get you home.'

He got up to help her into her coat, and she shrugged her way into the sleeves, pulled the headscarf from the pocket and tied it on as he paid the tab. He held the door open for her as she went out into the spring air, and there was still a little light left in the sky so they could find the motorbike easily.

She braced herself for another breakneck journey to Simpson Village. 'Would you mind awfully,' she asked, 'if we went a little slower?' She gave him a rueful smile. 'The insides of an engine are okay, but it's just I'm not used to riding pillion yet.'

'Whatever you wish, m'lady,' he said, and his face seemed to have lost its shadow. It lit up in a smile. 'In my condition, I count myself lucky to have any passenger at all.'

'In that case, you don't want to lose me,' she said as she climbed up behind him.

He set off as if he was carrying a basket of eggs, wobbling until he could get balance and easing back the throttle to a stately pace. Thank God. She might at least get home in one piece.

Back at Simpson Village, they put the bike in the garage together. 'Going to strip it down on Sunday,' he said. 'Want to join me?'

'I'd love to. Never seen inside a BSA.'

'Wear old clothes then. And wrap up warm.'

There was a moment when he looked at her and she looked at him. As if there was more to say. They stood in the dark of the garage a moment, the moment stretching, before he said, 'I can't wait for next weekend.'

'Me neither,' she said, excitement bubbling through her.

He stepped forward and reached out to kiss her on the cheek.

It was a brief touch, like a moth landing in the dark, but still, his touch kept on burning as they closed the garage doors together.

Above a single star glimmered in the darkening sky, and she shivered. Not from cold, but because she suddenly felt so alive.

But once back in her room, she wondered what she'd done. And the thought of Bren Murphy gave her a queasy feeling in the pit of the stomach.

*

The next day, Bren was lounging against the wall outside the gate as she cycled up. 'Morning, sweetheart,' he said in German, coming to grab the handlebars. 'Did you have a pleasant night with your friends?'

For a moment she was blank, but then said, 'Yes, yes. Very good. Coffee in Bedford.' She flushed at the lie. She was disconcerted that Bren had waited for her, and the fact he was standing so close made her nervous.

'I just realised, we're not on air until later tonight and I've some free time in the afternoon after rehearsal. How about you?'

She knew immediately what he was asking and was on her guard. 'I'm free from three-thirty until we broadcast,' she said. 'But I usually go to the canteen. There's not enough time to go home.'

'Fancy a walk? The woods around here look beautiful.'

She hesitated, wary. 'Most of it's fenced off or out of bounds.' She braced herself. After all, a walk couldn't hurt, and she had questions that needed answering. 'We could have a stroll down the road towards Woburn though. We'll have to be careful where we go, they don't like us wandering in case the locals ask questions.'

'If they do, they can't pin anything on us. An Irishman and his girl out for a walk.'

His girl. Surely he didn't expect to pick up where they had left off? So much had changed since then, especially after last night with Neil.

But after rehearsal Bren waited for her, and they set off together through the gloomy trees along the tarmac away from the village. At first they walked side by side, with Bren telling her about some of the stuff he was to broadcast. Once away from Milton Bryan though, Bren walked over to place an arm around her shoulders.

'I never dreamt I'd see you again,' he said. 'You look just the same, you know.'

'Yes. Older.' She tried to move away.

'Not older, gorgeous.' He stopped to draw her off the road and into a brake of trees.

Her heart was thudding under her coat and thin blouse, as he reached down to take hold of her by the shoulders. Before she could say anything more, his lips were on hers.

The kiss was long and deep and insistent.

'Where've you been all this time?' he whispered when he came up for air.

She couldn't answer because she thought she might slap him. She was angry with herself for responding so easily. She hadn't realised how much she'd missed simple human contact, but she remembered Neil's eyes, and it filled her with guilt.

And she knew it to be a sham on Bren's side. He didn't care for her; he was only doing it because he was up to something. Well, two could play at that game. She'd string him along a bit, find out what he'd been doing before he came to England.

He pushed his hands under her coat and untucked her blouse. His cold hands made her shiver as they found the warmth of her back, then slid around to the front of her brassiere.

She pulled away at the touch of his icy fingers.

'You cold?'

'A little. And anyway, we'd better not be too long,' she said. She mustn't let it go too far.

'Yeah. You're all goosy.' His hands roamed her stomach under her thin blouse. 'I'm going to move out of my billet,' he whispered. 'I don't like being in there with those snobby Englishmen. I'm going to find a place of my own. Then we'll have somewhere to go. Somewhere where we can be just us, together.'

She tried to draw away again, but he pulled her back, grinning.

164

'I want to get you somewhere warm, where I can take these off.' He tugged at the strap of her brassiere.

Just then there was the noise of an engine. Thank God. A heavily armoured truck nosed around the corner. Lilli started and hurried to tuck in her blouse and smooth her hair. It drove past without seeing them in the trees, but Lilli, flustered, headed for the road as soon as it passed.

'Better be getting back,' she said. 'I've to be in rehearsal soon, and I'd like a bit of practice time. Tell me about what you've been doing since you left Germany.'

'Plenty of time to catch up,' he said easily. 'No rush. We'll see each other again soon, won't we? What about tomorrow, Friday?'

She was reluctant. 'I've got something on, so it'll have to be another night.'

'What?'

'Oh, another girls' night out.'

'Okay.' He frowned. 'When then? We've got a lot of catching up to do.' He pulled her closer, threaded his arm around her shoulders again.

'I'll need to look at the schedule. Don't know yet when I'm broadcasting.'

They walked back up the road. She moved away, nervous in case someone from the station should see them. Bren put his hand over hers, and interlaced his fingers, and it felt odd, this gesture they used to have when she was eighteen years old. She felt as if a century had gone by since that time. He squeezed, and she had to remind herself, this was the man who had betrayed her. Twice. She wouldn't let him do it again.

'When did you leave Germany?' she persisted. 'Did you go home to Ireland?'

'Can't remember exactly, but yes, I went home.' He made small talk then about Ireland, about the Murphy clan, until close to the gate, he let go. 'Don't forget to tell me your schedule,' he said.

'I will.'

He left her at the studio door to go and see if his news items were ready for the evening broadcast. She watched his long, rangy stride as he walked away. He hadn't answered her questions, but with disgust, she realised part of her desire for him after he'd gone was simply wanting to prove she was enough – that she was better than Hilde.

She was under no illusions now though. She'd grown out of needing him to bolster her self-confidence. She knew he'd drop her if someone else prettier appeared on the horizon, or if it moved him up the ranks.

Besides, even though it was nonsense, the Nazi narrative of dirty Jews had stuck all over the world, even in the Isle of Man. She refused to be belittled and hurt again by Bren Murphy. And the soft look in Neil's eyes kept coming into her thoughts.

She went into the dark corridor and as she passed the research room she saw Max was in there, poring over a newspaper. She went in. 'Hey, Max. How's it going? Any good news?'

He looked up, grey. Before he even spoke, she was aware of a looming blur like a thundercloud. 'No. Last year we got a copy of the Warsaw underground newspaper, the *Liberty Brigade*. It told us the Nazis are murdering tens of thousands of Jews. Gassing them. In purpose-built camps. We didn't believe it. It seemed so improbable. But now we know – there's one at Chelmno in Poland – and it's been going on months.' He stabbed a finger down on the paper. 'Turns out it's system-wide. Not just in Poland, but everywhere.'

She sat down on the hard chair next to him with a thump. 'It can't be true. Someone would do something, surely?'

He was shaking, she realised, shaking with rage. 'Bastards.' He stood up and threw the paper down. 'And what am I doing? Sending them little snippets about how they might not get warm clothes, or enough potatoes this year, how the bigwigs are cheating with the rations. How their wives are unable to send a letter to the front reassuring little Fritz that his job will be secure when he comes back!'

'Max, I—'

'They're killing us. Don't you understand?' He grabbed her by the shoulders, his eyes wild. 'Like culling deer. Our scientists, our artists, our best men. Even women, little children.' He thrust her away to dash the wet from his eyes with his jacket sleeve. 'My mother and brother are still there. They shot my father but he ... he was the lucky one. They took Mother and Jacob away. A neighbour told me. He's only fourteen. Can you imagine the fear? How terrifying it must be?'

She held herself together like tying a string around her heart, and pulled a handkerchief from her bag. 'It's false news, just like ours,' she said. 'Here. We're doing what we can. It's not much, but it's what we can do. We have to believe in Delmer, that this propaganda works. For them as well as us.'

'Delmer's just a hack. To him it's an intellectual game.'

'Better here with Delmer than in the camps for enemy aliens where we can do nothing at all.'

She turned, her stomach churning with choked-up anger, and walked out of the room. Out past the switchboard room into the blast of fresh air. There, she gave a groan and hugged herself tightly. The words that had just come out of her mouth to Max were the words they expected women to say. Not the real words. Not the truth.

Was this business of death camps just propaganda? Like the news they themselves were doling out? She wouldn't put it past Hitler to spread rumours like that to destroy morale. She had a choice. To accept it, or to resist it.

She wouldn't believe it. Papa was still somewhere in Germany, somewhere safe. Someone kind would have taken him in, and he'd be sitting by a warm fire right at this moment tuning into a home-made radio and wondering where she was. The other thought was too huge to let in.

A crunch and spray of gravel and the coach from the villages drew up. She watched the skinny grey-faced prisoners of war clamber down, their red patches stark in the fading light. They were the orchestra for tonight's broadcast.

But if it was true ... *How many of you knew about this?*

The other truth began to bite. These men were safe. They might be cold, they might be hungry, but nobody was going to put them to death. What about Papa? Where was he, now? She saw the last man get off the coach but ran inside and slammed the door hard against them. She couldn't bear to be anywhere near them, let alone sing when they were playing.

She grabbed her coat and went to speak to Ron. 'Sorry, Ron, I can't do this. Find someone else to sing tonight.'

'Hey, wait a minute. You can't just walk out. Delmer will have a fit. What is it?'

By now the POWs were collecting their instruments from the side of the studio.

'I can't sing with those musicians.'

'Why not? You did yesterday.' Ron rubbed a hand through his sandy hair, perplexed.

'That's before I knew what they'd done.' The words came out strangled. 'Excuse me.' She pushed past him, almost ran down the corridor, and began walking as fast as she could towards the gate. She flashed her pass at the guard, and he merely glanced at it as usual.

Then she was out, away from that place. Only a few hours ago she'd thought this road beautiful, its stark winter trees, the glint of frost. Now it seemed menacing. Max was right; if the news was real, if it was true, then singing to the Nazis seemed too small a stand against the enormity of the atrocities in Poland.

A car passed, its headlights thin splits of light in the burgeoning dark. She headed towards Simpson Village, anger and pain powering her stride. She'd leave as soon as she could, go back to London, try to stay away from the authorities.

She'd been walking about fifteen minutes when she saw a single glow of light coming towards her. She kept walking, but the light wavered and the engine noise died.

'Lilli!' Neil was struggling off the bike. 'Stop!'

She put her head down and hurried past him.

'Wait! Don't make me run after you, you know I can't.'

She slowed, but kept on walking.

'I just want to talk. Give me five minutes, that's all I ask.'

She turned. 'You never told me,' she said. 'You never told me what they were doing.' She almost spat the words.

'What? What's going on?'

'The Nazis. They're exterminating people while we sing and give them the music they love. Max told me.'

'Come back.' He held out his arms. 'Please.'

Saying the words out loud had made her stop and bend over to try to hold herself together. Neil's footsteps hurried towards her and moments later his arms wrapped around her. He held her tight, in a clumsy bear hug.

'It's all right.' His words were close to her ear.

She turned to grip him around the waist. 'Tell me it's not true.'

'The rest of your family, are they …?'

'My father. I haven't seen him for five years. How can he face something like that? He'll be older by now, and he's not strong, not used to looking after himself. What if I never see him again?' She broke away, dashed away angry tears. 'He's all I have left. Time's passing too quickly and there's nothing I can do to stop it, and now I don't know if he's dead or alive—'

'Hush. Listen, Lilli. That's tough.' He paused as if to summon his thoughts. 'If he could speak to you now and tell you what to do, he'd be glad you're safe. I bet he'd say, "Keep on doing the work you're doing. Because every broadcast is a nail in the Nazis' coffin."'

'Oh yes, it all sounds so English and reasonable!' she snapped. 'You don't know what he'd say. You don't know him. He's not like that! He's bloody awkward and frustrating and he'll question everything – as if it makes any sense! He'll ask intellectual questions and try to argue back … oh you'll never understand, not unless you have someone still there in Germany.'

He pressed his lips together. She took the handkerchief he offered and blew her nose. She couldn't tell him about Bren, about how he could still be a Nazi, and she'd actually kissed him. It was all too much to deal with.

'Better?' Neil said.

'How did you know where I was?'

'Blame Ron. He put an urgent call through to Wavendon Tower. He guessed you'd head back to Simpson. But you'll come back to the studio, won't you?'

'I can't look them in the eye. The German prisoners.'

'You can. I know you can. You have more strength than you know.'

She shook her head and thrust him away. 'I'd be singing my heart out to people who would shoot me in the street, and I just won't do it.'

'Please.' He pulled her back into his arms. 'I know it's a lot to ask, but—'

'Then make the broadcasts more damning. Make the people see what sort of foul masters they are serving.'

He moved her hair gently away from her face. 'But we have to gain their trust first.'

'Trust? It's a foreign language in Germany right now. Promise me this charade is helping to defeat the Nazis.'

'I can't. I can't promise anything. Promises are too easily broken. But we're doing our best.' His voice was full of emotion. 'It's all we can do. It's small, but it's something. Something I can do. I can't fight, can't do anything else. No other unit will have me.'

She was quiet a moment.

'Hop on. I'll give you a lift back to Milton Bryan,' he said.

She hesitated. The thought of that bike was just too much. 'I'll walk.'

'I'll drive slowly, I promise.'

As she climbed up behind him, she tapped him on the shoulder,

170

so he turned. 'I'm sorry. I wasn't thinking. I know you lost your father too.'

He simply shook his head, put up his goggles.

So it was that they puttered back to Milton Bryan.

As soon as she dismounted, Bren was there looming over her. He glared both at her and at Neil. 'Where in blazes have you been? Everyone's waiting.'

Neil took off his goggles. 'Lilli just heard the news about the extermination camps. She just needed a bit of time away, that's all.'

Bren's eyes didn't flicker.

'I'm okay,' she said. 'It was just a shock.'

'Do you need a stiff drink?' Bren asked. 'I've got a flask of whisky in my briefcase.'

'No. I don't need anything.'

'Go on, it will warm you.' He took hold of her arm as if to guide her indoors.

'No, it will affect my voice.'

'A little snifter won't hurt.'

'She said she doesn't need a drink.' Neil stuck out his chin.

Bren gave him a look of pure loathing. 'I was only trying to help.'

Lilli held up her hands. 'Really, I'm fine. I don't need all this fuss.' She pushed past them and hurried in past Maureen and the switchboard girls.

Ron gave her the thumbs-up when she arrived, and shot a look of relief to Max as he passed her the music for the songs. The orchestra was already tuning up but she deliberately turned her back on their faces and concentrated only on the sound.

That night she closed her eyes and sang for those in the camps. A song of long, lonely blue spaces. As she sang, she tried to keep the break from her voice.

Chapter 17

On Friday Bren stuck his hand out from the bus shelter into the rain, and climbed aboard the Bedford bus, which was heaving with morning commuters. He'd far more freedom in England than he'd ever had in Germany, and it surprised him. Still, that was all to the good – nobody looking over his shoulder. The English were amateurs, ramshackle; not like the German command. As the bus rumbled down the lanes, he thought about last night's transmission. He'd enjoyed making the evening broadcast; he was good at his role and enjoyed the excitement of acting again.

He'd forgotten how good Lilli was – she'd been superb last night, her voice fragile but full of longing. He was surprised she hadn't heard about the death camps before. They'd been common knowledge to him for years. But the way Callaghan was protecting her rang alarm bells. He didn't want another man muscling in on his territory. Especially not Callaghan. Maybe he could arrange a little accident. That motorbike might develop some kind of fault. Harper and Green might be happy as long as it looked legit.

In town, Bren shook his umbrella and left it by the library door. He'd picked up the meeting time yesterday and was restless, prowling the place, keen to finally meet his contact Estofal face to face, and link up with his German paymasters to tell them what he'd found out. The librarian, a harassed-looking woman in glasses, briefly looked up as he passed.

He browsed, picking up three random books, scanning for Estofal. He passed a young woman in drenched factory overalls with a shopping basket and gave her a brief smile. 'Awful weather, isn't it?'

To his satisfaction, she blushed furiously.

He headed for the shelf where he'd previously found the message in *From Track to Highway*. Sure enough, a man was crouched there, a short, scruffy-looking individual, in a soaked raincoat. He stood up sharply as Bren appeared, and dropped the book he was holding. Hurriedly, he picked it up and thrust it back into the shelf before wiping sweating palms down his trousers.

Instantly Bren knew he was Estofal. He did look Portuguese with his dark mottled skin, eyebrow-thin moustache, and short stature. Bren guessed he was in his mid-fifties, too old for conscription. He gestured with furtive eyes that Bren should go outside.

Bren put his umbrella under his arm, took his books to the desk, and had them stamped. 'You were quick,' the librarian said.

'Knew what I wanted.' He glanced down at his books and he saw that he'd grabbed *Rambling for Pleasure*, *The Great Outdoors*, and *Anglers All*. Shit.

'Walker, are we?' the librarian asked brightly. 'I'm a keen walker too. Are you in the Ramblers? Great to get away from the smoke and into the country, isn't it? Not today though, obviously.' She giggled and he nodded politely while mentally gritting his teeth. He didn't want to get typecast or known for anything, so he flashed a smile, wedged the books under his arm, grabbed his umbrella, and headed briskly out.

A few moments later Estofal appeared, gave him the side-eye and hurried past, nose stuck forward through the drizzle like a dachshund. Bren followed about twenty yards behind. They walked down High Street and De Parys Avenue until

Estofal turned left past Bedford's impressive statue of Bunyan and headed towards the church, a fine-looking building with a square tower. Bren read the sign, *St Peter's*. So a protestant church. Still, he couldn't object. At least it would be dry. He hoped there were no vicars about to come out of the vestry, like Callaghan Senior.

The heavy door was open and the pews deserted. Their footsteps echoed on the tiled floor as they headed for a pew in the dank, dim interior. Bren sat down in the pew behind Estofal, who turned to face him, his greasy skin damp from the drizzle, his upper lip nicotine-stained under the moustache. 'I take it you're in there, then,' Estofal said.

'Yep. It's a fake broadcasting network.'

Estofal took off his rain-darkened hat and wiped back his sparse hair before replacing the homburg further back on his head. 'Okay, message from Pfalzgraf by radio. He suspected as much. That it would be some kind of black broadcasting. You're to find out which frequencies their stations are on, and which news is coming to England via leaks in German intelligence. That last part is the bit they're really steamed up about.'

'Delmer's got good sources, he's got contacts with the BBC and men phoning it in from all over the country.'

'Who sorts the intelligence?'

Bren lowered his voice. 'The main man for sifting through the stuff is a journalist – a Jew called Max Lieberstein. He decides what's in and what's out.'

'Can you lean on him?'

'You're joking. He's an idealist, hung up on his own principles. Wants to build Utopia. And though the place looks like the grounds of a country house, there are sentries at the gate all armed to the teeth. They've even got dogs. There's Callaghan in there too, our double-crossing agent. He goes between the studios at Milton Bryan and the hub of operations at Wavendon Tower.'

'What's he like?'

'Not what I expected. He looks a bit like Gary Cooper – mild, soft-spoken, self-effacing.'

'Self what?'

'Oh never mind. Looks harmless but he's the one who shot Otto Hefner, Canaris's right-hand man, so not one to cross. Callaghan vets the whole broadcast as it's going out and will pull it if it's not on script. Any suggestion I'm not on their side, and you'd be looking for another contact. One who's alive.'

'Can you take him out?'

'Who? Max or Callaghan?'

'Max. The man who writes the stuff.'

'It's possible. I've been warned off eliminating anyone. Too risky, it would put them on their guard, and anyway they'd just replace him with someone else.' He didn't mention his plans for Callaghan.

'You'll find out their sources though? Pfalzgraf wants exact details.'

'You don't know what you're asking. It's seamed up pretty tight.' Bren leant forward against the pew. Lilli crossed his mind, but he didn't mention her either, best keep that to himself. 'Trust me, I'll get what I can,' he said.

Estofal was twitchy, his gaze roaming round the church.

Bren tapped a hand on the pew to get his attention. 'Next meeting?'

'Don't know yet,' Estofal said. 'I've got a lot on. I'll leave you a message in *From Track to Highway*, or send word via another of my contacts. All right?'

'Don't leave it too long. I want out as soon as I can. It's a tight box and not a comfortable place to be in.'

Estofal, who had been fidgeting nervously the whole time, stood up. 'You and me both. Say, you haven't got a fag, have you?'

Bren always kept cigarettes as currency. He got out a squashed packet of Capstans and held it out. 'Don't light it in here.'

Estofal took one with a shaky nicotine-stained hand and

stashed it behind his ear. With a hurried wave, he rushed away. Bren heard the church door creak and slam.

Bren sat for a moment, on the hard shiny pew, frustrated. Estofal was a wreck. Experience had taught him how to spot a frightened man, a man on the edge, and Estofal had all the classic signs. Was he supposed to trust his messages to that shaking leaf of a man? He was reliant on him. Bren himself had no radio. He stood and rubbed a hand over his jaw. Harper had told him Estofal was the main man in this part of the world, the man with all the knowledge and contacts. Maybe Estofal had bitten off more than he could chew.

Just do your job, he told himself. If Estofal had been given the responsibility by Pfalzgraf, then he must be okay. First Lilli, now Estofal. This mission was turning out to be a problem he could do without.

*

Before returning to the studio for the afternoon rehearsal Bren went to the hardware shop and brought a small nut spanner. Then he headed for the offices of the local paper where he bought the *Bedfordshire Times and Independent*. He was intent on finding somewhere else to live. He wasn't a POW, so there was no reason he should have to live under supervision. It made his undercover activities twice as difficult.

He leant against the brick wall of the bus shelter and pored over the small ads. Ah, here was what he was looking for – an 'elderly widow seeking paying guests, four individual bed-sitting rooms for quiet working gentlemen'. 'Quiet working' gentleman – he could be that. He made a note of the address and set off immediately to check it out. Sefton Delmer wouldn't be happy, but he was sure he could buy him a bottle of whisky and persuade him it was all right.

Number 128 Lansdowne Villas was a tall Victorian terrace with a rusty doorbell, and the elderly widow was a Mrs Gammage, a blowsy forty-year-old with dyed black hair, too much lipstick, and a rather rapacious smile.

'This way,' she said, leading him up the stairs. He watched her ample behind swaying as she negotiated the stairs in her too-tight skirt.

She threw open a door to show him a neatly furnished room, no frills. Utility furniture and a bed that looked flat as a board.

'I don't cook for my gentlemen,' she said, waving her red nails towards an electric two-ring Belling cooker behind the door.

'Fine,' he said. 'There's a refectory where I work. The tyre factory in Bedford. It's a reserved occupation.'

'Ooh, Irish, are you?' she asked.

'Brought up in Dublin,' he said.

'Well, I won't hold it against you.' She gave a tittering laugh and stuck out her bosom. 'Rent's four shilling a week. D'you want to see the bigger room?'

'No, this'll do nicely,' he said. 'When can I move in?'

'Soon as you like, Mr …?'

'Kelly. Call me Ralph.'

She smiled. 'Nice. I'm Bar. Short for Barbara.' She ushered him out. 'Right you are, Mr Kelly. Bring me a week's deposit in cash and I'll give you the key.'

'Do I have a rent book?'

'Nah. Never bother. You trust me, I trust you. That's how it works.'

She meant she would never declare it as income. But it suited him. Cash and no questions asked, nothing to sign.

*

The brigadier at his billet at Aspley Guise was surly when Bren told him he was moving out and wouldn't require supper. 'My wife has cooked for five,' he said huffily.

'I'm sure the other two will eat my portion. Waste not, want not.'

'Was the room not satisfactory?'

'Perfectly. But I'm Irish. We're neutral and I don't like lodging with those Germans,' Bren said.

'Well, if you're going to be like that—'

'Goodnight, thank your good wife for me,' Bren said, and walked away with his suitcase before the brigadier could find an excuse to detain him.

When he returned to Lansdowne Villas, Mrs Gammage was even more heavily made-up, and blinked thickly mascara-ed eyelashes at him.

He handed over the dosh and she simpered at him. 'Thanks, Ralphie.' He did his best to force a smile.

She looked him up and down appraisingly and then went to fetch the key. The key was unpleasantly warm from her hand when she passed it over.

'There's another new chap moving in on Monday. A Mr Battle. Nice older gent, widowed, works for the council.'

He nodded, making a mental note to avoid Mr Battle, and hoping Battle would be more impressed by Bar's charms than he was. A quiet life; that was what he needed.

The room was icy, but a quick blast of the electric bar warmed it a little. He was still worried about Lilli. She hadn't fallen into his arms in quite the way he expected, and Neil Callaghan was sniffing round her like a bloody guard dog. He'd have to turn up the heat, make sure she wouldn't let anything slip.

And before meeting Estofal again he'd need to press Max for hard facts about where Delmer's outfit got their information. Names, sources, whatever he could get.

Chapter 18

The next morning Bren eased himself onto the table opposite Max in the canteen. 'How come you can get such up-to-date news?' he asked him, as he wolfed a sausage sandwich. 'Doesn't it have to come from Germany?'

'Our secret weapon,' Max said. 'The Hellschreiber – a genuine German teleprinter. Any messages or radio news from Germany gets sent straight here. Then we put a spin on it, and send out our broadcasts – with any luck, before their own news goes out. By the time we've finished, I bet the Jerries don't know which news is the real deal, and which is fake. They won't know if they're coming or going.'

'Where is it, this machine?'

'In the small room opposite Delmer's office. Great place to get away from Delmer and his crew. I'm a lucky boy, I have the key.' He tapped his jacket pocket.

Bren nodded enthusiastically. Still didn't explain where the actual information came from, or how they were intercepting the German Morse. 'So where does the decoding go on?'

'Haven't a clue,' Max said, as he wiped his plate with a slice of bread. He chewed a moment then said, 'They won't tell us. Some other place. It's all hush hush. And anyway, who cares, as long as we're getting it.'

'True.' Bren stood up to follow him as he got ready to leave.

Together they went back into the main building and over to Max's desk, which had not a single inch of its surface clear of papers, and where a copy of the *Frankfurter Allgemeine,* somewhat crumpled, awaited his attention.

Bren picked it up. It was yesterday's date. 'How the hell d'you get these so quickly?'

'Just luck. Prisoners. Captured U-boat men. We have to hope they've got something useful. Surprising how many have stuff like this, newspapers, typed orders – we frisk them as soon as they're captured. If our chaps find newsprint they get it couriered over. Guess they know by now how essential it is to us.'

Bren made an appreciative grunt, thinking he must tell Gestapo HQ to brief all U-boat men about not keeping anything like that in their crew quarters. Shame it would have to be done via Estofal. He would rather have enjoyed baiting the bigwigs about the stupidity of their recruits. 'Where else do you get your intelligence?' he asked, picking up another newspaper, and hoping his appetite for news from Germany didn't show.

But Max was bored with this conversation. 'Oh, here and there,' he said dismissively. He whipped the paper out of Bren's hand. 'Sorry, mate, but I've got to get a move on. There's three hours to fill tonight, and I'm up against the wire.'

Bren held up his hands. 'Understood.' Wouldn't do him any good to get Max's back up.

Later, he took him a cup of coffee from the canteen. 'Here, mate. I know you're busy, so I thought you could do with it.'

Max raised his eyebrows in pleased surprise. 'Thanks.'

Bren gave him a thumbs-up and left him to it. He needed to get a reputation as the good guy, the helpful one. That way they'd be more inclined to confide in him and give him the details he needed.

Callaghan arrived then with a new script from Delmer. He put it on the desk in front of him. 'Tonight's broadcast, Johnny,'

Callaghan said. 'Quite a lot of names and data you'll need to get your head around.'

Patronising jerk. 'Grand,' Bren said, aiming for a reassuring manner. 'I'll be word-perfect by the time I get my call.'

He felt for the spanner in his pocket.

*

Later that day, while Max was on his lunch break, Bren returned to Max's desk. His jacket was hung over the back of his chair as usual. Bren slid his hand into the pocket and grabbed the bunch of keys, before strolling down the corridor. Now to find the Hellschreiber. It took him a few attempts to find the right key, and his hands were sweating in case Max came back before he was done. At last, a click. He unlocked the door and went inside. The light was already on, and the machine inside the room was pushing out copy.

Bren bent to scrutinise the paper in the out tray. It was a crude news printout, with separate entries delineated by what looked like a line of perforation type. He peered at it, hoping for an indication of its source, but there was nothing. MI5 were obviously keeping it all under wraps.

He tore off a piece of the paper by the perforation, folded it, and stuffed it in his pocket to look at later.

In the rest of the room there was nothing else to see; no files, no papers. Disappointing.

He came out of the door to bump smack into Ron. 'Ah, Johnny,' Ron said. 'Is Max in there?'

'No. I'm looking for him too.' The first excuse he could think of. 'Thought he might be getting more copy.'

'He shouldn't have left that door open. Not with all the prisoners coming and going.'

'Sure he meant to lock it. Easily done, and he's very busy right now – said so earlier. I'll remind him,' Bren said.

'When you see him, tell him we've got a better way of getting information from the camps, a real beauty.'

'Sure. What way's that?'

'Hidden microphones. They let the Jerries have a bit of leeway, a chance to chat, and every communal place is thoroughly bugged. If they can shove officers together, then they do that. More chance to get a handle on strategy, see?'

'Then what? Is one of our men listening in?'

'Nah.' Ron grinned. 'Not one man. There's only a whole bloody unit devoted to it. Translators, the lot.'

Bren made a mental note to tell this to his contact. Two could play at that game, the Germans could use that ruse too, if they weren't already doing it. And at the very least they could warn captured men that the camps were bugged and to keep *stumm*.

He watched Ron go; he was swinging his heavy toolkit, a weighty bag that seemed to always be attached to him like an umbilical cord. Bren headed back to the studio, but not before slipping the bunch of keys back into Max's pocket.

*

Bren spotted Neil Callaghan talking to Max, and they were deep in conversation. Now was his chance, if he was quick.

Bren strode outside to where the motorbike was parked, under a corrugated iron roof near the bicycle rack. The rain had stopped and the bike was out of sight of the sentries at the gate. He glanced around to check nobody could see him, before crouching down next to the front tyre.

Earlier, he'd spotted Callaghan riding up from Wavendon Tower to Milton Bryan on the BSA. He'd seen the way he drove that thing – he'd overtaken them on the bend, going way too fast.

Time to manufacture something that would put Callaghan out of action for a while.

Bren pulled the spanner from his pocket, and loosened the

valve to the inner tyre. It was stiff but then he could easily bend the nozzle to get to the small nut that kept the valve pressed up against the tyre.

Carefully he twisted the spanner to loosen the nut. Ugh. Dirt had got under his fingernails. He loosened it enough so that the lug for the air would sheer off against the wheel rim if he took a bend too fast. It would cause an instant blowout. With any luck Callaghan would be going at breakneck speed when that happened, and hopefully the roads would still be greasy from the rain.

A quick visit to the gents to wash his hands so he didn't stink of dirt and rubber, and then he was back to work. The whole thing had taken less than twenty minutes.

Chapter 19

Lilli was in her lodgings preparing for broadcast while this was going on, lying on her single bed, shoes off, and learning the words of the songs. She was dreading seeing Bren again. *Johnny*, she said to herself, trying to drum it in. Now she'd pretended they didn't know each other, she'd have to continue the deception or it would look odd.

She hummed the tunes as she cycled over to Milton Bryan, her mackintosh hood up against the rain. English summer, green and wet. She braced herself, took a deep breath.

Bren stood up from the long metal table the minute she entered the studio. Already, he gave the impression of owning the space, with his expansive well-dressed presence. Most men looked shabby these days, but not Bren. His clothes seemed almost new, his shirt well-pressed.

'Miss Linde,' he said loudly, pulling out a chair for her. 'All set for tonight?'

She sat down. 'Hello, Johnny,' she said. 'Had a good day?'

'Reading round my script. Researching in the archive. It beats working for the GPO, that's for sure.' He looked around, as if to make sure Ron and the others could hear him.

'Did you work for the post office? I didn't know that.'

'Yes, I was a postman in Bedford before Delmer took me on.'

She lowered her voice. 'But you have a PhD. Isn't that a bit of a waste? How did you end up being a postman in Bedford?'

He sat down, propped himself on his elbows, face close to hers so the others couldn't hear. 'Ireland's neutral, so I came over hoping to do war work – in the foreign office maybe – because of my languages. But then I got a temporary job at the GPO in London, and it just stuck. Then they needed people in Bedford, so I transferred, and here I am.' He searched in his pocket and brought out a GPO identity card, placing it down on the table.

She stared at his photograph. It was him all right. But why was he showing her this? The story didn't ring true. The feeling reminded her of when he'd told her he was going to a football practice when really he must have been going to meet Hilde. Beforehand, he'd made a great thing about getting out his boots. She should have known then, that it wasn't right and he was cheating on her. And of course once she'd seen him with Hilde, the game was up.

What was it with men? Did they think you were too stupid to see through them? She glanced around, but the technicians were busy with the consoles and not listening to their chat.

'I was hoping I could take you for dinner next weekend,' Bren said. He looked into her eyes, to regain her attention. 'The weekend schedule's out, and we're not on it. What about next Friday night? We can have a proper catch-up then.'

'Not Friday – my girls' night out.' The orchestra with Neil. She tried to sound natural. 'But I'm free on Saturday evening.'

Immediately she felt guilty. But it would be her chance to find out what Bren was really doing in England.

'Grand. I look forward to it. I'll meet you in the lobby of the Swan Hotel at seven o'clock. They do a good dinner there, and you can bring your own wine.'

'It's a date,' she said. 'It will be great to have a proper conversation, after all this time.' She gave him her best smile.

Just then, Neil came in, deep in conversation with Max and Ron. 'You've got everything you need? And you know the running order?'

'Yep,' Max said. 'Miss Blum's typed it up so we've already got a proper prompt copy.'

'I thought I'd listen here tonight, rather than from Wavendon,' Neil said. His eyes flicked to Lilli and she felt herself redden. Her stomach was already fluttering just because he was in the room. 'Len should be along any minute to do the announcements. We'll have to keep him off the bottle, or he gets abusive to our German guests.'

'We'll do our best,' Bren said, shifting his chair closer. 'Hey, Lilli, want to go over your lines?'

She agreed, though she found him overbearing. She was aware of Neil the whole time, even though he was busy organising the POWs who had just come in and were on the script that night. Bren saw her look, and turned his back to Neil as if to cut out his presence.

The evening show went well, and Len and 'Johnny' were excellent in their roles as the newsreader and German military man. Lilli enjoyed syncopating the popular jazz songs Neil had chosen.

At the end of the broadcast, Neil came over and said, 'Lilli, it's late. Would you like a lift down to Mrs Littlefair's?'

Bren stepped up to interrupt before she could open her mouth to reply. 'She doesn't need a lift. She can go on the bus with Max and Ron.'

'They're cycling,' Neil said. He turned to Lilli. 'You can go with them if you like. I just thought you might be tired and need a lift.'

Lilli hesitated. She was not a fan of the bike, but she wanted to get away from Bren's continual watching. 'That's a nice offer. Yes please.'

Bren's face froze in an expression of thunder, which was quickly erased. 'Looks like you got yourself a lift, sweetheart,' he said in German.

186

Lilli waited as the studio was closed up for the night – a rigmarole that took a long time while they checked every switch was off and the studio locked up. Outside, Max and Ron had already gone off on their bikes, but the coach to Bedford was waiting and as it drove off she saw Johnny, in the shadow of the window, watching Neil wheel the motorbike out from the shelter.

Lilli prepared herself by wrapping a scarf around her nose and mouth, buttoning up her coat and putting on her gloves. She slung her bag of music over her back by the strap and prepared to cling on.

Meanwhile, Neil was revving the bike, and a cloud of black smoke buffeted against her shins. 'Hop on,' he said, giving her a broad grin.

She hugged him around the waist and they shot off into the dark, her eyes closed against the grit and wind and throb of the throttle. Neil seemed to have forgotten her earlier plea to drive slowly. Dark silhouettes of trees and hedges went by in a blur. They whipped through a village with blacked-out windows and no welcoming lights to greet them as they flew past. After more bone-rattling miles, she opened her eyes briefly to see they were coming up to Bow Brickhill on the left, and the bumpy part between Aspley Lane and Woburn Sands where there was a sharp bend in the road. Neil barely slowed and she dug her nails into his leather coat.

A sudden jerk before she was in the air. In a split second she stretched out her arms. Her hands scoured the gravel and her shoulder hit the ground so hard that the road seemed to crash into her cheek. Disorientated, she sat up to find she was in total dark, no sound, except for the whirr of a wheel spinning to a stop. The lack of sound was the most disturbing thing, though she could hear her breath rasp in her throat, a sound that was somehow the shape of sand. She tried to sit up but she was too winded. She gasped for breath.

'Lilli?' A panicked voice came to her from the road. 'Don't move. I'm coming to get you.'

She sank back down. Neil was there. He was alive, thank God. 'Is anything broken?' He crawled to be by her side.

'Ich weiss nicht.' The German words just came out. *I don't know.*

His shocked face came close to hers, leaning over, and seeking reassurance. He grasped her hand. 'Sorry. Sorry. Are you all right?' He touched her cheek. 'You're bleeding. A scrape.'

'What happened?'

'I don't know. Bike just skewed for no reason. You'd better move to the side of the road in case more traffic comes. I can't help because I think I've done something to my arm. Can you crawl?'

She eased her way slowly to the side of the road, feeling sick and shivery. *Shock,* she thought. She sat up and put her head between her knees. Her hip and shoulder hurt and her gloves were ripped. Her hands felt burning hot.

Neil struggled to drag the bike off the road, but one arm seemed useless and he couldn't manage to even lift it. 'A blowout,' he shouted. 'Front tyre. But the clutch lever's broken and there's damage to the brake calipers. I won't be able to ride it again.'

Thank God, she thought. As he was struggling a sliver of light sliced over the brow of the hill. A car. Neil stood out in the road waving his arm. The headlights with their narrow regulation beams bore down on them. For one terrifying moment she thought the car was not going to stop and would mow him down, but at the last minute it braked. Neil staggered to the driver's window and gestured towards Lilli, and the bike, still a heap in the middle of the highway.

A man and a woman got out, the woman ran towards her, tottering on platform shoes. 'Oh dear. Can you walk?' She bustled to help her up.

Meanwhile the driver, a grey-haired man in a suit, was helping Neil drag his motorbike to the side of the road. Neil's face was white and waxy. One arm was dangling by his side. They stood the motorbike back on its stand and looked it over. All the time Lilli thought she might be sick.

188

The couple insisted they both get in the back of the car. 'Don't touch the seats though,' the woman said. 'Your hands are bleeding.'

'Should have checked the tyres,' the man said to his wife under his breath. 'Would you believe it?'

'The tyres were new,' Neil said.

'Then you must have hit a nail somewhere.'

'But we only came from Milton Bryan.'

The man looked across to his wife in the passenger seat with a look that clearly said, *What a fool.*

'Dr McKay will know what to do,' the man pronounced, starting the car. 'We'll drop you at his house for him to check you over.'

'I just want to go home,' Lilli said.

'No. Dr McKay will look at you,' the man said firmly.

*

They were dumped outside the doctor's house, and the couple drove off.

'I did check the tyres,' Neil said. 'Only a few days ago. They were fine. Honest.'

Dr McKay, terse because it was so late, told Neil his collarbone was cracked and supplied him with a sling, then doused Lilli's cuts on her hands with purple iodine. Without a word, he handed her a tube of Germolene and gave Neil the bill.

Neil had no cash, but promised he'd return to pay it as soon as he could. After that, with much huffing and puffing the doctor shoved Neil's coat into the car because obviously he couldn't put it back on wearing a sling, and then drove them to Mrs Littlefair's.

Once they were inside the door, Lilli said, 'Thank goodness. That couple were awful. I think I need to sit down.'

Neil ushered her into his room, where she sank into a chair, wincing at the grazes on her hands.

'I'm really sorry,' he said again. 'I feel terrible, putting you through that. Are you okay?'

'Just a bit winded.'

'I'll have to get the bike fixed up before I can ride it again.'

'You want to get back on that thing with a broken arm?' She looked doubtfully at his arm where it was up tied against his body.

'It's the collarbone. And it's only cracked, not broken, and it's a good job it's the left side because otherwise I wouldn't be able to use my stick. It's lucky I wasn't going any quicker.'

She bit back the words, *You drive too fast.* 'Can't someone else fetch it back for you?'

'Maybe. Collarbone should be okay in a week or so, but I'll sweet-talk Ron to drop me there in his car and take a look.'

*

The next morning Lilli ached everywhere. She was so sore that she had to go down the stairs sideways. In the hall mirror she saw that her cheek had scabbed over, but it still felt tender and tight. Her hands looked like they were encased in purple gloves.

What a sight. It was a good job no one could see her on the radio.

Neil was waiting by the door. 'I hope you don't feel as sore as I do.'

'I feel about ninety!' She smiled at him.

'You don't look it. But I think you'd better come with me on the coach this morning.'

There were still broadcasts on Saturday, though not Sunday, which was reserved for the sort of fake Christian services favoured by the Nazis.

'What the hell happened to you two?' Maureen asked as they struggled into their seats.

'Accident on the bike,' Neil said.

'With what? A lorry?'

'No, a tyre blew.'

190

'Bloody dangerous things, motorcycles.'

At the studio Bren was already there. He turned sharply as they came in and stared at them as if they were exhibits in a zoo.

'Don't ask,' Lilli said, holding up a hand.

He rushed over, suddenly full of concern. 'What's happened? What have you done to your face?'

She explained.

'You're not to go on that bike again,' Bren said, steering her away so Neil couldn't hear his whispers. 'Callaghan's a dangerous driver,' he said. 'I absolutely forbid it. He could have killed you!'

'It wasn't his driving. It was a puncture or something.'

'I won't let you risk it again. From now on you're to go on the bus, or cycle. Okay?'

She didn't like him ordering her about, but just nodded. She'd do what she liked. Though she couldn't imagine getting on Neil's bike again. She'd got bruises on her bruises.

*

By the end of the week, Ron had fetched the motorcycle and it was back in Mrs Littlefair's garage. Neil had dispensed with the sling, though he couldn't lift up his arm very easily, and Lilli could see by his pained expression it still hurt.

Her hands were grazed and rough, and her hip had a bruise the size and shape of Germany. She'd used this as an excuse not to have another walk with Bren that afternoon. 'I'm still feeling rough after the accident,' she said. 'I'd rather just rest.'

'You do that,' he said. 'Best you take care of yourself. Get fit for next Saturday – our dinner date, remember?'

She nodded, but felt her heart sink. But maybe she'd get more information out of him about what he was doing here in England.

*

Sunday breakfast was a more leisurely affair, and Lilli was glad because she still ached all over. Neil said, 'Day off at last. Hurrah. I'm going to take a look at the BSA today, give it a clean-up.'

'I'll help, Neil,' Lilli said.

'Are you sure?' he asked. But his face had gone pink, and he was smiling.

'Lucky man, you've got yourself a mechanic,' Ron said.

So later Lilli was crouched uncomfortably next to the engine, a scarf wound around her hair to keep it out of her eyes. Her job was to pass the spanner and wrench and hold the thing still because Neil couldn't use his left hand properly. He was sitting on the cold concrete floor, legs splayed like a wooden doll. This odd position was obviously something he was used to.

'There's barely a scratch on it,' she said.

'Except for the calipers and the engine casing.'

'Like us,' she said laughing. 'Our engine casing took the worst of it!'

He turned to enjoy the joke, and a little glimmer of something passed between them. It was lovely, she realised, to be tinkering with the engine, and even better, with Neil. Lilli looked down to where they'd laid out all the parts. He passed her the plugs and valves to clean, while he looked at the starter motor.

A noise behind her made her turn. 'Oh, hello, Raymond.'

'Is it broken?' Raymond was dressed in a blue jumper and his hair had been pressed flat to his scalp with water.

'We don't know yet,' Lilli said. 'We're trying to find out. We had a puncture and the bike crashed.'

Raymond's eyes were round with interest. 'Did you hit a car?'

'No. Just skidded and fell off,' Neil said.

'Nothing the matter with these,' Lilli said to Neil, passing the plugs back to him.

'I'm baffled.' He frowned at the tyre he had removed. 'The tyres are perfect.'

'Will it be mended soon?' Raymond asked.

'We hope so,' Neil said. 'But if I give you this rag and the polish, you can buff it up for us. That's the most important part.' He winked at Lilli, handed Raymond the rag and polish, and got him buffing the headlamp.

'Look at this though,' Lilli said in a low voice. 'The valve to the inner tube's sheered right off. The air would have escaped almost instantly, and that's why the front outer tyre slipped off and you lost control.'

'I don't understand how that could have happened, the nut on the valve stem was wound tight before, and I would've needed a spanner to shift it.'

'Worked loose maybe?'

'Possible, I suppose. Anyway, I'll have to go to Derek's Garage on Main Street and get a new inner tube.'

'If you didn't loosen it, d'you think someone was trying to steal the tyres? Because of the rationing?'

'Possible. That, or they were trying to do me in.' It was a joke, but neither of them laughed.

The atmosphere thickened. Neil glanced over to Raymond, who was concentrating hard on wiping the handlebars.

'You're not serious.' Lilli's stomach swooped. In an instant the garage seemed colder and darker. 'Who would do that?' But then she remembered his father had been murdered.

They looked at each other. They couldn't say anything else in front of Raymond.

Besides, it was too ridiculous. And yet …

*

The next morning Neil stopped at the gate to talk to the security guard.

'You see anyone hanging around the bicycle sheds last week?'

The soldier shook his head. 'No, no one. You worried about kids?'

'A bit.'

'Your bike's safe. Nobody can get in without me or Private Garrard seeing them. He patrols the fence.'

So, an inside job then. It was the opposite of reassuring. For the next week, Neil was extra-vigilant. He kept going out to check on the bike, but saw nobody. Maybe he was overreacting; it was probably just a random accident. Still, he couldn't shake the feeling that someone, one of Otto Hefner's friends, had somehow found out where he was.

It put him on hyper-alert. He watched the prisoners with new eyes, escorting them on and off the transport, looking for any straggler who might have an opportunity. The thought someone would try to kill him on purpose made his palms sweat.

*

The motorbike had been repaired and it was the night of the concert. Lilli was nervous about getting back on the pillion, even though she knew the accident was a once-in-a-lifetime freak event. Before they'd set off she'd watched Neil check the bike over, examine the tyres minutely, and measure the contents of the fuel tank twice. And he'd driven sedately, but she realised this was because his arm still hurt from the accident.

Neil linked an arm with hers in the queue, and it felt good, though her mind would keep going back to her walk in the woods with Bren, and how tomorrow night she must have dinner with him. It made her feel guilty to be two-timing Neil, who didn't deserve it. Somehow, being in the accident with him had brought them even closer together.

The village hall was packed, with only a little space left at one end for the orchestra. The windows had been taped over with blackout paper, and the gas wasn't lit, but the number of people meant it wasn't as chilly as she expected. Though anywhere would be warmer than on Neil's motorbike.

They found seats in the middle of a row. It seemed everyone was going to huddle in their coats, hats and gloves, at least until the tea break. Through a hatch in the wall, she could see a gaggle of women preparing a tea urn, and setting out green utility cups and saucers in rows. Neil seemed to know a few people who she assumed were workers at Milton Bryan or Wavendon. A few she recognised as Poles who played in her band, and she nodded to them politely. None of them spoke, instinctively knowing an accent would cause antipathy among the solid middle-classes who formed the bulk of the audience.

Once the music began, there was no need for talking. She stole a glance at Neil. His expression was one of extreme concentration, as if he would suck out every nuance of the music. It was strangely moving to see his face lose its worry lines and become absorbed in listening. His hand reached to take hers in a warm grasp while the lights were low, and the feeling was both exciting and comforting.

At the interval, Ron spotted them and bounded over. 'Ah, Lilli! I didn't know you were here,' he said. 'How're you liking it?'

'They're good, aren't they?' Neil said. 'Especially that violinist at the front.'

'You wait there, boss, I'll queue for the tea,' Ron said. 'Milk, no sugar, right?' He pushed his way towards the hatch, which was already three deep.

'He's a good sort, isn't he? Knows I can't manage the tea and my stick.' She nodded, and he continued, 'It's fantastic to hear live music again.'

'It's painful, but a good pain,' Lilli agreed. 'I was too afraid to feel anything before. Papa would love this.'

'You're lucky you were so close to him. I miss my father too. I never thought I would. You see we never really got along. Not really, though we pretended. It's not easy being the son of a vicar. I never felt I quite lived up to what he expected of me. Now, I feel awful that there'll never be a chance to tell him how much he influenced my life.' A pause. 'He loved music though. I wish I could have brought him to this.' He gestured to the main hall.

'He'd be proud of you, if he could see the work you do.'

A shadow crossed Neil's face before he said, 'We're very grateful to you, you know. We needed a female voice.' He was looking at her with the spark in his eyes that made her stomach twist. 'You're far better than we deserve.'

'But I could do so much more, if they'd let me. You know, I tried to get transferred to work on the engineering side, but Delmer wouldn't have it.'

He stopped to look down into her face. 'You're really serious about it, aren't you?'

'He said I was a sabotage risk, being German.'

'Ridiculous. Anyone can see that's complete nonsense. This way.' He took her arm as the crowd was growing thicker and they moved out of the crush to the wall of the foyer, where Neil could prop himself up more easily. In the main hall, the orchestra had begun to tune up again.

'And I had an idea – I was thinking though,' Lilli said in a low voice, 'that if the Aspidistra mast is so powerful, and can change frequency so quickly, is there any chance we could use it to jump in and impersonate German ground control?'

Neil looked taken aback.

'What d'you mean? Jam them? They tried that and it fouled up the network. While I was away Ron had to go and sort it out.'

She shook her head vigorously. 'Ron told me the Germans blank out their broadcasts when Allied planes are attacking, to stop them finding their command source. So when they're off air, we could jump in.'

He blinked. It was obvious from his reaction it had never been tried.

'Oh, there you are! Lost you for a minute.' Ron arrived with a tray of tea, and they thanked him and took their cups and saucers. He moved off smartly though, having spotted Maureen by the hatch.

Lilli moved closer to talk in Neil's ear. 'What if our ground control were to impersonate theirs, and give false information to the Lutfwaffe,' Lilli continued, leaning in to whisper, over the noise of the orchestra tuning up. 'We could redirect the pilots away from the English bombers.'

'It's not possible. And anyway, who'd do it?'

'Len Hubbard? He could match his voice to that of Nazi control, and just think how many English lives it would save.'

Neil shook his head. 'It's too risky. It's not part of our remit. We're supposed to be a radio station, not getting involved with air traffic control.'

There was an uncomfortable silence as they drank their tea. Lilli was disappointed he'd rejected the idea out of hand.

Someone rang what sounded like a dinner bell.

'Oh! They're ready.' Neil broke the awkwardness. 'Let's find our seats.'

The second half of the concert was, if anything, even better than the first, and Lilli was enthralled. Neil though, looked as if his mind was somewhere else. He was frowning and his eyes were focused on his knees. He didn't take her hand, and she felt its lack. Perhaps grief over his father was getting to him.

At the end of it, there was a huge round of applause and everyone stood. Neil leant over to talk into her ear. 'I was too hasty. What you were saying in the interval, well, it's a brilliant idea. Our new man, Johnny Murphy could do it – he's a better actor than Len, and fluent in German.' She turned, surprised. She was still clapping but he grabbed hold of her hand to still it. 'I thought it through and I'm going to run it by Delmer tomorrow. It's just the sort of thing he likes – the sneakier, the better.'

'Really?' She couldn't help smiling. She leant over to speak in his ear again. 'They could split the frequencies, Aspi's plenty powerful enough.'

He grinned. 'You sound like Ron.'

'No, I sound like my father. He worked for Blaupunkt; he was their senior radio designer.'

'Ah.' The clapping had died away, and people were leaving their seats. She saw the understanding dawn on his face. 'You're a bit of a dark horse, aren't you?'

'Dark horse?'

'Sorry, yes, it's an English expression. It means sort of mysterious, or someone with hidden secrets.'

She gave him an astute look. 'Then I think you too are a dark horse.'

He shook his head, as if to dismiss it, and steered her through the crowd towards the door.

'Can we drive slowly?' Lilli said, seeing the dreaded motorbike parked at the back of the hall.

'Maybe I should get a sidecar,' he said.

She didn't answer. She could think of nothing more terrifying than to be locked in a capsule with no one to cling on to.

Chapter 20

'Got information for me?' Estofal asked. His fingers were never still, playing with the buttons on his cuff.

Bren nodded. They were in the church again, this time sun streamed through the stained glass to give Estofal a green-and-yellowish complexion. 'Seems the leaks are coming from our side. German intelligence is being decoded instantly over here and sent the same day to the broadcast unit via a new direct-line teleprinter. One of our Hellschreibers. God knows where they got that, but there's nothing I can do to stop it. Where the actual decoding goes on is so secret that even the suckers at the station don't know where it comes from.'

'Pfalzgraf won't like that – saying there's nothing you can do.' Estofal glanced nervously over his shoulder as if one of the Gestapo might be sitting there in a pew, watching. 'Have you found out where the transmitter is?' he asked.

A shake of the head. 'They're very tight-lipped about it, as you'd expect. Must be a bloody big thing though, more powerful than ours, because they've got another station going out from it now, aimed at German U-boats. Atlantiksender. It seems they're rounding up POWs with submarine experience and grilling them. Getting all the inside info about our U-boats to make it sound real.'

'I know, the big guns aren't happy. I've to tell you to find out where the English transmitter's located, so we can target it from the air.'

'I told you, I'm working on it. The trouble with our intelligence is, it's just too slow. By the time I get the message to you and it goes back to Gestapo headquarters, half a week's gone by. We're lagging behind the whole way. German messages get to our radio station in hours not days. Tell Pfalzgraf that there's no way I can stop the flow of information.'

'You think I can tell them that?'

'It's the truth.'

Estofal sighed. 'I need a few breadcrumbs to throw them, at least. This U-boat broadcast, it's put the wind up them. It's getting popular. People are tuning in. You know nothing more of the English plans?'

'Zilch. There's also something coming up they're calling Operation Dartboard. I don't know anything about it yet, but I'm trying to nail it down. They seem very excited about it; something new, to do with the Air Ministry and the Luftwaffe. I just heard the name mentioned in passing, but everyone's tight-lipped about it. I'll try to get more gen on it this week, but then I need to be out of there.'

'I'll message them about the teleprinter tonight.' Estofal looked at his watch. 'Got to go. Someone else to see.'

From this Bren understood he was not the only agent in town. He put a hand on Estofal's arm to stay him. 'Next meeting?'

'Don't know yet, I'll leave a message in the library.'

'No. How about you give me four days? This place is heating up and I want to be out of it as soon as possible.' He was thinking of Lilli. It was awkward, and being in those studios gave him claustrophobia.

*

Lilli sat nervously in a leather armchair in the lobby of the Swan Hotel. It was a swanky place, right next to the river, and seemed to be populated by high-up army officers talking strategy in whispers over whisky and soda. She crossed her legs, pleased with how they appeared, now she was wearing her only pair of seamed silk stockings, which had been a birthday gift years ago from Maddie. She had dressed to impress, in the green silk dress that was tight-fitting in all the right places.

'Lilli, my darling!' Bren's voice made her stiffen and turn. He'd made an effort too, she saw. He was wearing a suit and a blue-striped tie with a modest gold tiepin, surely not real gold, and had polished his shoes.

He bought her a dry sherry and made small talk about the weather before escorting her through for dinner at the Bedford Tudor Grill. Their table was pristine with a white linen tablecloth and napkins, and a window overlooking the river which slid by in surly grey.

She knew what it was all for, because it's what men always did. Tried to soften you up. The Tudor Grill might have grand pretensions, but like everywhere else in wartime, the food was the usual sausage and dried potato, with pale, watery-looking carrots. The gravy was its saving grace and made it edible, though only just. Their conversation was strained.

'You're a sight for sore eyes,' Bren said. He paid her a lot of compliments, which she tried to accept as gracefully as she could.

She decided to tackle him about the GPO. 'You must have made a lot of friends working in the post office,' she said. 'It's a big depot, Bedford, isn't it?'

'Funnily enough, no,' he said smoothly. 'I didn't get to know many folks, because I wasn't there long enough. Only been there a few weeks when I met Delmer in the bar here. We got chatting over a Scotch and a crossword. I helped him finish it. The cross-word, not the Scotch. Persuaded him to try an Irish.' He smiled, and she laughed along.

'Do you still have contact with Ireland? I remember you had an aunt still living there. Though if I remember rightly, you didn't get on.'

'Yeah. Sanctimonious old biddy. She thought I was too wild, that I should settle down to an apprenticeship in the docks.'

'So do you still keep in touch?'

He hesitated, shook his head. 'I've built my life over here now, and travel isn't so easy in wartime.'

It was a reasonable enough reply, but it still felt evasive. Every question she asked seemed to have a plausible answer, but one lacking in any detail.

They carried on eating, until the plates were empty.

Bren sat back and patted his stomach. 'Nothing like good English food, is there? Though you can't beat an Irish stew.' He poured more wine. 'Though I think Ireland should have taken a stand,' he continued. 'After all, the other half of Ireland's part of Great Britain. We were all one island once. It feels odd to stand by and watch those on the other side of the border being called up to fight.'

She nodded in agreement. 'You agree Hitler's gone too far then? Like the Baedeker Blitz?'

'The what?'

'The attacks on cathedral cities. From the Baedeker tourist guidebook?' He must have heard of them.

'Oh, those. Undoubtedly.' He drained his glass. 'Your voice is just as good as ever, you know.' He took her hand and caressed it with his thumb.

He'd dodged the subject. So maybe he hadn't been in England then.

'Will you turn professional after the hostilities cease?' he asked.

'Maybe. I love singing, but I wish I could sing some of the English songs.'

'Like what?'

'Oh, Glenn Miller's "Serenade in Blue", or that one by Dinah

Shore, "Blues in the Night". I like the slow ones. Do you like Dinah Shore?'

'Love those English singers,' he said.

She's American. 'What's your favourite song?'

He floundered a moment, and then said, 'I'll just get the bill.' He signalled to the waiter. She watched him covertly. He obviously didn't know anything about what was popular in English music. So, had he really been in London during the Baedeker Blitz, working at the post office, or had he still been in Germany? There was no way she could find out.

She wasn't giving up. Perhaps there'd be something at his house to give her a clue. Once he'd paid, he insisted on taking her back to his place for a nightcap. She didn't want to take their relationship any further but she'd do it if she could get some proof that he was up to no good.

Then she'd have to tell someone. Who? Delmer? Neil? It wasn't a conversation she'd relish. Why should they trust her, an enemy alien? She remembered Webster the driver telling her to behave herself or she'd be sent back to the Isle of Man, and Delmer implying she couldn't be trusted.

Her thoughts were interrupted as Bren insisted on helping her into her coat. He draped an arm around her shoulder as they walked, and she tried not to pull away. Everything about him now irritated her.

On the way to his apartment he pushed her into a doorway, and leant down to kiss her. She steeled herself and let him do it. Better he should think her amenable and pliable, so he'd let down his guard. It was a moment before she could pull away and begin walking again. He hurried to catch up with her, taking her arm as they walked past a football pitch now turned to allotments.

'How long have you been at Milton Bryan?' he asked.

Lilli stiffened, instantly on her guard. 'I came just before Christmas. It's exciting, isn't it,' she said, 'what they're doing here, destroying the morale of the German armed forces?'

203

'Doubt it has that much effect,' Bren said. 'And anyway, I hear we're not the only RU in the network.' RU was short for research unit, which was what the workers were told to call Milton Bryan. 'Max says there are a few other units round here. Not just transmitting in German, but in Norwegian, Bulgarian, all sorts. Seems half the prisoners of Europe are in Bedfordshire. D'you think all these stations broadcast from the same transmitter?'

How did he know all this? She was wary. His question might be sensitive. 'I guess so.'

'Where is it? Is it nearby?'

She hedged, unwilling to tell him she'd been there. 'Uh huh. Miles away.'

'You've seen it?' He stopped her with pressure on her shoulder.

She found it hard to lie with him staring down at her like that. She wriggled away from him. 'Once. But when I went all the signs were down, and they didn't really want anyone to know its location.'

'Understandable, I suppose. In the countryside, is it?'

She had to answer or he'd know she suspected him. 'It's in a forest, quite a way from here. The other side of London. We had to stay overnight.'

'Overnight? And they let you?'

'Ron arranged it. The passes and everything.' She was suddenly aware that she was giving more information than she was getting. She must get out of this conversation.

'Security sounds lax,' Bren said, 'if they let someone German like you in.'

'Not at all,' Lilli said, floundering. 'There are two twelve-foot-high perimeter fences and armed soldiers to stop anyone going in without a pass. Ron knows them all though because he's a technical whizz.'

'Bit like Milton Bryan, then.'

'No.' She was getting rattled, and tried to put him off. 'Altogether a notch up from us. A bit intimidating really, out in the middle of nowhere. And their guards were military. Ours look ancient, like they've escaped the English Home Guard.' She paused. 'Better be quiet now, we're getting near houses again.'

'Somewhere down towards Sussex then?'

No way would she give him that information, she was already squeamish about how much she'd said. 'I don't understand the English geography, so best ask Ron. I expect he'll take you over if you're interested.'

Bren was quiet then for a bit as they walked past the houses. Their footsteps echoed on the tarmac pavement.

'Here we are,' he whispered. 'Let's go in quietly so we don't disturb the other lodgers.'

Bren's lodgings were clean, and she scanned it quickly for anything suspicious, but the room was small and functional, lacking any colour except for a ghastly coral-coloured woollen bedspread.

I should have gone straight home.

It was chilly, and she was reluctant to take off her coat, and nerves were making her shaky. Bren had always been unpredictable. She felt a sudden frisson of fear leap up her spine.

'Drink?'

She was unsurprised to find he'd splashed out on a black market bottle of wine. 'No, thanks. I think I should tell you—'

'Oh, go on! Let's celebrate a bit. After all, it's not every day we finally get a chance to be alone. Just us.'

'Bren?'

'Better get used to calling me Johnny. Let's get drinks first, then we can talk.'

She watched him uncork the bottle, and glug a large amount into two tumblers. She scanned the room again, noticing a suitcase under the bed, library books on the table. She wandered over to look at them. Books on rambling. She opened one, and closed it again. 'Doesn't your landlady mind you having lady visitors?' she asked.

'Definitely,' he said. 'But she's out at bingo in the Women's Institute Hall. I'll sneak you out before she gets back.'

He passed her a glass, and sat down on the bed, as she had taken the only chair. He held his glass out towards her. 'Prost!' he said in German. 'I can't believe we've found each other. The Irish would say, with luck like that we've been touched by the fairies.'

She raised her own glass before taking a sip. 'Look, Bren, I mean Johnny, dinner was really nice, and I appreciate you taking me out, but this has all been quite a whirlwind. I'm not sure I'm ready for a full-blown relationship again yet.'

He frowned, held up his hand as if to stop her.

She carried on over it. 'I'm sorry but it's been a lot to come to terms with, this war,' she said, feeling stupidly, the need to apologise. 'Being uprooted like that. It's not the same for you; Germany was only ever temporary for you.'

He made a sharp movement of his head. A denial. 'You're putting the brakes on? But we've only just found each other. We've always had so much in common, like our love of the English poets, like our—'

'I know, but I'm not the same person I was when I was a student. Too much has happened since then, and I was naïve and didn't understand anything.' She put the glass down. 'Of course, I'd like us to stay friends but—'

He stood up and came to crouch next to her. 'We're the same people underneath, aren't we? Surely it's worth taking a chance?' He reached for her free hand and interlaced his fingers in hers. 'Come on, Lilli, give us a smile.'

'I don't want to rush,' she said, reluctant to look him direct in the eye.

'Who's rushing?' He brought her hand to his lips, kissed her fingers softly. The feeling of it made her stomach turn over, whether from desire, fear, or revulsion, she didn't know. Letting go of her hand, he reached to push his fingers into the thickness of her hair at the nape of her neck, and draw her towards him.

She resisted, but it was hard to do. Underneath her dislike, the old attraction was still hiding there, all the old habits of being together. It would be easy to fall into the trap.

She braced herself as he touched the graze on her cheek where she'd had the accident. 'That Callaghan's a danger with his maniac driving. I want to look after you. I love you, Lilli,' he whispered. 'I think I've always loved you.'

No. That couldn't be true. But she let him kiss her on the lips, a full, deep kiss, the way they used to, and it felt so strange to be in his arms again. Was he a traitor? Had she imagined that word on the stairs? It was all moving too fast.

'Let me carry you,' he said. He picked her up and took her to the bed.

His kissing became urgent. The back of Lilli's dress was swiftly unbuttoned and Bren's shirt was off.

Lilli was desperately searching for an excuse to escape when the downstairs door banged.

'Shit,' Bren said. 'Mrs Gammage. She's home early, and she doesn't want women in our rooms. She might throw me out if she knows you're here.'

'What shall I do?'

'You'll have to stay until the morning.'

'I can't.' She was frantically fastening her dress, fumbling with the buttons. She threw her coat on over it. 'I need to be on that last bus or Mrs Littlefair will have the police out looking for me. It's all right for you, you're Irish, you're no risk to security. But I'm German. What's the time?'

'Just before nine-fifteen. Curfew's not till ten.'

'That time already?' She was horrified. 'I'll have to make a run for it to the bus station.'

'No, don't go. Can't you stay, pretend to them you went out early in the morning?'

207

'Are you crazy? I'm a registered enemy alien! I have to toe the line, or heaven only knows what they'll do to me.' She was hopping into her shoes and grabbing her scarf from the chair.

'I'll come with you,' he said.

'No time,' she said. And she was out of the room and running down the stairs. *Stupid. Stupid.* She berated herself as she went.

She knew no more about him, but had almost fallen in with his demands. Fortunately, the stairs were lit, and the door was unlocked. She pelted away down the path, only glancing back once, in time to see a corner of the front blackout blind drop back.

Someone had seen her go. No time to worry about that now, she had to make that bus.

In fact the panic was unnecessary, for the bus was running late due to an air raid warning and she had to wait in the wind-buffeted bus shelter along with a few other night-workers, puffing away on their cigarettes, and shivering in the damp.

The bus trundled in and she hoisted herself aboard, into the stale smell of smoke-ridden upholstery and wet coats. She stared at her reflection in the dark bus window, into her own troubled eyes. She felt guilty about Neil. They hadn't even kissed, not like the fumbling in the dark with Bren, and yet though she hardly knew Neil, she trusted him and she didn't want to hurt him.

She hadn't managed to close it off with Bren. He was different from how she remembered him, less impulsive, more uptight and controlling. Perhaps it was that they'd both grown up, seen what war can do. But there was a domineering feeling about him that made him hard to resist. She had to remember The Night of Broken Glass to remind herself what she was doing.

Her father, lying, telling the Brownshirts she was out.

She'd find definite proof Bren was in league with the enemy, then tell someone. She must try to get in his flat again, but this time she'd have her wits about her. She'd persuade him to go out to the shops for something – then she could search his things.

But what about Neil? The feeling she had about Neil was

small, like a tiny spring shoot. But it was undeniably there, and to pretend it wasn't would be foolish.

She was playing with fire. She dreaded one of them finding out about the other.

*

The next morning as Bren bounded down the stairs, Mrs Gammage stopped him at the door. Damn, the old witch must have been waiting for him.

'I told you, no women or shenanigans in my house. Only respectable working gents.'

Bren put on a puzzled look.

'Did you have a young woman visit you last night?'

'A woman?' He should win a prize for acting. The odious old bat couldn't prove whose room Lilli came out of, and he could protest his innocence.

She scrutinised him. 'Frank says it wasn't him, and Mr Battle is away. So that only leaves you.'

'I don't know what you're talking about. Is there some sort of problem?'

Mrs Gammage narrowed her eyes under her black-painted eyebrows. 'Now look here, Ralphie, I don't want any trouble. Working men only, and no callers. Am I clear?'

'As crystal, Mrs Gammage. Perhaps you were mistaken and she came from next door.'

'Call me Bar.' She allowed a coquettish smile to play on her lips. 'And I'm not bleeding stupid.'

There was silence and a kind of unspoken truce. 'I assure you, there'll be no trouble from me,' he said, pushing past her. 'Now if you'll excuse me, my bus will be along shortly.'

He set off to the station, it would be quicker than the push-bike. It was only a few stops to Milton Bryan and he used the time to read an English paper from the newsagent on the corner. Best be up to date with the Allies's news, and try and see what Delmer's Operation Dartboard was about, before meeting Estofal again.

The bus rattled along, through lanes ruffled white with may blossom, and verges of bluebells, but Bren saw none of it. His mind replayed what Lilli had told him yesterday, about this mega-transmitter somewhere in a forest. She'd been useful already – definitely worth cultivating her, and she obviously had no idea he was an agent. The position of the transmitter would be information that Pfalzgraf would want. Perhaps he could pump Ron, as he was so enthusiastic about it. Feign interest in the technical stuff and ask for a tour.

And he'd make another date with Lilli. He'd be happier knowing she was tied to him more tightly, so he could control who she was seeing and what she was doing. He didn't want her telling anyone about his Nazi Party friends or any doubts over his legitimacy to be working at Milton Bryan.

*

Bren waited until Ron had removed his headphones then walked over to where he was hunched over a console.

'Pretty interesting, the way all this works, isn't it?' Bren said. 'Have you always been a radio buff?'

Ron turned, his face pink. 'Ever since I heard my first broadcast. It was magical. Just to hear voices coming at you from nowhere. It always fascinated me, how they canned those voices. Took my first radio apart as soon as I could get hold of one. I was about seven. My dad went nuts. After about my third one I'd learnt how to reassemble them, and it just went from there.'

'It's amazing we can reach Germany,' Bren enthused. 'Lilli says everything goes through a big transmitter. And Max was telling me it can also change wavelength to hop onto their broadcasts. I'd like to see that.'

'It's not wavelength, it's frequency. It's that we can split it, so the power can go to different places, reach wherever we need it.'

Bren nodded. 'Is it possible to get a tour of it? It sounds grand.'

Ron shook his head. ''Fraid not. Its official staff only. Last time I nearly got caught taking unauthorised visitors in. And I'd get sacked, or even charged with treason, if they caught me.'

'Aren't you on their staff list?'

'Yes, but they've tightened up security in the last few months – since February when Goebbels declared "total war" against the Allies. Now we can only be approved by Delmer or Harold Robin himself, and a standard pass won't cut it. A memo came round telling us the place is strictly off limits.'

'Where is it?'

'Near Crowborough. Ashdown Forest.'

'Shame,' he said, aiming for a light tone. 'I'd like to see the machinery that sends our voices into the ether.'

'When the war's over, I'll take you on a trip.'

'Thanks, pal. That'd be great.'

He left Ron putting his headphones on again, and headed to his pigeonhole to pick up the script for today's broadcast. *Crowborough. Ashdown Forest.* He'd got a location, even if not a tour. That should please Pfalzgraf.

He'd have to do a recce to get co-ordinates though, and find some excuse to get away from here and go take a look, though from the sound of it, and what Lilli had said, it was pretty secure. He'd have to go carefully.

He watched Max come in and the easy way Ron greeted him, and a stab of envy made him tighten his lips. For a moment, he wondered what his life would have been like if he hadn't been an agent, if his friends had been real friends, and his world had been less lonely.

Chapter 21

Lilli was early to the studio, because she wanted to be there before lunchtime. Under the guise of practising her lines for the news broadcast, she waited until she saw Delmer go past the window heading for the canteen.

As soon as he'd gone by, she slowly creaked open the door to his office, which was next door to Max's, leaving it ajar.

Strangely calm, but listening hard for any sound of Delmer's return, she opened up the filing cabinet, looking for the staff files. The buff-coloured files were labelled with metal tags bearing stickers with the names of personnel in surname order. She thumbed through the Ms, looking for Johnny Murphy's file. Ah, there it was. She opened it up. Not too much stuff, but it might solve the mystery of what Bren had been doing before he came here. Then as an afterthought, she took out her own file. Lilliana Bergen. Hers was thicker.

Aware time was ticking by, she thrust it back. One file missing might not be noticed. But she didn't want to link herself to Bren's missing file if Delmer should spot it was gone.

Taking documents off the premises was forbidden. They'd signed the Official Secrets Act to say so, on day one. Now her breath caught in her throat as she shoved Bren's file inside the leather satchel that she wore over her shoulder to carry her music.

A draught, and the door swung open. Expecting Delmer, she took a step back, clutching the bag to her chest.

Bren. He looked just as startled to see her.

'I was just collecting my music,' she said, patting the bag, which now was almost burning her chest. 'The door was open and I saw it on the desk.'

He frowned. 'You shouldn't be in here. Delmer wouldn't like it.'

Nor should you.

He stared a moment, but offered no explanation as to why he was there.

A moment of uncomfortable silence, until the slap of footsteps down the corridor made them both hurry out of the room. Lilli clutched the bag and on her way down the corridor passed Delmer, who was striding towards her holding a plate with a sandwich, and a cup and saucer slopping tea.

'Were you after me?' he said.

'We were just passing and saw you left your door open,' Bren said.

'Did I? I only nipped out to get lunch.'

'Thought you might fancy a drink at the Swan later,' Bren said, 'when we're done with the broadcast tonight.'

She heard Delmer agree, and it made her uncomfortable. What was Bren doing in Delmer's office? The same as her, she guessed, spying.

After the broadcast she braved the sentries, her heart in her mouth. The men at the gate knew her well and after the first few weeks had given up checking the familiar faces on the way in and out. Still, the thought of actually leaving the building with Bren's file in her possession made her body break out in a cold sweat.

But as usual, the sentries were used to the sight of her on her bicycle, her music bag over her shoulder, and they waved her on down the road towards her billet at Simpson Village. She prayed Delmer wouldn't need the file before she had a chance to return it.

Once she was at home, she laid out all the documents on the bed. There was a copy of an Irish passport, and a couple of references from the post office. A pay slip, and clocking-in card. With amazement she read the references given by the head of the post office, 'Murphy is a good worker, trustworthy and helpful.' Huh. She'd see about that. She resolved to follow them up the next day.

As she pawed through the papers, the thing that struck her the most was that the history seemed pretty thin. It was odd that there was no record of any other kind of work, except the GPO and the university, no details about the theatres where 'Johnny' supposedly did his cabaret work, no flyers or cast lists or theatre programmes. There was no hint about any previous career or training as an actor. And of course nothing about his friends the Brownshirts. It was the sort of file you'd give to an agent as a cover story.

Wait a minute. Now she was looking at it, all spread out; that seemed to be exactly what it was. Without 'Johnny's' exuberant personality and charisma, this was all pretty bald.

All night she wrestled with it, until early the next morning she cycled to the Bedford Post Office, and asked to speak to the postmaster there. She had to wait a good half an hour before she was invited up poky narrow stairs and into the postmaster's office, a sweaty, enclosed little box with a sash window painted out black, and a coal fire blazing.

The postmaster, a Mr Greenland, balding and bespectacled, left her standing without offering her a seat, as if he couldn't wait to be rid of her. 'I'm a busy man,' he said. 'If it's about the WI raffle then—'

'No. I'm from the government base at Milton Bryan.' She showed her pass.

He scrutinised it, then looked up at her. 'You're not English, are you?'

'No, refugee working for the British.' She rushed on before he had time to think. 'I've been sent to enquire about one of your employees. A man named Murphy? Johnny Murphy. Irishman?'

'No. No one here by that name. Or anyone Irish. What's this about?'

Lilli took the passport photograph out of the file and slapped it down.

Mr Greenland studied it. 'No. Never seen him before, I could swear it.'

'So who wrote this?' She pulled out Johnny Murphy's references, and singled out the letter of recommendation on official post office paper. Placing it before him, she smoothed it out.

Greenland pulled it across the desk, frowned, and rubbed at his moustache. 'I never wrote this. And it says Edwards. Mr Edwards was my predecessor – died fifteen months ago. I took over after him. But I'm pretty sure that's not his signature either. I know what his writing looks like.'

'So it's a forgery.'

Greenland turned it over on his hands. 'Can't see any other explanation. I've never set eyes on it before.' He sat up straighter, his expression full of outrage. 'If someone's been impersonating someone in the GPO that's a criminal offence.'

'Can I go through to the sorting office, see if anyone recognises this photo?'

Greenland shrugged. 'You can, but I don't think anyone will have seen him. I keep a tight eye on all my employees.'

Tight enough that anyone can get access to official paper and forge a reference.

Lilli manoeuvred her way awkwardly down the dark stairs to the ground floor and into the sorting office, a place busy with the clatter of sorting machines and wheeled trolleys. She went round asking if anyone recognised the man in the photo, closely followed by Greenland, who by now was just as curious as she was.

'Hang on a moment,' said one old chap who was shoving

batches of mail into pigeonholes. 'I've seen his face before. He took the mail sometimes on the Wavendon round. Haven't seen him for a long while though. Why? What's he done?'

'Some of the mail didn't reach its destination,' Lilli improvised. Mr Greenland was flabbergasted.

'Hope you get him then,' said a postwoman who'd overheard.

'Now listen,' Greenland said. 'I don't want this getting out. It would reflect badly on the branch and I'm not far from retirement—'

'It's all right, Mr Greenland. This is just between us. I shan't be putting in an official report. We just want this man stopped and arrested.'

Mr Greenland frowned, but looked relieved.

Lilli got back on her bike and pedalled back to Milton Bryan wondering what to do. It seemed obvious that Bren had produced fake documents and probably wasn't who he said he was. But why? What was his endgame? Should she talk to Neil?

*

Neil was watching Lilli sing, mesmerised by the expression on her face and the way her hips swayed to the tune. He'd come up to Milton Bryan again supposedly to deliver the next day's script to Miss Blum for typing. In reality, he was hoping he could get another date with Lilli. Once the band began packing up their instruments, he tried to catch her eye, but he was too late. Johnny Murphy was there before him, bounding over, and placing an arm proprietorially on her shoulder.

He watched covertly as Johnny steered her away towards the door. At the last minute she turned to look towards him, her brown eyes contrite, and he almost stepped forward to speak to her, but Johnny pushed her out of the door.

'They're pretty close, those two,' Ron said, seeing him staring after her. 'He's a quick worker.'

'Suppose so,' Neil said. He was surprised how much it stung, to see Johnny Murphy wind Lilli around his little finger.

'She's nice though, isn't she?' Ron said. 'Can't say I blame him.'

'Uh huh.' Neil was deliberately casual. How could he compete with Johnny? He'd always found it hard to talk to women. Johnny, handsome and confident, was fast becoming the star of the show. Sucking up to Max and Ron, bringing them cups of coffee, laughing at their bad jokes, drinking in the Swan with Delmer. Johnny never brought Neil a coffee, and glared frostily at him if he went near Lilli, even just to give her the music for the broadcast.

'I'm taking Maureen out on Saturday,' Ron said. 'We're going bowling. D'you think I should wear a suit, or just my shirt and jumper?'

Neil blinked. What did it matter? 'Oh, shirt and jumper should be all right.' What did he know? 'Ask Johnny, he's Mr Man-about-town.' The words came out more bitter than he intended.

Ron gave him a puzzled frown.

He'd had no chance to talk to Lilli even though he'd waited all morning, and it was galling. He'd try again tomorrow, but for now, he had to be getting back to Wavendon Tower before the broadcast proper. He swung his way down the corridor, but as he passed Delmer's door Delmer stuck out his head. 'Ah, Neil. I thought it was you. Heard your stick going by. Come in a minute, would you.'

Neil went in and sat down. Delmer and he had become closer colleagues since he started there, and the two men had grown to like and trust each other.

'How's it going?'

Neil gave him an update.

'Ah yes I heard about the accident. Rotten luck. Your shoulder okay now?'

Neil brought his hand up to it. 'Still a bit stiff, but on the mend.'

'You're not having trouble with Music Hall Len, then?' Delmer lit himself a cigar. 'I hear he's a bit too fond of the whisky.'

'No more than usual. We feed him coffee and keep him busy.'

'And the new guy, Murphy, he's a belter, isn't he?'

'He's good at his job.'

'I sense a "but". A cloud of choking smoke came Neil's way.

Neil shrugged and tried not to cough. 'He just rubs me up the wrong way. And sometimes his stories don't make sense. I know we're in the business of lies, but lying to your colleagues isn't good.'

'How d'you mean?'

'I heard him telling Ron he'd always been interested in the technical aspects of radio, but then he told Max he'd no interest in the equipment whatsoever. It just seemed a bit odd, like he tells us all what he wants us to hear.'

'So, he's a bit two-faced. Nothing new in actors. They can all be a bit self-centred. And he's a great voice for Atlantiksender. I was talking to him last night over a drink and he's really passionate about doing his bit as a submariner. The navy picked up one of the captains of the U-boats and he's a mine of useful insider jargon. Murphy impersonates him brilliantly, and the station's going down a storm in the boats – they love the music and the fact it's so personal.

Neil nodded along, trying not to feel jealous at this glowing report of Johnny's success.

Delmer was still spouting. 'Our insider's given us the captain's nickname and even the names of the women in the ports where they drink. Trust like that means we can feed the Jerries false information about where our troop carriers are, and where the supplies are coming in, and they think it's all real. We're sending U-boats after our supply ships in totally the wrong direction – works like a charm.'

'That reminds me,' Neil interrupted, 'Lilli told me she came to see you. About training to be a broadcast engineer.'

'Oh that. Quite impossible to have a German on equipment.'

'Her father used to work for Blaupunkt, did she tell you that?'

'The German radio company? Really?'

218

A nod. 'She gave me an interesting idea; one I think can work.' He explained about taking over German Luftwaffe command.

Delmer's eyes lit up. He stubbed out the cigar. 'So we wait for them to briefly come off air, then we intercept? Good God, you're right. Could it work? We started Operation Dartboard a few weeks ago – sending German air crews in the wrong directions – but we usually use recordings of the real operators, ones we made on a previous night, but this …?' He stood up and paced, his hands shoved into the pockets of his suit trousers. 'It's a bit underhand.' He grinned. 'Just the way I like it. As long as MI6 doesn't cotton on, we could test it.'

'Aspidistra has the power to do it. It's just an extension of what you're already doing. Aspi's already got the ability to drown out German broadcasters, this is just intercepting.'

'But we'd need copycat broadcasters that sound just like the Germans.'

'I could get the boffins in the recording studio to record and label a few voices, so we can match them.'

'Splendid! So you're saying Miss Bergen's worth listening to … as well as becoming the U-boat sweetheart.'

'I believe her father was once a professor of mathematics at the University in Nuremberg too. One of their brightest and best. Missing now of course. She'll do anything to bring the Nazis down. For her, it's personal.'

'Hmm. And is she managing to keep a distance from all you men buzzing round her like flies round a honeypot?'

Neil felt his face grow hot. 'She's very professional.' The words came out defensive, though he tried to rein them in. 'Murphy's taken a shine to her though, won't leave her alone.'

Delmer eyed him and sucked in his breath. 'Never a good idea to have personal relationships within the PWE, you know that. It can get awkward.'

Neil looked down at his shoelaces. 'Don't worry. I'll keep my eye on them.'

'If we get this Luftwaffe operation on the go, you realise you'll be the one who has to organise the switch-over?'

'Thank you. I hoped you'd say that. It gets pretty dull at Wavendon and I'd love to be more involved up here at Milton Bryan.'

'You've got it. Just keep it under your hat. It's unethical stuff and MI6 would have a fit if they knew.'

Chapter 22

A few weeks later

Bren looked at his watch. Twenty minutes late and still no sign of Estofal. Last time he'd met him, he'd told him what he knew about the site of the Aspidistra transmitter. Estofal had been relieved to have some sort of information, though he was evasive about Pfalzgraf's reaction to it all. He'd been anxious to get away, said he'd got business with a printer in Luton, and meetings set up with other groups of operatives nearby. Bren hoped they were a bloody sight more efficient than Estofal was.

Bren got up and strode around the church, staring at the huge stone arch and the carved wooden altar screen. He peered up at the dark-hued stained-glass window of Christ with the message under his feet, *I am He that liveth, and was dead.* The words seemed false, foreign. He repeated the words floating above Christ's head, 'Holy, holy, holy.' Nonsense words, like a child's nursery rhyme.

A draught as the door opened, and Estofal shambled in. He peered out of the door again as if to check he wasn't being followed before shutting it.

He took a pew. 'New instructions from Pfalzgraf,' Estofal said.

'They did air reconnaissance of Ashdown Forest. It's too awkward to bomb. They can't get a fix on the target, so they want the sabotage to happen on the ground.'

'Meaning?'

'You've to gain access somehow and do the job.'

'Gain access? Do they know what they're asking?'

Estofal shrugged. 'I've been detailed to give you assistance with finding the right materials. Pfalzgraf says you've been trained at Brandenburg, and once you've assessed the site, you'll know what to do.'

Bren sucked in his breath. 'Woah. I'm not going to be responsible for that amount of carnage.'

Estofal shrugged. 'That's their orders.'

'Then if it's done at all, it'd have to be done at night. According to Ron, my contact at Milton Bryan, about sixty personnel work there, but I guess there'll be less night staff.'

'They just said to take out the transmitter. Make sure it can never work again.'

'That's all well and good, but the place is fenced off. And there'll be security on site.' Bren ruminated a moment. 'Where am I supposed to make this device?'

'There's a rented garage at the back of my house, where I store stuff and run my fake insurance business. If you tell me what you need, I can pull a few strings with my contacts, get what you want. After that, you'll need to make the thing, and find a way to get in there and do the job.'

'Sabotage is a high-risk activity.'

'You're not the only one at risk, you know. Having a radio aerial hanging out of your window is not exactly risk-free. Nor is going about trying to get hold of explosives.'

'Okay. I get it. Tell them I'll find a way to get in there and check it out. Once I've seen the mast, I'll drop-box you with what I need. I'll use the standard food codes for the chemicals. You learnt the decoding manual?'

'Yep. Know most of it by heart, gelatine equals gelignite, et cetera. Check our drop box again in two weeks, okay, and I'll arrange a meeting to update you with what I can get.'

'Gotcha.' He'd get a map from the library and mark out the high ground in Ashdown Forest. It must be on a hill, he reckoned. Everywhere within, say, a thirty-mile radius. Shouldn't be hard to find if it had a bloody great fence around it. If he could find it, he might be able to get in there and disable it somehow. A bomb wouldn't be necessary if he could do it another way. He felt his excitement rise. This was more like it. Actual action, instead of all this pussyfooting around. 'Just one thing.'

Estofal raised his eyebrows.

'If it's a blow-up, I'll need to get out of there quick. I'll not do it unless there are watertight plans to get me out or give me a safe house.'

'I'll sort something.'

'Make sure you do.' He knew from experience this was the part they often neglected. Alix and Dieter, two of his training camp buddies had been caught that way – done their job, then been abandoned in France with no way out. Dead, the pair of them. He wouldn't want to be hanging around once the damn thing blew.

*

Lilli opened the front door with her key and dragged herself into the hall, longing just to collapse into bed. The broadcasting schedule left little time for leisure, which in one way was a relief, because she always had an excuse for not going out with Bren, but on the other, she had little time for Neil either. They were like ships passing in the night. Yet she always hoped to see him, and hung around the hall hoping to catch a glimpse of him.

She slid off her jacket and hung it on the hooks by the door, glancing at the hall table as she went by. She'd given up looking for mail from Germany after all these years. So she was surprised when Mrs Littlefair heard her come in, and stopped her in the hall.

'Letter for you, Lilli,' she said.

'For me?' The envelope was a mess; it had been ripped open, then stuck back together with sticky tape, and the ragged edges were torn and dirty.

'Thanks,' she said, as Mrs Littlefair bustled away.

Straight away she knew it was from Maddie; she had written to her a while back to let her know her address, and to tell her she was now doing 'clerical work' for the civil service.

Maddie's writing was large and expansive.

Hello old bean, I got this rather mysterious letter yesterday addressed to you. It had been all round the houses, even to the Isle of Man! I had to open it, I'm afraid, before deciding if I should send it on. It is good news, I hope? Here the hospitals are overcrowded and I'm dead on my feet half the time. Oh this bloody war. How I wish it would stop …

The letter went on with more small talk about shifts, and air raids, and the man Maddie was dating, but Lilli had seen the other envelope within – smaller, and postmarks and censor marks were all over it. She recognised one as a Manx postmark, and gave a shudder.

Gently she prised it open. A flimsy piece of paper like tissue. Airmail.

Her heart almost stopped.

The letter was German handwriting, all curves and loops unlike the upright way English people wrote.

To Lilliana.

Your father is alive. A letter came to you, by hand from [Censored]. It was a very short message written in pencil. He says he is sorry he had to leave you. He says he is well,

224

in a town with others, and not to worry. I am not able to
tell you more or send it on. I had to burn it. I am sending
this to your friend Maddie and I hope she will tell it to
you.

Maybe we will meet again, until then, God be with you
both.

Elise Kirchner

Lilli stood a moment in the hallway, to read it again and again. *With others.* Presumably other Jews and objectors to the Party.

Her father was alive. In vain she tried to read the name of the place Frau Kirchner had written under the censor's block, but it was impossible. She wished she could touch the letter her father had sent, see his untidy scrawl of writing, but she understood why Frau Kirchner couldn't keep it. Too much of a risk.

It took her a few moments to calm down enough to go up to her room where she could read the letter again. It was news she longed to shout from the rooftops, but immediately she felt guilty. Max's father had not been so lucky, and Neil was still getting over the death of his father.

And besides, who knew if Papa was still alive now? The message had travelled all over England. But the thread of hope made her want to whoop with joy.

*

The next day, Lilli badgered Max for a familiar tune she thought her father might know. She knew that the idea he could be listening was far-fetched, that even if he had a radio, he might not hear their station. But it was the only thing she could do to try to let him know she was still thinking of him and was well.

She asked Max if he could find her the music for 'Junger Mann im Frühling', one she and Papa used to hum together whenever it came on the wireless.

'Oh, that old thing,' Bren said. 'I don't see why anyone would want to listen to that.'

'Some people like it,' she said, and moved away to study the lyrics, wondering if there was some way she could make her father understand it was his daughter singing.

Then she smiled. Got it! They used to sing the accompaniment together between the verses, with a 'badum dum, da dum dum dum'. She'd put that in.

She crossed her fingers that no one would notice it, and just think it some new arrangement she was trying. She was sure sending messages like this was against the Official Secrets Act.

*

After the broadcast, Neil came over to see Lilli and talk about the new plans for Operation Dartboard.

'That was something new, the improvising in that song you were singing,' he said. 'Sounded good.'

'Lilli?' Their conversation was interrupted by Johnny Murphy, who came to take her arm. 'There you are. You look tired. I'll walk you to your bicycle and make sure you get off home.'

He glared at Neil as he escorted her out.

'Oof,' Max said to Neil. 'He hasn't forgiven you for the accident, has he?'

'Guess not,' Neil said.

'Don't worry, I'm going now too. I'll cycle down with her.'

'I'll catch you up later, Max,' Neil said. 'I've got a few things to do for tomorrow.'

After Lilli had gone, Neil sat down at the big metal table to sort the scripts from the evening's broadcast for archiving. He became aware of the door opening and a draught, as Johnny came back in.

At first Neil thought he'd forgotten something, but then Johnny leant over Neil's shoulder. 'Ah, the good man, up to his ears in papers as usual,' he said in a sneering tone.

Neil turned, perturbed at being interrupted.

'I know you like Lilli,' Johnny said, his face inches from Neil's. 'But I just want to make one thing clear. Lilli's my girl. So just keep out of my way unless you want trouble.'

Neil stood up. 'Now just wait a minute—'

But Johnny was sauntering away as if nothing untoward had happened.

How dare he? Neil's face flared as if he were on fire. The cheek of it. It would be demeaning to be fighting over a girl. And didn't Lilli have any say in it?

Should he tell Delmer? He baulked at the idea. It would sound so petty, and hadn't Delmer warned him of precisely this?

But he wouldn't be bullied, he knew that much. If there was one thing he'd learnt from his dealings with Otto, it was to stand up to bullies. He'd catch Johnny Murphy tomorrow and make it perfectly clear he wasn't going to be browbeaten.

*

Neil propped his stick against the wall, and stood up tall with his shoulders back as he waited outside the door of Milton Bryan studios for the bus which brought people from Bedford. His throat was dry and he rubbed at a tic in his cheek which had come on all of a sudden because he knew he was no match physically for Johnny Murphy. He could see Johnny through the window of the bus, putting on the charm to the bus driver. As Johnny got off the bus, one of the last passengers, Neil swallowed, mentally preparing himself.

Johnny glanced towards him, but looked away, ready to walk past ignoring him.

'Johnny? I need a word.'

'I've no time,' Johnny said, trying to barge past.

'You'll damn well make time,' Neil said, grabbing him by the sleeve. 'I didn't like the way you spoke to me yesterday. If I want

227

to talk to Lilli Bergen, I will, and nothing you can do will stop me.' The words came out in a burst. 'She's a colleague, and we're supposed to be adults here. I won't be talked to like that.'

Johnny's palm shot out to give him a shove in the chest so he nearly over-balanced. 'You're pathetic. D'you think she wants you? No. She's just sorry for you, that's all.' He moved closer, backing Neil up against the wall. 'Now leave her alone.'

Neil stood his ground. 'I won't be bullied by you. If Lilli wants to spend time with me, then who are you to say she can't?'

'She wouldn't want a Nazi like you,' he said. 'Delmer told me about your shady past.'

Neil was still reeling from this information when a fist came out of nowhere and hit him square in the belly.

He staggered back and crumpled against the wall. His stomach hurt like hell, but his pride hurt more. Delmer must have told Johnny about his involvement with the British Union of Fascists, and it filled him with shame. And worse, he knew he'd have to do something about Johnny Murphy. But what? Complain to Delmer that he'd told Johnny about his past? He couldn't do that. He'd die of humiliation. But one thing was certain: he wasn't going to let Johnny take Lilli from him.

Chapter 23

Lilli was overwhelmed with the attention Bren was giving her, though she now knew he had never worked for the post office and his whole back history was a lie. She'd returned the file the next day, which was almost as terrifying as taking it.

She was determined to find out more, so this was the third time she'd gone back to his lodgings, each time on a Tuesday when Mrs Gammage was out. She'd examined the contents of the bathroom cabinet, and had a good look around, but frustratingly, found nothing in the least incriminating. There was a key under the soap box which she guessed belonged to his suitcase but that was all. Strange place to leave it, so he was definitely hiding it. She left it where it was, because she couldn't search his case while he was there in the room.

She'd managed a peek in the wardrobe and seen a GPO uniform, so somebody, not the post office, must have supplied him with it. Who? The Gestapo? Thumbing through the hangers she found what looked to be casual clothes a walker might wear. Two suits she'd seen him wear at work. Shirts, with Bedford laundry labels. Rough twill trousers and an old tweed hacking jacket. Odd, she'd never seen him wear those. She longed to search his suitcase but couldn't do it without arousing suspicion.

Today he seemed terser than usual, and she soon found out why. 'Ron told me he'd seen you at a concert. With Neil Callaghan.'

'Oh. Yes. It was the Aerospace Orchestra. Neil had booked it for a friend, but then the friend couldn't go, so he asked me.' A white lie, but it made her squirm.

Bren looked hurt. 'What the hell? You lied to me. You said it was a girls' night out. Why didn't you tell me you were going with another fella?'

'You'd only just arrived, and I didn't know how I felt about it. It was all too new, and I didn't like to let Neil down. Not when you and I weren't going out properly.'

'I told you, Lilli, you've always been the one for me. We're made for each other. I've been waiting to ask you because I didn't know if you'd say yes, but look here—' He delved into his pocket and brought out a box. 'It's only second-hand, but—'

He opened the box to display a ring. It looked like a diamond, flanked by two small sapphires. Lilli was so shocked she couldn't speak.

'Will you marry me, Lilli?'

She looked up at his face, which seemed hopeful and slightly nervous.

God, he couldn't be serious. Play for time. 'Are you sure? We've barely had any time together.'

'That's because we're at war. And in war anything could happen. I want to know you'll be there by my side. Always. That when the war's over, I can take you back to Germany as my wife.'

The thought of going back brought such a rush of mixed emotion, she couldn't speak. Tears sprang to her eyes.

'Aww. Don't cry.' Bren seemed to take this as a good sign. 'Try it on. Go on.'

He eased the ring from the cushion inside the box and took firm hold of her left hand. He slipped it on her ring finger and then kissed it. 'It looks like it belongs there,' he whispered.

She looked down at how it sparkled. *No. This wasn't supposed to be how it went at all.* 'It's lovely,' she said, about to give it back, 'but—'

He stopped her by kissing her deeply on the mouth.

'Thank you,' he said, looking deep into her eyes. 'I was so afraid you'd say no. I love you, Lilli.' He kissed her again.

Overwhelmed with confusion at this rapid turn of events, she wasn't quick enough to pull away.

'Stay,' he said.

She didn't reply, but immediately realised that if she did, she might be able to get into his suitcase. They moved to the bed, and after they had petted a while, he wanted to do more.

'After we're married,' she said. She'd take advantage of this situation if she could. 'Let's wait.'

He continued to press her, and she resisted, until he mumbled a few more endearments then fell asleep. Lilli fastened the front of her blouse again and lay there for a long time, thoughts ricocheting around her head.

Bren had said he was afraid she'd say no. The old Bren had never been afraid of anything. She glanced over to where he was sleeping. How could he sleep? He'd taken off his shirt, and his face was quiet and still.

Was this real? Did he really want to marry her? No. She was sure not. An inner instinct told her it was about control; that Bren was doing it to stop her telling anyone his real name. She stared down at him, detaching herself from the encroaching memories of the past. Bren didn't stir, but as she moved, the engagement ring flashed in the light of the bedside lamp.

Get a grip. Search his case. She began to ease herself off the narrow single bed.

He stirred then. 'Turn off the lamp, Lilli.'

She did as he asked, and he hitched the bedclothes over them and wrapped an arm over her thigh. She was still, almost holding her breath, until she was sure he was asleep again.

The bed creaked as she moved but he didn't wake. She left him

231

lying there while she gently eased his case from beneath the bed. It was thick, dark in the room, so she had to do everything by feel. As she withdrew it, her hand recoiled from the cold porcelain of a chamberpot, there presumably because he shared a bathroom. The case was heavy, and made a scraping noise on the lino as she dragged it out. She froze in mid-movement in case he woke. The case felt sturdy, with metal locks, probably brass. She tried to slide the catches, but they wouldn't budge. Locked.

She tiptoed to the sink and feeling for the edge of the cabinet, reached up for the key.

Her eyes were accustoming themselves to the dark, but she was still feeling her way back to the bed, terrified she'd trip over something on the way. A few moments later she was on her knees again on the threadbare rug by the bed.

Bren stirred and reached out. She left the key in the lock, praying he wouldn't get up, and slid back under the eiderdown and into bed as his arm came to rest over her belly. She let it lie there until she was sure he was sleeping again. She stared up at the ceiling listening to his breath huff in and out. After what seemed like an age, she slowly extricated herself inch by inch from underneath his arm.

She kept her thumb on the catches of the case to keep them silent as she opened it. The first thing she felt was the smooth surface of a leather holster, with the cold handle of a gun.

Her hand snapped back. She felt it again, uncertain of what she was feeling and afraid to press something she shouldn't. Her fingers drew it out and traced the shape of the barrel. Some sort of revolver? He was armed. She glanced up. His regular breath told her he was still sleeping. She brought her face close to the gun and squinted at it in the dark.

That thing could be loaded. Gingerly, she slid it back and lifted up the clothes in the suitcase, feeling a soft cap, a pair of spectacles in a case, and papers – what felt like a folded map, and a thick wallet. She prised it open and immediately recognised the crinkle of notes. So, he was well paid, whatever he was doing. In the side pocket there was a cigarette case, which she ran her thumb over to feel a bubble of glass. No. Not a cigarette case. Bren didn't smoke. She brought it up to her eyes to examine it. A camera. She daren't open it in case it made a noise, but she was pretty sure it was a camera. There was also a compass with a luminous dial.

He turned over and the springs creaked.

'Lilli?'

Hurriedly she put everything back, breathless with fear, and closed the case.

'Sorry. Just needed to use the chamberpot,' she said, dragging it out.

Fortunately she was able to go, and as she did so, she locked the case. She stuffed the key under the pillow as she climbed back into bed. She'd need to return it later.

Morning came, and a little light stole in under the door from the hall. She slipped the key into her pocket, got up, and dressed. As she tried to put on her shoes, she stumbled and the sound woke him.

'Is it that time already?' he asked.

'Yes. I need to go. The early bus is in fifteen minutes.'

'Now we're engaged, we could live together all the time,' he said.

She'd be living with an armed man. Why did he need a gun?

'Lovely idea. Let's talk about it later,' she said, and she grabbed her coat and hat, and slipped out of the door. As she tiptoed down the stairs the door to one of the downstairs rooms opened.

A black-haired woman in a print housecoat emerged, an angry expression on her face. 'Who the hell are you?'

'A friend of Johnny's.'

'Who?'

Bren emerged at the top of the stairs. 'It's all right, Mrs Gammage. This is my fiancée, Lilli.'

'Fiancée? You never told me you were engaged. I said single men only.'

'I needed somewhere to live.'

'I'll have none of that in my house. You'll have to find somewhere else.'

Lilli didn't want to hear this argument. 'I'm sorry, I'll miss my bus.' She pulled open the door and escaped into the misty dawn. The first bus was on time, cold and empty except for her. She jumped aboard and only then remembered she'd stolen Bren's key.

He'd miss it, she knew he would. And it was too late to return it. If he found it on her, he'd know she'd been snooping. She got off at Simpson, panicked, and threw the key straight into a hedge. The implications of the gun were just sinking in, and her hands began to shake. If he had a gun, he might use it.

At her house she glanced at the hall table as usual to see if there was another letter from Maddie and was about to go up the stairs when the door to the kitchen opened, and Neil was heading towards her, a plate of toast balanced on his free hand.

'I just stepped out for a bit of air,' she said, defensive. She didn't want him to know she'd been out all night. Guiltily, she remembered the ring, and stuffed her hand in her pocket so he wouldn't see it.

'Have you had breakfast? There's some bread left.'

She smiled and tried to act normally. 'Smells good. Maybe I'll get some.'

'It's the stale stuff from last week. It's all right though as toast. I'd kill for a bit of jam, but there's none left. Ron's a demon with the jam.' He paused. 'I've been meaning to catch you. I wondered if you'd like to go to another concert.' He had a steely determination in his attitude. 'The railwayman's choir's doing "The Messiah" at St Peter's in Bedford next Thursday. We're both off-shift then.'

She had a sudden urge to confide in him, tell him about Bren and the gun. 'Neil, there's something I'd like to run by you.'

'Another grand idea?'

'No. Something else. I just need to talk to someone, but it's confidential.'

He took a step towards her. He'd seen she looked serious. 'Hey, is something the matter?'

'I don't know. Is there a place we can talk without being interrupted?'

'You can come into my—'

Max and Ron clattered down the stairs in their usual morning rush. 'You ready, Lilli?'

She hesitated a moment. 'I need my music. Hang on while I get it.'

'Come on,' urged Max. 'We're already late.'

She ran upstairs to get the scores, cursing Max and Ron's bad timing, then hurried down.

'I'll see you later,' she said to Neil. She turned to Ron. 'Let's go.'

'I'll find you at the studio,' Neil called as she lifted a hand in farewell. Max threw open the door and they all headed for the bicycle shed.

*

Neil watched them go. Trust Max and Ron to arrive at just the wrong time.

Once inside his room, Neil put his plate down and cursed himself. What an idiot. He bet she'd been out last night with Johnny Murphy.

Lilli's eyes had been troubled. She was probably going to tell him she didn't want to go out with him again. The toast suddenly looked unappetising. He sighed. Delmer was right. Never get involved with other staff members.

Chapter 24

Bren was packing. He'd been unable to smooth things over with Mrs Gammage and she'd ordered him to be out by the end of the week. Stuff that. He'd leave today.

But now he'd have to find somewhere else to live.

After laying out his stuff on the bed, he went to get the key to his case.

He lifted up the soap dish, but there was only empty space. Confused, he searched the shelf, shifting his razor and shaving brush, the indigestion remedy and the spare tin of toothpowder. It wasn't there.

It could have fallen in the sink. He peered down the plughole, but there was a strainer in it so it couldn't have gone down there.

Had Mrs Gammage taken it? He wouldn't put it past her, the old harridan.

He pulled the case out from under the bed and examined it. He should have kept the key with him. The case didn't look like it had been touched, but instinct about these things made him suspicious. What if Mrs Gammage had seen the gun? Was that why she wanted him out?

It was disturbing. Not because he couldn't get into the case – of course he could – his time in the commandos had taught him those skills. But because he'd been at this game long enough to know every glitch was a warning. The back of his neck prickled.

He searched the room again on his hands and knees, and all his pockets. Had he dropped the key somewhere? He thought of Lilli with irritation. She wasn't as pliable as he'd thought. Even an engagement ring hadn't persuaded her to give in to his advances and have sex. Would she have taken the key? No. Didn't seem likely. She'd shown no awareness of the suitcase, and was in bed with him the whole night.

He picked the lock, and examined the contents. Nothing missing. But it looked like someone had been in it, the clothes were rumpled. He shoved the rest of his possessions into a carrier bag and with his pick, re-locked the case. He'd have to move on, and quick. Good thing he'd given Mrs Gammage a false name. Ralph Kelly from the tyre factory would cease to exist in about five minutes from now.

He grabbed the case, the bag, and his work briefcase, and scooted quietly down the stairs and out of the front door leaving it swinging. He'd never go back. Having to find somewhere else was a nuisance. But perhaps now he was engaged to Lilli, they could find somewhere together. It would only be for a few short weeks, long enough so she wouldn't give the game away that he wasn't really Johnny, but Brendan Murphy.

Besides, he'd got as much as he could from being at Milton Bryan. It was time to find the transmitter and disable it. And it would give him the greatest pleasure to get rid of that snooty toad Callaghan. He'd been half-tempted to beat the shit out of him, and he would have, only Harper's warnings rang in his ears.

That morning he got the bus to Milton Bryan as usual and picked up the script for the day's broadcast before dumping his bags in the switchboard room for safe-keeping. He waited until Lilli arrived in the green room, a dingy back-room where they all gathered for coffee, and then he grabbed his coffee cup and spoon, rattling it to get everyone's attention.

'I have an announcement,' he said. 'Come over here, Lilli.'

She was wide-eyed, and shaking her head. He ignored it.

The others gathered.

'Just thought I'd let you all know … Lilli and I are engaged!'

A hubbub of cheers and congratulations.

'Lilli darling, you're such a dark horse!' enthused Max. 'Let's see the ring.'

The switchboard girls had heard the noise and all hurried in to crowd around and have a look. Bren stiffened as he saw her draw the ring from her pocket and put it on. The fact she hadn't been wearing it made him tense up.

Ron clapped him on the back. 'Heck Johnny, you're a quick worker! Congrats, old chap. When's the wedding?'

'We haven't set a date yet, but you'll all be invited.' More congratulations, and he was suddenly the centre of attention.

He glanced over to Lilli, who was red in the face and looked rather tearful. He regarded her dispassionately. She was not as won over as he thought. He'd have to take extra care.

In the corner he saw Neil, his face thunderous, ignoring it all, shuffling papers around on his desk. At the same time he saw Lilli's gaze go over to him, and her lips press together.

So that's the way it is, Bren thought. *I got there just in time.*

He went over to Lilli and grasped her by the hand. 'I wish we could have champagne, but I suppose we'll have to make do with the canteen coffee, won't we, darling?'

He leant over to kiss her on the cheek. She smiled, but it was a smile pinned on like a tail on a donkey. Bren was astute enough to see it and it set his senses jangling. Perhaps after all, it was Lilli who'd taken the key. He'd have to press her a little.

*

Lilli hated all the fuss, but it would seem strange, and like sour grapes to burst the celebratory bubble. She'd have to play along – just until she got sure-fire proof of what Bren was doing and could go to Delmer. And that would be an awkward conversation – telling Delmer he obviously hadn't vetted his employee properly.

She brought her attention back to the room. Someone handed her a cup of coffee that actually smelled like coffee. Everyone seemed so thrilled for them. She watched Ron scurry off, intent on telling Maureen the good news.

Maureen came rushing in, squealing, full of hugs and enthusiasm. 'Our two great stars getting together,' Maureen said. 'It's so romantic. Like in the films. We need a bit of glamour in this ghastly war. Why didn't you tell me?'

'It was all a bit of a whirlwind,' Lilli said. 'He only sprang it on me last night.'

'At least he won't dump you like that awful boyfriend you had,' Maureen said. Lilli blanked her real reaction and but continued to smile.

'How's it going with Ron?' Lilli asked, to get Maureen off the subject.

A shrug. 'He works so hard,' Maureen said. 'It's difficult to prise him away from the station. The minute anything technical goes wrong he has to be there, on the other end of whatever plug it is that needs fixing.'

'Could be useful though. At least he'll know what to do if something breaks down.'

Maureen smiled. 'I hope it's catching.'

'What? Fixing stuff? I can show you. Just ask.'

'No silly! Getting engaged.'

After the fuss had died down, Lilli settled at a table to study her music, and a shadow fell over it. She looked up to see Neil at her shoulder. Guilt washed over her, that she couldn't speak what she was feeling, not with everyone watching. Her face felt like it was on fire.

'Just wanted to say congratulations,' he said, his expression cool and reserved. 'I suppose that was what you wanted to tell me this morning. I wish you both every happiness.' His eyes wouldn't meet hers. He paused a moment. 'Though I can't pretend I'm not disappointed, because I thought we had an understanding, and I definitely would have liked to get to know you better.' Now he looked direct into her gaze. 'The real Lilli, the one who likes mending engines, not the siren on the broadcasts.'

She felt a tug of emotion, and a desperate need to unburden herself. 'Please, I'd still like to explain, if you can find a minute.'

'It's all right. You don't need to say anything else.' He turned to go, and she had the sudden urge to shout, *It's all a mistake.*

'Neil, wait!'

The door slammed shut behind him, making Max look up from his papers, and a few moments later she heard the roar of his motorbike outside and then the noise of its engine fading away.

She'd have to try to get Neil by himself tonight, when she was at home at Mrs Littlefair's.

Later that afternoon Bren came over to her after the rehearsal. She was angry about how he'd sprung the engagement announcement on her, but bit back the words. Two of the other technicians nudged each other and exchanged amused glances.

'I'm going to look at a flat,' Bren announced. 'I was telling Maureen and the switchboard girls, Mrs Gammage has thrown me out. She saw you leaving and threw a fit, started preaching morals at me.'

'Couldn't you persuade her to let you stay?'

'You saw the row we got into. It didn't end well. Anyway, Maureen saw I'd left my bags and asked me why they were there, and to cut a long story short – she says her neighbours have a vacant upper floor flat with its own entrance. Two pounds a week. The couple who were tenants have just been moved to a different hospital. He was a doctor. Now we're engaged, we could take it on.'

She froze. 'Where is it?'

'Bedford again. The other side of town. I rang the landlord and he's keen. Get your coat, Ron's going to drive us over there.'

'That's a lot further out than Simpson Village,' she said, playing for time. 'It won't be so convenient. It's nice to be close to the base.'

'But we'll be together. We can start to build a proper life, and that's what we both want, isn't it? We've wasted too much time already with this damn war. Come on, darling, get your coat.' He strode over to the coat stand to fetch it.

Ron appeared brandishing his car keys.

She should have stopped it earlier. Now it was like she was on a runaway train. This was a bad idea, but she knew making a scene would just alert Bren to the fact she was not the naïve woman he thought she was, so she kept quiet. After all, would anyone believe anything a German woman told them about all-round Mr Popularity Johnny Murphy?

It would look odd to object, so she followed him out to where Maureen was already waiting in the car, smiling and waving. Bren sat in the front with Ron, while she and Maureen had the back seat. She noticed Bren's collar was sharply pressed, his hair oiled back. It should have made him attractive, but she just wondered why he took so much trouble.

When they got there, the house was a pleasant 1920s semi-detached in a tree-lined street. It had been divided into two by the owner, a Mr Barrett, who insisted on accompanying them around the back to the entrance to the upper apartment.

'This is my fiancée, Lilli,' Bren said.

Mr Barrett smiled at her. 'Very pleased to meet you. Friends of Maureen's will always be friends of mine. I've known Maureen since she was a nipper. I work with her dad.'

On the way round, Bren told him that they all worked at Milton Bryan for the Ministry of Defence, and the old chap seemed impressed. 'Good to see you young folk taking on responsibility. Fought the Boche in Belgium in the last war,' he said, 'but now I'm in webbing manufacturing. It's a reserved occupation.'

They followed him up the concrete steps to the first-floor apartment, and Mr Barrett opened it up. 'It's been vacuumed,' he said.

Lilli wrapped her coat tightly over her chest. The floors were grey linoleum with pressure dents where a table once stood. A stiff-looking brown sofa was against one wall, which was papered in faded yellow flowers that might have been popular when it was built several decades ago. It was sparsely furnished, with a sideboard and a moth-eaten standard lamp, and ice-cold despite the sunshine. Thin brocaded curtains hung limply over the blackout blind. Her heart sank.

As she pushed open the door to the kitchen, she heard Bren ask, 'Where's the nearest call box?' and Mr Barrett's reply, 'End of the street. Nearest bomb shelter's the Andersen shelter in next door's garden. Don't think you'll need it though, we've seen no action round here.'

She was just thinking, *It's tiny. No room for a bookcase, or anything*, when she heard Bren say, 'Good. It looks grand. We'll take it.'

'Can't we see the bedroom first?' Lilli asked, shooting out of the kitchen, looking for any excuse not to commit to it.

Bren smirked and raised his eyebrows at Ron, who took a moment to understand Bren's meaning, before giving a nervous giggle. Lilli wished she hadn't asked.

'This way.' Mr Barrett led them through the door, where the bedroom housed a dark wood wardrobe with a pock-marked mirror and an over-large chest of drawers. They all stared at the double bed, and Lilli grew pinker, realising what they all must be thinking. 'We'll get twin beds,' she blurted. 'Until we're married.'

'When can we move in?' Bren asked. 'I need somewhere immediately.'

'Shouldn't we discuss it first?' Lilli said desperately. 'It's a big step.'

'It's empty now,' Mr Barrett said, beaming.

'I've got some spare kitchen things you can have,' Maureen said. 'It'll be topping to have you so near. We can be a foursome.'

'Thank you, Maureen, that's a lovely thought, but—'

'Then it's all settled,' Bren said.

Mr Barrett passed the key to Bren and said, 'You can take it straight away. I'll get you a rent book sorted and I collect the rent on Fridays, okay?'

'We'll get moved in this evening then.' Bren pocketed the key and the men shook hands.

'Oh, but I need a bit more time,' Lilli said. 'I'll need to discuss it first with Mrs Littlefair, she'll be relying on my money, and I know they don't like' – she nearly said 'Germans' – 'employees to be living away from a houseparent.'

'It'll be all right,' Ron whispered, taking her aside. 'Johnny's not German, so he can act as your houseparent. Mrs Littlefair will be fine about it, you'll see.'

They were all so kind, but it made her want to weep. She was quiet all the way back to the base, while Maureen and Ron chattered to Bren about how friendly the nearest pub was, and how there was a launderette nearby.

Once they got back to Milton Bryan, Lilli grabbed Bren by the arm and took him to one side, in the corridor outside the studio. 'You should have talked to me before agreeing to the flat.'

'What do you mean? You were there!'

'I know, but you didn't give me much of a chance to speak. You rushed me into it with no time to think. Somewhere else might be better.'

'That's ridiculous. If you didn't like it, why didn't you say so?'

'I couldn't. Not with Maureen there. She's his neighbour. It would have looked rude.'

'I thought it was ideal. So close to your friends. Don't you want to move in with me?'

Tread carefully, Lilli. 'Of course I do. I just feel I'm being pushed, that's all, and it's not what I would have chosen.'

'Most women would be glad of it, our own space already, and no one to tell us what to do. I thought I was doing the right thing, so I did, making sure we could get set up straight away.'

She tried to think of an excuse. 'I guess it just feels too much like settling down.'

'For heaven's sake! Before, in Berlin, you once said you couldn't rely on me. And now it's the opposite. I'm doing my best here, and you're just throwing it all back at me.'

Her stomach was churning, she felt as if she was in a battle she hadn't even asked for. The two parts of her were at war; the part that fell in love with Bren all those years ago, and the part that knew he was the man who had betrayed her, the man with a gun in his suitcase. She couldn't reconcile the two things. *Trust your instinct*, a little voice inside her head insisted. But she wasn't brave enough, not in this country where she was a foreigner, and not without concrete proof.

'I'm sorry. Perhaps I'm just tired.' The excuse slipped out easily, but she knew for certain she didn't want to live with Bren.

'It'll be fine, you'll see. And I know you can make it nice, make it a home.'

She nodded to try to keep the peace. *It would take a lot of love to make that place a home.*

'By the way,' he said, 'you haven't seen a key, have you? A key's gone missing at Mrs Gammage's and I wondered if you'd seen it. It was under the soap dish.'

'A key?' She turned large innocent eyes on him, tried to keep them steady.

'You'd tell me, wouldn't you, if you had?' He took a step nearer, loomed over her.

'I haven't seen a door key.' She deliberately misunderstood.

His eyes narrowed. 'The key to my suitcase.' He grabbed her wrist.

'I haven't seen your key,' she said, twisting away. 'You've probably just mislaid it.'

He gave her a long look, but then shrugged, seemed to let it go. 'Just bloody inconvenient. Let me know if you come across it, will you?'

'Of course,' she said. But she'd seen the part of Bren that scared her, and her heart was thudding in her chest as if she'd been running.

Chapter 25

That evening once the red light went on for recording, Lilli read her script and sang through the numbers as though in a trance.

'You all right?' Ron asked. 'You look a little under the weather.'

'Fine. I'm fine. Just tired.'

'I've still got the car. I can give you a lift home. We'll miss you, when you move out, me and Max. It was nice having a woman about.'

She accepted the lift gratefully, a dread unfurling in her stomach. How could she get out of living with Bren, without alerting him to her suspicions? And what could she do about Neil? She couldn't stop the flutter in her stomach every time she saw him.

The car drew up in the dark and they bustled into the darkened hall. A slice of light under his door showed that Neil was still awake. If she moved out, this would be her last chance to get him on his own, to explain.

Ron headed towards the kitchen, but Lilli took a deep breath and knocked softly on Neil's door. He opened it almost straight away squinting into the darkness. His face took on a closed expression.

'I need to talk to you,' Lilli said. 'Can I come in?'

He held the door open to let her in, and closed it after her.

She stayed standing up. 'Look, this is going to take some explaining. Will you promise to listen, and not shoot me down in flames until I've told you everything?'

He still looked wary, but gestured to the one chair. 'Be my guest.'

Her stomach was doing somersaults. 'I'm going to speak quietly because I don't want anyone else to hear. Okay?'

A nod.

'I don't want to be engaged to Johnny Murphy. I only did it because I wanted to find out why he's pretending to be someone else.'

'I knew it.' Neil sat down on the bed and closed his eyes a moment. 'I knew you weren't suited.' A pause. 'What d'you mean? How can he be somebody else?'

'Please, keep your voice down and just listen. Hear me out. It's complicated and goes back a long way.' She hesitated trying to find the right words. 'I knew Johnny in Berlin. He was Brendan Murphy then. We were …' she swallowed, '… lovers.'

'You knew each other before. Of course. I thought it was too quick, the whole engagement, as soon as he announced it. It seemed too sudden.'

'My father was arrested and taken to a camp and I suspect it was Johnny – Brendan – who betrayed us to the Nazis. But I have no proof. I tried to put it aside. For five years I heard nothing of Brendan Murphy. Then he turns up here.' In a halting voice she told Neil about how the only proof she had was that one word. *Irländer*. 'So you see, he has no idea that I know anything about it, and besides, I was in a panic and I could have been mistaken.'

Neil was silent a moment. 'What are you going to do?'

'That's not all of it. He's armed. He's got a gun in his suitcase.'

'Jesus, Lilli. Are you sure?'

'I've seen it. I was looking for some sort of evidence—'

'You mean you've been doing this all on your own? Acting like some kind of secret agent? Why didn't you go to Delmer or—'

'There was no proof! Who would believe me, a German? They all think he can do no wrong. The wonderful Johnny Murphy who's so charming and helpful. But I've been to the post office and he never was a worker there. His pass, his letter of recommendation, it's all false. Some sort of cover story.'

'What are you saying? Wait a minute. That means—'

'Yes! I know for a fact Brendan hated the English. He talked about it all the time in Berlin before the war. But now he's here and I want to know why.'

Neil rubbed a hand through his hair. 'You're telling me he could be some sort of spy for the Germans?'

'I don't know.' She stood up and paced. 'It seems sort of crazy, when you say it like that. Like something out of a movie. And he's Irish; he could be completely innocent.'

Neil shook his head. 'He punched me. In the stomach where no one would see.'

'What?'

'He was trying to stop me seeing you. That's the kind of man you're dealing with.'

'But why would he—'

'I thought he was just jealous.' Neil leant forward to keep his voice low. 'He doesn't know you suspect him?'

'Who can tell? With Brendan nothing's ever straightforward. He charms people, manipulates them. He did it to me in Berlin, but it took a betrayal to make me realise it. And I know he doesn't want me to reveal his real name. He gave some excuses as to why, but they were quite thin. And since then, he's pressured me, and to be honest, it's making me uncomfortable and I don't know how much longer I can stand it.'

'Then give him his ring back, tell him you're not ready to be engaged to him. That you've had second thoughts; that you need more time.'

She shook her head. 'But if I can do it, if I can live with him, I've the chance to find out more. I owe it to my father; to get the proof he's in the pay of the enemy, get him stopped. Give him what he deserves.'

'But what if there is no proof? You'll be living with a violent man – one you don't even want to live with, and for no reason.'

A deep sigh. 'I told you no one would believe me.'

He jumped up. 'I believe you, of course I do. But hell, Lilli, I don't want you taking risks. If he's an agent, I know what these people are like, and they're bloody dangerous.' He paced round the room, then suddenly turned. 'If I tell you something private, will you swear not to tell another living soul?'

'It depends what it is.' She was expecting some light-hearted confession, but he was not smiling.

'It's not easy.'

'Go on.' She sat down, folded her hands in her lap.

'My skills in German got me into deep trouble. When I was in London a few years ago I was targeted by a group of pro-fascists. Not Germans, but English Nazis. It was the worst time of my life.'

'What did they do to you?'

He let out his breath, and said, 'No. It was me. I did awful things, things I'm ashamed of.'

'What? Wait a minute. Pro-fascists? You're telling me you were a fascist?'

'Keep your voice down! I was scared. They threatened me, blackmailed me until I did what they said. They made me steal secrets from the files. You've no idea – I thought I'd die of stress. It didn't end well.'

She swallowed. The words came out in a croak. 'You're kidding me.'

A shake of the head. 'After I nearly died in the bombing, I vowed I'd never lie again, that I'd always tell the truth. But in wartime you've no idea how difficult that is. Especially when they offered me a job here, in the Ministry of Lies.'

'So what happened? How did you get out of it?'

'I shot one of them, in the end.' His mouth worked and his eyes grew glassy.

My God. He couldn't be serious. But one look at his face told her that he was. 'Did he die?' Her question was a whisper.

Silence. But his eyes sought forgiveness.

'I told you. I try to always speak the truth.'

The enormity of what he'd just told her wouldn't sink in. This man, this mild-mannered man in front of her, the man she was so drawn to, in the frayed collar, with his stick and his shelf full of books, had taken someone's life. She licked her dry lips. It couldn't be real, what he was telling her.

'I did warn you. The truth is hard. But if Johnny is one of these people, they are not reasonable like us. They have a loyalty to a warped dictator and will stop at nothing to see him succeed. It's not about what's really best for the people, it's about them. Them having the right to dictate what's best for us all, d'you see?'

She didn't know what to say. The silence stretched again, until she whispered, 'I can't believe you killed someone.'

'Sometimes, neither can I.' His face had gone very red. 'Telling you was a risk. Because I have to live with it every single day, the guilt and the horror. If it wasn't wartime, and he wasn't the enemy, I'd be in prison. And I can live in fear of people finding out, or choose carefully who I tell. But I think because of what you told me about Johnny Murphy, I owe it to you. Because it might come out, and I want you to be able to trust me.'

His gaze was intense, and she couldn't meet it, couldn't stand its glare. She played with a strand of hair instead.

His hand reached towards her but then fell away. 'And of course it's up to you what you do about Johnny, but I'd advise caution. I can't tell you what to do. All I can say is; if he's really the enemy, you're playing with fire.'

'I want to get to the bottom of it. I want whoever betrayed my father to get what he deserves. To get the full measure of the Law.'

'Then I'll be here for you. Find out what I can. But the

250

moment things start to look dodgy, you must call me or Delmer. Understand?'

'Promise me you won't tell anyone,' Lilli said. 'We can't scare him off – not until we have definite proof.'

He reached out to her, as if to enfold her in an embrace, but she shook her head. She needed time to process what he'd told her.

'Right now, life's complicated enough,' she said.

*

Once Lilli had gone, Neil paced in his room, picking up books and putting them down, re-ordering the shelf of tin soldiers that he'd brought with him to remind him of home.

He'd ruined it with Lilli. Who would want to live with someone who killed another man? His mind circled, thinking through what she said. It had dredged up all his old emotions about the British Union of Fascists, unpleasant memories that made him break into a cold sweat. He paused, weighing one of the lead soldiers in his palm, and remembering the noise of the London air raid. He'd shot Otto, who'd once been his best friend, because of his sister Nancy. Because he had to try to save her life.

Johnny Murphy was armed. The fact had taken a moment to sink in. Now Neil sat down onto the bed, as if he'd been punched again. The murder of his father took on a darker, more sinister cast. It somehow connected in his mind with this whole affair of Lilli and Johnny. Was Johnny part of the BUF?

Things began to fall in his mind like toppling dominoes. And what about the accident on the motorbike? It was a bit of a leap, but his instinct gnawed at him. There was no need for guns in anything they did at Milton Bryan.

Johnny had said Delmer had told him about his involvement with the BUF. But what if it was the BUF itself who'd told Johnny that?

Lilli was right; Brendan, alias Johnny, Murphy could just deny everything unless they had definitive proof. They had no hard evidence at all. Neil dragged open a drawer and grabbed a notebook.He had to write it all down, so he didn't forget anything. It calmed the tight feeling in his chest, just the idea of making a list. He'd do a bit of digging, ask Delmer how he met Johnny; find out all he could about him. He'd ask Max if he could go through his card index as well. He uncapped his fountain pen and wrote down:

Murphy, Brendan, Johnny?
didn't work for GPO, so what was he doing?
actor in cabaret?
met Lilli University of Berlin. PhD in German.
Motorbike sabotage? Killer?

There must be something on record about Brendan Murphy. Some record of his acting credits, surely? He'd start with that, see what that turned up. Because he sure as hell didn't want Lilli living with that creep of a man.

Chapter 26

A few days later Lilli moved into the new apartment. At least here, Bren would have nowhere to hide. Moving in was easy because she owned so few possessions, and anyway Bren had taken over the place. His favourite Irish whisky was already on the table with a glass and the newspaper. His shoes were lined up neatly next to the door. When she opened the kitchen cupboard, it was full of unfamiliar enamel pans and mismatched crockery from Maureen.

Someone must have had a word with the powers that be, because now Lilli was engaged to Bren, or Johnny, as he liked to be called, there seemed to be no more doubt about her being an enemy alien. It was assumed that he was vouching for her reliability, and this in itself was galling.

Lilli had a bucket of hot soapy water and was cleaning the paintwork and windows to remove dirt and any traces of the previous occupants, but Bren didn't offer to help. He was restless, irritated with the things she was doing to make the flat habitable.

'I'm sure it's clean enough, now,' he said, frowning. 'Do you want to take the paint off?'

She couldn't explain that it was because she was nervous, that she had to do something – anything to keep busy. As she polished and dusted, Bren spent his time reading the daily papers cover to cover, and keeping fit. The keeping fit involved press-ups, and lifting two bricks that he'd got from outside, and then running as if he was training for some sort of marathon.

The first thing she bought for the apartment was a radio. She wanted to listen to the news on the BBC.

'I don't know how you stand that infernal noise first thing in the morning,' he said, the first day she tuned in.

'I like to keep up with what's happening. With how the war's going.'

'We have enough of that at work, don't we?'

Reluctantly she turned it off until he was out. He was often out on small errands, going to the paper shop, going on his run, or what he called 'getting some air'. It was like living with a ghost – he seemed to drift in and out. She couldn't see his suitcase anywhere. Where had he put it?

One morning he told her he was going to the library. 'Sorry, Lilli, but I might be all day. I'm going to do some research. I need a bit of background to the Great War, to make my character of the submariner convincing.'

'I'll come with you then. I'd like to get some books out. It's ages since I read a good—'

'No, you stay here. Mr Barrett said an electrician's coming today to fix the light switch in the bathroom.'

'Why? What's the matter with it?'

'It was flickering, I asked him to get someone to look at it.'

'I could do that. I'm good with electrical things. I did a lot of it when I was in the Isle of Man.'

'No need for you to do it, and besides there's a proper electrician coming. You just need to wait in for him.'

A proper electrician. She didn't like to tell him she could probably run rings around any electrician. She bit her lip – anything to keep an even keel, and it would give her a chance to search his things again.

As soon as he was out, she searched all his pockets and looked for the case with the gun. No sign of any of it. She yanked open the drawers one by one.

His clothes were carefully arranged, underwear folded, shirts and ties hung in the wardrobe, all smelling of the pungent Bay Rum aftershave he used. He insisted on ironing his own shirts and polishing his own shoes. 'I know how I like it done,' he'd said. There was no sign of the locked case and it niggled at her. She began to wonder if she'd been asleep and dreamt it.

She'd feel a proper fool with Neil if all this was just her mind playing tricks.

Neil. She wondered what he was doing. The fact she was sharing her life with Bren and not with Neil, where her heart lay, gave her a sharp pang.

She hung around all morning waiting for the electrician, peeling potatoes for the midday meal and doing her smalls washing in the Lux flakes in the sink, but nobody came.

At lunchtime she decided to fix the light fitting herself. She switched the light on and off with the pull cord. It was fine. Not flickering at all. Puzzled, she took off her shoes and stood on a chair to take out the bulb and look at the socket. After that she turned off the trip-switch at the mains, and unscrewed the socket to examine the wiring. All good. It was strange. Must have been some sort of power outage. Or more likely – just an excuse to keep her at home.

Well, she wasn't going to stay in all day now it was fixed.

She'd do a bit of sleuthing on her own. She'd go and see his old landlady in Bedford, Mrs Gammage. See what she could tell her about the mysterious life of Johnny Murphy. Maybe she'd tell her who he met and what he did when he wasn't at work.

*

The door opened and the woman glared at Lilli from the doorstep. 'Whatever it is, I'm not buying any,' she said, hand on hip. She was heavily made-up with thickly plastered powder and red lips.

'I'm not selling anything,' Lilli said. 'Do you remember me? I'm Johnny Murphy's fiancée.'

She frowned. 'Who? Who did you say you were after?'

'Johnny. He rented a room from you. Upstairs, second door on the left.'

'Oh, you. The one seeing that Ralphie. A right double crosser he turned out to be. Owe you money too, does he? Well, you won't get anything out of me.' She made to shut the door.

'Please. I just need to know a bit more about him, who he saw, things like that.'

She looked Lilli up and down. 'Went off with someone else, did he? Doesn't surprise me. Proper ladies' man, he was. Kept trying to look up my skirt when I went upstairs.'

'Did he bring any other women here?'

'No. Now that I think of it, he didn't. He was always out at work. Worked at the tyre factory in Bedford. Long shifts, he said. Nights, often. He'd come in late, sleep late.'

'You called him Ralphie. Was that the name he had on the rent book?'

She drew back her chin. 'He never signed nothing. Told me his name was Ralph Kelly. Has he done something wrong? Because if he has, I want nothing to do with it, see. I run a nice clean boarding house here and I don't want no trouble.'

'He gave me a false name, that's all. There won't be any trouble. Did he have any visitors except me?'

'No. Never got no mail, neither. Thought that was odd. Most folk have family that write, or bills come for them.'

'There's nothing else you can tell me?'

'Only that I wish I'd never set eyes on him. Owes me a whole month's rent and his notice money. I should have listened to Mr Battle. Now there's a gentleman. He said, "Never trust an Irishman", and he was right. If you see Ralphie Kelly again

– or whatever the hell he's calling himself – tell him I want my money.'

As Lilli walked away, she puzzled over it. Another false name, and false employment. Why would he do that? Why not just say he worked at Milton Bryan? The only reason she could think of was so he wouldn't be traceable.

The yellow telephone directory in the box down the road gave the address of the tyre factory and she rang them from there to find out if they knew a Johnny Murphy or a Ralph Kelly.

They put on another Irishman called Declan, who told her he was the only Irish person that had ever worked there. So as she'd suspected, that was a dead end too. So was he really at the library, or was it more lies?

She caught the bus home again and began to prepare the evening meal.

Bren tread on the steps outside. He breezed in and thumped the pile of books down, and Lilli went and picked one up, to see what he was reading. Three books on the Norman Conquest. She spread them out on the table. 'I didn't know you were interested in history.'

He shrugged. 'I'm interested in a lot of things. I thought some books about a war in the past might help me make sense of this one. Help me be a war-weary submariner.'

She opened one at random, leafed through it. 'It says a hundred thousand men were killed in the invasion of England. How awful. Do you think it's like that in France?'

No answer. He poked his head into the kitchen, where steam bubbled from under a pan lid. 'What's cooking?'

'Only tinned meat and potatoes I'm afraid. But there are some scrubbed carrots to go with it.'

He sat down and picked up the newspaper. He was staring at it, but she knew he wasn't reading because his eyes had that faraway look as if he was somewhere else.

'The electrician didn't come,' she said.

'What? Oh. Never mind, I'll look at it myself later.'

'I had a good look. There's nothing wrong with it.'

'That's good.'

Where had he been? He had a life full of unexplained gaps and his conversation had become a series of platitudes. They ate together, but it was awkward, and he made her on edge, drumming his feet under the table, his face creased in a frown.

'Are you nervous?' she asked him. 'About tonight's broadcast?'

He looked at her with complete condescension. 'Good God, no. It's only a few lines to read. I'll take a look at them later.'

During the time at the studio Bren was too busy reading his lines to find time for conversation, and by night-time they were both drained after trying to keep their wits during the live broadcast. It didn't stop him from wanting to make love though, although his kissing seemed more cursory than it had been at the beginning, thank goodness, and he wanted to do everything with the lights out.

When he got more urgent, she pushed him off. 'Let's wait,' she said.

A heavy sigh, designed to make her feel bad. 'Why? We'll be no different then, with a marriage certificate, than we are now. It's like you're teasing me, every night, holding something back.'

'I'm not. Johnny, I—' But it was too late, she felt him roll over and turn his back on her. She felt bound to make these excuses, but didn't know how much longer she could push him away. His back was like a stone wall. She gripped the bedcovers with both hands, feeling small and vulnerable. She had to get away from him soon, she could feel pressure building, blue-black, the shape and colour of an approaching wave in a storm.

*

Neil made a point of appearing at Milton Bryan every afternoon; and she knew it was because he was keeping an eye out for her.

She was always relieved to hear the sound of his motorbike, or to find him suddenly in the green room before the broadcast.

'You all right?' he'd mouth quietly, and she'd nod, unable to say more because others were in the room. They had a language of shared glances. It was reassuring, but she felt guilty she'd found out nothing further about Bren, and wondered if Neil would think her story just some sort of attention-grabbing.

In the middle of the night she woke up, having one of her nightmares where her father was being taken away and she was locked on the other side of the door. She sat upright in a cold sweat and went into the living room to try to calm down. On the table were the library books untouched. Bren hadn't even opened them. There was a train timetable there though, one she hadn't seen before. He'd marked the trains to London, and then to Tunbridge Wells. He'd underlined the times.

There was something going on, but she didn't know what.

It didn't take her long to find out.

'What are you doing?' Bren appeared behind her, his voice sharp.

'I couldn't sleep. I came to get a drink, but then I saw these timetables.'

'Yes. I have to go away for a few weeks. Sorry. I meant to tell you, but it wasn't fixed up until yesterday.'

'Away? Where?' Suspicion rose up in a tide. She told herself to calm down.

'I can't tell you. I've been taken on by another arm of the Political Warfare Executive and I've to go to London.'

Act the outraged girlfriend. 'But we've only just moved in here!'

'I know. I expect it will only be for a couple of weeks, darling, then I'll be back.'

'What will you be doing? What sort of work? More broadcasting?'

'I can't tell you. The Official Secrets Act and all that. But it's war work. I'm sorry, I know it's a hell of a bind, but I can't tell you any more than that.'

259

'But when did they ask you? You didn't have an interview, or anything.'

'The letter came when I was still at Mrs Gammage's. I'm to go a week on Friday, and I'd almost forgotten about it, what with moving and everything.'

Mrs Gammage had definitely said he had no mail.

'How could you have forgotten about it? That's ridiculous! And now you're going to leave me stuck out here while you gallivant off?'

'It's not gallivanting, I told you. It's a job for the PWE.'

'You should have told me.' The new petulant Lilli did sound convincing.

'I know. It was hard to keep it quiet, but I couldn't say anything until it was definite.'

'Do they know yet at Milton Bryan?'

'I'll tell Delmer today. He'll need to replace me with someone else.'

So whatever it was, Delmer was going to know about it. Lilli took the breakfast things to the kitchen to wash them, trying to work out what was going on in Bren's life.

'Bren?'

He turned, 'What?'

'Can I call you Bren at home? It feels strange calling you Johnny. Like it's not really you.'

'It's safer if you get used to Johnny. If you accidentally call me Bren, people will start to ask questions. If they start to ask questions about me, then they might start to ask questions about you too.'

A pause, in which the silence in the room grew thicker. 'What do you mean? What questions? I don't understand.'

He approached and put a hand on her shoulder, explaining as if to a child, 'We'll be suspects if they ever find out we were friends with Willi and Gustav, paid-up members of the Nazi Party.'

She stepped back. 'But I was never their friend. You know I wasn't.'

'You mean you never had that affair with Willi Wendt?'

The blood in her veins turned to ice. 'Of course I didn't. What are you talking about? That's complete—'

'Gustav told me. And it tore me up.' A pause. 'That's why I started up with Hilde. But if it were to come out that you were sleeping with the enemy …' His face was deadly serious.

'You can't believe …?' Heat rose to her face. 'Gustav is a liar.'

He was still staring at her with mild almost mocking eyes. She understood in a flash what was happening. It was a threat, she was sure of it.

'They'd consider you a risk to me, darling, now I'm working for the Political Warfare Executive.'

She gave him a look of daggers, turned, and went from the room.

Her hands shook with rage as she put on her hat and coat. She had never been near any of those Brownshirts. Gustav couldn't have really said those things about her. It was just Bren twisting the truth to get her to do what he wanted.

I see you, you bastard, she thought.

By the time she came back, ready to go to the studio, he was waiting, already in his summer jacket and lightweight trilby. He looked handsome as always, chatting easily with an older woman as they waited at the bus stop, laying on the banter. They travelled together, his foot still tapping on the floor of the bus, and his eyes scanning the landscape blindly as if he were watching some film inside his head.

'Bren?' She tried to speak to the old Bren, the youth she used to know, but he didn't turn away from the window. 'You know perfectly well I never did those things. It's all lies.'

A tightening around his mouth. 'Let's leave it, shall we?'

When they got inside the offices at Milton Bryan, Bren walked straight to Sefton Delmer's office and knocked. A few moments later and he'd gone inside without a backward glance.

Lilli paused outside the door, wishing she could hear their

261

conversation. But the walls were too thick to pick up anything, so she braced her shoulders and headed for the recording studio. She almost stumbled. His accusations had knocked her off balance. He couldn't really believe it, could he? Willi and Gustav had always despised her because she was half-Jewish. They'd called out at her, saying Jews polluted the streets.

But one thing she was certain of – Bren, or Johnny, was hiding something, that much was blindingly obvious.

*

Half an hour later, Bren came out of the door and leant against the corridor wall to let out a sigh of relief. That had gone better than he'd hoped. He'd been worried Callaghan might have squealed about how he'd threatened him, but nothing was said. Despite the fact Delmer was smart and would spot any inconsistencies in his story, Delmer had believed the transfer nonsense he'd spun him – that because of Johnny's German-speaking skills the PWE were sending him on an undercover mission behind enemy lines.

'Don't tell Lilli,' he'd said to Delmer, wringing his hands. 'This is terrible timing for us. I've told her I'm going to be working away for a few weeks, but obviously not what I'm doing.'

Delmer was impressed. The work he'd done on softening them up had worked. They saw him as 'the good guy'.

'Sorry to leave you in the lurch,' Bren said.

'Never mind, old chap. It can't be helped,' Delmer replied, and shook his hand, giving him the sympathetic look that meant *you are a brave and considerate man*. 'At least you're not going to the BBC.' He smiled. 'I expect we'll find someone else, and I wish you good luck.'

Just as he was replaying this conversation and congratulating himself, Neil Callaghan came past. No stick this time, but he had one hand on the corridor wall for support.

'Excuse me,' Callaghan said icily, squeezing by.

'Be my guest,' Bren said, giving him a contemptuous smile. He guessed Callaghan hadn't told Delmer about their fight because it would be humiliating.

He stood away from the wall in one languorous movement, and followed Callaghan to the recording studio. Callaghan was a thorn in his side. He wished his contact Harper had been less keen for him to bide his time and insisted he eliminate Callaghan first, but the motorbike trick hadn't worked, and he couldn't think of another convincing 'accident'.

The studio had that hot burned-dust smell of electrics. Today they were doing a test for what they were calling an 'intrusion operation', where the English announcer would take over from the German one in a seamless transition. Their first attempt was to be on the night shift.

Bren felt a momentary pang for the pilots of the German Messerschmitts who'd be blamed for not stopping the bombers. Poor sods. While they searched in the wrong direction, Allied bombers would reach their German targets with zero resistance. Whole cities could be decimated that way. Even Berlin.

He sat down to pick up his script with the detailed wrong co-ordinates. He had to admire Delmer's idea; the sheer brazenness of it.

Unfortunately Callaghan, Delmer's sidekick, had wheedled his way into running that particular project on the ground, so Bren knew he'd have to toe the line for now. Callaghan, meanwhile, was at the console and had asked Ron to get up the recording from German command on the tape.

'Hey, Johnny, have a listen to these recordings of yesterday's announcements,' Ron called. 'Right up your alley, mate.' He tapped the chair next to him where there was a pair of headphones waiting.

'You'll need to practise the same intonation and accent and mimic him exactly,' Callaghan added, still with that ice in his tone. 'We need the two voices to be indistinguishable.'

Bren suppressed his desire to punch his lights out and put on the headphones anyway. The accent he was listening to had a slight touch of Bavarian. He could imitate it, he thought, with a little practice. He had to do it to keep them all sweet, even if it stuck in his craw. If only they'd asked someone else to do it, rather than him. All those Hooray Henrys in their planes deserved any German flak they were getting.

It would be his last few days here, because after that he'd be on his way to Ashdown Forest to try to get inside the compound and disable the mast. Then this whole malarkey would be obsolete. He smiled at the thought of the damage it would do. It would show the bloody English a thing or two when they realised they'd been duped and he claimed it for the IRA and the Gestapo.

*

Neil picked up his stick and left Johnny Murphy in the studio mouthing the accent over and over. Johnny seemed the same as he always did, charming, a bit jokey, full of good humour. It made Neil grit his teeth. He knew what the man was really like underneath – the humiliation of being knocked down by him still festered.

As he walked down the path to the lock-up, he pondered it all. He was certain Lilli was right; that Johnny had betrayed her family, but the evidence just wasn't enough. Just the sound of someone on a stairwell. Even the fact he'd falsified his CV. He imagined trying to tell Delmer and knew it would look like a) he was accusing his boss of negligence, and b) that he had a vendetta against Murphy.

Yet the more Neil saw of Brendan-cum-Johnny Murphy, the less he trusted him. But again, Neil thought, with his own track record – the fact he'd once collaborated with the BUF, he wasn't exactly the best person to throw accusations around. Especially since they were both fighting over the same girl.

Neil wanted to see how the new POWs were getting on. They were to broadcast a satirical radio play about a Nazi officer's mess room. He found them in the lock-up rehearsing their scripts. The lock-up was like a prison cell but with a gate of bars so he could talk to the men through it. They seemed to have it all under control and he exchanged a few pleasant words with them. Only last week one of them had said he was grateful to be out of the reach of enemy fire and that he worried about his children's school. It made Neil sad, that the English were still killing civilians with their aerial bombing raids. *Stop thinking about it.*

On the way back, Delmer stuck his head out of the office. 'Neil, we've got a problem.'

Neil swung himself in to hear what was going on.

'Johnny's been called up for an SOE job. Behind enemy lines. So we're losing him.'

Neil sat down with a thump. The SOE? Was that what the gun was about? His whole GPO cover story? 'But I thought he'd just got engaged to Lilli Bergen?'

'Yes, poor sod. He's leaving us on Friday. Any of your POWs up for the job he does? We need someone with excellent English so he can understand the details of what we're asking, but also someone who can imitate German air command.'

Neil struggled to take it in. Had he misjudged Johnny Murphy? He could only manage a strangled, 'Where's he going?'

'You know I can't tell you, even if I knew. He's told Miss Bergen he's on another PWE broadcast job in London. But it means we're short of a voice.'

'Not sure there's anyone capable at the moment,' Neil replied. 'I'll sift through them when they're on air tonight. There's a couple of possibilities, but they're not actors.' He'd be glad to be rid of Johnny Murphy. His mood lifted, but he was astute enough to hide it.

'Don't suppose we'll be able to get anyone as good as Johnny,' said Delmer. 'But so long as they can speak German, mimic High Command and issue orders, that's all we'll need.'

'Okay boss, I'll see what I can do.' Neil stood up to go.

'And by the way, I promised Johnny I'd not tell Lilli where he was going, so I trust you to do the same.'

Neil sighed. 'I won't lie to her.'

'Just avoid the question then. The last thing we need is some emotional woman in the studio.'

'Lilli's not like that.'

Delmer shook his head impatiently. 'I know that. But you can see it would get awkward and no one's supposed to know, not even spouses. It's all classified. I'm only telling you because the intrusion ops are vital, and I'm relying on you to get us out of this mess and find us another voice.'

Neil hobbled back to the recording studio. His leg was giving him gyp again. He thought of his sister, Nancy, who'd been part of the SOE for years, though pretended to everyone, including her family, she was in the FANY. He wasn't supposed to know about that either, but he did. You'd have to be as thick as two short planks not to see it. All those fake postcards with bland messages that she'd sent over the years. He bet she was in Holland again; her Dutch was impeccable. He wondered where Johnny Murphy would be sent; Germany probably.

When he got back, Lilli was rehearsing, a good tub-thumping number called 'Erika'. He stopped to watch her. He was only here to make sure the intrusion op ran smoothly, and he'd missed seeing her sing live. She looked tired though today, and not like her usual lively self.

She finished the number with a flourish and thanked the band.

'How're you doing?' Neil asked when she was done.

'Still nothing I can pin on him,' she whispered. 'Though I went to see his old landlady. He was using a false name. Ralph Kelly.'

'Did she say anything else?'

'Nothing we can nail him with. It's so frustrating.'

'I hear he's going away.'

'Can't keep anything a secret in this blasted place.'

'Has he told you anything about it?'

'Not a thing. I'm torn to shreds over how loyal I should be, and if he's really on some mission working for us—' She paused as Ron came by with some other technicians, and shrugged apologetically, moving off towards the piano again.

Neil buttoned his lip. Delmer's words haunted him. He knew he mustn't tell Lilli what Johnny was doing. He could really be going in somewhere as an agent, and Neil knew only too well what the chances of coming back alive would be.

He hung around until the broadcast, hoping to get another chance to talk to her, and watching the evening programme go out. He stayed on the earphones until it was time to listen in to the German channel which, when they detected incoming allied planes, would cut out.

Ron was poised at the controls and Johnny was ready to cut in with the announcement once the German military transmitters went off air. Johnny looked unhappy and tense, but had the new script in front of him.

Through the loudspeaker crackled the voice of German command before it suddenly died.

'Here we go!' Ron said. 'Switch over. You're on, Johnny.'

The red light came on and they all held their breath as Johnny's voice rang out. Calm and precise, he seemed a natural at impersonating Nazi bomber ground-control. Neil heard him give the fake co-ordinates and deliberately send the German squadrons of night fighters to completely the wrong sectors. Neil held his breath, hoping this would mean they'd lose sight of the incoming Allied bombers.

At the end, as soon as the red light went off, Johnny pushed back his chair and rubbed the sweat from his forehead.

'Did you get it on tape?' Neil asked Ron.

'Hope so,' Ron said.

'What do you mean?' Johnny asked. 'Are you recording me?'

'We thought we could use the recording again another night,' Max said. 'Sow more confusion.'

'But I didn't give permission for that.' Johnny's voice held a flinty edge. 'You never told me it would be used more than once.' He moved towards Max's desk and stood over him. 'I demand you destroy it. I don't want that tape hanging around forever. Who knows what else it could be used for?'

Neil leapt in. 'Calm down. No need for there to be an argument over it. If Johnny doesn't want us to use the tapes again, then we won't. But we'll need a new recording for every night in that case. I take it you'll at least do that, Johnny?'

Johnny seemed to suddenly realise where he was. 'Sorry, everyone, just a bit nervous. Yes, of course I'll make new recordings. We want to outfox the Germans any way we can.' He smiled around the room, but Neil frowned to Ron, uncomfortable. They'd all seen the slightly bullying way he'd harangued Max, and a few smiles weren't going to mend it.

'I suggest we call it a day,' Ron said. 'We're all tired and it's late.'

Neil gave Ron a grateful nod. As he was putting away the microphones and placing the papers back in the paper rack, Neil kept one eye on Johnny. It riled him to see Johnny thrust his arms angrily into his overcoat and head for the door, leaving Lilli to struggle hurriedly into her coat and collect his briefcase where it lay on the table.

Neil worried about her, going home with someone who was so obviously in a bad temper. Maybe the thought of such a dangerous mission abroad was getting to him.

'What was all that about?' Ron asked.

Neil shrugged, just as Maureen put her head around the door. 'Call for you, Mr Callaghan.'

Neil hurried to the phone and heard the click-clunk as he was put through.

Delmer. 'Congratulations, old boy. Bloody marvellous. Whole payload of bombs dropped with not a sniff of a Messerschmitt, and our men are on their way home. Glorious stuff! Radio control says the enemy planes were way off course. Buy that singer of yours a drink, will you?'

If only I could, thought Neil. *If only I could.*

*

'Tom, I need you to do some digging for me.' Neil was in the public phone box. He pictured his friend Tom in his bed-sitting room in London, the room full of poetry posters, and heaps of books piled up on the floor.

'What about?' He could hear Tom's wariness in his tone. 'It's not Nancy, is it?'

'No. I've heard nothing of her.' Tom was sweet on Nancy. 'No, I expect she's fine. It's about a man who's working with us. I need him checked out. Anything at all you can find out about him.'

'I don't know if I'll be able to find out much. Is he one of ours?'

'That's what I need to know. The name's Murphy. Brendan Murphy – expat Irishman. About twenty-six years old, six foot one, studied German at the University of Berlin.'

'What's he done wrong?'

'Nothing – yet. He's claiming to be from the SOE, and I hear through the muddy grapevine that they're about to fly him off somewhere. But he's … well, he's behaving strangely and I want to know if I can trust him. If he could be an agent for the Abwehr.'

Tom's voice came back through the crackle of the earpiece. 'Well, if anyone should have an instinct for that sort of thing, it's you.'

Neil didn't take this as a dig, but as a compliment. He knew Tom Lockwood well enough to know they were friends. Tom had understood his past like nobody else. And even better than that, he'd forgiven him.

'You'll search the records for me? I guess he's going to be posted to Germany, but I could be wrong.'

'You'll owe me a pint if I do.'

'They're on me.'

Chapter 27

'Mr Kelly?' The librarian called to Bren as he went by. She called again.

His heart gave an unpleasant thump as he realised she was talking to him.

'Your books are overdue.'

'Oh yes. Sorry. I've not quite finished them yet.' *Calm down*.

'Well, we can't let you take out another six until you bring them back.'

Bren frowned, impatient. 'I'm just browsing.' He had been obliged to use his fake name at the library because that was what used to be on his rental address. He turned away and headed for the section where he normally met Estofal. He wasn't there yet, so he picked his way along the shelves, taking out the odd book and shoving it back. He hoped Estofal had been in contact with the Gestapo.

Estofal arrived about ten minutes later, looking worse than Bren had ever seen him, sweating, and his eyes bloodshot and darting left and right. 'See anyone come in after me?' he asked. His breath reeked of whisky.

'I wasn't looking.'

He followed Estofal to a bench by the river where the August heat was making the pavement melt and give off the choking smell of tar. The sun beat down on his hat, as he watched the ducks swim past.

'Pfalzgraf threatened me,' Estofal said in a low voice. 'They're saying it's urgent now. Delmer's transmitter's interfering with German Luftwaffe control. Some bastard's impersonating one of their broadcasters, causing rank chaos in the air with aircraft all sent in the wrong directions.'

Bren didn't react, but watched as Estofal fumbled to get out a wallet from his briefcase, and hand it over. 'False travel papers. You're an inspector doing factory inspections again. The train tickets are there too – open ended. They want you to get over there and take the transmitter out as soon as you can.'

'Christ, it's not that easy. I told you; I need to recce it first.'

'Good, that's good.' Estofal looked distracted. He glanced over his shoulder. 'Have a look, see if there's a motorcyclist behind us.'

Bren glanced behind at the street. Ordinary pedestrians strolling, walking their dogs. Delivery vans trundling by. Nothing.

'Thing is, I think I'm being followed. There's been someone watching my house. A man on a motorbike. Looks like a cop. Whenever I catch sight of him, he speeds off. And yesterday I distinctly heard another click when I used my transmitter.'

'What sort are you using?'

Estofal glanced around to check no one could hear. 'The old Keksdose – the standard-issue biscuit tin. Only any good for Morse, but using it makes you pick up clicks and whirrs.'

'You think they're onto us? Who? MI5?'

'Could just be paranoia, but I'd take care if I were you. Once you've done the recce, you'll need to come to my garage to make the device. I'll have the gear ready for you. But take extra precautions and make sure you're not followed. Here's the address, memorise it, then burn it, okay?'

*

The next day, Bren shut the daily paper with venom. The headline boasted of German cities obliterated by English bombs. Delmer's outfit had sent the German Luftwaffe on a wild goose chase. Bren massaged his temples. He knew his impersonation had led to this carnage. He'd done three of these 'intrusion' broadcasts now, and each one rankled. The IRA had trusted him to sabotage English factories, and now here he was doing the very opposite and decimating German manufacturing.

He stood up and went to the window to look out over the back garden, which was a series of beds with vegetables and a greenhouse and a disused potting shed where he'd hidden his suitcase. He heard Lilli washing dishes in the kitchen, the hiss of water into the bowl, the clank of cutlery. Domestic life didn't suit him. He felt too big in their upstairs flat, claustrophobic, as if he couldn't breathe properly, and he hated having to do what the English told him to. It felt disrespectful to his IRA friends. He longed to hear another Irish accent.

When Lilli came through, drying her hands, he said, 'Got a meeting tomorrow in London. A bod from the Political Warfare Executive.'

'London?' She frowned. 'What about?'

'My new job. They're going to brief me. Several different meetings. I'm sorry, darling, but I'll be gone three or four days.'

'It must be something important then, if it takes that long.'

'I won't know, will I? Not until I get there.'

'You should have told me last night.'

'I know, but I was distracted. It's been a lot on my plate, all this intrusion stuff.'

She merely stared.

He'd offended her, he thought. He knew he'd not paid her much attention recently to keep her sweet. Maybe he shouldn't have insulted her with the stuff about Willi Wendt.

'Wish me luck then,' he said, going to embrace her.

'Good luck,' she said, remaining wooden in his arms, and it

made him want to shake her. She seemed dried up now, not the young girl that used to fall into his arms in Berlin. Good thing she didn't know what she was really wishing him luck for, spying on the transmitter. He picked up his small overnight bag, then kissed her goodbye; a peck on the cheek from a dutiful fiancé. *Just a few more weeks and he'd be rid of her.*

*

Ashdown Forest was bigger than Bren thought, but the ground crackled dry underfoot, and with not as much tree cover as he'd hoped. He spent a few hours avoiding the main trails, looking for the site, so it was now mid-afternoon. He took out his binoculars and scanned the trees. He was dressed as a walker, skirting through the woods rather than by the road. From what Lilli had let drop, there were dogs. He'd try to survey the compound without setting them off.

He heard the rumble of traffic and saw two military cars grind by on the road. A few moments later, their engines cranked down through the gears and they idled, so they must be at the gate. Bren slowed, creeping through the undergrowth until his binoculars showed a tall wire fence about fifty yards away.

Twelve feet tall. Razor wire. Double layer. He homed in through the binoculars on the door to the bunker, twisting the focus knob until he had it clearly in his sights. Damn. Solid steel by the look of it, and another armed guard outside with a machine gun.

He crept a bit further forwards and scanned downwards to locate the main gate with its armed sentries. And yes, there were dogs, so he definitely couldn't get much nearer. There was no sign of a huge mast, just a bunker-like structure, and what looked to be several antennae. The underground part had an installation of cooling pipes snaking around the top of it. He scanned to the left. Several wooden Nissen-type huts dotted in the trees. He guessed the actual aerial was mostly underground, and so the hardware would be bombproof from above.

No chance whatever then of blasting it from outside, not through all these trees and a bunker, so it would have to be an inside job. Not good news.

Keeping a safe distance, he picked his way silently around the edge of the compound, but there seemed to only be one gate. Hard to disable the main gate. Perhaps he could cut his way in through the back somehow? But then, how would he get into the bunker itself? The door seemed to be solid steel.

His best bet would be to go in with a member of staff. But then how would he get out before the thing blew? He'd have to think of something. He hit the ground and squirmed nearer on his belly, trying not to make a sound. Above him, birds sang, and he could hear the distant voices of the guards as they checked the passes of the men in the cars. Engineers judging by their overalls.

It was watertight. He'd have to wrangle his way in. Persuade or encourage Ron to bring him. The device would need to be small, like the Coventry bomb, and operated with some sort of timer. Get in somehow, plant it, and get the hell out. He'd aim for the control room, a big enough device to stand a chance of taking out the whole place.

He lowered his binoculars and shuffled backwards before standing. Looked like Ron was going to get a new best friend.

*

When Bren returned, he didn't go home, and intended to stay with Estofal, but couldn't make telephone contact. Instead, he stayed overnight in a boarding house, making plans and calculations to assemble the device. The next day, in Estofal's garage Bren was at the workbench, slowly funnelling the explosive into the tube. Estofal's breath, sour from cigarettes, wafted over him as he did it.

'You didn't answer my call,' Bren said.

'Can't. Think I might be bugged.'

'Just move back a bit, can't you,' Bren said. 'You're in my light.'

The garage was dark and damp, and the only light was from one small side window. But still, the work bench was adequate and Estofal had supplied him with a large leather holdall suitable for carrying the heavy battery and the device, once it was done.

'That man was back,' Estofal said.

Bren didn't look up. He was concentrating on inserting the wiring.

'The man on the motorbike.'

'He hasn't approached you?'

'I've seen him twice since I last saw you. Thing is, I think he's tailing me.'

'Have you spoken to Pfalzgraf about it?'

A shake of the head. 'I can't tell him. If he thought I was a danger to the network, he'd arrange an accident. And maybe the man's one of his men.'

'Why would one of his men be following you?'

A shrug. 'Keeping tabs on us?'

He glanced up. 'How long have you been doing this? Being a contact, I mean?'

'Thirteen months. Too long.' He fiddled with a cigarette in his hands.

'Don't light up!' Bren snapped.

'I wasn't going to. Thirteen months. Unlucky thirteen. They say most men last for six, max. Thing is, I want out. I made a few enquiries, about going back to Europe.'

Out? To run from German intelligence was impossible. All you could do was stay useful. Bren finished what he was doing, and began to load the holdall. 'Just lie low for a while. Do nothing suspicious. Just be an ordinary citizen. Whoever the tail is, he'll soon get bored following you about, if all you do is sell insurance.'

'I was wondering, you must have contacts in Ireland. Could they help me, d'you think?'

'No. Sorry, old chap, but I'm not getting involved. You've stayed alive all this time, so you must be doing something right. If I were you, I'd just move on. Move somewhere else. Take up selling insurance for real.'

'Ha bloody ha.' Estofal gestured to the holdall. 'I'll be glad to see the back of all that stuff.'

'You'll have to hang on to it a bit longer. Can't keep it at home, nowhere safe to leave it. I'll come back for it the night before I do the job. I'll leave you a message in our drop book, when to expect me, okay?'

Estofal shifted from foot to foot. 'I'd rather you took it with you now.'

Someone had really put the wind up him. 'Just a few more days, okay?' Bren stood up tall, and fixed Estofal with a look, and Estofal caved, as he knew he would. He was no match for Bren and he knew it.

'Soon as you can,' Estofal mumbled.

'When you get my message about the "go" date, you'll arrange my transport out, right? Safe house, then Dublin.'

'Yes, yes. You got it.'

Bren frowned. Estofal didn't look like he was listening or paying attention. 'One o'clock, we said. But the getaway car must be there in the forest by noon. Four miles down the track, like I showed you on the map.'

'Like I said, my contact Sheridan will be waiting where we agreed.'

Later Bren pondered over Estofal. Poor sod. He was losing it. If someone really was after him, would he blab under torture? He had to assume yes. Yet getting him away to Ireland would be too much risk, too much involvement.

He needed to get rid of Estofal. He'd become too dangerous. But he couldn't shut him up until the job was finished.

Chapter 28

While Bren was away Lilli managed to finally find Neil alone in the canteen, sitting at one of the tables reading a paper. He stood up immediately, concern on his face.

She sat down opposite him without even ordering.

'Thank goodness,' he said. 'I've been worried sick. Been trying to catch you for days, but you're always surrounded by people.'

'I've been run off my feet with rehearsals. Now we're on air more frequently there's so little time to prepare.'

'I found something out from Delmer,' he said, leaning forward, 'and I weighed up whether or not to tell you, because it's classified information.'

She raised her eyebrows in question.

'I could get into serious trouble if Delmer finds out I've blabbed. But I can't lie to you when I know something, not something important like this.'

She leant in ready to listen.

'Johnny's working for the Special Operations Executive. Secret agents who go abroad.'

'Oh.' A sense of deflation rather than relief. She took a moment to think. 'Will they send him to Germany?'

'I don't know. I shouldn't even be telling you, but I thought you had a right to know.' His eyes were disappointed. 'Sorry, Lilli, but it seems that's what all the subterfuge is about, not because he's an enemy agent, but because he's one of ours.'

'Oh,' she said again. 'Probably why he had a gun in his suitcase too. I suppose he signed the Official Secrets Act like the rest of us.'

'It's a dangerous occupation, going behind enemy lines. Takes exceptional courage. You know the risks?'

She nodded. She did. But she found it hard to feel anything at all.

Neil swallowed. 'Do you want me to butt out of it now? After all, he's your fiancé and you'll need to think about the fact he might be gone a long time, and he might not come back. Spend time with him while you can. You owe the man that. You don't need me getting in the way.'

'You're never getting in the way.' She meant it and reached for his hand, but too late. He'd stood up and was folding his newspaper. 'What I said still stands though. If you ever need a friend, I'll always be there for you.' There was a slight emphasis on the word 'friend'.

With that, he hurried away, slightly pinker than he had been when she arrived.

She watched him go, and tried to quell the wringing feeling in her stomach. She supposed that there was no excuse now to mistrust Bren, and yet she still did. She still remembered Berlin, and no matter what sort of man Bren was now, she couldn't forgive him for that. Obviously Neil thought she should give up trying to spy on him, that Bren was working for the SOE and not for the Germans at all. She knew Neil didn't like Bren, but how typical of him, that he'd put that aside to admire the fact Bren was doing his bit for the Allies.

It was this that hurt most of all, to lose Neil's trust in her instincts about Bren. At the same time, she knew with certainty, no matter what sort of a hero Bren was now, she could never be his wife.

*

Bren came home the following day, full of himself. 'Good news, darling, they're letting me stay on here a little longer after all. With these things, timing is everything.'

'Oh that's wonderful,' she said. But inside her heart gave a lurch. As she prepared their evening meal – she wondered how long she could go on living this lie. If Johnny was innocent, and really doing work for the British, then she was treating him in a way that she would hate to be treated herself. Was all her animosity towards him unfounded?

She watched him covertly, knowing the golden glow she had for him had long since fallen from her eyes, and now she saw him only as a manipulative man who was too self-obsessed to think of anyone else. The sheer business of sharing a life with him, of keeping up the pretence was exhausting.

That night he didn't reach for her. His desire for sex had evaporated almost immediately after she'd moved in.

The next day when he told her he was going to the library again, she said, 'Finished with those already? You were only there a few days ago and you've barely started them.'

'I lost interest,' he said. 'It's the war, and the fact my job keeps changing. It makes me restless, but I need something else to distract me. I thought history would be the answer, but it's not. I'll go and change them for something else. I'll be back in time to get to the studio this afternoon.'

Lilli saw him thrust the books into his briefcase and dash out. *He's even tenser than before*, she thought. It was like he bristled with some sort of static electricity, a red fuzz that spiked around him. She lifted a corner of the blackout blind to watch him stride down the road, but fearing he'd see her, dropped it back. There was something furtive about the way he kept looking back over his shoulder. So he was working for the Special Operations Executive, was he? She'd soon see.

On impulse, she grabbed a jacket and hurried out of the door.

She'd watch where he went. Go in the café opposite and see if he really did go to the library.

The day was bright with a cool breeze and she fastened her jacket buttons as she went. Too much wind for a hat. The 57 double-decker bus to town would be along any moment, and she'd try to catch up with him that way. There was an older woman there waiting in the shelter, string bag over her arm, but no sign of Bren, so he must have walked.

She was just on time, for here was the green bus lumbering around the corner. She stuck her hand out for it to stop, paid her fare to the conductress, then after pressing the bell for it to go, she hauled herself up the narrow metal stairs to the top deck.

She sat down behind a man in blue mechanic's overalls and wound the ticket stub round and round her fingers. The bus ground into motion. They had only gone about a half mile when she saw Bren marching along the pavement. To her dismay, he hailed the bus. She turned away, hiding her face.

How the hell would she explain what she was doing? She could say she wanted to go to the hairdresser, perhaps. Some innocuous excuse.

But to her relief, he didn't come upstairs, so he must be sitting down below.

She'd have to wait until the stop after the library to get off, or he'd see her. When she heard the bell ding for the library stop, she stood, but clung to the rail at the top of the stairs. To her surprise, Bren didn't get off. She went to peer out of the window. Was she mistaken?

She waited on the bus watching each stop. Still he didn't get off. Finally, she saw him alight just at the edge of town. She scrambled down the stairway to the door, just as the bus was leaving.

'Oh sorry!' she said. 'I nearly missed my stop.'

The conductress yelled to the driver, who braked again, and Lilli jumped off as it was still moving. By now Bren was about a hundred yards behind her. She nipped smartly across the road and behind a parked van.

He hadn't seen her, but her blood was still pounding in her ears. Holding her breath, she crouched out of sight hearing his footsteps slap past and turn down a side street into a quiet cul-de-sac. Peering around the privet hedge on the corner, she saw him walk purposefully down the street to where there was a row of three prefabricated garages behind some red-brick semi-detached houses. He seemed to know exactly where he was going, and went to open one of the double doors of the middle garage. She watched his dark figure disappear inside.

When he emerged again after about ten minutes he was in a hurry, glancing feverishly from side to side, his face set into a mask. In one hand there was a weighty holdall that he hadn't had before. He rested it on the ground as he fumbled to make the door stay shut, finally aiming a hard push. It still gaped open but he didn't wait. He was still scanning the street as he set off again, hurrying, straining to carry the bag. About halfway down the street he stopped, put the bag down, and rubbed his face. In that moment she saw something she'd never seen in Bren's face before – fear.

She knew it would look odd, her following him, so she ducked down behind the privet hedge out of sight. His footsteps came past, and he was moving fast, as if he was running away. Once the footsteps had passed again, she gradually stood up.

As she was watching, a man on a motorbike veered out of another side street. The bike let out a cloud of exhaust smoke as it shot past her, making her wince and step back into the hedge. It was a different sound from Neil's, more like a black roar.

Soon as the air had cleared, she turned to walk down to the garage, curious as to what Bren might have been doing in there. She'd seen no sign of anyone else, so she guessed the lock-up must be empty. The green paint on the double doors was peeling and grass sprouted out of cracks in the concrete base. The corrugated asphalt roof was rust-stained and full of dead moss. Warily she glanced back to see if the owner of the garage might wonder what she was doing there. She supposed, if anyone asked, she could say she was Johnny's fiancée.

She pulled the door further open to let the lozenge of sunlight inside.

No car. That was her first thought. And a smell. Something putrid that made her gag.

But then the draught from the door caught something that was slowly revolving, hanging from the rafters.

A man's face, bloated, eyeballs white. A shoe on the ground.

Her first reaction was to slam the door shut.

She was panting with fright. She must be mistaken. She steeled herself to open the door again.

There was no mistaking it. That was the smell. A man, hanging by the neck. Obviously dead.

She fought back nausea, shut the door again.

Who was he?

What had Bren got to do with it?

Think, woman, think.

She must find a telephone. She ran first one way, then the other. No phone box.

Should she fetch the police? An ambulance? From the smell, he'd been dead a few days. But what could she say she was doing there? Maybe Bren had gone for the police. Yes, that must be what was happening. That was why he was walking away so quickly, to fetch help.

But so far nobody had come. And he had taken a holdall from there.

Lilli walked back to the corner, but the garage remained silent and still behind her.

She waited about five more minutes, gripping her handbag to stop her hands shaking. Finally, she plucked up courage to walk up to the middle of the three houses and knock.

'Yes?' The door opened. An elderly man, stomach like a sack, in collarless shirt and braces.

'Is that your garage? The middle one in the block?'

He looked at her through narrowed shifty eyes. 'Why? What's it to you?'

'You own it?' she insisted.

'I rent it to a man to store some stuff. Is there a problem?'

'What's his name? Is it Mr Murphy?' Was Bren renting it for some reason?

'Nah. Mr Estofal. Man from the Ministry of Health, he said. Needs to store his health and safety stuff there. He's an inspector, lives in a flat around the corner. Why? What's it to do with you?'

'Can you repeat his name?'

The landlord obliged. Estofal. A name she'd never heard of. She took a deep breath. 'Sorry, but I think he's dead.'

A frown of disbelief.

'I was looking for someone else, and I went in by mistake … and … maybe you should go and take a look.'

She left him staring after her as she hurried away.

'Wait, miss!'

She didn't want to get involved, and she didn't want Bren to be involved either. She'd done what she could.

Breaking into a run, she turned out of the cul-de-sac and headed for the town. She had to get away from there. So many unanswered questions. And the stench still hung in her nose.

Her side was crippled with a stitch by the time she got to the high street. She pushed her way into the Blue Door Café and ordered a coffee, strong and black. She knew she looked dishevelled, her face red and sweaty.

She paid with her ration card, added a spoon of sugar (two points extra), then took a gulp of coffee and forced it down. The man's face kept appearing in her mind. A suicidal man. Who was this Estofal, and what had he to do with Bren? Why was Bren lying to her about going to the library?

284

She needed an excuse as to where she'd been. So after she'd calmed down she went to buy a few things, though she felt guilty, wondering if the dead man had a family, whether the paunchy man in the house had gone to the garage and found the body. But with her brown-paper packages of four ounces of rationed bread and a few paltry vegetables, she caught the bus back to the flat. Time was getting on and she'd need to change ready for the broadcast later in the day, if she could force herself to be calm enough to sing.

At the flat, the blinds were up, she noticed. Bren must be back. When she got inside, he was at the dining table reading the paper, his tie neatly knotted and a pile of books on the table. He looked unperturbed.

'I just popped out for some groceries,' she said.

'Mhmm.' A reply that showed he wasn't listening. She glanced at the books. A new selection; rambling books again. 'Did you get to the library?'

It was a foolish question, but he noticed nothing amiss, and just grunted another assent from behind his newspaper.

'We could have a walk together sometime,' she said, 'I didn't know you were keen on rambling.'

'Yes, sometime,' he said. His voice was unenthusiastic.

She went to put her shopping away in the kitchen, noticing there was no sign of the brown holdall she'd seen him take from that garage.

She went through to the bedroom, and there was no sign of it there either. On the pretext of getting changed she searched his drawers and under the bed. He still had said nothing about where he'd been that morning.

'Have you had a sandwich?' she asked, peering round the door from the hall.

'No. It took longer than I thought at the library. There was a queue.'

She turned over the books on the table. 'Don't you want a good novel?' she asked. 'Graham Greene is very good.'

'I like that stuff,' he said. 'Things about the English countryside.'

She stared at him. 'Do you have any friends round here, apart from the people at Milton Bryan?'

He started. 'What?'

'Nothing. Just, you were a long time at the library. I wondered if you'd called on a friend. Someone from the post office, maybe?'

'No. I don't keep in touch with anyone there. I told you; I wasn't there long enough.'

Or at all. His tone closed down further conversation.

He was definitely hiding something, but it could just be SOE business. She prowled the house again, looking for the brown holdall, but it was a small flat, and she couldn't see it anywhere. First a missing suitcase, now a missing holdall. Every now and then the image of the hanged man would loom up in her mind, so her chest grew tight and panicky. She would have to tell Neil. Maybe he'd think she was making this up; it sounded so bizarre.

When it was time to leave for the studio, she was still rattled by the morning's events. She was wondering if the man in braces had called the police. She turned it over and over in her mind, who Mr Estofal was and why Bren hadn't mentioned him. Perhaps he didn't want to upset her? That would be the charitable view. Or perhaps Estofal was someone that worked at Milton Bryan. Was that it? The Official Secrets Act.

At Milton Bryan, Max handed her a script and told Bren he needed to discuss his role in the evening broadcast.

She got on with looking over her broadcast sheet which Max had given her, at the lyrics of 'My Girl's Gone Bad'. After about twenty minutes Neil arrived.

She looked up from her papers as he approached.

'All set?' he asked, taking a seat next to her.

'Yes,' she said. 'I like the song. It's one I've done before, but in English.'

'Where's Johnny?'

286

'Gone with Max to the canteen.' She hesitated. 'About our conversation yesterday, can I ask you something?'

'Fire away.'

'Have you ever heard of anyone called Mr Estofal? A ministry man? Could be from the Ministry of Health? Someone from the SOE?'

He shook his head. 'The name's not familiar. Why?'

Just then Bren returned, telling Ron some story that was making them both laugh. Neil stood up straight away.

Lilli dropped her voice to a whisper. 'Nothing. Forget I mentioned it. And whatever you do, don't say a word about it to Johnny.'

Neil raised his eyebrows.

'I mean it, Neil. Don't say anything. Promise?'

Chapter 29

Bren brought the coffees to the table and put one down in front of Ron, who was reading the paper. Bren took a deep draught of the bitter brew and swallowed it. Truth be told, since seeing Estofal strung up like that yesterday, he needed some caffeine. He glanced at his cup. Not that this shit would have much caffeine in it. Probably mostly chicory.

Had Estofal hanged himself? It was made to look that way. But Bren wasn't so sure. He smelled a rat. Estofal had told him about being followed, and that had rung alarm bells in Bren's mind. He'd probably been eliminated. But by whom? The Nazis? The English?

He toyed with his spoon, juggling it between his fingers. Why would anyone kill Estofal, unless they thought he was a danger? Had he given 'them' any names beforehand? The spoon clattered to the floor and it made him jump, and his heart leap.

Ron picked up the spoon for him, and Bren willed himself to take a deep breath. He watched Ron pull his cup and saucer closer, and absent-mindedly dunk his biscuit, as he pored over the back page sports.

Bren steadied himself. No reason the plan for Aspidistra couldn't still go ahead. It was what Pfalzgraf would expect, and he sure as hell didn't want to end up like Estofal. *Get to Aspidistra. Do your job.*

'Hey, Ron,' he said, 'Max says you're from the north of England. Which team d'you support? Blackpool?'

'You're kidding!' Ron was scathing. 'Waste of space. The first division's up the spout. Blackpool's ground's been taken over by the Air Raid Patrol folk. They even put in a blooming barrage balloon. No. I stick with the third division friendlies – Oldham Athletic and Rochdale. But my main interest is rugby. Used to be in the Rochdale Hornets before the war.'

'Really?' Bren had no interest in football or rugby. 'I'm a Liverpool fan myself.' Sounded plausible though – everyone knew about the close ties to Ireland through Liverpool. 'Your rugby team any good?'

'You've not heard of the Hornets?'

'Of course I've heard of them. But I suppose they had to stop, like everything else.'

'Yeah. It's a bugger. I've not been home for months. I'm stuck here. Mind you, I wouldn't do any other job but this. I worry what I'll do when this lot's over. When we've won, I mean.' Bren's face must have looked blank. 'When the Germans surrender.'

Bren hadn't thought that far ahead. Now he was forced to consider the idea of Britain and Ireland under German control. He didn't much like it. But then again, he didn't like Ireland being under English control. Which would be worse?

Ron had stood up, so Bren followed him out of the door and along the narrow tarmac path to the studio entrance.

He wanted the English taught a lesson. That they couldn't just go around riding roughshod over everyone as if they had a God-given right. If the Germans would do that then he was all for it.

'I guess if the war ends we'll all be redundant,' Bren said, hurrying to catch him up. 'And I'll miss my chance to see the biggest transmitter in the world. I find it all fascinating. It's really

289

opened my eyes. I knew nothing about radio before, now it's like I've opened the door into a magic cave.'

'Really?' Ron grinned and stopped walking. 'You've caught the bug! Just like I did.'

'You know what I hate? The thought of this place being shut down. But most of all, missing seeing the transmitter in action. The Aspidistra. They'll probably de-commission it once it's over. I'd like to see it working, while it's still sending my voice all over Germany. Something to tell my old ma in Ireland when I get home. Have a proper guided tour.' His ma had been dead a long time, but never mind.

Ron almost blushed. His freckled cheeks grew red and shiny. 'I said before, I'll take you sometime, if you like.' He set off walking again.

'I'm free this weekend.'

Ron hesitated. 'I meant when the war's over. I wasn't thinking—'

'Oh go on. I'd love to see it. Lilli said you gave her a tour.'

'But that was in the beginning. I told you before, you'd need a pass. They've got really picky about who goes in and out.'

'Come on, it would be fun.' He slapped him on the shoulder.

Ron was not good at resisting pressure. He gave a shake of his head but it wasn't very certain.

'Go on, everyone else has seen the damn thing.' Bren kept up the intensity of his smile until Ron was forced to look away.

'I suppose I could try to arrange something,' Ron said. 'They're not keen on tourists on site though; like us, they've got work to do.'

'We won't interfere with their work, but we might not get another chance. Saturday all right? I've no broadcast Sunday, it's the God slot.'

'All right. I'll try to find a good reason and sort us out some passes, okay?'

'Ah, that'll be grand. You're a real pal,' Bren said.

*

A few days later Lilli was studying her script when Neil appeared at her shoulder. He had a flat leather case under his arm. 'Come take a walk with me?' he asked.

'Why? What's up?'

'We can't talk in here. Let's take a turn around the grounds.' If he was suggesting walking then it must be important.

She grabbed her cardigan from the back of the chair and followed his limping gait down the corridor. On the way she saw Maureen plugged into the switchboard. Maureen raised an eyebrow at her and grinned. Lilli knew it would be easy for gossip to start if she were seen with anyone but 'Johnny'.

The lawns were vibrant green and peppered with daisies. A blackbird made its sweet, piercing song. The fact it was summer was often forgotten when you were in a blacked-out studio. It looked like the sort of scene where you could picnic, were it not for the armed guards posted around the walls. Once they were out of earshot, Neil paused, leant an elbow on his stick.

'I've been through Max's archive,' Neil said, tapping his case. 'I know you said to leave it alone, but I just couldn't. I still think there's something not right with Johnny Murphy, and I worry about you every single minute. What you're getting into. So I looked into Estofal.'

Her heart lifted. So he didn't think she was just some hysterical woman who had got it all wrong. 'Go on.'

'There are two references to a man called Estofal there. Of course it's an alias. He uses several names; Pereira, Machado, Estofal. One link that came up is in connection with a sabotage of a train depot in Crewe two years ago. He got away, though several other far-right saboteurs were arrested. The other is that as Estofal, he went on the run last year. He was suspected of infiltrating the post office in Bedford and sending classified mail to the Germans. Apparently he's still in the area, which I have to say I thought was rather remiss of those in charge of policing him—'

291

'Unless of course, they were using him as bait to catch other saboteurs.'

'Are you a mind-reader? That's exactly what they're doing. I went to the police at the station and had a word with the Superintendent there. He was reluctant to speak to me at first until he'd phoned someone at the SOE to check me out. There's an undercover policeman, let's call him Bingley, set to keep an eye on him.'

'Then they'll be lucky. I think Estofal's dead.'

Neil stopped again. 'How? I mean why?'

Lilli put a hand on his sleeve. 'If I tell you, you must promise not to tell. Just like I promised not to tell anyone about your secret.'

'Okay. But let's keep walking a bit. I'll pass you some music so it doesn't look so suspicious.'

He opened the case and handed her a sheet of music before setting off to stroll again. Lilli told Neil what she'd seen in Estofal's garage and how she was following Bren, and how he'd taken a holdall from the scene.

He stopped dead. 'For God's sake, Lilli! And you haven't told anyone, or reported it?'

'I thought Bren would. And maybe he has. But he didn't bring the holdall home, and he's deliberately avoiding talking to me about any of it, and I don't know why. If he's an SOE agent, then could it have something to do with that? Is he tailing Estofal for some reason because Estofal's in the pay of the Nazis?'

Neil sighed. 'I don't know. If we see no reports of it in the news, of Estofal's death I mean, then we can be fairly certain his case is of interest to MI5 and they want it hushed up. You're sure it was him? Estofal?'

'That's what the man who owns the garage said, but I'm not sure of anything. Even whether he'd done it himself, or if it was some sort of – how d'you call it? – foul play. There was a low stool there, like it had been kicked over.'

'Good God. And you saw it?'

She didn't answer him.

'You okay?' He grabbed her by the wrist and turned her so he could look into her face.

'Just a shock. I'm fine.' She brushed it off.

He put a hand on her shoulder. 'And you say that Johnny, I mean Brendan, didn't do anything about it?'

She pressed her lips together and gave a shake of the head.

'It worries me. There's something off about the whole thing. If Johnny wasn't involved somehow, then why would he hide it from you?' Neil let out a sigh. 'Trouble with all government agencies is that the left hand never knows what the right hand is doing. We had this all the time when I worked at Baker Street. Secrecy's all very well, but when we end up keeping useful information from each other, it becomes a problem.'

'What shall we do?'

'I'll do some more digging. Find out about Estofal and get a photograph of him, a mugshot, so we can identify if it's really him. You must try and press Johnny, see if you can get any clue as to what he was doing there. Try and track down the holdall you mentioned. It might have some clues as to what's going on.'

'Will you tell Delmer?' The last thing she wanted was to cause trouble. She dreaded being sent back to the Isle of Man, especially now she had this connection with Neil.

He shook his head. 'It could be bona fide SOE business, and I know better than to interfere. But I'll keep at it behind the scenes.'

'I can't tell you what a relief that is. I thought you'd given up on me. That you thought I was imagining it all.'

'You thought that?' He looked stricken. 'No. I just wanted to tread carefully to keep you safe. In case you got hurt.'

He was looking at her with soft eyes. She wished she could reach out to touch him, but knew that people could be watching, and news of an affair with Neil would certainly make it look like he had an ulterior motive for accusing Bren.

293

Neil seemed to read her mind. 'We'll get him eventually. Stay strong.'

*

Neil hurried to fetch his motorbike. Who was Estofal, and did he have something to do with the Special Operations Executive like Johnny?

There was nothing for it, he'd have to call his old contact Beauclerk at Baker Street and ask him. Tom wouldn't be any use; he wouldn't be senior enough to have access to old MI5 files. He'd have time to ring before the evening broadcast if he opened the throttle. But he didn't want to use one of the phones at Milton Bryan or Wavendon; it was too sensitive for that. He'd have to use a public phone box.

At Mrs Littlefair's he parked the bike and saw that Ron was busy, with the bonnet open on his car. 'Hello, Ron,' he called. 'Engine trouble?'

'No. Just filling the radiator. I'm taking a long trip over the weekend and I want to make sure she doesn't overheat.'

'Sounds great. Going somewhere nice?'

He banged the hood shut. 'Just a drive.' He didn't meet Neil's eye. 'Johnny and I are going on a jaunt. Getting out into the country.'

'You and Johnny?' He couldn't keep the incredulity from his voice.

Ron looked even more shifty. 'Yeah. We get on well. He's interested in broadcasting.'

'Probably because he's an actor.' His tone came out more barbed than he intended.

'No … I think it's not about getting acting work. He seems pretty interested in everything we're doing here. The technical side of broadcasting. Says he wants to work in radio when this show's over.'

'Really? I thought he might go back to Ireland.'

'I suppose he might. If Lilli wants to. He's never mentioned it to me, though.'

Neil raised his hand in farewell and let himself in. Max was there at the dining-room table with a sandwich.

'Ron's outside fixing his car,' Neil said.

'I know,' Max said, without looking up. 'He's taking Johnny on an outing tomorrow.'

'Aren't you going too?'

'I wasn't invited.' The words sounded bitter.

'Have you fallen out?'

Max looked up. 'With Ron? No.' He chewed his lip a moment. 'But Johnny's a pain. He was ignoring Ron when he first came, as if Ron was beneath his notice. Now he's all over him. But I think it's because Ron has a car. He's not interested in Ron. He just sees him as a free ticket.'

'Guess you're not Johnny's biggest fan.'

'You can't talk though. I can practically feel the daggers between you and him.'

'Rubbish. I treat him like everyone else.'

Max gave a snort of derision. 'By avoiding him, you mean? He's good at his job, I'll say that much for him. What does Lilli see in him? He blows hot and cold. At the beginning he was stuck to her like a rash. Now he's living with her he barely acknowledges her existence. There's something odd about him, he picks people up when it suits him, then drops them. Now he's doing it to Ron and it makes my blood boil.'

'Ron'll see through him if he pretends to know anything about radio.'

'I'm not so sure. Look at Delmer. He thinks the sun shines out of Johnny's arse. The intrusion broadcasts have been a massive success, so old Johnny-boy can do no wrong.'

'Where are they going, Ron and Johnny?'

'Ron's taking him to see Aspidistra.'

Neil felt something cold wash over him. If Johnny Murphy

was an enemy agent, and not working for the SOE, that was the worst possible idea. He'd have to try to stop them, if he could. But first, he'd have to try Beauclerk, and pump him about Estofal – a conversation he didn't relish, because Beauclerk was so war-weary, it was like wading through sludge.

He set off for the telephone box, pondering. Was Johnny working for the SOE? Now he thought about it more clearly, it seemed unlikely. Neil had been at Baker Street, knew how they operated. Why on earth would they send someone all the way down here? It didn't add up.

Now someone was dead, and it made him fearful for Lilli.

When Beauclerk's secretary put Neil through, Beauclerk's voice sounded raspy as hell. 'Better be something important,' he said. 'I was just about to go home.'

'I need to know all you can tell me about two men – Johnny Murphy and a man called Estofal. They could both be working for the Abwehr.'

'Ah yes, Theodor Estofal. Not a name you'd forget. Someone's already been to see me about him. Someone from MI5. Thought he was something to do with us, so I did some digging. Apparently Estofal did himself in, only a few days ago. Is it about that? I can't say I'm surprised. He got caught stealing mail.'

'And?'

'Sacked from the GPO last year. But get this—' A cough, and a sound like Beauclerk couldn't get his breath. 'MI5 got the police in, and Estofal was charged, but only with petty theft. Got a suspended sentence and a discharge. Fishy, isn't it, such a light sentence? Now I hear he's been under government surveillance a while. Only found out this week though that he's …' he cleared his throat, 'no longer with us.'

'What about Murphy? Brendan Murphy alias Johnny Murphy.'

'No. Not ringing any bells. Give me twenty-four hours though, I might come up with something.'

*

At the same time as Neil was talking to Beauclerk, Bren was in the public telephone box just down the road from his apartment. That morning a postcard had arrived in a sealed envelope with the simple message: *EGD 7601*. A phone number. At last, Estofal's demise had prompted some action.

'Edgware 7601?' The voice sounded like Harper's.

'Murphy,' Bren said.

A brief pause. 'Black Bull. Seven o'clock. Contact will say, "How's Jane?" You answer, "Fine."' The line went dead.

*

At just before seven, Bren was in the bar of the Black Bull, propping up the counter, and expecting to see Harper or Green. He'd been there only a few minutes when a short, dark man approached, and clapped him on the shoulder like an old friend. 'How's Jane?' he asked.

They went through the contact ritual.

'What're you having, mate? Guinness?'

The Irish drink. This'd definitely be his contact. 'I've got one already,' Bren said, but waited for the other chap to get his half a Guinness, before they walked to a quiet corner.

There, Bren was able to get a better look at his 'friend'. He was a younger man with the stooped shoulders of a clerk, and greasy collar-length hair over a sports jacket.

'You can call me Barry,' he said in an undertone. 'Harper sent me. Said to tell you to cease activity immediately. Our recently deceased Portuguese friend was supposed to be running all sorts of networks here. Turns out he was unreliable.'

'What?'

'Estofal's dead.'

Bren feigned shock.

'But it's worse.' Barry glanced round to check they were alone in the room. 'He had no network, no contacts except you and

297

Harper, who had no idea that all the information he was ferrying back to Germany from Estofal was a pack of lies. He'd invented networks, contacts that didn't exist, sabotage that never happened, you name it. Told the Abwehr what they wanted to hear. It was a cushy number – until they sent you. And then he had to actually do the real job. And he just wasn't up to it.'

'Jesus, Mary and Joseph. Let me get my head around this … but he took information from me to … you know who, and gave me instructions. Instructions I'm now acting on.'

Barry lowered his voice further. 'I know. Thing is, we don't know which of his instructions are real, and which are fake. Which of his contacts are real and which are fake. It seems he invented stuff when he felt like it, anything to keep the big boys happy.'

'So who killed him?'

'He killed himself, we think. He'd made one or two cock-ups that were hard to get out of, and he knew Pfalzgraf had rumbled him.'

'He asked me if I could get him out to Ireland.'

'And we don't know, but we suspect the cops had their suspicions and were following him. That's why you've got to stop. His neighbour reported he'd hanged himself and after that, the Special Branch were round there like a shot. They've got access to his house now, and they're combing through it.'

Bren didn't tell him he'd got the stuff from his garage.

'But the thing is,' Barry said, 'we don't know what's in the house or his lock-up. So whatever you're doing, you've to stop, because the whole thing's an unholy mess, and Pfalzgraf needs to set up a more reliable line of command.'

Bren tightened his hands into fists. 'Stop? So in that case, how the hell do I know you're who you say you are?'

'You ever been to a betting shop in Birmingham? Name of O'Donnell?'

'Okay, okay. I believe you. So what do I do now?'

'Nothing. You've to await further instructions.'

Bren felt his heart begin to race. He leant in to whisper urgently, 'But I'm in the middle of a sabotage op! It's tomorrow. I've got everything I need. Estofal was supposed to have arranged the getaway.'

'I've been instructed to tell you only one thing – sit tight and do nothing until we can work out what's good information and what's not, and if Estofal had any other contacts. Contacts on the wrong side.' He downed the rest of his Guinness in one long gulp, stood, and said, 'See ya, mate.'

And he was out of the door before Bren had time to protest.

Bren sat there staring at his glass, his fists curling and uncurling. He couldn't stop now. It was all sorted. Everything was ready. Ron was going to pick him up and get him in to Aspidistra. He's psyched himself up for it, and he was pretty sure Pfalzgraf wouldn't object if he blew the mast sky high. The only questions were, who else knew about it, and if he could get out of there. He'd have to make some sort of contingency.

But he sure as hell hadn't done all this prep for nothing.

Chapter 30

Lilli had searched the whole flat for the holdall but found nothing. It was only in the last few minutes that she had the idea to search outside. There was a potting shed supposedly used by Mr Barrett the landlord, though he seemed to take no interest in it. The key to it was in the kitchen drawer, along with the key to the greenhouse, the outside coal store and the privy. She grabbed the keys and moments later she was searching the coal shed. Nothing but coke and dust. Greenhouse next. Nothing amongst the plant pots and propagation boxes, though she opened the cardboard boxes under the workbench, but there was no sign of it.

The potting shed. Last chance. She turned the rusty key in the lock, but it turned more easily than she'd imagined. She moved aside several stacked tea chests with terracotta plant pots, and an old tin watering can. Feeling like a thief, she heaved one aside, but there was nothing beneath but more beer crates full of pots. She hauled out an old carpet with a roll of bird-netting on top of it and peered underneath.

Bingo. The holdall.

A heavy-duty canvas one, with leather straps and a good strong zip. So Bren was definitely hiding it for some reason. But why? And what if he came back for it?

She grabbed it by the handles and lugged it out onto the concrete floor. It was heavy, as if it had metal bars inside and banged against her legs. It was dirty, and the handles were oily. She was scared she'd find guns or knives in it. Some sort of murder weapon.

Warily, she unzipped it and let the bag fall open. At the bottom, lengths of metal pipe. Two packs of taped stuff – could be sand, or drugs, or something soft and powdery in hemp bags. A bunch of wiring. Random lengths, with a soldering iron and flux in a separate screw-top jar. Wire clippers, and what looked to be a charge. And then something in what looked like a metal biscuit tin.

She prised it open.

A portable radio. She recognised it instantly. The transmitter was built around a single KL2 tube valve. But Bren had protested he knew nothing about radio.

She took out the components piece by piece. Could probably be crystal-operated as well as free-running. There was a battery here and wire antennae and what looked to be a type of Morse key that her father had shown her.

It was then that realisation dawned. It was too familiar. This was a German set. The spare valve was in Telefunken packaging. Not an English set at all, but a German set. Probably made by the Abwehr.

Was this Estofal's set? Was Bren spying *on* him, or *for* him?

Hastily she pushed all the parts back, only then realising that Bren might have checked the contents himself and he'd guess someone else had been looking inside.

Carefully she started again and put everything back piece by piece exactly where she had found it. A further search under the old carpet revealed the missing suitcase. She didn't open it. She was too scared of the time it would take. Her footprints were clearly visible in the earth around the shed, so she scuffed at it with the toe of her shoe, trying to make it appear as if no one had tampered with it.

She wasn't stupid. The radio was something used by a spy, and the other stuff in the bag looked like sabotage equipment. Was Estofal a saboteur? She had no more time to wonder, for though her blood was almost fizzing with adrenalin, the bus to Milton Bryan was due and it was time to go to work and do her job on air. Bren would already be there. He was supposed to be jumping in for a German announcer during a raid over Hamburg. British bombers were due to drop a payload of bombs over the German city in retribution for the dreadful attack on Birmingham near the beginning of the Blitz. No one in England had ever forgotten it. This was in retaliation; the first of several night attacks to show the Allies might.

Hurriedly, she washed her hands and dressed. By the time she'd caught the bus to the studio, and sorted her thoughts, she'd understood for certain Bren was working for the Nazis. Because he hadn't reported Estofal's death. Had kept it to himself. And the radio meant he'd be able to contact the Germans at any time, in fact probably had been doing it ever since he came to Milton Bryan.

The bus was late and she had to run breathless up the drive and into the studio where they were all already waiting for her. She entered in a daze, and stopped inside the door, half in, half out of her jacket. Of course. She should have seen it. Estofal must have been Bren's contact and perhaps it was his radio. No wonder Bren was clearing everything out; he had to do it before the police came looking. It was obvious now she'd seen it.

In the studio she was distracted, with one eye on Bren and the other on trying to rehearse and do her job. Now she looked at him with loathing. But at least he had to stick to the script here. If he didn't, they'd soon have him locked in the POW cell.

The routine for broadcast was pretty smooth by now, and it all went off without a hitch. Bren was impersonating both the captain of a U-Boat off Norway, and then later, German High Command once their airwaves went dead.

She had to admire his skill. She watched the bulging tendons on the side of his neck as he ranted into the microphone.

You're a traitor. The thought was so clear, it made her inhale sharply. They were both playing games, and the games had become too real. Everything between them had just been a smoke screen to get her to keep quiet about his real name and his links to the Abwehr.

She'd have to go to Delmer.

As soon as the recording lights were off, she marched out of the studio and rapped on Delmer's office door. No answer. She knocked again.

Max brushed past her in the corridor. 'Oh Lilli, Delmer's not here today, he and his wife have gone up to London to some fancy dinner at the BBC.'

She turned away frustrated. She'd have to speak to Neil.

'What are you doing?' Bren was striding towards her.

'I just wanted a word with Delmer.'

'What about?'

'Just to talk through the sort of music we're doing,' she said brightly. *Don't blow it at the last minute.* 'Which numbers are most popular.'

'Whatever you sing sounds good to me,' he said. The sharpness had faded from his eyes. She guessed she'd appeased him with the right answer. 'Let's get home,' he said. 'We're in time for the bus.'

She held herself together. One more night. She could manage one more night until she could speak to Delmer. They walked together out of the building arm in arm, and through the main gate and onto the road. There Bren dropped her arm.

It's just an act, she thought. *It always has been.*

There were two others at the bus stop, so they didn't speak. She was on tenterhooks. Once on board the bus, Bren turned to her and said, 'Ron's taking me out tomorrow in his car. I hope that's all right.'

'With Ron?' She replied on automatic. 'Yes, of course it's fine.'

Thank goodness. She'd be able to talk to Neil; maybe get in touch with Delmer.

'Ron's got to do some work in London. We'll leave early, have a bit of a pub lunch, play a game of darts. But I'll be back late. And Ron said to bring an overnight bag in case he has too much to drink and doesn't want to drive.'

An overnight bag. And what about the one in the shed?

'What will you do with your day?' he asked.

Think. 'There's a jumble sale in the village hall and I thought I'd try to get some second-hand fabric for curtains.' She was burbling, trying to cover her confusion.

'What a good idea. It'll cheer the place up. I'll be going early. About eight.'

'Can Ron get petrol coupons? I thought they wouldn't let you use them for leisure. Is it for work?'

'Yes. Delmer set it up.'

Delmer, who was out at a fancy dinner at the BBC.

Feigning exhaustion, she turned in almost immediately, but Bren didn't sleep as he usually did. She felt him toss and turn on the other side of the bed, and get up several times in the night. Lilli too was restless, a deep underlying tension. What should she do about the holdall? She must cycle over to Simpson and show it to Neil before telling Delmer. Get some moral support.

In the morning she began to cook breakfast as usual, and saw that Bren had his good raincoat ready and a bulky overnight bag by the door. The paperboy had already been and the newspaper was on the table.

She glanced at the headline as the egg boiled. 'Looks like the raid on Hamburg was a success,' she said.

'I don't see how you can see anything as a success when it flattens a whole city.'

She ignored his snappy manner and put the single rationed egg in his eggcup, barely able to breathe for tension. She watched Bren eat his bran flakes and a boiled egg, unhurried and methodical in his usual routine. The clock ticked on the wall, in sharp staccato dots like full stops. Bren stood up and put his raincoat over his arm. 'I'll wait for the car outside. Don't want to wake the Barretts below if they're having a lie in.'

It was this air of normality that finally made her snap. Suddenly, she couldn't bear it any more. The skin of reality was splitting and she could see the dark spaces beneath. She thrust his hat at him in an angry gesture. 'Bren?'

'What?'

'You've never cared about me, have you?' She slid the ring from her finger and held it out on her palm. 'It was all an act.'

A sigh of impatience. 'There's no time for this now. I know it's difficult, me being away from home—'

'Did you tell the Brownshirts where we lived?'

His face froze.

'In Berlin.' Now she was calm. She placed the ring deliberately on the sideboard. 'You did, didn't you? When they came for my father I was in the next room. I heard them say that you had given them our address. "Der Irländer" they called you.'

'No, you're imagining it. You're just overwrought.'

'And what about Mr Estofal. Am I imagining him?'

He took a step back. 'I don't know who you mean,' he said. But his eyes were suddenly dark as pinpricks – hard; calculating.

'The man who hanged himself in the garage. He was your contact, wasn't he?'

He took a step nearer to her, threatening. 'How do you know that?' He grabbed her shoulder.

'I followed you. Saw him hanging there.'

'You did what?' He let go, shoved her away.

'You heard me. I watched you come out of his garage – and you never said a word.'

'Was it you? Did you fetch the police?' He took a step towards her again. 'You fool. You've ruined everything.'

305

'No. But I couldn't believe you'd just leave that poor man hanging there—'

'Estofal was a clown. He thought he could hoodwink the Gestapo. He had it coming.'

'It's over, Bren.' She steadied her voice. 'I can see through your lies. I have ever since the beginning.'

'Over? It was never anything anyway. You think I'd marry you?' He gave a derisory laugh. 'You flatter yourself.'

'You bastard. Because of you they've taken my father God knows where. D'you know how it feels, to not know if I'll ever see him again?'

'Then you're better off than me. My father is dead. Machine-gunned in the back by the English for nothing, except being a Catholic.'

'So you think that excuses it? An eye for an eye, is it? You gave us away, knowing what they'd do to us.'

'It's not personal. The Party view it as a cleansing process. Just like the Irish would like to be cleansed of the English. After today—' His voice was interrupted by the pip of a horn outside. Ron, come to pick him up.

Not personal. After her father had been rounded up like a beast? The words echoed in her head.

'Don't you dare run out on me!' She tried to stop him as he snatched his overnight bag, but he pushed her so hard on the shoulder that she stumbled back into the wall. By the time she caught her breath, the door had slammed behind him.

She raced to the bedroom to look out of the window, and saw the wardrobe gaped open. He'd taken most of his clothes, three pairs of shoes, and his best suit. It floored her.

The bastard. He was doing a runner.

She banged furiously on the window, as he emerged from the shed, the canvas holdall in his hands. No! That was her evidence.

Another pip of the horn.

Sprinting to where the stairs led down the back of the house, she almost leapt down them, screaming, 'Ron! Wait!' but the car was already accelerating away.

She stood breathless on the pavement, uncertain what to do. She was about to run to the phone box to call the police when Neil's motorcycle shot around the corner into her drive in a flurry of dust.

He ripped off his goggles and leather helmet. 'Lilli. I need to talk to you.'

'I know. Bren's working for the Germans,' she said breathlessly. 'He's gone out with Ron and he's got a holdall with him with an Abwehr radio.'

'Slow down,' he said. 'What's this about a radio?'

'It's a signal radio, a German one. He took an overnight bag too. Said he and Ron were going to London; that they might stay over, but he took an overnight bag and all his clothes are gone.'

Neil blinked. 'But Ron didn't take a bag. He said he'd be back very late this evening. I tried to dissuade him from taking Bren to Aspidistra. Said it was off limits.'

'Aspidistra? Bren said they were going to London!'

'I tried to stop him, but Ron thought I was just being an obnoxious manager, and said Mr Robin had given it the okay. Ron's flattered Bren is so interested in Aspidistra.'

'Of course! Because Bren's working for the Abwehr.'

They looked at each other a moment, the weight of implication sinking in.

'And listen to this,' Neil said. 'I called some SOE friends. Bren's nothing to do with them. So I rang the newspaper archive, the registrar of births, marriages, and deaths. It seems Bren's impersonating his cousin. The real Johnny's still at home in Ireland, completely oblivious. But get this – Beauclerk just got back to me, and Brendan Murphy's name came up – to do with a bombing in Birmingham.'

'I don't understand. Who's Beauclerk?'

'My old boss. He called me in a funk at the crack of dawn. Brendan Murphy's linked to a sabotage unit of the IRA.'

'You're joking.'

'An IRA bomb,' he insisted. 'The Irish Republican Army.'

'Yes, yes, I know who they are.' She stood still. Sabotage. Bren still had the holdall with him. Everything in it suddenly made sense.

She tried to interrupt, but Neil was continuing, the words spilling breathless from his mouth. 'I'd no idea the Nazis had links to the IRA until I spoke to Beauclerk. Murphy's not one of our agents. He's one of theirs.'

Lilli swallowed. 'He's got a gun; he keeps it in the suitcase. Not in the house. And bomb-making equipment. At first I thought it was all to do with the radio. But there was a battery, and a tube with wires and an alarm clock.'

His face grew hollow. 'Shit. Aspidistra's fully staffed. What can we do?'

'Get hold of Delmer? Tell him to get someone on the guard-house to search them as they're going in. Tell them Johnny Murphy's armed and to arrest him.'

Neil was already poised to run. 'Quick. Where's the nearest phone?'

She pointed. Before she could move, Neil charged towards the telephone box in a lop-sided, painful run. She yelled after him, 'His London number. Delmer's in London!' By the time she got to the phone box, Neil was red with sweat and pain and was dialling and fumbling in his pocket for coins.

He shook his head. *No answer*, he mouthed at her through the glass.

'Hold on a bit longer,' she said, willing Delmer to pick up.

But eventually he had to give up. 'No go,' he yelled from the door.

She watched him dial 999, thrust coins in, and speak rapidly into the receiver.

'I called the police,' he said, 'but the woman on the other end sounded dozy, like it was some sort of hoax. She said to wait at the box and they'll call me back.'

A groan of frustration. 'We can't wait. Who else?' she asked, in a panic. 'Max?'

'No use. A foreigner like him won't have access to anyone high up enough.'

'But we have to do something. Bren's armed. What if he threatens Ron?'

'How big was this pipe with the wires?'

She held out her hands to about a foot's span.

Neil shook his head, his face pale. 'God, he could blow the place sky high. There's nothing for it, I'll get on their tail, try to overtake, warn the guards. Here – the number for Delmer. Keep trying, and wait for the police to call back.' He began to scribble something on a piece of paper.

'No. I'm coming with you. Delmer might be away all day. We need to get to Aspidistra.'

'You'll slow me down,' he said.

'I don't care how fast you go. It's a long shot, but I might be able to talk to Bren. Convince him to stop what he's doing. And I can run fast, which as you've just found out, you can't.'

Neil threw up his hands, which seemed to mean yes.

They sprinted breathlessly back to the motorbike, where Neil thrust his scarf into her hands, then lowered his goggles over his face as he kick-started the beast. Scarf firmly wrapped over her nose and mouth, she jumped up behind him. They were roaring down the street before she realised she hadn't even locked the door, and her handbag was still on the bed.

'Do you know the way?' she yelled into his ear.

But there was no answer as he tore down the road. Fortunately there was little traffic because leisure driving wasn't allowed, and although the war didn't stop on Friday nights, weekends were always quieter. She was terrified the bike would get another flat tyre, and prayed they wouldn't get stopped, for what possible excuse could they give, that didn't sound barking mad?

They'd gone about forty bone-shaking miles when Neil veered into a petrol station.

The attendant came out in his overalls, but Neil said he'd do it himself. Obviously he was taking no chances with the fuel tank. He had his identity card and some extra coupons because of his disability, and they were able to fill up the tank. Lilli got off to stretch her legs a moment. Her back ached, and her thighs shook too, from gripping on. The young attendant seemed to take an age with the coupons.

Come on, come on. She willed him to hurry. 'How far do you think we are behind them?' she asked, hopping from foot to foot.

'Dunno. Ron's a steady driver, but this old thing's not as fast as a car, so even though we're pushing it, it will be another few hours in the saddle, I'm afraid.'

She wiped the grit and grime from her face and prepared to cling on again.

*

As Ron drove, Bren was mentally going through the arrangements he'd made with Jim Sheridan, the taxi driver Estofal had said he'd contact. Of course Estofal hadn't done it, so Sheridan had to be bribed on the telephone, with the promise of a crisp pound note and no questions asked, to wait, then take him to O'Donnell's in Birmingham. Bren had never met the man, but had to trust he'd be waiting with a getaway car on the other side of Ashdown Forest in an access road used only by loggers. If not, it would be a scramble across country.

Ron was keen to make a running commentary on every car on the road – its make and model and how many miles it did to the gallon. Bren let the fool prattle on as he ran through in his head the minutiae of what he had to do.

He cracked his knuckles as the car dawdled along. He wished Ron would drive faster; it made him grind his teeth the way Ron did everything at a snail's pace. Frustratingly his mind kept going back to Lilli. It griped at him that she'd uncovered his agenda. He'd thought himself too clever to be outwitted by a woman like her and it had upset his equilibrium.

'Shall we stop for lunch?' Ron asked.

'What?' It took Bren a moment to realise he was being asked a question.

'Lunch? My legs are stiff.'

'No, let's press on. More time looking at the transmitter then. Why don't we share the driving? You can navigate as you know the way.'

'I'm all right to carry on. If you're sure you're not hungry?'

'Had a big breakfast. And I fancy a drive of this, she's a beauty.'

Ron was reluctant, but Bren kept insisting. And now it meant he, Bren, had got the car keys in his possession. Very useful indeed. Bren smiled, and put his foot down hard on the accelerator.

*

On the road to Aspidistra, Lilli almost fell off when the motorbike skidded to a stop at the gate, in a cloud of dust and grit. She stuck out a foot to keep her balance.

The soldier at the gate stepped in front of the barrier. 'Can I help you?' he asked politely.

Neil took off his goggles. 'We're friends of Ron Bottomley. Has he arrived yet?'

'He forgot something and we want to give it to him,' Lilli called.

'Mr Bottomley's already inside, and I'm afraid I can't let you in without a pass.'

'We didn't have time to sort one out, and it's an emergency. But here are our identity cards.' Neil signalled Lilli to get hers out.

Oh Lord. Her stomach sank. It was still in her handbag. 'I

can't,' she hissed at him, 'I was in such a hurry I left it in my bag at home.'

The guard eyed her with suspicion. She realised her slight accent was cause for concern.

'I'll vouch for her,' Neil said, bracing his shoulders. 'I'm Neil Callaghan, personnel manager at Milton Bryan, head of one of the research units that broadcast via Aspidistra.'

The guard held out his hand for the pass then beckoned over a second guard to check the pass.

'That seems in order sir,' the second guard said. 'But we still can't let the lady pass unless under the express orders of Mr Robin, or Mr Bottomley.'

'You go in without me,' Lilli said.

Neil shook his head. 'Did Ron have a friend with him, another man?' Neil asked.

'Yes, his colleague, Mr Murphy. His pass was quite in order. They arrived about fifteen minutes ago.'

'Well, if you won't let me in,' Lilli said, 'can you get on the switchboard to Ron, and get him to speak to me?'

'I can try. No guarantee we'll get him though. What did you say your name was, miss?'

'Lilli Bergen. Ron and I used to share the same lodgings.'

He stepped back into the guard house and picked up a telephone. She saw him dial 0 and then heard him ask the internal operator if someone could bring Ron to the line.

Her palms were sweating and a speck of dust in her eye meant it kept watering. She kept glancing at the doorway to the bunker, terrified she'd suddenly see the place go up.

*

Inside the underground chamber, Bren was having a tour of the base. They'd failed to check Ron's weighty box of tools and batteries, which he always carried with him. Just as well, for when they'd stopped at

312

a petrol station, on the pretext of getting a rug for his knees, Bren had carefully buried the pipe bomb and the timer, wrapped in a blue towel, at the bottom of Ron's toolkit underneath a few tools.

So now, as they strolled inside this concrete holy-of-holies, Ron's car keys on their leather fob were snug inside Bren's trouser pocket.

Bren was relaxed now he was inside the bunker. It had gone without a hitch. Now he just needed to find a place inside the Aspidistra building to conceal the device, and then he would make an excuse to leave. Feign illness perhaps, or claustrophobia and the need for some fresh air.

It was going to be hard to set the device, without Ron getting suspicious. First of all, he'd have to wangle his toolbox from him somehow, then find a place to prime the bomb.

He was getting a good idea of the layout, though he had to keep one ear on Ron's ramblings about megahertz and aerials. He glanced around the room they were in now, scanning a bank of what looked like grey, gun-metal lockers, except each had a frequency dial set into it. There were a few men in braces and shirt-sleeves working at these, standing around with headphones on.

Here, underground, it was warm and damp, an atmosphere that seemed to be made entirely of men's cigarette smoke. The engineers nodded to Ron deferentially as he sauntered by, and carried on working.

But the rack of consoles gave Bren an idea. A locker would be the ideal place to conceal the device. 'Do you have a locker here for your stuff?' he asked Ron.

'Nah. Don't bother. I'm here less frequently now, and I just tout my kit everywhere I go.' He gave it a shake, to indicate it, and Bren gritted his teeth. The wiring in the device was delicate. He didn't want to have to remake the damned thing.

Ron carried on giving his guided tour, while Bren listened with a look of intense interest. 'There are three three-hundred-foot masts, plus all the supporting masts,' Ron said, his face shiny with enthusiasm. 'Did you see as we came in, how all the supporting

313

buildings have uneven roofs or are buried under trees? That's to hide them from the Jerries' reconnaissance planes.'

'Have there been any bombings here?' He bloody hoped not.

'Nah. The ceiling's four foot thick. Reinforced concrete. Mind you, there's an evacuation procedure if there's an air raid.' He pointed down the corridor, and above the door in front of them was a sign painted in red:

EVACUATE THIS AREA IMMEDIATELY SIREN SOUNDS

Bren prayed for no siren. He was still looking for somewhere to hide the bomb. 'Are there WCs inside the bunker?'

'No, sorry. You have to go out – there are some next to the canteen, or there's a block around the back. Or the bushes opposite the front entrance, that's what we all do.'

They were now going down the main spine of the complex and into a vast generator hall. Bren mentally noted the route as they went. After all, once the timer was set, he'd have to leg it back to the car.

'Concrete walls again for blast protection,' Ron said proudly.

He smiled to himself. They wouldn't protect if the blast came from the inside.

Around the wall was a gantry with hoists for moving the heavy machinery into place. The room was a hive of activity – more than thirty people were here at desks, and the workstations were fitted with headphones and radio sets. Along one side, a row of pasty-looking secretaries hammered away, the keyboards rattling and pinging in the vast space, all illuminated by the newfangled fluorescent lights that made everyone look washed-out.

Too many people here to do anything. 'What's through there?' Bren asked, pointing at a red metal door.

'Boiler room,' Ron said. 'It's an oil-fired heating system. We need to keep the equipment at a stable temperature. Latest design, but not as reliable as the old coke ones. I had to take a look at it once, the water wasn't heating. Now it's checked regularly.' He swung the door open into a cellar-like room with several large tankers and a massive boiler roaring away. A chalkboard showed the times the boiler had been serviced. Two hourly, and only done fifteen minutes ago.

This is it. Bren smiled to himself. Close to the main hub, and the thought of all those oil tanks going up was a dream. Shame he couldn't do it at night. There'd be a lot of collateral damage. Now he just had to get rid of Ron and somehow detach him from his toolkit.

Ron was already heading for the row of desks before the sloping metal consoles which were bristling with an array of dials, knobs, and switches. Ron went over to the man sitting there in shirtsleeves and a green sleeveless pullover, and put a hand on his shoulder. The engineer started and almost jumped out of his seat, but when he saw Ron his face broke into a smile. 'Ron, old chap! Haven't seen you for ages! How's tricks?'

'Fine. Just thought I'd come and check the aerial allocators are still working. That there's no interference. This is my friend, Johnny Murphy. He's got bitten by the radio bug. Johnny, Mike.'

'Hello,' Mike said, smiling up at him briefly before sliding his headphones back on and returning to the console. He passed a second set to Ron. 'Hey, Ron, have a listen. There's something interesting here. When I tune in to this frequency,' he turned a dial, 'then the station drops out completely.'

Ron didn't need a second invitation.

As soon as they were both engrossed, Bren picked up Ron's toolkit and slipped across the concrete floor and into the boiler room. One of the men saw him go, but paid him no attention. Good, being with Ron had made him part of the furniture.

Inside the boiler room he spotted a broken metal-and-canvas chair and shoved it under the door handle to stop anyone coming in.

Kneeling, he opened the toolbox, took out all the things he needed, and began to lay them out on the floor.

*

315

Meanwhile, in the transmission hall, Ron and his friend Mike were tuned in to the diplomatic wireless service which kept dropping out of range.

'Hey, Johnny,' Ron said, turning to hand him the headset, 'have a gander—'

But Johnny was nowhere to be seen. He'd probably gone for a pee, Ron thought. He was about to put the headphones on again when one of the secretaries, Jean Briggs, came rushing up. 'Call for you sir, on the switchboard. From the gatehouse. It's urgent. Can you come?'

'For me? You sure?'

'They're insistent, sir.' Ron rubbed a hand through his hair and let out a frustrated sigh. 'Sorry, Mike, got to go,' he said. 'When Johnny comes back, tell him where I've gone, will you?'

Ron headed up the corridor, disgruntled, with Jean hurrying alongside. 'What's going on, Jean?'

'There's a Mr Callaghan and a Miss Bergen at the gate. They've got no passes and they want you to vouch for them.'

Neil and Lilli. He knew Neil disapproved of this outing. The cheek of it, thought Ron. Checking up on him on his day off.

Jean was still talking. 'They say you left something behind, and they need to hand it over.'

Ron frowned, sure he hadn't left anything. It made no sense. Still, upsetting the bosses was never worth it, and there was no harm in letting them in. Probably Lilli just wanted to keep an eye on her fiancé, he thought. Women. Always an enigma.

The girl at the switchboard passed Ron the receiver and flipped the switch for him to speak. The guard explained the story again. 'Yes, yes,' Ron said, impatient. 'Tell them to come in. I'll meet them at the entrance.'

*

Lilli and Neil made their way through the double fences towards the entrance to the bunker.

To Lilli's relief Ron was waiting just inside the door, looking harassed. 'What's up?' he asked.

'Where's Johnny?' Neil went straight in with the question.

'Gone for a pee. He'll be back soon. You can join us for lunch.'

'Listen, we need to go somewhere private to talk. Johnny's not who he says he is.'

'What?' Ron looked blank.

'A private room, Ron.'

'Okay, okay. I don't know what all this is about, but there's the engineer's room just down there on the left.' He led the way and they all hurried in.

Neil closed the door behind them. 'You need to evacuate the building. Quietly and efficiently and as soon as humanly possible. Johnny is an IRA sympathiser, probably armed with a bomb that could blow this place sky high.'

'Ha ha. You're joking, right?'

'No. Dead serious. He's a Nazi saboteur.'

'But Johnny's been with me all the time—' He stopped dead, paled. 'My toolkit. I left it …?' He looked confused.

'Where did you last see Johnny?'

'In the main transmission hall.'

'Ron, it's not a joke,' Lilli begged. 'We have to get people out. If it's a false alarm, that's better than a catastrophe. Is there an alarm?'

Ron seemed to grasp it all of a sudden and his face turned crimson. 'The air raid siren. Operated from the control room down the corridor. That's the quickest. It'll get everyone out to the shelter next door.'

'Then go.' Neil said.

Ron dithered a moment, but then seeing their tense faces set off.

A few moments later the siren began to wail. Ron came rushing back in. 'I don't know what to do. People think it's a false alarm. Nobody's moving.'

'Then we'll have to bloody well tell them to move,' Neil said. He hobbled out of the door and down the corridor. The other two followed him as he threw open each door and yelled, 'Not a drill! Get out! Quietly, quickly, just leave everything. No bags or coats, just get out.'

As he went, more worried faces began to stream past them in the corridor.

'What about Johnny?' Ron asked.

'He'll hear the siren and evacuate if he hasn't gone already. But he might have left the bomb somewhere and—'

'Shit.' Ron clapped a hand to his forehead. 'He's got my car keys.'

'Then he'll be coming out,' Neil said. 'How many exits are there?'

'Just the main entrance to the bunker and the main gate. The place is secure.'

'Then get the hell out of here.'

Ron stood stock still, his hands wringing together. His face had turned even redder under its freckles. 'The bastard. He pretended to be interested! He told me he was … Oh Christ. It's my fault. I'm not letting him blow this place up. I'm going to find him.'

'Are you mad? He's armed!' Lilli said, grabbing his arm. 'We should check everyone's out and then get out ourselves.'

'And leave this place to blow? No way.' Ron wrestled free of Lilli's grasp.

'Ron! Wait!' yelled Neil.

In the space of a breath Ron was storming down the corridor, bumping and battling past everyone coming out. Lilli dodged after him, shouting back over her shoulder, 'Neil! Go to the gates, alert the guards! Try to stop Johnny, as he comes out.'

'Lilli! Come back!' Neil's frantic cry was barely audible over the wail of the siren.

But she knew he wasn't fast enough to run after her, and she had to try to catch up with Ron before he did anything stupid.

Ron was hurling open every door as he went, searching for Johnny. His rage was like a cloud of angry red wasps, an almost visible mist. By the time Lilli caught up with him in the transmission hall it was completely empty.

318

'My kit was here,' Ron said, hand trembling, pointing at the floor.

Lilli had her hands over her ears. In here, the siren noise was deafening. A noise like blindingly blue light.

Search the place, Lilli tried to make herself heard over the siren. Anything that looks wrong.

*

Two minutes earlier, inside the boiler room, Bren had taken what he needed from Ron's bag, and checked his gun was loaded in the holster strapped under his arm. He was taking no chances with getting out of here once the thing was primed.

He checked the items on the floor again. Battery. Switch. High explosive charge. Timer. Tweezers to connect the wiring.

He found this methodical laying-out calming. He set up the device underneath the boiler itself, thus ensuring maximum explosive power. Now it was just him and the device. When it was done, he placed it gently on the floor ready to wire it to the alarm.

A sudden screeching noise disorientated him like waking from a dream.

His hand jerked. A momentary blank confusion before he realised it was a siren. Damn. An air raid? A siren test? What were they playing at?

It had to be a false alarm. Had to be.

He winced. It would be turned off in a moment. No need to worry; maybe they tested it every week.

He focused his attention into the narrow beam he needed, wiring the alarm clock to the bomb. Ten minutes should be enough. Long enough to get out, not long enough for someone to find it. He set the timer, gently ratcheting the key round. He exhaled, rose slowly with no sudden movement, and walked to the door where he gently shifted the chair from under the handle.

The siren was still blaring as he pushed open the door. He hunched his shoulders against the noise and prepared himself to walk speedily out of the bunker.

But before he could even get out into the corridor, Ron Bottomley cannoned into him.

'You bastard. You thought you could fool me, did you? Thought I was some sucker that would believe all your crap?'

'Hello, Ron,' Bren said, in a jovial voice. 'I heard the siren and thought I might be able to switch it off in here.' He shrugged, put an arm around Ron's shoulder. 'Come on, it'll be a false alarm, but we'd better get out, like everyone else.'

Ron pushed him away. 'Where is it? Don't you come the innocent with me! Callaghan's here and we know you're planning on blowing this place up.'

The instant the words were out of Ron's mouth, Bren whipped the gun out from under his jacket, lunged at Ron, and grabbed him by the arm, twisting it up his back. He pressed the gun to the side of his head and shunted him forward. 'We're going out whether you like it or not. Now walk, or I'll blow your bloody brains out.'

Pushing Ron ahead as a human shield Bren thrust him towards the door, but before they got there, the handle turned, the door opened, and Lilli's white face appeared right in front of him.

Chapter 31

Lilli saw the gun at Ron's head, and backed off into the corridor.

'Try to stop me, and he gets it,' Bren said calmly, stepping out. 'You've got about eight minutes to get out of here before the thing blows. If I were you, I'd follow us out. There's nobody left inside.'

'They won't let you get out. They know who you are. That you're Brendan Murphy, not Johnny. The guards on the gate will stop you.'

'If they do, they'll lose their best engineer. Now back off.'

Instead, she took a step towards him. 'Bren, just stop. Leave Ron alone. This is madness, you have to—'

Ron twisted then and lunged away, but a second later threw himself at Johnny's legs in a rugby tackle. Johnny crashed to the ground and the gun flew out of his hand. Lilli dived for the gun as they wrestled.

Ron sat on his chest, trying to pinion Johnny as he struggled to get up, and for a moment they tussled, until Johnny gave a grunt and threw Ron over.

Then he leapt to his feet and ran out of the door and up the corridor. Ron grabbed the gun from her hand and fired but it went wide, ricocheting off the wall in a spatter of dust. The recoil made him stumble backwards.

'Let's get out of here,' Lilli yelled over the siren's noise.

'No!' Ron was panting. He threw the gun to the floor and pointed to the boiler room. 'It must be in there somewhere. We have to disable it.'

'No! You're crazy. Eight minutes he said!' She tried to pull him away.

'It's less than that now. And we have to try.' He wrenched away and headed for the door.

She hesitated only a moment before going after him. *I have to make him see reason.*

'Okay. Look everywhere,' he shouted.

Nothing. Lilli dropped to her knees and began to scour under every appliance. 'Please, Ron! Let's go. It's hopeless.'

Just at that moment the alarm ceased. Perhaps it too was on a timer. What a blessed relief.

A moment where she could hear her own breath, her own heart. And then – the ticking of a clock. Like an orange note, pinging, metallic. She lay flat. A package in the dust – under the oil tank. A long paper-wrapped package wired to an alarm clock. 'It's here!' she yelled. 'Underneath.'

She inched herself flat on her stomach to where she could read the dial. The clock showed six minutes to one. Six minutes left.

'*Sheisse.* Six minutes. Should we run?'

'Just look how it's connected. Is there a battery?' Ron was on his hands and knees next to her now.

She crawled nearer, not daring to touch it. How was the wiring attached to the clock? She followed two long snaking wires with her gaze. A brown wire and a black wire. One must be the earth. Which?

'The brown wire,' Ron said. 'What's it attached to?'

'You look.' She let him crawl half-underneath the boiler, as she sat back on her haunches, ready to up and sprint. But then she saw the toolkit. Ron's bag that he never let go of. She dragged it towards her, and frantically searched inside for a pair of bull-nosed pliers.

322

She glanced up. How had the time shrunk so quickly? Five minutes. She cursed again under her breath. Not enough time to get out of here.

Now they had no choice.

*

Neil had assembled everyone outside the perimeter fence, scanning every face as they came out. One of the women was taking a roll call from the clipboard of papers at the gate – workers who'd signed in, any visitors. The men and women streamed out, annoyed at being interrupted, wondering what was going on, and looking to the sky for enemy bombers.

'This way!' Once the name was checked, Jean, ever efficient, was sending them onwards to the air raid shelter, a double Andersen-type shelter in a farmer's field nearby.

Neil watched the last stragglers coming out. No sign of Ron or Johnny or Lilli. He thought he might faint. Where were they?

'Jean,' he called, urgency making his voice hoarse, 'there are three more still inside. I have to go in and fetch them.'

'What is it?' she asked, frustrated. 'Why will nobody tell us?'

'Sabotage. A bomb. Inside the bunker somewhere.'

'Good God.'

Neil stumbled towards the door. His legs were unwilling to move. His ears were full of blast sounds from before; when he'd been caught in the bomb in London. Of shattered images of being buried under rubble, of doctors in masks, of pain, and fire blazing in burning buildings.

He pushed the fear down into his gut.

Jean yelled after him. 'No, sir! Don't—' But too late he was already halfway down the ramp.

Thudding feet. A figure running out.

He lurched forward to help as the person emerged into the light. He stopped dead when he saw it was Johnny Murphy, alone.

'Out of my way,' he said.

Neil stood his ground. 'Where's Lilli?'

'How should I know? Still down there,' Johnny said. 'Stupid bitch wouldn't come with me.'

'How long until it blows?' He stood in Johnny's path.

'Two minutes. You'd better get out of my way. Unless you want to go the way of your father.'

'You bastard.' Without thinking Neil leapt towards Johnny, and grasping hold of him by his shirt, drew back his fist. But Johnny was bigger and heavier, and with a grunt, threw him to one side. Neil smashed against the metal door frame as Johnny took a quick, frantic look behind, then dodged past and sprinted towards the gate.

'Stop him!' yelled Neil, clutching his injured shoulder as Johnny burst out of the front of the building.

Through eyes watering with pain, Neil made out a guard firing his Lee-Enfield as Johnny ran for the gate.

Neil staggered back to his feet. The first shot had hit. But Johnny jerked and stumbled and didn't stop, just ran zig-zag fashion out of the gate. The guard fired another shot catching him a graze on the back of the leg.

He was heading for the cars. Another guard was in pursuit with a machine gun. The rat-a-tat of fire shattered the back window, but Johnny leapt into Ron's car and screeched away, leaving only the smell of burning rubber behind, and a spatter of blood on the dusty road.

Neil blinked. It had taken only moments for Johnny to get away, but moments were seconds. Seconds he didn't have.

'Clear the area!' yelled the guard.

But Neil ignored him and turned back inside the tunnel. Lilli was still down there.

*

324

Find the live wire connected to the battery.

Lilli wished her hands wouldn't shake so much. Two and a half minutes on the clock. Should she disconnect the timer first or was it booby-trapped? She tried to understand Johnny's mind. What would he have done?

'Can you reach it, the brown one?' Ron asked.

Lilli didn't answer. She was flat on her stomach peering into the dark. She was the one they'd decided would cut the wire because it was a narrow space and Ron was too bulky to get his arm underneath without risking the device going off.

'You need to disrupt the link between the power source or switch and the explosive. Then the bomb won't go off. But the clock might not be accurate, so sooner the better.'

But there was no time to think. Missteps during this process would risk blowing the place to smithereens.

'I think I have it. Two wires from the switch, one black, one brown, right?' The brown wire seemed to her to be soft and sweet like toffee. The black wire sharp and shiny like metal with a peculiar buzzing sensation about it.

'Good, good. Then cut the brown one. That's the live one.' Ron passed Lilli the pliers. They were damp with his sweat.

'You sure?' Her instinct was screaming. *No. It's the black one.* She turned to him. 'Go, Ron. Get the hell out of here!'

He didn't move. 'I'm not going, not until you've done it.'

'It's this black one. I'm certain.' Lilli took a deep ragged breath. She summoned her father in her mind. What would he say? *Step by step,* he'd say. She opened up the pliers with the wire-cutting edge.

The clock ticked. Sounds like tiny gunshots. She hesitated. Maybe Ron was right. 'Shall I do it?'

'Black or brown, who knows what the bastard did. We have to risk it. We'll die anyway if we don't do something. Just go slow and easy.'

There was no more time to think.

Carefully Lilli peeled the waxy paper away from the terminal

325

where the wires connected. She mustn't disturb the deadly explosive materials inside while she dismantled the wiring.

She said a silent prayer, and took one last look at Ron. He gave a silent nod and she saw him stiffen.

She eased the mouth of the pliers over the black wire. She'd trust herself this one last time. *For you, Papa.* It would have to be now.

She took a deep breath, leant in, and cut.

*

Neil knew he was crazy. That he was walking into danger, into another bomb, but he kept on moving. He couldn't think of Lilli still down there. What if she was injured? What if Johnny had shot her?

He kept on walking, cringing inside, expecting any moment might be his last. Until he heard a great shout, a noise of whooping.

As he approached the transmission room he saw two figures leaping up and down, clinging to each other in a crazy dance.

They saw him and turned, faces suddenly fearful.

'Neil!' A lone figure detached itself from the other and wove up the corridor towards him, swaying slightly as if drunk.

'Lilli!' he cried.

She broke into a run. He held out his arms and as she ran into them, he grabbed her, dragging her away. His one thought, to get her out of there as soon as he could.

'It's all right,' she said, resisting his pressure. 'It's safe.'

'There was no bomb?' He had a sudden vision of the guards shooting Johnny for no reason.

'We disabled it,' Ron said. 'Lilli cut the wire. She was bloody amazing.'

'It's safe? You're sure?'

'We left it where it was,' Ron said. 'The materials and the pipe will need to be used as evidence.'

Neil hugged Lilli tight and she burst into tears.

'Sorry, sorry,' she said, through sobs.

'What are you sorry for? It's okay,' he said. 'Let's get you out.' Christ alive. Had she actually defused a bomb? He couldn't believe it. His adrenalin was still flowing like liquid fire through his veins.

Ron had set off towards the front entrance, his expression dazed, and now Neil grabbed her arm to hurry her as fast as he could limp, he just wanted to get her to a safe space.

As they came up through the passageway, the tarmacked road to the entrance was deserted. There was nobody there. It was eerie, like arriving on Earth after a major disaster.

As they approached the gate, a guard came out pointing a machine gun at them.

'It's over,' Neil called to him. 'The bomb's been made safe. But we need our bomb disposal squad to go and check it out before anyone goes back in, and make sure there are no more devices left there.'

'Yes, sir. But I must ask you both to go to the shelter now with everyone else.'

'Johnny Murphy, did he get away?'

'I'm afraid so. But as soon as we were aware there was a problem we telephoned the Sussex police to surround the place. He won't get far. And I'm afraid you must all stay here. They're unhappy with how you got into the facility. Brigadier Jones is on his way, and he wants a complete debrief. He's angry at the breach of security and risk to our communications.'

'What about the risk to his people by his less-than-rigorous vetting procedures for new recruits?' Neil said. 'We'd all be dead now if Johnny Murphy had had his way.'

'I don't know about that, sir. I'm just following orders.' The guard shrugged and smiled.

'Let's do as they ask,' Ron said. 'It's my fault. I let him in, with a false pass. I'll be for it. And I feel like I've had more than enough excitement without asking for trouble. I feel like such an idiot.'

'No,' Lilli said. 'Look at the way you brought him down, the Hornets would be proud of you.'

Ron led the way shakily out through the gate. Neil took Lilli's arm and walked with her past the wire fence towards the field. Ahead of them was a field of plough with starlings scratching at the surface. As they approached, the birds scattered with a flurry of wings, wheeling like black confetti into the sky.

Neil stopped, suddenly taken with the blueness of the sky, with the shapes of the trees. 'Just a minute,' he said. He wrapped his arms around Lilli's waist and leant down to kiss her. To his delight, she stayed there, pliable under his kiss, her lips soft and warm.

'I've wanted to do that ever since the first time I set eyes on you,' he said.

'Then what took you so long?' Her eyes, still a little shiny, looked up at him with her candid gaze. 'Will I have to defuse a bomb every time?'

He laughed, and it turned into a sort of hysteria. They both laughed and laughed, clutching their stomachs.

'Oy!' Ron who had gone ahead was yelling and beckoning. As they approached the shelter they could see there was a crowd outside. A huge cheer erupted.

'Thank God,' said Jean. 'I thought you were all goners.'

'We would have been,' Ron said. 'But for Lilli. You have her to thank that the mast is still standing.'

'And you,' Lilli said. 'We did it together. I've never seen anyone dive to tackle a man the way you did.'

A shadow crossed Ron's face. 'He would have shot me, you know, once he'd got me into the car. I know that.'

'Where is he?'

'The suspect was wounded,' Jean said, 'but he got away, in Ron's car.'

'They'll get him, won't they?' Ron pleaded.

*

Bren skidded around the bend, trying to keep control of the car with his good arm. His shoulder was weak and one arm wouldn't work properly. He was aware as he yanked on the wheel that he'd heard no blast. He mentally went through it all, trying to see if he'd done something wrong. They'd be behind him soon enough, he'd seen men scrambling army jeeps as he reversed out in jerks and starts.

A pheasant shot up in front of him and he swerved, almost hitting a tree. He put his foot down again and heard the tyres squeal as he headed up the hill again towards the rendezvous point.

What a pig's ear. He'd be out of it soon though. If he didn't bleed to death.

He was still listening for a blast. Nothing.

He pulled off left down a narrow track, between banks of gorse and scrubby trees. Sheridan had better have the car waiting.

The track was pot-holed and it gave him pain in his wounded shoulder every time the suspension hit a bump. His calf was dripping blood onto the accelerator making it slippy as hell. At last, he saw it, a dark car parked in the trees. Sheridan. He pulled off the track and abandoned the Austin with its doors gaping open as he ran towards the car.

The back door of the sedan swung open. He leapt in. 'Go,' he shouted. 'They're on my tail.'

'Good afternoon, Mr Murphy.' The man in the front seat swivelled, and raised a gun to his face. 'Detective Inspector Howe of the Bedford police. You're under arrest.'

A trap. He tried to get out of the door but it had an automatic lock.

He glanced out of the windows. An army jeep was just bumping up the track behind them and as he watched, armed soldiers leapt out to surround the car. The British Army. The men he'd hated since he was seven years old.

'As you can see, Mr Murphy. You are going nowhere.'

Chapter 32

The debriefing took a long time as they were called to testify individually. Lilli told them all she knew of Brendan Murphy. By the end of it she was so tired she could barely stand. Jean had ordered a staff car to take them all back to Simpson Village, and Neil insisted Lilli be taken back there, as she couldn't face going back to the flat she'd shared with Johnny. Neil too couldn't face a motorbike journey this late in the day. Ron snored all the way home, to their amusement. At Simpson, they staggered into the house through the dark and the hoot of owls.

Mrs Littlefair showed Lilli to her box room from before, and Lilli fell into it gratefully.

She slept like the dead and was still groggy by mid-morning when there was a soft knock on her door. It was Neil. 'You all right?' he asked, holding out a mug of tea.

Just the sight of him made her smile. 'I'm fine. It all seems like something I've made up. Something I imagined.'

'Funny,' he said, putting the tea on the bedside table, 'that's what I think too. One minute I've got this nice quiet desk job, then I'm running down a corridor towards a bomb.'

'Think what would have happened if it had gone up.'

'Don't.' He sat beside her on the bed. 'Do I get another kiss? I promise there are no bombs involved.'

She hugged him tight and he got his kiss. Then they sat for a long time on the edge of her bed, their hands entwined. It felt strange to be so close to him, this man who fascinated her but who felt so familiar. She couldn't get enough of his face, of the way he looked at her with that half-puzzled, half-admiring expression. He told her all there was to know about his life in the SOE and how he had come to be blown up by a bomb. She watched his face as he told her the tale, seeing him struggle to be truthful with eyes that changed tone like the weather. It gave her such a churn in her stomach that he was trying to be so exact in telling her all, even the parts that painted him in a poor light.

She squeezed his hand, to show she understood. 'I don't know if I can tell you the truth about Bren,' she said. 'It's all such a muddle in my head, still.'

'It doesn't matter,' he said. 'I can wait. We've all the time in the world.'

She leant up against him. 'We were inches away from losing Aspidistra,' she said. 'What were you doing in there?'

'I came back for you,' he said, simply.

'You fool,' she said, smiling through tears.

*

Later that afternoon she was in the dining room having a pot of tea with Neil when Max told them Delmer was at the door.

Neil went to let him in.

Delmer was full of apologies. 'The Aspidistra is irreplaceable. I've read the reports, Neil, and I couldn't believe I was so blind about Johnny Murphy. You saved us thousands of pounds and I don't know how many lives.'

'It was Lilli and Ron, not me.' Neil brushed off the praise with a gesture, and Delmer squeezed himself into a chair at the table.

331

'We've arrested Murphy and he'll be charged with treason, threats to endanger life, and whatever the hell else we can throw at him. Undoubtedly, he'll plead he's Irish, and can't be tried here, and no doubt try to get himself expatriated, but we'll do our best to ensure he gets what he deserves.'

'What'll happen to him?' Lilli asked.

'Best not to speculate. A long prison sentence at best. At worst – well, let's not think about that.' He put a big paw on her hand. 'Ron tells me your heart is engaged elsewhere anyway. And I must say, I was a chump not to see it, and I'm glad.' He patted her hand before releasing it and turning to Neil. 'Look after her. Tomorrow is business as usual. We need our songstress, and the war doesn't stop for one unforeseen event.'

Neil looked at Lilli with a question in his eyes.

Lilli said firmly, 'We'll be there, Mr Delmer.'

'Oh, and Ron's happy to take you on informally, as an apprentice engineer,' said Delmer, 'so long as it doesn't interfere with our usual programming. No promises, mind; we'll have to see how you go on. And it goes without saying, this whole sabotage thing is to remain just between us,' he added. 'The guards have been changed, and as far as the personnel at Aspidistra are concerned, it was a routine practice air raid drill.'

'Will they buy it?' Neil asked. 'It was all pretty panicky.'

He laughed. 'You're asking me that? People will buy anything if you sell it to them hard enough. Now then, is there any more tea in that pot?' He helped himself to the last of the biscuits.

When they'd had their tea, they went to the door to see Delmer out.

Delmer's shiny black Wolsey was parked at the kerb, and Raymond, dressed in his Boys' Brigade uniform, was hanging over the wall.

'Smashing car, isn't it?' Raymond said, as Delmer climbed in. 'Look at them hubcaps. Are you going out on your motorbike today?'

'No, not today. We had quite a busy day yesterday,' Neil said, as Delmer eased away.

'Raymond!' A piercing shout from next door. 'Get back in here right now! Your tea's on the table!'

Lilli turned to Neil as Raymond rushed off. 'Strange, isn't it,' she said, 'how life just goes on. No one will ever know about yesterday.'

'We will,' Neil said, leaning down to kiss her tenderly on the lips. 'And it's a good thing we know the truth, because it's something for us to share, and we'll be able to tell our children, one day, once this war's over.'

Our children. The world suddenly exploded with possibilities. *And my father,* Lilli thought. *So much to tell him.*

One day, Papa, we'll be together again. And until then, I'll be singing for you every night.

A Letter from Deborah Swift

Thank you so much for choosing to read *The Shadow Network*. I hope you enjoyed it. If you did and would like to be the first to know about my new releases, please sign up to my mailing list.

Sign up here! https://dl.bookfunnel.com/e6izwznl1e

I was inspired to write this story because understanding the propaganda in the news we read is so crucial, and because we tend to think of fake news as a modern phenomenon. I was fascinated to find the concept existed in WW2, and you can find out more about the real history in the notes at the back of this book.

I hope you loved *The Shadow Network* and if you did I would be so grateful if you would leave a review. I always love to hear what readers thought, and it helps new readers discover my books too.

Thanks,
Deborah

Twitter: https://twitter.com/swiftstory
Website: https://deborahswift.com/

The Silk Code

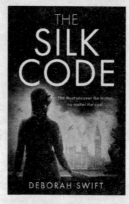

Based on the true story of 'Englandspiel', one woman must race against the clock to uncover a traitor, even if it means losing the man she loves.

England, 1943:

Deciding to throw herself into war work, **Nancy Callaghan** joins the Special Operations Executive in Baker Street. There, she begins solving 'indecipherables' – scrambled messages from agents in the field.

Then Nancy meets **Tom Lockwood**, a quiet genius when it comes to coding. Together they come up with the idea of printing codes on silk, so agents can hide them in their clothing to avoid detection by the enemy. Nancy and Tom grow close, and soon she is hopelessly in love.

But there is a traitor in Baker Street, and suspicions turn towards Tom. When Nancy is asked to spy on Tom, she must make the ultimate sacrifice and complete a near-impossible mission. Could the man she loves be the enemy?

An utterly gripping and unputdownable WW2 historical fiction novel, perfect for fans of Ella Carey and Ellie Midwood!

Historical Notes

Fake News in WW2

> 'We must never lie by accident.'
> Sefton Delmer about the WW2 radio station
> Soldatensender Calais

In wartime Britain there were three branches of propaganda, known then as 'white', 'grey', or 'black,' though we probably would not call them that now. White propaganda came from a known source and was completely transparent. Grey propaganda, on the other hand, was the subtle promotion or amplification of a political opinion by entities self-proclaiming themselves as 'objective' or as neutral. However, with black propaganda the audience were oblivious to the fact they were being manipulated, and did not feel that they were being pushed in a certain direction. This was because black propaganda pretended to come from a source that was not the true source.

Grey propaganda was used very effectively by Goebbels to help drive Nazi ideology. In Britain the campaign to undermine Goebbels's propaganda was led by the Political Warfare Executive, which ran a number of black propaganda radio stations. The first such station, Gustav Siegfried Eins (GS1), featured a Nazi extremist called 'Der Chef', who accused Adolf Hitler and the Gestapo of going soft. It undermined the German soldiers' trust in their leaders by reporting on their alleged corruption and sexual improprieties.

The two stations mentioned in this novel are the British radio station Soldatensender Calais, supposedly a radio station for the Wehrmacht based in France, and Atlantiksender, a shortwave radio station for German submariners. Both were under the direction of Tom Sefton Delmer, a British journalist who had resided in Germany and spoke perfect German.

There were British black propaganda radio stations broadcasting in most of the languages of occupied Europe. Many of these were based in the area of Woburn Abbey in Bedfordshire.

The Aspidistra Transmitter

The radio signal for these 'fake news' radio stations needed to be strong enough to appear as though it came from Germany and had to be more powerful than anything that was then available.

By coincidence, the Radio Corporation of America (RCA) had created two high-powered radio transmitters which could not be used in the US, because of a change in American law. The RCA were eager to sell them to Britain. So Harold Robin, a Foreign Office radio engineer, saw their potential, and travelled to America to examine them, and then worked to improve them. He adapted a transmitter so it was able to move frequency in a fraction of a second, at the flick of a switch.

The powerful ex-RCA transmitter, eventually installed in Sussex, England, was named Aspidistra, referencing the popular Gracie Fields song 'The Biggest Aspidistra in the World', in which an Aspidistra houseplant grows until it 'nearly reached the sky'.

In fact, most of the technology was buried underground at the site at Crowborough, though its antennae were visible – three guyed masts, each 110 metres tall, directing the signal broadly eastwards. The Art Deco–style transmitter building was housed in an underground shelter which had to be excavated by the Canadian army troops who were stationed nearby.

After the war, Aspidistra was used by the BBC. It made its final transmission on 28 September 1982, before being finally switched off by Robin, the man who had been responsible, forty years earlier, for bringing the transmitter from the US and setting up the station at Crowborough.

German and Irish Saboteurs

As far as I know there was never any attempt to sabotage or bomb the Aspidistra transmitter, though I enjoyed making it a possible target for a German agent and saboteur. However, German agents were sent into Britain to sabotage British targets – mainly military, industrial, and transport facilities. Their aim was to create maximum disruption, and to lower the morale of British civilians.

In reality, the German spies were less efficient than my fictional Brendan – the German spies had poor English-language skills and little knowledge of British customs. One German spy was arrested after trying to order a pint of cider at ten in the morning, as he didn't know that landlords weren't allowed to serve alcohol before lunchtime. Two other agents were stopped because they were cycling on the wrong side of the road. The twelve spies we know of who landed in Britain as part of the so-called Operation Lena in September 1940 were nearly all captured.

The German war machine was generally very efficient, so it remains a mystery why these men were not better trained. For this reason, I chose to link my saboteur to the Irish Republican Army (IRA), and the Coventry IRA bomb. It is a little-known fact that the IRA and the Nazi regime were in collaboration during the war.

At lunchtime on 25 August 1939 an unknown bomb-maker cycled into the city of Coventry with a five-pound bomb in his bicycle basket. The device, wrapped in brown paper and with an alarm clock timer, was left outside Astley's shop where it exploded fifty minutes later, killing five people and injuring seventy, and causing devastation to the surrounding buildings. For a while, the authorities and the public were wary of anyone Irish, but because of close ties to Ireland this vigilance soon waned.

The Coventry plot was linked to three other 'bicycle bomb' plots in London which were part of a concerted campaign by the IRA. The S-Plan (Sabotage Campaign or England Campaign) was a campaign conducted by members of the IRA to protest against control of Northern Ireland by the British.

The Nazis made links with the IRA as far back as 1936, when IRA member Sean Russell sought German support for IRA activities and engaged in talks with the German Foreign Office, regarding IRA–German cooperation. When war was declared, the Germans saw the IRA as a useful ally should the Wehrmacht invade Britain. However the IRA saw Germany only as a stepping stone to a united Ireland, and these two motivations were not easily aligned. The IRA's collaboration with the Nazis against Great Britain made the ideal background for me to construct the character of Brendan Murphy.

The Rushen Women's Internment Camp

Lilliana Bergen is fictional, but many women like her were interned as enemy aliens in Rushen Camp on the Isle of Man. Before May 1940, not a single person interviewed by the polling group Mass Observation suspected refugees to Britain of espionage, or suggested that they should be interned.

But in April 1940, after the German occupation of Norway made the invasion of Britain seem more likely, Colonel Henry Burton persuaded members of the House of Commons worried about what he termed 'enemy aliens', that it would be 'far better to intern all the lot'. Soon this view began to prevail, based on little evidence – for most Germans in the country were refugees, fleeing Nazi oppression.

Act! Act! Act! Do It Now! was the headline of a newspaper

article by G. Ward Price, on 24 May. 'All refugees … should be drafted without delay to a remote part of the country and kept under strict supervision.'

'You fail to realise,' Price wrote, 'that every German is an agent.' This of course could not possibly be true, as many had fled the Nazi regime, but it is a good example of grey propaganda in action.

These unfortunate people, many bewildered and innocent of any crime, were rounded up without warning and sent to various transit camps, or to prison cells to await dispatch to more permanent accommodation. Women and children were sent to the south of the Isle of Man. At one point this end of the island was cut off from the rest of it by a barbed-wire fence. Men were held on the other side, and their camps were enormous, housing about 26,000 prisoners, increasing the ordinary population of the island by a third. All these 'enemy aliens' were civilians and many of them had been in England since early childhood, or had come to England more than a generation before.

The Rushen Women's Camp held 3,500 internees, housed with landladies of seaside boarding houses, or families with spare rooms who were paid a guinea a week for taking in their 'guests'. The women of Rushen Camp were a mixed bunch, as not only did it accommodate Jewish and political refugees, but also economic migrants who had come to Britain in the 1930s, and a few others who were pro-Nazi sympathisers.

Within the camp, the women organised themselves to stay busy – there were classes for painting, dressmaking, and typing, as well as languages, and they even spent time on the beach. This did not mean life in internment was easy, as the strict rules and regulations, plus the loss of freedom to travel, or see relatives or husbands on the other side of the wire, were difficult to bear.

Unlike my character Lilli, who was able to escape these privations, the last remaining internees left the Isle of Man in September 1945. Many women however had befriended their hosts and some stayed on as part of the Manx population.

Selected Further Reading

Black Propaganda in the Second World War – Stanley Newcourt-Nowodworski

The Black Game – Ellic Howe

The Secret History of PWE – David Garnett

Bodyguard of Lies – Anthony Cave Brown

Spy Capital of Britain – Stephen Bunker

Radio War – David Abrutat

The Anatomy of a Spy – Michael Smith

Forgotten Voices of the Secret War – Roderick Bailey

Operation Lena and Hitler's Plots to Blow Up Britain – Bernard O'Connor

The Island of Extraordinary Captives – Simon Parkin

WW2 Internment in the Isle of Man – Culture Vannin (https://www.youtube.com/watch?v=7iLKvMFmhEA)

The Night of Broken Glass – edited by Uta Gerhardt and Thomas Karlauf

Acknowledgements

My thanks go to the whole team at HQ Digital, especially to Audrey Linton, my excellent editor. At home, my husband John is forgiving of the long hours and obsession that a novel demands. Without him, everything would be so much harder! Novels such as this one require a lot of research and I owe particular thanks to Tom Halls for his knowledge of motorcycles, the Open University for information on the Political Warfare Executive, the National Archive for material on Sefton Delmer, and *Nuts and Volts* magazine for technical radio information. All radio and broadcasting errors are my own! I'd also like to acknowledge *Radio Aspidistra*, a BBC drama documentary radio broadcast that first introduced me to the idea of black broadcasting and fake news in WW2, and inspired me to research and write this novel. .

If you have enjoyed *The Shadow Network*, I'd be really grateful for an online review or rating. You can keep in touch with me by joining my monthly newsletter, where you will get a free short story as a welcome gift.

Join Newsletter https://dl.bookfunnel.com/e6izwznl1e

Dear Reader,

We hope you enjoyed reading this book. If you did, we'd be so appreciative if you left a review. It really helps us and the author to bring more books like this to you.

Here at HQ Digital we are dedicated to publishing fiction that will keep you turning the pages into the early hours. Don't want to miss a thing? To find out more about our books, promotions, discover exclusive content and enter competitions you can keep in touch in the following ways:

JOIN OUR COMMUNITY:

Sign up to our new email newsletter:
http://smarturl.it/SignUpHQ

Read our new blog www.hqstories.co.uk

https://twitter.com/HQStories

www.facebook.com/HQStories

BUDDING WRITER?

We're also looking for authors to join the HQ Digital family!
Find out more here:

https://www.hqstories.co.uk/want-to-write-for-us/

Thanks for reading, from the HQ Digital team